I0630634

THE CHANTING

Beverly Terhune

JERSEY PINES INK
https://www.jerseypinesink.com

This is a work of fiction. Names, characters, businesses, places, events, locales and incidents are either the products of the author's imagination or used in a fictitious manner. Any resemblance to actual persons, living or dead, or actual events is purely coincidental.

All rights reserved. All rights reserved, including the right to reproduce this book or portions thereof in any form whatsoever.

Cover art— Dar Albert, Wicked Smart Designs

Interior design—River Cove Production

Copyright © by Beverly T. Haaf, 2023

Printing History
Popular Library Edition/1991
Jersey Pines Edition/ 2021

The publisher is not responsible for websites or any other such content not owned by the publisher

For information, address the publisher at: Jerseypinesink.com

ISBN: 978-1-948899-23-9

JERSEY PINES INK
https://www.jerseypinesink.com

Memories of summer evenings;
The voices of two mothers, each calling
three children in safely for the night
The memories linger yet . . .

THE CHANTING

Beverly Terhune

Chapter 1

THE SOUNDS OF THE BABY CRYING pulled Janet from a deep, dreamless sleep. The crying, thin and fretful, sharpened, weaving its way in and out of her dawning consciousness.

The sound faded. Janet decided Becky had returned to sleep, but she would check on her anyway. She sat up, untangling herself from the bed covers, mindful of not jostling her husband, Clay, who would be annoyed if she disturbed his rest.

She slipped her slim legs over the edge of the bed and reached for her robe. Her fingers closed upon a soft, plush fabric. How strange, she thought. It felt like her fleece wrap instead of the thin cotton she wore in this southern heat.

She and Clay had moved to Alabama for his new job, and it was here that Becky had been born in April 1984. Dear Becky. So small, so perfect—so new to the world.

Janet smiled, hugging the memories, although now in the summertime, Becky was no longer brand new.

Becky . . .

Janet caught her breath as the room suddenly seemed to shift around her. She gripped the edge of the mattress and the sense of motion ceased. She heard Becky again, an odd cry, the cadence strangely rhythmic, the child's voice sounding huskier than usual. Alarmed, Janet got to her feet. Not bothering to hunt for her slippers although the floor seemed oddly cold, she hurried toward the door.

There was no door!

Bewildered, she strained to pierce the dimness.

Enough moonlight filtered into the room so that she felt she should be able to see, yet nothing looked familiar. She realized she had somehow gotten turned around so that she faced a flat, featureless wall. Off to the side, instead of one window, there appeared to be two. She tried to blink away her double vision. Her eyes found the black shape of the door opening, the door left wide as always so that Becky's slightest sound could be heard. She hurried toward it.

Her head and toes struck painfully against something solid and unyielding. She stumbled back, gasping, almost losing her balance. Clearing her head, she realized the door was shut. Her heart started to thump. She stared at the dark rectangle, as tall and narrow as an upended coffin. It bore no resemblance to the ivory-colored panel she'd painted after they'd first moved in. The surface looked more like varnished wood, the dark color having deceived her into thinking it yawned open to the corridor outside.

Confused, she felt along the door, found the knob, turned it and stepped into the corridor. Blackness, thick and womblike, enveloped her like a cloak. Confusion deepening, she wasn't sure which way to turn. The Cabbage Patch Kids lamp in Becky's room must have burned out. But she knew the way, she told herself, trying to fight off unreasoning panic. She knew the way, yet as she moved along, the corridor seemed alien. The baby's cries echoed as if several children were crying. Had her hearing been affected when she bumped into the door? Now that she was almost to the nursery, Becky's cries sounded more distant. That made no sense. Janet reached urgently toward the doorway of the child's room.

Becky's room was gone!

Frantic, Janet ran her hands over hard, cold plaster. The door was walled up, sealed over, trapping Becky inside! Her seeking hands found a ridge that should not be there. It felt like wood. Waist-high and flattened like a chair rail. Her pulse pounded. She was lost. Lost, unable to find her way around in her own house. Her heartbeats seemed to clog her throat. How had she gotten so mixed up? What was happening to her? Her breath came in stricken gasps as she searched for the light switch.

She slid her hands along the wall.

She couldn't find the light switch! What was going on?

Janet feared to take another step. She had no idea where the stairs were. One step in the wrong direction and she might tumble down the entire long flight. Sweat trickled along her ribs. She longed to call for Clay, but she held her tongue. He would be furious if she awakened him for such a foolish reason—getting lost in their own house.

Then, ever so faintly on the dark air, there came a suggestion of smoke, a mere wisp of odor. It was gone in an instant, yet its hint was enough to jolt her into action.

"Becky!" she screamed, blindly beginning to run, thinking of nothing except reaching her child. "Becky!"

Light exploded with eye-searing brightness.

"Janet?" a voice called. "What's the matter?"

Janet came to an abrupt, disbelieving stop as she recognized the voice of her sister. What was Fran doing here in Alabama?

"Janet?" Fran called anxiously. "Are you all right?"

Stunned, Janet watched as her sister hurried forward, the hem of her thickly quilted robe flapping about her sturdy, athletic legs.

"I heard you bumping around," Fran said. "Jan, are you okay?"

As if in a fog, Janet lifted a hand to touch her bruised forehead. "I walked into the door," she said. It was difficult to speak. "Somehow, I—I was all turned around." She put her hands to her ears. "Things sounded strange, all distorted."

She remembered thinking she smelled smoke, only there was no smoke. "I got up because the baby . . ."

Her voice trailed off, leaving nothing except an awkward, painful silence.

"The baby," she said, knowing as she repeated the word that something was wrong, terribly wrong.

"Oh, honey." Fran's face constricted. "Honey, you've been dreaming."

"But I heard . . ." Dazed, Janet looked around. She saw the painted plaster and the tan and black floral design Fran had stenciled above the wainscoting. Her hazel eyes widened as she recognized the walls of the restored craftsman-style house in Princeton, New Jersey, where Fran lived with her husband Warren.

Suddenly everything became achingly clear.

She had arrived at Fran's that morning. It was October, not summertime, and it wasn't 1984, it was 1986. Clay hadn't been sleeping beside her. She was staying alone in Fran's guest room because she and Clay were getting a divorce. She couldn't have gotten up in response to Becky's cry because Becky had been gone for over a year. She smothered a sob. That small white casket, closed forever, that sweet face, sealed for all eternity in the smothering darkness. It all came back to her, the awful truth sinking in, crushing her like a leaden weight.

"It wasn't Becky I heard," she said in a dull monotone as if reciting a lesson she must learn. "It was somebody else's baby."

"You were dreaming," Fran repeated softly. "Nobody living nearby has a baby. Nobody on this block."

Ignoring her sister's words, Janet ran a shaking hand through her dark, feathery curls. "It wasn't Becky I heard crying, because she didn't cry that night. If she had, I could have saved her. I was always alert to her slightest sound."

"I know, honey. I know." Fran slipped an arm about the smaller woman. "Let's go down to the kitchen. It's your first night here and you're getting adjusted. No wonder you felt all turned around when you awoke. I'll make hot cocoa and we can talk."

Shaking her head, Janet moved free of Fran's touch. She drew a breath. "I'm all right." She pulled herself together enough to manage a normal tone. "Really, I am. I'll stop by the bathroom and then go back to bed."

She was aware of Fran's worried eyes following as she stepped into the bathroom.

"Take a couple of aspirin," Fran called.

Janet hesitated, then drew a paper cup from the dispenser, ran the water, and swallowed two aspirin. As she stepped out, she saw Fran watching; Fran, always the big sister.

Janet forced a smile. "I'm fine now, honest." She hoped that the commotion hadn't awakened her brother-in-law. But even if it had she supposed Warren would never react with the kind of anger Clay would have shown. Poor Clay, always protecting himself from injustices, most of them imagined. Despite all that had happened, she could only pity him.

Back in the guest room, Janet looked at the moonlit rectangles of the windows and wondered how she could have deluded herself into thinking she was still in the Alabama house. Shivering from cold, yet reluctant to return to bed, she folded her arms across her small breasts, remembering their fullness when they had been swollen with milk. Drawn to one of the windows, she peered out.

The three-quarter moon was screened by clouds that transformed the sky into a pale, inverted bowl. The scene was black, white, and gray, as cold and impersonal as a stopped frame from an old film. Nearby houses were hidden by dark shapes, hunched and brooding; shapes that by daylight would be revealed as magnificent oaks, tall drooping hemlocks, pines, and maples.

She remembered when she and Clay had visited Fran to show off little Becky just after she was born. It had been the end of May and the weather was beautiful. In the afternoon they had walked around Fran's block, Janet so proud of what she knew was the most beautiful baby in the world. They came to a house that was at the opposite end of the block from Fran's. There was a FOR SALE sign in front of a circular driveway. They had paused to look.

The large house was painted a warm, light yellow and it had tall windows. Although the house was old, everything appeared to be in perfect repair, including the romantic-looking cupola on the top of the roof. Without speaking, she and Clay found themselves walking around the property, experiencing the shimmering sense of peace and beauty in the yard and garden. On the sidewalk again, Janet remembered imagining that the front door would magically open and invite them in. Standing with Becky cuddled in her arms, she had found herself wishing that they had never moved away, wishing with her whole heart that the yellow house could have become their home.

Her memories broke off abruptly as she once again heard an infant's cry. The sound was thin and incredibly pure as if it floated from someone's open window. She strained her eyes almost as if expecting the sound to become visible, glistening like a silver thread in the moonlight, inviting her to follow it back to its source. As mysteriously as it had begun, the cry ceased as if it had never been.

A shudder vibrated through Janet's slender frame. Fran said none of the neighbors had a baby. Even if she were mistaken, would anyone keep windows open on such a cold night? Her own was certainly closed. She touched the icy slickness of a pane with trembling fingers. Behind it was a storm window.

How could the sound have reached her?

Chapter 2

THE SPARKLING SUNSHINE THAT TEASED JANET'S eyes open in the morning failed to dispel the shadows of her restless sleep. She remembered how she had awakened in the night, thinking that Becky was still alive and crying for her. Troubled, she stared around the sunny bedroom, mentally retracing her mistaken steps of the night before. She saw where she had gone wrong. The direction which would have led to the hallway in the Alabama house led only to a blank wall here.

It occurred to her that she might have been sleepwalking. Even though she had never had a sleepwalking experience in the past, it offered a perfect explanation. Then, frowning, she remembered having heard the crying again, after she returned to her room. She certainly had been wide awake then, hadn't she?

She reached for a sweatshirt, tights and leg warmers to keep off the chill. Everything about the night's episode was disturbing. She no longer wanted to think about it, and she hoped her sister wouldn't want to talk about it either.

Downstairs in the kitchen, she found Fran already dressed for her day in a grey power suit, the jacket hanging over a chair. She was busy putting bacon into a microwave. When not in use, the device was concealed by a ruffled curtain. Fran, a nostalgia buff, had gone to great lengths in preserving the quaint kitchen despite the modern eighties features available. The kitchen featured an old working refrigerator, its white porcelain coils piled on top like a hairdo. There was also a wide, stork-legged sink. Both sat in proud display. The modern double-door refrigerator freezer and a dishwasher were inconveniently hidden in the pantry. A charming conceit, Janet thought, but perhaps not as false as what she was doing; pretending to live in the present while her heart remained in the past, holding a phantom child to her breast.

"Morning." Fran turned the knob that started the bacon cooking. Her cheery briskness announced in sisterly shorthand that no reference would be made to the previous night unless Janet initiated the subject.

Relieved, Janet took a seat at the oak table. "Has Warren already left for classes?"

"About fifteen minutes ago." Fran broke eggs into a bowl. "Scrambled okay?"

"Perfect," Janet said.

Warren, who had authored what was considered the definitive book on the subject of medieval musical instruments, taught at Princeton University. Janet remembered that Clay had considered Warren's special area of study ludicrous.

"Medieval instruments?" he had guffawed. "What kind of clown would sign up for his classes?"

"Court jesters," Janet had responded, smiling to keep it light. Keep it light . . . keep it light. That had been the watchword for peaceful coexistence with Clay.

Clay had a degree in computer programming, but he couldn't find a job where he was happy in the workplace. He blamed it on "East Coast cut-throat thinking." He decided they should move to the South. Janet researched and found that the job market was good in Georgia, but the position he accepted was the one in Alabama.

Fran poured juice and coffee. When the oven timer buzzed, she removed the bacon and transferred it and the eggs to a platter. She took a seat across from Janet, smoothing the spread collar of the white blouse that she wore with a black string tie.

"Dig in," she ordered. "I saw you at the train station yesterday and thought you were as thin as a scarecrow. I'll buy some good old Philadelphia-style scrapple to go with your eggs tomorrow. Bet you couldn't get that in Alabama. I'll start putting some meat on your bones."

"You're right, I doubt they knew what scrapple was, but you're as bossy as ever, aren't you? Like the witch from the gingerbread house, inviting me in to fatten me up."

At thirty-three, Frances, nine years older than Janet, was built on a Junoesque scale, with corn-yellow hair crimped and sprayed into a large halo, setting off her powder-blue eyes, wholesome smile and deep-cut dimples. Janet's own appearance was dramatically different, her hair a moderately styled cap of dark curls, her figure petite, her expression reserved. Her hazel eyes were tilted exotically and fringed with dark eyelashes. The ancestry of the sisters was English and Norwegian, but their father had joked that Janet's looks proved that a Gypsy once swung on a branch of the family tree.

"I'm glad I don't have to dash off this morning," Fran said. She was the owner-manager of The Magic Spoon, a tearoom at a small shopping area just outside of Princeton. "There's something we have to discuss." Her tone was serious. "It would be too soon to ask this except I have a special reason. Have you given thought as to what you'll do now that you're on your own?"

Janet couldn't help sighing. Here it was, she thought: *advice time.* Fran had married a widower, and after helping guide his two teenage sons into adulthood, she had channeled her considerable energies into making the Spoon a relaxed yet trendy luncheon refuge for young suburban housewives. But now, with a dependable staff, it was obvious she had regained time for her favorite mission—telling others what to do. Actually, a lot of her ideas were good. It was just that she tended to come on awfully strong.

"I've thought about a job," Janet said. "Probably secretarial work."

Fran grimaced. "Said with the joyous anticipation of jabbing a stick into your eye. What about journalism? Any ambition to take it up again?"

Janet remembered her once cherished enthusiasm to transform the world through the power of the press. She had pinned a slogan on her bulletin board that read, "Look out world!" She was the one who should have been looking out. Reasoning that she could always finish her education later, she had dropped out of her journalism classes at age twenty to help Clay finish his own schooling. They married as soon as he received his degree. She remained loyal as he abandoned one brief job after another in his sour struggle to find a niche where he felt his superiority would be recognized and jealous colleagues would no longer conspire against him.

"The reason I brought this up," continued Fran, "is because the community adult school needs a newsletter editor. It's held on certain evenings in the Princeton High School building. The person who formerly held the newsletter position had gathered most of what was needed for the next issue and then she left. They need someone to edit the material and get the newsletter in shape for publication as soon as possible. If there's a chance you're interested, you should apply before they grab someone else. Not that I'm trying to push. Maybe what you need most is a chance to rest, but then again, a distraction might be better. Here's one of the old newsletters." Fran handed over a publication. "The job wouldn't pay much but it's in your chosen field and it's a way to update your work experience and meet new people."

Janet had heard worse suggestions. "I'll need to go for an interview."

Fran poured more coffee for them both. "You will, but Ida Aaron, the director of the adult school, often lunches at The Magic Spoon. She's also a friend. That's how I know about the newsletter. I can arrange for you two to meet—if you're interested, that is."

Such restraint, Janet thought, amused. It didn't take second sight to know Fran was concerned about her rattling around the house all day with nothing to think about except the loss of the baby and a divorce that would soon be granted. The episode during the night had surely intensified Fran's concern. And, no wonder! To have dreamed so vividly that she heard the baby crying, waking to think she was still in Alabama and then trying to act on it.

Fran pulled her purse from the chair beside her and took out an appointment book. "Even if you're not interested in the newsletter, I think you'd enjoy meeting Ida. How about lunch next Monday?"

"That sounds fine." Janet realized she had already made up her mind to apply for the position. When Fran and Warren had invited her into their home for an indefinite stay, it had been as a family member, but she had no intention of sponging. Although she had enough money to get by for a while, she needed some type of employment. As Fran had pointed out, the newsletter would be a way to get started in the work-world again.

Finishing her breakfast, Janet glanced out the window and saw a Siamese cat streak by, followed by a dark-haired little girl. The child's open jacket revealed a lace-trimmed red taffeta dress. Her ponytail was caught back with a red ribbon. The child, who looked to be about eight years old, paused and looked toward Fran's house.

Janet was startled because it appeared that the child looked directly into her eyes. An illusion, of course. The little girl stood in bright sunlight and couldn't possibly see anyone sitting inside the house. All the same, what Janet felt when she looked at the little girl was an odd sense of recognition, although she knew she had never seen her before. It was puzzling. There were still times when she saw an infant with golden curls and large blue eyes and she would think: *Becky*! But there was no reason why this older, dark-haired child should arouse feelings of familiarity.

She said to Fran, "Who is that little girl playing out there? Is that how children around here dress for school—so fancy?"

"That's Gina," Fran said, taking a look for herself. "She doesn't attend school because she's handicapped. It looks as if the poor child had to get herself ready this morning." Fran's voice reflected disapproval. "She's a foster child of the Stocktons, the couple on our block holding the get-together we're taking you to Saturday night."

"That solar energy thing?"

"Yes," Fran said. "Tommy and Veronica Stockton are wealthy and given to crazes. The latest one is energy conservation. They've invited a speaker to the party in the hope of firing up the rest of the block on the subject. Gina is a craze from a few years back. She's an orphan, a survivor of an earthquake disaster in Italy. Tommy knew about an agency that cares for orphaned children and helps them become familiar with the language where they're being placed." Fran shook her head. "When it's hot tubs, racquetball ball, and solar power, who cares if you pick up a trend then drop it a month later? But no one should be allowed to do that with a child. I think she's a fad they've grown tired of."

Janet frowned. "They don't treat her properly?"

"As far as material things go, Gina has everything." Fran stood and slipped into her jacket. It had brass buttons and shoulder pads that were stylishly hefty. "But Tommy is away a lot on business and Veronica travels with him and calls herself his secretary. She thinks of herself as the Eighties Woman, doing it all herself: wife, career, keeping a house and raising a child, but that's not what's happening. She has a tutor for Gina and the live-in housekeeper, Mrs. Oswald—we call her Ozzie—is responsible for hiring all the help for the house and grounds. Ozzie also serves as the nanny because Veronica is away so much with Tommy. Veronica's nice enough, but—" Fran shrugged. "You can make up your own mind when you meet her."

Chapter 3

AFTER FRAN LEFT THE HOUSE, JANET was drawn to the window again, hoping for another look at Gina, but the child was no longer in sight.

Fran did have strong opinions, Janet thought. Was she exaggerating the situation with her neighbor? Janet hoped so. What sounded like treating a child with benign neglect was just wrong.

She sat down again at the table and leafed through the newsletter, seeing it included articles, artwork and photographs by the students. Was the editor's job solely to oversee the mechanics of the publication, or did it also entail writing copy? Janet remembered interview assignments as a student and felt she could pick up the skills again. She set the newsletter aside. There was no point in wondering about it. Fran's friend, Ida, would tell what she needed to know to apply.

After carting the breakfast things to the hidden dishwasher, she went back upstairs and pulled on jeans and a sweater. Downstairs again, she tucked a house key into her pocket and went outside.

The autumn sunshine was thin despite its brightness, but Janet rejected the impulse to go back and borrow a warm jacket from Fran's closet. Let the temperature drop, let the wind blow—she could take it. She was learning strength and independence the hard way and had no intention of slipping backward.

After the deaths of their parents, Fran had watched over her during high school with such smothering protectiveness that she had entered college ripe for a rebellion she hadn't been equipped to handle. All water over the dam. Both sisters had changed. Although Fran was still BIG SISTER, the discussion about the job showed she was trying to offer suggestions rather than take total command in her old way.

Ignoring the chill fingers of wind tugging at her hair, Janet looked up and down Quince Street. Fran's house was the only house on that block that actually faced that street; the three homes on the long sides of the block faced their respective side streets. An odd configuration, Janet thought. She wondered which direction would take her past the Stockton house. She decided to go around the block starting from the left of Fran's.

The homes she saw there all had wide side yards and short back yards. She came to the middle house and saw the name "Stockton" stamped on a brass marker near the door of a home with a pillared, Federal-style façade. The front door was a blue that was so shiny it looked as if the paint had been varnished.

Janet continued walking until she reached the corner at Parke Street. She had intended to circle the block but the cold had seeped into her bones. Time to go back.

As she turned, she caught a swirling glimpse of red. She recognized Gina weaving through evergreen that formed a line between the long end of Fran's property and that of the yellow house.

As Janet watched, an old woman, hunch-shouldered and shapeless, emerged from the latticed porch at the rear of the house, hurrying despite stiff, arthritic movements.

Seen at a distance, the profile of the woman's face was like a nutcracker, the prow of her nose and jutting chin threatening to meet. She was dressed from head to toe in black. Her black shawl covered her hair and was knotted under her chin babushka style. The perfect witch for a real gingerbread cottage, Janet thought.

Focused on Gina, the woman clapped her hands sharply, startling the cat into streaking off. Gina looked up. The woman made urgent gestures, clearly signaling the child to leave. As if performing a well-practiced role, Gina didn't hesitate before slipping back into the evergreens. The branches closed around her as neatly as if she had been swallowed.

Chapter 4

THE OLD WOMAN LOOKED STORYBOOK SCARY, Janet
thought, but Gina's behavior indicated she wasn't afraid of what must
be the neighborhood crone. If anything, it was the old woman herself
who acted fearful. Maybe she disliked cats. Or children.

Janet waited until after the black-garbed figure had painfully
retraced her steps back into the house. Would Gina reappear? A cloud
moved over the sun and the wind gusted sharply. Feeling the sting of
grit, Janet noticed a child's sandbox. What looked to be a little pink
Barbie convertible was half-buried in the sand along with other colorful
plastic toys. Did Gina play there with another child?

She spotted Gina again, this time emerging from the evergreens
and heading toward the Stockton's rear yard. Janet decided the child
was going home. She should do the same, go back to Fran's and finish
unpacking the luggage she had brought with her on the train.

A half-hour later she had emptied her two suitcases and organized
the closet and bureau drawers. She had gotten rid of her heaviest
clothing before moving to Alabama. Now that she was back up North,
she would need a warm coat. That evening, Fran was taking her
shopping. She should make a list of what she needed.

Pad and pencil in hand, she tucked herself into the cozy window seat only to find her attention drifting out through the glass. The sun was shining again, and the yards in view were spread below like a series of little parks. She found herself remembering the abandoned toys in the sandbox and she thought about Gina. The child's handicap didn't seem to be physical. Perhaps she suffered from a learning disability. Was she now studying with the tutor Fran had mentioned or was she home alone? Janet imagined her in an immaculate but sterile living room, her red taffeta skirt crisp around her knees as she sat waiting for a party that would never happen.

With a sigh, Janet resolutely applied her thoughts to her clothing list, wishing the melancholy image of a lonely child hadn't stolen into her mind.

She printed the words, "Winter Coat" and then let the pencil rest idle, her gaze again traveling to the window. From her elevated view, she admired beds of russet and wine chrysanthemums, a wrought iron bench and an old-fashioned grape arbor. She looked across the yards of the houses that faced the streets on either side of the block, and then to the end property and a huge copper beech. The broad trunk of the tree supported smooth gray limbs stretching skyward in a magnificent tangle that seemed created for the capering of elves and other woodland sprites.

Janet leaned forward, thinking that as autumn leaves drifted free, she would have an increasingly better view of the yellow house that had so captured her when she and Clay had visited Princeton with Becky. Funny how she felt nothing of the allure she had felt back then. She hadn't even thought about looking at it today, but she did remember how inviting the rear garden had appeared in the spring; as if it had been created to welcome little children.

And that was where the black-garbed woman lived. None of her business of course, but it seemed wrong that a person living in the yellow house would chase a child away.

Chapter 5

THAT EVENING, JANET WAS IN THE Princeton Shopping Center. Epstein's department store had the perfect coat and she'd found several other things she liked. In the dressing room, she admired the jacket of a wool suit she'd decided to purchase. Hoping to make an extra outfit, she'd tried on a black and tan pleated wool skirt she thought would coordinate with the heathery fawn of the suit. It had been too big, and Fran had gone to find another in a smaller size.

When Fran reappeared, she carried several garments. "Sorry I was so long," she said, "but I looked around to see if there was anything else you should try while we're here."

Janet frowned. "A second skirt is all my budget can handle."

"I know, but still . . ." As Fran leaned to place the clothing on a chair, her shadow, bowed and dark, loomed against the compartment wall, reminding Janet of the old woman she had seen that morning.

"Tell me something," she said as Fran handed her a flared plaid midi skirt with a belt, "that property that meets your back yard—do you know the elderly woman who lives there?"

"You must mean Rose. Dressed like a mourner, right?"

"She was wearing all black, yes." Janet pulled on the skirt and zipped it. "Oh, I do like this plaid, but look—" She slipped her fingers easily inside the high waistband. "Too big."

Fran wrinkled her nose. "Skinny thing. I was afraid of that. I brought along another, but the colors aren't the same."

Janet's thoughts returned to the old woman as she slipped off the skirt and tried on the replacement and it fit perfectly. "Anyway, I saw her, Rose, outside this morning. She seemed sort of odd."

"Odd?" Fran dimpled. "Tactful description. The poor thing with her apple doll head—"

Janet interrupted. "Apple doll? I thought of her as witch-like."

"I can see what you mean," Fran said with a shrug, "but her skin is so wrinkled. Remember when I showed you how to make apple dolls? We carved out eyes, nose and mouth in a peeled apple and let it dry and it turned into the face of an old person. Anyway, Rose can spend hours wandering about her back yard, muttering to herself. Watching her can be spooky. Not that I know much about her. The family hasn't been here long. The house only sold last month."

Surprised, Janet remembered the appeal that the house had once held for her. "I figured such an attractive place would be snapped up right away. Why would it stand empty for so long?"

"Who knows, but it did. Take off that skirt and that jacket too." Fran turned to another garment she had brought in. "Try something different."

"You didn't bring another suit, did you? I've already decided on this one."

"No. Just try it on. Here, have a look. Ta-da!" As Janet turned to look, Fran held up a dress, a lovely chiffon with a full skirt in a soft apricot shade. "I figured you could wear it tomorrow night."

Janet liked the dress at once, but she said. "I hadn't planned on buying anything dressy. Isn't my beige one okay? You said that tomorrow evening was just a neighborhood get-together."

"For the Stocktons, a 'get-together' means a cocktail party with delicious food." Fran handed over the dress. "You owe yourself a treat. And for goodness sake, in a livelier shade than beige!"

The dress had a high-necked bodice and semitransparent sleeves that seemed especially designed to flatter thin arms. Janet found that its color brightened her complexion and brought a sparkle to her eyes.

"And no more about your budget," Fran said. "If you like it, it's an early Christmas gift."

"Oh, Fran . . ." Janet pivoted before the mirror, viewing her reflection from different angles, aware of how the full skirt moved sensuously against her legs.

"Big sister still knows best?" demanded Fran.

"This time, yes," admitted Janet. Fran did so enjoy being right. She pivoted again. "Yes," she repeated, smiling at Fran. "And thank you. I like it very much."

Janet helped with the Saturday chores the next morning. After the kitchen was cleared, she went outside to sweep Fran's front walk. It was a beautiful autumn morning, crisp and invigorating, without the cold of the previous day. She wondered if Gina was playing around the neighborhood. The prospect of being in the child's home that evening and meeting her foster parents both intrigued and pained her. She hoped that Fran had exaggerated the couple's failings.

With the sweeping finished, Janet was cutting chrysanthemums for a bouquet when she saw Rose coming up the other side of the street. In her dark, foreign-looking attire, she seemed out of place, as though superimposed upon the scene by clever camera work. Seemingly oblivious to her surroundings, the old woman shuffled from the sidewalk and into the street. Halfway across, she stopped and cast confused glances from side to side. It was clear that she was lost.

There was no traffic and Janet hesitated, waiting for Rose to start moving again. When this failed to happen, she took matters in hand and went to her.

Up close, she marveled that she had imagined anything sinister about the old woman. She could see that she had probably once been handsome, but she was now wrinkled and toothless, her eyes a milky grey. Yet she looked well-cared for. The grizzled hair peeking from the folds of the babushka appeared clean, as did her black skirt, blouse and belted sweater.

"It's a pretty day, isn't it?" Janet said companionably, undeterred by the woman's empty stare. She touched her arm in the hope of guiding her toward the pavement. "The entire weekend is supposed to be nice before it turns cold again."

Rose cocked her head in a birdlike way. "Hot," she mumbled vaguely, looking past Janet's shoulder. "So hot. Everything burning hot."

Janet wondered if this was some sort of reverse comment about the weather. Rose's accent was unidentifiable, and her missing teeth caused a lisp which further distorted her words.

"All gone, all gone." There had been a bright, if empty, note in Rose's voice at first, but it changed, becoming fearful. "All gone!" Her eyes darted anxiously, and then briefly focused on Janet. "They were with us," she said, as if imparting an urgent message, "then they were all gone."

Despite the wrinkles and stooped shoulders of the figure before her, Janet felt she confronted a bewildered child. Making an instinctive gesture to comfort as well as distract, she offered one of the chrysanthemums. "Here, take one of these. Look, a bright orange one."

Calming, Rose accepted the flower and held it to her breast. "All gone, all gone," she lamented mournfully, gazing once more into space.

Taking her arm and saying she would walk her home, Janet led her safely to the sidewalk. Rose trudged along willingly. They were halfway to the yellow house when a black Oldsmobile purred to a stop against the opposite curb. The driver's door opened and a smartly dressed woman in her late fifties emerged. Her coloring was exotic, her complexion olive-toned, her hair a glossy black. As she hurried toward them, Janet observed the cut and fit of her double-breasted black suit, the pearl buttons catching the light. Her pearl and ruby jewelry looked genuine, and the upswept style of the woman's hair emphasized a face of classic beauty that transcended age.

"Oh, Rose," the woman cried in relief as she reached them, touching the older woman's arm. "Oh, Rose . . ." Looking at Janet, she nervously moistened her lips, showing a hesitant, uneasy reserve that seemed at odds with her sophisticated appearance. "Thank you for extending kindness to my sister. I am sorry you have been troubled." Her voice was soft and the phrasing of her words had a stilted, unfamiliar cadence, although the actual pronunciation held no accent.

"She's been no trouble," Janet assured. "I was just seeing her home."

The woman's eyes were like golden-brown cabochons, cat's eyes, tiger eyes. They widened, as if in alarm. "How do you know where she lives?"

"Because we're on the other end of the block. I'm staying with my sister, Fran Elwin. My name is Janet Fairweather."

"Oh, the Elwins, yes, I understand." The woman appeared flustered, but her voice was controlled as she said. "I am Muriel Renner. My husband and I . . ." she gestured toward a figure that was only a shadow in the closed car, "we went shopping but at our first stop, which fortunately was nearby, Rose became separated from us."

While listening, Janet had been covertly comparing the two women. Making allowance for the ravages of age, she could now see a certain similarity between the bone structure of Rose's face and that of her much younger sister. Remembering how the old woman had repeated the words *all gone*, Janet said, "I think Rose tried to explain about being lost. She must have been hunting for you."

"And I have been driving up and down, hunting for her," Muriel answered, faint exasperation in her tone. She observed the chrysanthemum which Rose held like a small sunburst against the dark sweater. "I see you have given her a flower. It is a surprise she accepted it. She allows few people to approach her." Softening a trifle, Muriel allowed herself a brief smile and then reverted to formality. "Thank you again." She took her sister's arm. "We will be leaving now."

The woman led Rose to the car and helped her into the back. She closed the door with firm deliberation as if emphasizing that the woman should stay where she was put. As Muriel resumed her place at the wheel, Janet caught only a glimpse of the male figure in the passenger seat before the door closed again.

The car drove off soundlessly, its sparkling windows and glossy black finish reflecting the light like mirrors. Janet watched until it turned the corner.

"I just met two of your neighbors," Janet said when she returned to Fran's house where Warren was helping Fran wash windows.

"Oh, which ones?" Warren asked

"Muriel and Rose from behind you." Janet returned the broom to its closet and placed the chrysanthemums she'd cut on the table.

"Did you also meet Dr. Renner?" Fran said.

"Muriel's husband is a doctor?"

"Yes, Dr. Herman Renner. He's a retired child psychologist."

"I didn't meet him—he stayed in the car. The fact that he's a doctor explains Muriel's elegant clothes. Not that she wouldn't be beautiful anyway."

"Isn't she gorgeous?" Fran said. "If I could only look as good when I reach her age!"

Warren, a big-boned, darkly bearded man, observed his wife's jeans and bandanna-wrapped hair. "Then right now," he said in a teasing tone, "you would have to look as glamorous as she must have looked at thirty-three."

"Oh, shut up," Fran admonished good-naturedly. "Instead of making wisecracks, why don't you go into the dining room with the stepladder and get things ready for me to do the windows there."

After Warren left, Janet said, "Does Muriel have an accent, or what? I couldn't figure it out. And what an unlikely pair of sisters." She grinned mischievously. "Now we know what folks say about us."

"Twerp!" Fran grinned back at her. "The Renners are from Argentina. Muriel is unquestionably an aristocrat, but Rose looks like a peasant." Going to the sink, Fran ran fresh water into the scrub bucket. "We had a party to welcome the Renners to the neighborhood.

I don't know what they did with Rose, but she didn't come. Hired a sitter maybe. Muriel's awfully reserved and seemed nervous. She clung to her husband's side all evening and barely said a word. Old Herman is more outgoing, only in a condescending way. Not actually offensive, understand, but it's clear he considers himself a cut above the common herd."

"Renner?" The name puzzled Janet. "I'd expect a Spanish-sounding name from Argentina."

"He's originally from good old Freud-land, Austria. I told you he was a psychologist, didn't I? To escape the Second World War, he fled to South America, where he met Muriel. They've been married for almost forty years. As young as she still looks, she must have been in her teens. They moved to this country because of his health." Rolling her eyes, she added, "His heart specialist is in Manhattan, so don't ask me why he bought a house in Princeton."

"Manhattan is only an hour away," reasoned Janet. "A lot closer than Argentina."

"Well, I suppose that's true enough," Fran agreed with a laugh. "He struck me as a scholar, so being near the university might be the draw. Still, it doesn't seem practical."

Janet's brief glimpse of the figure in the car had told her nothing about the doctor's appearance. Curious, she asked, "Will the Renners be at the party tonight?"

"Probably not. Those flowers are so pretty. Here, let me get you a vase." Rummaging in a cupboard, Fran said over her shoulder, "I think Dr. Renner made a special effort to attend that first neighborhood gathering. Even then, he had to leave early. You can tell he's not well just by looking at him."

Janet was disappointed. The image of Rose and Muriel stood vividly in her mind and she felt an interest in meeting the doctor. But regardless of how he looked and acted, she was convinced that the Renners were all wrong for the yellow house. The place had impressed her as needing young people with a growing family.

Chapter 6

ON SATURDAY EVENING JANET WAS MORE than grateful for the warmth of her new coat as she walked between Fran and Warren to the Stocktons' party. The way Fran had wordlessly jockeyed her into that position amused her. It was clear that Fran felt her little sister needed the protection of their larger, more bulky bodies.

Back when Fran started dating Warren, Janet had felt instant approval simply because of his size. At that time, Fran had just broken up with a fellow so frail and scrawny she could have worn him on her charm bracelet. Warren's burliness made a perfect complement to her full-figured proportions. Later, when Janet had gotten to know him better, she learned he also balanced Fran out in other ways, tempering her tendency to steamroller people for their own good and serving as a quiet foil for her lively enthusiasm. The serenity of their home was due as much to his sure stability as to Fran's more voluble warmth and caring.

As they walked along, Warren nodded his shaggy head as he related an amusing incident from his day. Janet wondered if he was trying to make sure she felt at ease when going to meet a crowd of new people.

She decided to participate in the conversation instead of plodding along between them like a package that needed special care.

"I intended to go around the block yesterday," she said, "but I got cold and didn't even get halfway. The layout of the block seems odd, with the two houses on either end having deep back yards that meet in the middle, while the houses facing the side streets have almost no back yards at all."

"Wide side yards though," Fran said.

"Yes, but still . . ." Janet decided her attempt at conversation had fallen flat, but then Warren spoke.

"I thought the same thing when Fran and I bought here," he said. "The house where the Renners live is clearly the oldest home, probably built in the middle of the last century. The deed to our house, Fran's and mine, stated it was constructed in 1910. All the homes on the side streets are newer, probably post-war in the forties and fifties. I imagine that the Renner house originally stood alone. Then the rear half of their property was sold to the people who built our house. Building lots on both sides were sold off later."

"That makes sense," Janet said. "Big plots of land can be expensive. Didn't people way back have caretakers to maintain appearances? The Renner house was probably built by people with money."

She recalled that after she and Clay and Becky had returned to Alabama after their Princeton visit, she remained enraptured by the yellow house. A library book about American architecture told her that in the 1800s, houses modeled on the villas of Renaissance Italy were termed "Victorian Italianate." What she had called a *cupola* was, in an Italianate house, called a *belvedere*.

"Here we are at the Stoctons' place," Warren said as he steered them toward the blue front door. A mercury-vapor lamp theatrically spotlighted the columned facade, showing the eye-catching changes that had been made since Janet saw it the previous day. On the left of the wide stoop sat three candlelit jack-o'-lanterns and a tall shock of beribboned Indian corn.

The jack-o'-lanterns welcomed Janet with flickering eyes and leering, gap-toothed mouths. An errant breeze wafted the smell of scorched pumpkin across her nostrils, reminding her of Halloween nights long past: cider-crisp darkness, sweaty costumes, and tightly clutched candy bags. She remembered shrill giggles smothered by colorful masks and frantic dashes past vacant lots. Had that shadow been a ghost? Had there been monsters behind that tree?

"I bet Gina helped carve the pumpkins," she said as Warren reached toward the doorbell. "That's always so much fun for kids."

"Maybe," Fran answered doubtfully. "They're carved awfully well. I don't know who would have taken the time to supervise."

The door was opened by a man in a brown tweed suit worn with a white shirt and a brown striped necktie. "Hi," he said. "I'm playing doorman for our hosts."

"And doing a good job of it, Arthur," Fran said with a laugh as they stepped inside, herding Janet along with them and making introductions.

Arthur turned out to be another neighbor on the block. He took their coats and slung them over his arm. "I'll put these upstairs," he said and was gone.

So this is where Gina lives, Janet thought, seeing the open doorways of lighted rooms on either side of the spacious foyer clouded by the haze of cigarette smoke. No sign of the child. For just an instant, she recalled that strange moment when she'd seen Gina through Fran's kitchen window and felt she was someone she should know.

"Here comes Veronica," Fran said.

Janet had no more time to look around before Veronica was upon them, a striking woman with an upsweep of champagne-colored hair, heavily mascaraed blue-gray eyes, and a broad, out-thrust jaw that no amount of artful shading could minimize.

"Fran's little sister!" she rhapsodized, pressing both of Janet's hands in cool, beringed fingers. She also wore diamond earrings that matched the diamond brooch on the wide padded shoulder of her turquoise satin dress. Snaring them with fragrant clouds of perfume, she moved them into the adjoining space she called the "music room." There, a tuxedoed waiter ferried refreshments. Billy Joel's "The Longest Time" played on what must have been an excellent stereo system because the music enhanced but didn't compete with the people talking and laughing companionably.

The walls, draperies, carpeting and the upholstered pieces in the room were white, the starkness dramatized by splashes of brilliant color. A vivid Scandinavian tapestry hung over the white marble fireplace where flames danced brightly. A sectional couch in a conversation area was flanked by tall crystal vases holding tropical blossoms. There was no hint that a child inhabited the house.

Having paused long enough to allow Janet to absorb the décor's impact, Veronica said to her, "Now, you're from Alabama, aren't you dear?"

"I only lived there a few years," Janet said, aware of Fran hovering protectively at her elbow. She trusted that Fran hadn't revealed the tragic details behind her move.

"I'm a Southerner too," Veronica confided with a glistening smile and Janet realized the woman hadn't really listened to her reply. Her voice now exhibited a slight drawl that had been absent before. "My Tommy is also from the South. We're Virginia Stocktons, not the-founder-of-Princeton Stocktons like everyone always assumes."

Feeling she was expected to say something, Janet ventured, "I know there is a Stockton Street in town."

"Oh, so you're aware of local history?" said Tommy Stockton, who had stepped up in time to hear Janet's comment. Cigarette in hand, he wore a three-piece gray suit with a sapphire stud in his gray silk tie. "You'll want to meet Kirby Orchard. He's around here someplace."

Veronica introduced Janet to her tall, glossy-handsome husband. His hair was a flaxen shade similar to Veronica's, and his manly jaw was even wider. Janet thought they looked like a pugnacious Ken and Barbie. Did they have a life-sized pink Corvette?

Tommy flagged the waiter who carried a tray of beverages. Janet chose one and Tommy said proudly, "Mateus is an excellent party wine, pleasing guests who are not connoisseurs. Excellent," he repeated and then said, "Stockton Street was named for a Quaker from Long Island, who gets the credit for founding the town of Princeton back in the 1700s. The old Quaker meetinghouse that Stockton built still stands. But, as Veronica has possibly mentioned, we're the Virginia Stocktons."

"Oh, Tommy, I just explained," giggled Veronica.

"We'll circulate on our own," Warren offered pleasantly as Tommy parted from his wife, excusing himself to meet new arrivals.

"Why bless me, but no!" corrected Veronica, laying a hand on Janet's arm. Her southern drawl was thickening like corn starch gravy over a flame as she said to Fran, "You and your lovely husband can circulate. You already know everyone! But there's someone your sister must meet."

Swept across the room, Janet found herself brought to a stop before a plump Friar Tuck of a man, probably in his early fifties. His thick glasses covered pale, friendly eyes and his bald head was neatly circled by a fringe of gray hair. He had been engaged in conversation with a younger man, but upon Veronica's arrival, they both turned toward her with polite and expectant attention.

"Kirby," said Veronica, "this sweet little neighbor here has been just dying to meet you! She's Janet Fairweather, Fran Elwin's sister from Alabama. Janet, this is Kirby Orchard."

Kirby smiled. "A pleasure," he said.

Veronica turned to the younger man, who appeared close to thirty. "Janet," she said, "you also must meet our guest of honor for the evening, Ben Yates."

"A pleasure indeed," Ben said. Dressed in a casual looking green corduroy sports coat, a tan shirt, and darker brown trousers, he had pleasant, irregular features and crisp-looking brown hair.

He was about to say something more when Veronica hooked him by the elbow. "Come along, Ben, dear. Sorry to drag you away, but so many are eager to meet you. A chore, I know, but so necessary to help your talk tonight serve its best purpose." Her drawl had mysteriously fled.

"Well," said Kirby, the expression on his jowly face pleasant as he and

Janet found themselves alone. "Such an intriguing introduction from Veronica. Why have you been so eager to meet an old duffer like me?"

"I don't exactly know," she answered honestly, sipping her wine—indeed pleasing to a non-connoisseur like her, she thought, amused by Tommy's lofty comment. She mentally backtracked to the conversation when she had first heard Kirby's name.

"Actually, Tommy Stockton suggested we meet," she said. "He didn't explain why, but it might be in connection with Princeton's history. Does that ring a bell?"

"Exactly the right note," Kirby said with a cheerful nod, puffing his waist-coated chest and considerable paunch with unconscious pride. "I'm a cinema arts instructor by profession, but local history is a hobby. You have questions about the town?"

Janet laughed. "That was a misunderstanding. But tell me about your film classes. I once took a film history class and I adore the work from the thirties and forties."

Kirby beamed. "As do I!" He launched into an elaborate discourse of old films. He was interrupted when Fran breezed by, checking, Janet was sure, to make sure little sister wasn't languishing in a corner. She was asked if she wanted more wine, but she glanced at her empty glass on the table and declined. One was enough for her. Fran introduced her to a silver-haired couple, their neighbors, the Gilroys, and then moved on. Janet lost sight of Kirby as the Gilroys took her to meet others.

She soon began to feel weary. Her curiosity about Gina had made her anticipate the evening, but with the child nowhere in sight, her energies started to flag. Dropping out of the conversational stream, she found herself remembering when she had proudly donned her first maternity dress. Back then, she had been filled with bright hopes for the future. It was dismaying to feel the sting of tears. Lord! A single glass of wine and she was getting maudlin.

The traffic had started to drift in the direction of the dining room. She allowed it to carry her along. The scent of food made her realize she was hungry. The vague thought crossed her mind that judging from the delicious aromas, the banquet table promised to be a lot less artificial than the hostess. She couldn't help wondering if Veronica was always so "on."

In the dining room, a long, white-clothed table was spread with a tempting array of dishes. Janet had just picked up a plate and moved into line when she heard a masculine voice intone near her ear. "Beat me to it. I intended to find you and ask if there was something I could bring to you."

Janet turned to look up at the guest of honor, Ben Yates, seeing a warm twinkle in his gray eyes. She smiled, but at the same time, felt herself shying away. He was attractive, but . . . Then she wondered what was wrong with her? Her failed marriage didn't leave her scared of men. Besides, he was simply being pleasant. Her problem was she didn't get out enough. But now, here she was.

Smiling, she said, "It's good that you didn't. It's quite a feast. I wouldn't have wanted to miss anything."

He grinned. "For you, I would have made a million trips." Taking a plate, he stepped into line beside her.

She felt an unexpected sense of pleasure and was glad of her flattering new dress. Light, nonsensical talk with an attractive stranger . . . it was a party, wasn't it?

"What's that dish over there?" she said, "Curry, but with slices of what—papaya?"

Shrugging, he spooned some onto his plate. "Don't know, but I'm game for adventure." He looked at her. "I'm glad I found you again. We had just started to talk and then Veronica swept me away."

"She's the hostess. She has a job to do, introducing people to other people."

"A job she takes seriously," he said as they moved on down the table. "I'll let you in on a secret." He bent closer. "We're gathered here tonight in the name of status. Shall we install a few solar panels, put in a glass room with lots of thermal mass? What we want to know is, what's the latest in conspicuous consumption?"

Janet tilted her head. "Sounds as if you're a cynic."

His laugh was good-natured. "Not really, but I guess I am sounding that way. Our hostess manages to set a certain tone if you know what I mean."

Janet smiled, thinking she knew exactly what he meant.

They turned from the table and probably would have hunted for a place to sit together but Veronica rushed up.

"Oh, Ben, good! You've already filled your plate. Could you bring it along to the library?" She turned to Janet. "I'm just so sorry to be taking this dear man away from you again, but there's literature I want to distribute after his talk, and I must have his approval first."

With little choice except to go, Ben flung a look over his shoulder. "Later," he mouthed to Janet as Veronica led him off.

For a moment, Janet felt very alone. Then, seeing Warren seating himself on a cream-colored settee, she joined him.

All this white," he sighed, uncomfortably balancing his plate on his knees, looking like a grizzly at a tea party. With no place else to put it, he'd placed his punch cup carefully on the snowy carpet by his feet.

Janet found it relaxing to be with someone she knew after making small talk with strangers, including Ben Yates although he'd been a pleasant passing moment.

A tan cat padded up and nosed Warren's drink. It was the Siamese Janet had seen with Gina. Pleased, she thought that if it was the little girl's pet, her life must not be as empty as Fran had made it sound. She imagined Gina snug in her bed, confident that her foster mother would save her special treats from the party. Yes, that's surely the kind of mother Veronica was.

With the arrival of fruit and chocolate-rich French pastries, the crowd was directed to take their desserts into the living room, where Ben would give his talk. Fran, like a brood hen, wanted Janet close under her wing, but she and Warren had seats in the front and Janet preferred a place farther back. She settled on a chair along the wall near the foyer. Where a guard might sit, with a view of both the front door and the room. The thought amused her. She looked toward the front of the room and Ben.

He was really quite nice looking, she thought. She was glad she had come. Getting out and associating with people was good for her.

She waited expectantly as Veronica introduced Ben to the gathering saying he'd just returned from Arizona after doing important work there.

Arizona, Janet thought. Someone who traveled a lot in his job, a charming man, but she was in no position to think about anything other than getting her life in order.

Ben started to speak, his pleasant tenor carrying clearly. Although it was evident that he believed energy conservation was of vital importance, there was nothing of the fanatic in his approach. Janet wasn't sure whether he was an architect or a builder. Fran could be counted on for the answer. Listening to him speak, she judged that he was a person who could take things seriously without taking himself too seriously as well. A comfortable trait.

Caught up in her thoughts, Janet only gradually became aware of the smoke drifting from the fireplace. Certainly, Tommy should be jumping up to fix the draft or something, but no one moved. The smoke wasn't visible. There was only an increasingly evil smoldering, more repulsive than anything she had smelled from a fireplace before. She surveyed the crowd, seeing the broad shoulders of the men in their suits and dinner jackets and the women in their low-backed party dresses all leaning toward Ben in rapt attention. How could they sit and be oblivious to a reek that was worsening by the second?

It suddenly occurred to her that the smell probably wasn't from the fireplace. It must be from the jack-o'-lanterns outside. Instead of guttering themselves lifeless, the candles had started to consume their hosts. That charred, nauseating odor, so thick on the air that she could barely breathe . . . burning pumpkins. It was the only explanation. And she alone had detected it because she was the closest to the front door.

Unnoticed by the others, she slipped into the foyer. Hidden from the view of the living room, she peered through the glass door panel, thinking that if flames jumped to the dry corn shocks, there was no telling what else would go up. The Halloween display was too far to the side of the wide stoop for her to see, but at least there was no flickering reflection of flames. Relieved, she quietly eased the door open and stepped outside, confident she could easily take care of the matter by scooping up earth from around the bushes near the side of the stoop and smother the fire.

Janet stepped dead. Illuminated by the outside lamp, the jack-o'-lanterns grinned placidly, the candles within them safely extinguished to blackness. Baffled, she stared. If not burning pumpkins, then what? She sniffed, unable to detect even a hint of the smell. The source of the burning had to be inside after all. Only, why had no one else seemed aware of it?

She was still standing in perplexity when she heard the thin, distant wail of an infant. Attention captured, she tilted her head, realizing that there *was* a baby in the neighborhood. Through some trick of the chill night air, the sound echoed, making a chorus of lost, lonely cries. Memories of Becky leaped into Janet's mind. Biting her lip, she waited tensely for the crying to cease. *Go to your baby, mother*, she begged silently, tears springing to her eyes. *Go to your baby while you can.* Blessedly, the sounds faded.

Shivering, arms hugged about herself, Janet waited another moment, and then eased back inside the foyer.

It wasn't until the door was closed behind her that she realized that the foyer no longer held a smoky odor. Unbelievably, that dreadful smoldering, that stench, was now totally gone. Only the mingled scents of the party . . . the foods and drink, cigarettes and perfumes, filled the air.

Chapter 7

JANET LEANED AGAINST THE INSIDE OF the front door, grateful that she couldn't be seen from the living room where Ben continued his talk.

What had happened to the smoky smell? It seemed impossible that the dreadful odor could have dissipated so completely. Had it been her imagination? No one else in the living room had seemed aware of it. Was she having an olfactory hallucination? The thought frightened her. She ordered herself to calm down.

She suddenly felt a hard, nervous spasm in the pit of her stomach and knew she was on the verge of being sick. After not having much of an appetite for ages, she realized she had gone wild, bingeing on a bizarre combination of unaccustomed foods. She could hardly expect anything but trouble. That Indian dish. Delicious, but with what kinds of spices and herbs?

A cheering thought momentarily overrode her discomfort: perhaps the phantom smells had been due to an allergic reaction. Yes, why not? She had heard of such things. Her stomach squirmed again and she hastened toward the steps.

A lamp at the head of the staircase guided her toward the bathroom.

Carpeted, she thought in dismay as she rushed in and shoved the door shut behind her. Without a doubt, she was going to spill up all over Veronica's downy soft rug before reaching her desired destination.

But once on her knees, the pull of imminent sickness blessedly lessened. She rested her arms on a puffed and padded toilet seat and gazed bleary-eyed down at the rug. It was a shade Veronica's designer probably called pale raspberry, but a grateful Janet was thinking it was more the color of soothing, quieting Pepto-Bismol.

When she finally rose to her feet and stared at her reflection in the mirror over the sink, she saw that her complexion was pale and the hazel color of her eyes was washed out, almost bleached, giving her that zombie look she'd had during those first months after Becky's death.

Becky, dead.

The words seemed to toll in her mind like a mournful iron bell. She stared hopelessly into the mirror, wondering if the time would ever come when sorrow would cease to catch her unaware; when she could hear a baby cry without her first thought being that it was her child. The crying she had heard earlier . . . if only by some miracle it could have been her own dear baby. If only she could rewrite history and go rushing to her, reaching her in time.

She felt in no condition to return to the party. Maybe it had been too soon to get out and try to socialize, especially among so many strangers. She decided to wait upstairs until after Ben's talk. Once the crowd started milling around again, she would find Fran and say she was calling it a night.

Stepping into the hall, she looked to a lamp-lit room where coats, so many of them beautiful full-length furs, lay spread across a bed. She decided to wait there. As she headed toward it, she heard the blurred, distant murmur of Ben's voice from below. To one side was a bay window that overlooked the Stockton back yard. What was probably a sunny hideaway by daylight was now murky, the multiple panes of glass admitting a ghostlike glow that spread over a small upholstered bench.

Janet was startled by a movement to one side.

Gina.

The little girl, dressed in a long nightgown, stood in the shadows. She had apparently been looking out the window until Janet had appeared, then she had drawn back. Her small figure showed indistinctly in the poor light, her dark eyes soft smudges of blackness in the moth-white triangle of her face.

Janet looked at the child and once again felt an odd stirring of emotion. She struggled to settle herself.

"Gina," she said, moving forward and forcing calmness into her voice. She sank to the bench so she wouldn't continue to tower over the child. "I'm sorry if I scared you." When Gina offered no response, Janet continued in a soothing tone. "Actually, I guess we scared each other, didn't we? Say, I bet you're wondering how I knew your name. You know Mrs. Elwin? Fran Elwin? She's my sister, and I'm staying with her, right down the block. We're just a few houses away."

Gina continued to stare at her mutely. Her dark eyes, lost in the shadows, gave no clue as to what she might be thinking. With a sense of defeat, Janet realized she child had probably been told not to talk to strangers. The little girl had been minding her own business in her own house and then a strange lady popped up and started quizzing her. No wonder she held her tongue.

"I'm sorry, Gina," Janet said softly, feeling a surprising depth of regret at the child's silence. "Maybe we'll see each other again, sometime when your mother is with you. Then you'll know it's okay."

Reluctantly, she arose from the bench. The view from the window caught her eye. The moonlit panorama showed a perspective far different from that of her window at Fran's, yet the dramatic silhouette of a particularly massive tree off to the left must be the copper beech in the Renner yard. The house, the beech tree . . . the scene was beautiful, yet at the same time, oddly disquieting.

She felt Gina's fingers touch her arm.

Startled, she heard the small voice; the sound so thin that Janet wasn't positive that Gina had spoken at all. She felt the small fingers close upon the fabric of her sleeve, pulling with a strange urgency.

"Yes, Gina?" she said. Janet lowered herself to the bench, again putting herself on eye level with the child, whose face now seemed to swim in the misty half-darkness.

"Yes, Gina? Did you want to tell me something?"

Gina spoke in that same eerie fashion, only this time the sound traveled clearly: "I heard your baby."

Janet gasped, feeling as if a blade of ice had been drawn along her spine.

"I heard your baby," the child repeated. Lifting her hand to Janet's face, she looked deeply into her eyes. Those gentle fingertips, moving in a warm, smooth caress against the frozen marble of Janet's cheek was the only reality in a world gone suddenly mad.

"I heard it tonight. I heard it before," came that small, disembodied message. "I heard your baby crying."

Chapter 8

IT WAS LUNCHTIME ON MONDAY. JANET sat with Fran and her friend, Ida Aaron, in a booth at the Magic Spoon. The walls of the restaurant were decorated with antique wooden kitchen implements, a collection of iron weather vanes, and stencils of Pennsylvania-Dutch hex signs. One of the signs, composed of a stylized blossom, reminded Janet of clover. Hex signs were supposed to be a farmer's protection against demons, don't let lightning strike my barn, keep my cows giving sweet milk. Years ago, she had a four-leafed clover tucked in her wallet. She wondered what had happened to it. Whatever, she had lost it, along with the luck it was supposed to bring. Yet maybe, she thought, *just maybe*, things could change.

After general conversation during most of the meal, Ida Arron, a slim redhead with Madonna-style crimped hair topped with a blue satin bow, asked Janet to tell her something about her work experience.

In preparation, Janet had mentally reviewed what to say: she had three years of college with a major in journalism. She had also been on the staff of her high school newspaper, but she had nothing to show for any of it. Clay had found all her old papers and threw them away.

"That's the past," he had told her. "You're starting a new life with me." And she, besotted, had been charmed. That had been her, the so-called *modern woman*--independent enough to go to bed with a man at the drop of a hat, but still letting the man make the rules. Ha!

She told Ida about her studies and then explained that she'd held a short-term job with a commercial printer. That had been after one of Clay's moves. She'd done cutting and paste-up which was an exacting task. She was a fast and accurate typist and knew word processing.

"The program I used was Word Star," Janet said, "but I also learned DOS and was excited about new programs coming out from the Microsoft Company but I never had the opportunity to work with them."

Smiling, Ida said, "I think you'll be excited about our school's program—a step up from what you've seen in the past. There are templates you can use that easily make professional-looking layouts." She lit a cigarette. "You'll be putting the newsletter together with material gathered by the previous editor, staff interviews and photos done by the students attending the high school. They receive extra credit for their work. We use the newsletter as a teaching experience, and of course, an advertisement for the adult school."

Ida began discussing the adult school program itself, the history and how it worked together with the high school, sharing office materials, and so on. Janet's mind returned to the memory that had held her for the past thirty-six-plus hours: Gina's small voice, so ghostly in the otherworldly mood of the Stocktons' moonlit hall and those haunting words, *I heard your baby. I heard your baby crying.*

What had caused the child to link the sound of a baby with her? Janet wished she had retained the presence of mind to ask, but in her shock, she had said nothing. Gina had left the hallway and Janet was left with confusion. How could the little girl have known a crying infant could represent only one thing to her, *Becky, dear lost little Becky*. She felt as if Gina had magically seen into her grieving heart.

Still talking, Ida placed her Virginia Slim cigarette in the ashtray and circled around to the present day and said how pleased she thought Janet would be with the school's word processing program.

"I'll have to learn it first," Janet said, wondering. It almost sounded like she was getting the job, like it was already settled.

"With your experience, I'll expect you to catch on easily," Ida said. "I'd like you to go to the adult classes at the high school tonight, see it in action, and then tomorrow, come to the high school office around eight-thirty. Crystal, our computer expert, will get you started."

Janet guessed she had the job, and knew she was right when Ida started discussing the terms. She would be paid for completing the newsletter, and she could spend as much time as needed in the office learning what she needed to do the job. The remuneration was more than she had expected and Ida said the paperwork would be ready to sign when she came in the next day. Janet had never had an interview go so smoothly and quickly.

Lifting her cigarette to take another puff, Ida said, "You basically can set your own hours as long as the job is ready to go to the printer on the date we discussed." She brushed smoke from her eyes. "I've got to tell you, I'm excited to have you aboard. The previous girl was familiar with the program, but she simply typed in what she had collected from others. It was accurately done but without style or polish. Your background should make an improvement in the overall publication and the students will also learn from it."

After a bit more conversation, with Janet confirming that she would attend the adult school that night and was looking forward to getting started the next day, the luncheon was over.

After Ida left, Janet was quiet.

Fran broke the silence. "Well, Jan," she said, "are you pleased or not?"

Janet looked up. "I know Ida's your friend, but that was the phoniest interview I ever sat through. What did you do, pay her?"

She expected her sister to be annoyed, but instead, Fran laughed. "I put together old papers I'd saved from your high school and college years. I showed them to Ida ahead of time. I don't know why she didn't mention them, but she went into the interview knowing a lot more about you than you realized."

"Why didn't you tell me?"

"I figured that with moving several times, as you had, you might not have any of your old papers handy and if I asked and you didn't, you would have come to the interview a nervous wreck. I just took a short-cut."

That was Fran, Janet thought, a mastermind behind the scenes. Finally, Janet took a deep breath and had to smile. "Okay, big sister, I guess the word is thanks."

On the way back to the house to drop Janet off and then return to The Magic Spoon, Fran turned the conversation to the Stockton party.

"How did you like Kirby Orchard? He's a love, but when inspired, his wit can be wicked. He once did a routine about a couple who had been picked up by a spaceship. He handled it as if he were reading from a *National Enquirer* article, but we soon realized he was parodying how Veronica and Tommy would report such an experience. So funny. I can't remember exactly what he said, but it was deliciously mean."

Unable to resist, Janet mimicked Veronica's sugary drawl. "We're not the Martian Stocktons, we're the Venusian ones."

Fran exploded into laughter. "Yes, yes, exactly! You've got their number." Turning the car from the highway to the street that would eventually lead to her block, she said more soberly, "Actually, Veronica can be all right if you catch her without Tommy. Then she stops acting as if she's auditioning for a part in a play."

Regretting her crack about the Stocktons because it was encouraging Fran to continue discussing the evening, Janet once again relived those strange moments with Gina. Her inner ear still reverberated with that eerie message: *I heard your baby crying.*

A flash of understanding came to her. Swallowing a gasp, she didn't see how she could have been so stupid. How could she have thought there was something almost supernatural in Gina's words when the truth was obvious?

There had been no need to introduce herself to the child. Alert to the new face in the neighborhood, Gina had known perfectly well who she was. She had probably heard Fran say something to Veronica like, "My sister is coming to visit with me a while. She recently lost her baby." *Lost*. That was the word people always used. "Her baby had seemed so healthy but then she lost it. Such a terrible thing."

So on the night of the party, when Gina heard a baby crying from some nearby house, she had made what seemed a logical connection. The child didn't know that the word "lost" was a euphemism for "death." She remembered Gina's pale, upturned face. Had she believed her information would help locate the missing infant? Janet was touched by the thought.

For a moment she felt warmed, but then she started wondering what else Fran had revealed about her to her friends. Although she found it too painful to discuss details of Becky's death she didn't mind if others knew it had happened. Her marriage breakup was different. It was no one's business unless she chose to reveal it herself. She had assumed Fran would realize this, but there was no assurance. It made her uncomfortable to think she might be meeting strangers who had chewed over her marital woes.

Clearing her throat, she ventured, "Fran, I want to know something. I'm not going to be mad, or anything—I mean, I'll understand, but have you said much to people about Clay and me splitting?"

Fran took her eyes from the street that was bright along the curbs with the fool's gold of fallen poplar leaves. "I couldn't say much—you've never shared any details."

Janet flushed. "I suppose that's true."

"Suppose?" Fran's voice rose and it was obvious a nerve had been struck. "Look, I assumed you were the most blissfully contented wife in the Western hemisphere. I had misgivings about Clay. I felt he was jealous of any relationship you had outside of him, which included me. But I hadn't a clue your marriage was in trouble until you wrote and said you were getting a divorce. It was clear that you didn't want big sister to mix in. I guess you had too much of me calling the shots when you were young."

Janet was surprised at her sister's insight. Had Fran allowed her to gradually test her wings as she grew up, she doubted she would have flown off so wildly at her first taste of freedom. But she also knew that her sister had always been motivated by her best intentions.

"I'm sorry, Fran," she said, reaching across the seat. "When I was a kid, I told you everything."

Fran's voice softened and went husky with emotion. "I learned a lot from watching Warren's kids grow up. Things I wished I had known with you."

Her natural buoyancy asserted itself. "But back to your original question. I didn't speculate about your troubles to anyone. When you called to let us know about Becky's death we rushed to you immediately. You and Clay were, of course grief-stricken, but I never dreamed your marriage was in trouble. This year when you wrote that you were getting a divorce you gave no details. When I invited you here and you came, it was obvious you didn't want to talk about it. As difficult as it's been for me, I've respected it."

"Oh, Fran," Janet said, tears coming into her eyes. "I've been so wrapped up in myself that I've never realized how I hurt you."

"I figured you had your reasons, Jan, and when the time was right, you would open up. As far as other people, all I've said is that you're staying with us while you make some personal decisions."

"Wait a minute," said Janet as Fran pulled the car into her driveway and switched off the engine. "Okay, nobody on this block knows my marriage broke up, but if you mentioned that my baby had died, that's all right. I just don't want to go in detail about it."

"Well, they don't know anything about it from me," Fran said. "You and Clay only visited once with Becky and never met our friends. I had no reason to say mention any of it." Fran studied Janet's face. "What's the trouble, Jan? Would it be easier had I told people about Becky? Knowing how you've been, I assumed—"

Janet shook her head. "That's not it. It's just that somehow the word must have gotten around. How else would Gina have known about it?"

"Gina? What are you talking about?"

"When I went upstairs at the Stockton party, Gina was in the upstairs hall. That baby was crying again and this time, Gina heard it." Janet couldn't suppress a tone of self-justification. "You see, there really is a baby somewhere in the neighborhood."

"The one you heard crying that first night?"

"Well, it has to be, doesn't it? And Gina had to have learned I lost a baby because why else would she have thought it was mine?"

"What makes you think she believes that?" Fran's voice was oddly flat. "How would you come to that conclusion?"

"Because Gina said so, of course." Janet was irritated by Fran's quizzing. "When I saw her upstairs she had apparently just heard the sounds of the baby. She looked directly at me and said, 'I heard your baby. I heard your baby crying.'"

Even as Janet repeated the words, they retained the power to make a chill run down her spine. Trying to shrug it off, she said to Fran, "I don't know why you're so defensive I just told you it was all right if you'd told people that much."

Fran's expression, which had been unreadable, began to break up, her lips trembling, tears appearing in her eyes. "Oh, Janet," she breathed softly. "Oh, Jan . . ."

"What is it now?" Janet was annoyed with her sister's odd behavior "What in the world is wrong with you?"

"It's not me, Jan, it's . . ." She reached for Janet's hand, "What you're telling me Gina said about your baby couldn't have happened, Jan. None of it. Remember I told you she was an earthquake victim? She's the only survivor of her family, and the experience caused a terrible shock. She's perfectly healthy except that she's lost the power of speech. That's her handicap, Janet. She never could have told you anything about hearing a baby. Gina can't talk. She couldn't have told you a thing."

Chapter 9

THAT EVENING, JANET CALLED A TAXI to take her to the high school. Fran wanted to drive her, but she would have none of it, or rather, she would have nothing to do with Fran.

When Fran had dropped her bombshell about Gina's supposed inability to speak, Janet had refused to accept it.

"All right," she'd argued, "Maybe Gina was speaking in a sort of whisper, but I understood her perfectly."

"And she said she heard your baby?" Fran's wholesome face had reflected dismayed concern. "Even if by some miracle she did manage to speak, it would be Italian, not English."

"Oh, is she rumored to be deaf as well?" Janet shad aid with uncharacteristic sarcasm. "If she's been in this country any time at all, she's picked up some English. Besides, you told me that agency helps prepare children for the county where they're placed. Certainly enough to say a few simple words."

Once inside the house, Fran had insisted on phoning the Magic Spoon to explain she wouldn't be returning that afternoon.

"This is ridiculous," Janet snapped when Fran hung up.

Fran's lips were drawn in a thin line. "Maybe, but I can't go back to work and leave you. You should see yourself. You're as pale as a ghost."

"Can you blame me? It isn't exactly pleasant to discover my only sister thinks I'm a lunatic."

"That's not true. But you have been under a terrible strain. It's understandable if your nerves act up in funny ways."

Sure, nerves, Janet thought sourly. A nervous breakdown was more what Fran really meant. The conversation was pointless. Janet ended up seeking refuge in her room. Thank goodness there had been no occasion to mention the burning smell. She could just see Big Sister frantically dialing the Fruitcakes Anonymous hotline. Janet made a sound of disgust. Whether Gina's words made sense or not was no longer the question. The child had spoken, she had heard her, and Fran could like it or lump it.

Warren wasn't home from his seminar by dinner time, so Janet stayed in her room rather than face Fran alone over the dining table. When her taxi arrived, she merely called a brusque, "I'm leaving," over her shoulder as she went out the door. As she rode off, she supposed Fran was watching from a window, but she refused to look back.

Arriving at the high school, she gaped at the ivy-covered stonework and leaded windows of the Gothic-style building.

"This looks like one of the university buildings," she observed aloud as she got out and paid the driver.

"It's the school you wanted, miss."

Yes, she thought. My first step in a new job, a new life.

She walked up the steps and through the high school's front door with none of the trembling butterflies she might have expected.

Inside, she found adults of all ages in the hallways, eagerly chattering. The newsletter from Fran had the classes listed on a diagram. She fell in with a group going up a wide staircase to the upper-floor classrooms. Once there, she walked along a corridor and found descriptions posted on cards outside various adult school classrooms: YOUR LOG CABIN

HOUSE, ELIMINATING CLUTTER, COLLECTING DOLLS and CHOOSING A HOME COMPUTER.

After wandering around, she returned to the first floor and stepped into the auditorium, which offered a theater workshop. The auditorium was an impressive space with long, velvet-draped windows, an ornate balcony, and a stage that would credit any professional theater.

"Princeton High is like no other high school you can think of, right?" asked a plump, balding man who had gone in ahead of her. He had turned and caught her look of awe.

"Neither outside nor in," she agreed, still staring. "My school looked like a brick box, and our auditorium was also our cafeteria and gym." She shifted her gaze to the man and recognized him as Kirby Orchard.

"Oh, hi," she said, "I'm Janet Fairweather. We met at the Stocktons' party."

"I remember. I'd never forget such a pretty face," Kirby said. "You're a relative of the Elwins."

"Fran's sister," she said. The space was large enough so that they could talk quietly without disturbing the people gathered by the stage where a woman wearing bright red lipstick and a grey striped suit with puffy shoulders spoke with crisp authority to the group.

Janet looked back at Kirby. "You're part of this class?"

"What, with the Joan Crawford look-alike up there?" He chuckled. "No, just peeking in. My class starts a half-hour later in a regular-sized room. Are you here for this?"

"No, I'm just looking around," Janet said.

By mutual agreement, they returned to the hallway and Janet told him about her job to edit the newsletter.

"Ah, then you'll be including information about my Old House Genealogy class."

"I thought your subject was films," Janet said.

"That's on a different night. Here's this one." He took the newsletter she carried, found his name and pointed out the brief description, which he read aloud: "How to research the history of your house."

"House history?" she said.

Kirby nodded, rubbing a hand over his balding head. "That's an off-shoot of my interest in local lore. Wonderful houses in the Princeton area. House genealogy satisfies that urge to root through the past in the same way as family genealogy, but without the risks." Seeing her frown at the word risk, his tone became mischievous. "To learn that your roof once sheltered a rumrunner is fascinating stuff, but to learn that great-grandma had a fling with the hired man is hard for some to take."

Janet laughed. "Well, I hope to eventually settle somewhere near my sister. If I ever find my own house, I'll take your course and have fun learning how to dig out its skeletons."

As they talked, they walked down the corridor.

"Fun it is," Kirby said. "You'll learn that some houses even have intriguing patterns. I helped the Umsteads, the former owners of your sister's house, study its background. We learned that in its long history, all the owners have been middle-aged or elderly people."

Janet looked thoughtful. "That's probably because it's fairly small. There are only two bedrooms and one bath."

"Then it would then make an ideal first home for a young couple, wouldn't it? But that's never happened."

Janet narrowed her eyes. "Are you hinting that something besides practicality is afoot?"

He shoved his glasses up his snub nose, as he quoted from Shakespeare's Hamlet. *"More things in heaven and earth, Horatio."* He smiled, then said, "Odd as it sounds, it seems that invisible factors must attract certain types of people to certain homes—not always, but in enough cases to add an extra thrill to my research."

"It sounds as if you're talking about haunted houses."

With a wink, he lowered his voice to an ominous note. "Maybe I am. But I can't list that in an adult school newsletter, can I?" He glanced at his watch. "Time to head for my class. If you're just wandering around getting the feel of the place, continue on and follow signs to the cafeteria. Have a cup of coffee and meet people involved in the school, instructors as well as students."

"Good idea," she said. "Thanks."

In the cafeteria, she found coffee and ginger cookies were being offered, which made her realize how hungry she was. Foolish to have been so annoyed with Fran that she'd skipped supper. As Fran would have lectured years ago, "Don't cut off your nose to spite your face." Or in this case, to spite her stomach.

She was heading toward the refreshments when she was surprised to see a familiar tall figure turning from the table with a cup of coffee in his hand.

Ben Yates, tanned and fit, his jeans and crew-neck sweatshirt worn over a collared shirt, emphasizing his vigorous outdoorsy appearance. The bright cafeteria lights brought out touches of chestnut red in his dark, wavy hair.

Seeing her, his face broke into a pleased smile. He stepped around people and came up to her. "Janet, good to see you again. Are you taking a class?"

"No," she said, showing her surprise at seeing him. "I didn't expect to see you still in town. Aren't you from Arizona?"

"No, I'd just come back from there when we met at the Stocktons', but I have an apartment not far from here. Let's get you a cup of coffee and you can sit with me for a moment."

The next thing she knew she was telling him about the work she would be doing for the adult school newsletter and thinking that pretty soon she'd need to print flyers announcing, "Janet's New Job."

As for what Ben was doing at the school that evening, he said that questions had come up in one of the classes about solar power. He'd been invited to step in and answer them.

"I'm supposed to show up in about fifteen minutes," he said, glancing at his watch, "then I intend to go out for something to eat—more than cookies and coffee." He gave her a thoughtful look. "Since you're involved in the school, why not come with me to the class, see what's it's about, and afterward join me in getting some food. You said you had come here by taxi, so after we eat, I'll drive you back to your sister's house."

Ordinarily, she might have hesitated, but she was still annoyed enough with Fran to feel defiant.

"That sounds good," she said. "Actually, I'm starving."

She did, however, find a pay phone in the school lobby to call Fran and say she would be late. Her only explanation was that she had run into someone she knew. She hung up before Fran could ask questions.

It was clear that Ben was interested enough to want more of her company, but was she ready for . . . for what, a social life? She was still in her early twenties, and while she wasn't ready to think again of marriage and a family, maybe it was time to venture out a little.

When Ben was done answering questions in the class, he and Janet left the school. He drove them to a little eating place on Nassau Street, a spot frequented by university students.

There was a short walk after he parked his car, a blue Chevrolet Cavalier sedan. He pointed out several landmarks along the way, saying that Scott Fitzgerald, who had been a Princeton student, had made mention of them in his writings.

In the restaurant, over hamburgers, french fries, and more coffee, they exchanged get-acquainted information. Although Ben traveled frequently, his company, a construction firm that specialized in energy conserving architecture, was in the Princeton area. He was thirty-one and a New Jersey native.

"And, as of six years ago, I'm single," he added meaningfully.

She frowned. "Did I ask that?"

"No. But having told you maybe I can ask the question back." He looked at her left hand. "I don't see a ring."

She didn't know how she felt about the conversation becoming more personal, but after a moment of silent debate, she said, "There was one, but that's all over now except for receiving the final papers."

"That's a lot more recently than my six years."

"Yes," she said and found herself responding honestly and in more detail than she had planned, although not about Becky—she wasn't ready to tell him about that. "The marriage was a mistake from the start and maybe we were both at fault." She was thinking that Clay had never

51

deceived her. She had wanted to see someone other than the actual man. Maybe her idealistic blindness had been unfair to them both.

"A lot of times, the fault is simply being too young," Ben said, combing his fingers through his hair. The red-brown waves had a crisp look, but Janet suspected they would feel soft.

His tone reflective, he said, "I had known my girl all through high school and our wedding was immediately after we graduated. Once in college, we both knew we wanted different things out of life. We tried to make a go of it, but it didn't work. Thank God, at least we didn't start a family in the hope it would be a cure."

Color leaped into Janet's face. *A family. Becky.* And there had been no cure, only additional pain. Hiding her flush, she looked down for a moment. When she dared look up again, her voice held forced brightness. "We'd better leave. I don't want my sister to worry."

Outside, they found waning moonlight filtering through a haze of clouds. Although the sky glowed, only a pale reflection was cast downward, painting halos around the street lamps and playing tricks with the shadows.

"How far to your sister's place?" Ben asked, stopping beside his car.

"It's on the same block as the Stocktons' house."

"That's not too far from where we are now," he said. "It's a nice night. Let's walk."

She realized he wanted to prolong the evening, and so what? She was sick of analyzing things.

"It is a nice night," she agreed.

"Sounds like a yes," he said, and they started walking. He tucked his hand into the crook of her arm as they crossed the first street and she made no protest when he left it there as they continued on. She told herself she could hardly feel it through her jacket. If she had worn her heavy winter coat, she probably wouldn't even know it was there.

They fell into a mutual silence. The only sound was that of their feet crunching through the leaves. At Fran's block, he turned a street too soon.

"We're one more down," she corrected. "The house faces Quince Street."

"That's the far end of the block, right?"

"Yes."

"Then we'll go around the long way," he said.

Janet could tell he was smiling.

When they resumed walking, his arm still linked with hers, she found his nearness companionable rather than threatening. She appreciated the way he modified his long stride to match his pace with hers.

They had come to the yellow house almost before she realized it. Her steps lagged.

The house was set back from the street, allowing space for the half-circle drive in front. The Renners' black Oldsmobile sat like a dark animal, hunched and waiting for a command. Alongside the house, a path allowed access to the rear. The house was in darkness except for a misty light in the belvedere.

Ben started to move on, but she resisted. She thought she heard some sound.

"Janet?" Ben questioned.

"Listen," she said quietly. "Did you hear that?"

"Hear what? No." He paused, then said, "Oh!"

"You heard it?"

"No, I thought I saw something. A squirrel maybe. Only squirrels aren't out at night. Anyway, there was some small animal moving through the shrubs along the drive. That's what you must have heard."

She shook her head. "No, it wasn't anything like that. There it is again! Listen."

Her body stiffened as the sounds of a child's whimpering clearly reached her ears. The soft cries of distress seemed to come from behind the house.

Ignoring Ben's sharp whisper for her to stop, Janet hurried to the path that led into the rear yard.

Chapter 10

SCARCELY AWARE OF BEN AT HER heels, Janet moved until she stood in the back yard of the yellow house. The moon was hidden behind a cloud. She could barely make out the shapes of the beech tree branches against the sky. She looked toward Fran's but could see nothing because of the row of evergreens between the Renners' property and that of her sister. The smell of leaf mold lay heavy in the moist air. Suddenly uncertain, she paused, turning her head from side to side, listening.

"Janet!" Ben whispered urgently, catching up with her. "What are we doing?"

She didn't answer.

"Janet!" Ben whispered again.

"Shhh!" she hissed, silencing him. Once again, the whimpering reached her ears. It seemed to be quite near. She turned toward the sound, then caught her breath in surprise.

In the far corner of the garden, flanked by a growth of dark bushes, there was a child, a little boy who looked about four years old.

Janet blinked, hardly able to believe the way he was dressed for an October night, naked except for a pair of white, drawstring drawers. He looked unhealthy, his body painfully thin, his belly bloated. Apparently unaware of being observed, he continued to weep softly. He was angled so that she couldn't see his face. A certain awkwardness of his stance convinced her he had injured one of his legs.

"Come on, let's go," Ben said, his tone low, but imperative. "We can't go prowling around somebody's property without good reason." His voice, hushed as it was, was enough to start a dog yipping. Ben took hold of Janet's arm. "Let's clear out, and now!"

"But, Ben, that child—" Her eyes returned to the little boy. He was gone. She pulled free and was about to look for the boy when a light in the second floor of the yellow house went on, laying a bright, rectangular slab across the grass.

"Now, we've done it!" Ben took Janet's arm again, and this time she went willingly as he hauled her toward the border of evergreens.

Feeling through the branches, he muttered, "Good, no fence." He turned against the trees, clasped Janet to his chest, and plowed his way backward, his arms and broad back protecting her from the stabbing pine needles. Gasping, they emerged safely on the other side. Still in the circle of Ben's embrace, Janet was quiet a moment, catching her breath. Then, becoming aware of the male strength of his body against hers, she tried to move away.

He resisted for a second, whispering into her ear, "Will you put in the newsletter that a certain evening school participant is also quick, resourceful, and brave?"

"A regular knight in shining armor," she whispered back and was relieved when his grip relaxed. It had been a long time since she had stood enfolded in a man's arms. Hoping he couldn't tell how flustered she felt, she moved to peer back through the evergreens. As she watched, the light in the upstairs of the house went off.

"Guess they figured there was no cause for alarm after all," Ben said. "What were you chasing in there?"

Janet turned with surprise. "Didn't you see that little boy?"

"I didn't see anyone."

"Well, he was there, only he must have gone to a nearby property, one that faces the side street. The way he was crying, I'm sure he was in trouble. I think his leg was injured. We shouldn't leave until we learn what's going on."

"You mean he went through where that dog is?"

"Yes, I suppose that makes sense."

"Then he belongs there. Listen, the barking has almost stopped. If a stranger trespassed, it would be raising more of a ruckus, not less."

Although Janet saw the logic of Ben's reasoning, she wasn't ready to abandon her argument. "That still doesn't explain why a child would be out so late, hurt and crying. And he was dressed only in some kind of underwear!"

Hearing her distress, Ben slipped a comforting arm about her. "He probably went outside on an adventure and got scared. I remember getting scared my first night outside in a tent. Little kids are like that." He gave her a reassuring squeeze. "Hear how the dog has calmed down? The boy is probably back safe in his room by now. Let's get you home. Where's your sister's place from here?"

"We're actually in her back yard." Distracted by the pressure of Ben's arm, she pointed, using the movement to draw away from him. "It's that house there." Still flustered she directed Ben across the garden and around to the front entrance to Fran's house.

Fran must have heard them because she opened the door. "So, you're Janet's mystery friend!" she exclaimed when seeing Ben. Shaking her blonde head, she stepped back so they could come inside. "Here's my little sister, new in town, but phoning to say she had run into a friend." Fran's laugh showed her frustration. "I couldn't figure it out."

Janet smiled as Fran pretended dismay when Ben said he couldn't stay for coffee. She knew darned well her nosy sister couldn't wait for him to leave so she could learn everything that had happened at the adult school.

"You must come back another time," Fran told him at the door. Then she asked, "By the way, did you two come through the back yard? I was in the kitchen and I thought I heard voices."

"We cut through the block," Ben answered. "Janet thought there might have been a child in one of the yards, hurt or something. She heard crying sounds. But I guess it was nothing to worry about."

At his words, Fran flashed Janet a quick, anxious glance, then told Ben, "I'll walk you out." She edged him out the door before Janet could react.

With a sinking heart, Janet knew Fran had misread the situation, linking the crying child with the episode of the crying baby. Now, she was taking Ben out to quiz him, never stopping to realize she'd end up convincing him the woman he had walked home was a mental case.

Standing frozen at the door, she watched their progress down the walk. Her worst fears were realized when Ben abruptly veered off and vacated the property at a fast clip.

"Thanks a bundle, Sis," she said bitterly as Fran came back inside. Vivid in her mind was Ben's touch, that brief moment in his arms when it had seemed he'd been reluctant to let her go. To be held, comforted, protected, to be *wanted*. She hadn't realized how much she had missed that part of life. Now it was over between them before it had begun.

"Oh, Janet . . ." Fran's tone of apology changed to defensiveness. "All right, yes, I told Ben about the other night . . . about you thinking you heard the sounds of crying then too. But I also told him about your own baby, and I know he understood."

"Lovely," Janet snapped. Turning, she walked stiffly into the living room. "After your private chat, Mr. Benjamin Yates will be keeping his distance."

"Jan, he's not that kind of man, I'm sure of it." Catching up, Fran tried to take Janet's hand. "Come on, let's sit down and talk."

Janet pulled away. "Talk about what, my wild imagination? The fact that you think I belong in a loony bin?"

The sisters were still squabbling when the doorbell interrupted.

Fran, who went to answer, exclaimed Ben's name and then said, "A cat? Ben, why are you carrying that cat?"

Hardly daring to believe that Ben had returned, Janet hurried to the hall and saw him standing with Gina's tan cat in his arms.

Seeing her, he grinned broadly. "Mystery solved! While I was talking with your sister, I caught sight of this cat on the prowl. Remember when I spied movement in the bushes at that other house? All of a sudden, I remembered my mother's Siamese cat. Everyone always said it made sounds like a crying baby. I put that together with something your sister said, and well—"

As if in response to Ben's words, the animal, wanting to get down, uttered a surprisingly human-sounding meow of complaint. Understanding, at last, Fran cried, "Oh, Janet! All along, what you mistook for a baby, was only the Stocktons' cat, Pagoda." Her expression was relieved, but contrite. "Honey, I owe you such an apology. To think my fussing was caused by a cat!"

Taking the animal from Ben, she placed it on the stoop. The creature immediately tried to dash back inside the house. "No more of your sneaky cat tricks," Fran ordered with a laugh, turning the animal around. "You're a naughty girl, Pagoda! Go home!" She stamped her foot. With a wail that did indeed sound infant-like, the cat darted off. Fran looked gratefully at Ben. "I don't know how to thank you. Things are so simple once they're straightened out. Would you believe that my sister and I were actually having words over this?"

"Glad I could help," Ben said, looking pleased.

This time when he left, it was Janet who walked him outside and when they parted, he promised with a smile, "I'll call you."

With his promise warming her heart to a surprising degree, she went back inside, where Fran apologized again. "Janet, I'm so sorry. To think I doubted you without ever considering another explanation. I'm ashamed of myself. Will you forgive me?"

The warm glow Janet had felt with Ben faded. So, everything was explained, was it? She swallowed painfully. She knew that she and Gina hadn't mistaken a mewing cat for a crying child. Besides, how could Fran so blithely forget the discussion of whether or not Gina could speak? But why stir things up? She hated arguing. If Fran was willing to believe the presence of the cat explained everything, so be it. For now, at least.

Chapter 11

IT RAINED ON TUESDAY, A NASTY drizzle that drained the autumn coloration from the scenery. Janet didn't care. She was too excited about learning the newsletter word processing program. Fran dropped her off at the high school on her way to the Magic Spoon, and she said she would take her back to the house again whenever she called.

Sisters again, Janet thought as she waved goodbye to Fran outside of Princeton High School's gorgeous Gothic front entrance. Janet knew Fran always had her best interest at heart, and she also knew she was still fragile because of Becky's death, but from now on, she vowed, she would keep her mouth shut about anything Fran found too hard to accept. Like hearing a child speak and seeing another child after dark. And none of *that* was the cat!

Ida met Janet and led her through a hallway crowded with high school students changing classes and on to the school office where she introduced her to Crystal, a pretty redhead with a Molly Ringwald pouty mouth. Crystal said she was a former high school graduate who had been hired as the school office's computer expert and would also help with adult school computer needs.

Ida left after saying she would be back in the afternoon to see how they were doing.

"I want to be an illustrator and also create better games," Crystal told Janet as she adjusted the flowered scarf draped over the neck of her white cable knit sweater. The girl's brown plaid skirt was long enough so that only the toes of her brown boots peeked out as she moved.

Continuing, she said, "I got good comments on a submission I made for a MacPaint contest in the MacWorld Magazine." She went on to say she had four younger siblings, so money was tight. "I want a career in something my parents don't understand. I'm saving up to go to New York City on my own. I'm after a job in my field. I'll not only learn a lot, it will keep me in rent money."

Janet admired Crystal's determination and found the girl to be a good teacher, patiently introducing her to the working of the school's computer and the PageMaker program. The computer, the printer, the new program—all new and all exciting.

So much to learn, she said to herself. She went at it with an energy she hadn't felt in a long time. She worked all morning, had lunch in the cafeteria, and then worked with Crystal in the afternoon.

Ida poked her head in. "How are things going?" she said.

"Crystal's been wonderful," Janet said. "I'm taking home printed material that the previous editor did. I'll do editing and then plan how to lay it out once I'm more comfortable using PageMaker."

"Janet wants a consistent look to the newsletter," Crystal said, "The previous issues were all circus. The previous editor used different fonts for each headline and differing fonts for each article."

Ida nodded, the yellow satin bow on the top of her head bobbing. "Janet's after a more professional look," she said in a tone of approval, smiling at Janet.

At the end of a good day, Janet called Fran saying she was ready to go home. That evening, Kirby Orchard, who lived on a neighboring street, phoned to say that if she would be interested, he would give her a ride to the adult school on his first class night the following week.

She accepted but had to admit to herself that she was disappointed that the caller hadn't been Ben. Maybe he'd had second thoughts. A woman who had lost a child and who was in the process of a divorce might seem a bit much, even for a casual friendship. Plus, he was a man in business and an extremely attractive one. No doubt he had plenty of demands on his time, ones that didn't come equipped with possible complications.

Besides, what was she thinking? She was in no position to start a relationship, no matter how attractive Ben was.

Two days later, Janet was home early because of Fran's schedule and fortunately, that was when Ben called. He was somewhere in western Pennsylvania. The connection was so filled with static that he said goodbye before his three minutes were up, but not before promising to call again when he reached home that weekend.

With elevated spirits, Janet noticed that the heavy rain was slackening. She decided a walk around outside would be good before going back to the newsletter. She checked the stew she had prepared and put in the Crock-Pot—it had hours to go—then borrowed a hooded raincoat and a pair of Fran's old boots and went out the back door.

Gone was the bone-chilling weather of the past week. The air outside smelled pleasantly earthy and the rain had become a foggy mist. In the rear of Fran's back yard, she moved to where she and Ben had pushed through the evergreens. She peered through the long-needled branches to determine where the little boy she'd seen had stood.

She remembered that the Renner yard had seemed dark until the upstairs house light cast a bright rectangle across the lawn. How could she have seen the child so clearly? She guessed it was because his body and clothing were lighter than his surroundings.

When she had asked Warren about the children living in the neighborhood, he had said Gina was the only youngster he knew of. If he was right, then the little boy must be a visitor. And judging from his malnourished appearance, he must suffer from some illness.

She was still thinking about the child when the door to the Renners' latticed back porch opened.

Rose emerged, garbed in her funereal black. Stiffly, she made her halting way down the steps and across a brick path to the wet grass. Her expression was harried, and her shrunken lips moved as though she were talking to herself.

With helpless sympathy, Janet watched through the greenery as the woman embarked on a slow circling of the yard, wringing her hands as she trudged. Like the grim shadow on a sundial, she doggedly shuffled through the carpet of leaves on the slight incline, laboriously tracing and retracing her path. Janet realized that the poor soul was undoubtedly senile, but her repetitive actions made it look as if she had been placed under an evil spell.

Rose's foot slipped and she went down on one knee. Janet held her breath. Rose attempted to rise to her feet, but her efforts were futile. Her arthritic knees were apparently too weak to enable her to get up without assistance.

Janet pushed through the pines with their stabbing needles, getting wet as the rain-laden branches released showers. Feeling as if she's been wrestling wet porcupines, she burst through to the other side and paused to shake water from her hair. Rose, intent on her struggles, paid no attention to Janet's arrival.

Janet pushed back her no-longer-needed rain hood and went to Rose. Kneeling, she used the same matter-of-fact tone as on that previous Saturday. "These fallen leaves are slippery, aren't they?" Janet said. "Here, just sit down and rest a moment while I have a look at you."

Rose didn't protest as she was examined for possible sprains.

Janet found no swelling. "Does anything hurt?" she asked, gently rotating the woman's black-stockinged ankles.

Rose replied with a sensible complaint, "Wet—grass wet."

"Yes, and I imagine you feel soaked." Deciding no harm had been done, Janet said gently, "Here, let me help you get up."

Rose darted an anxious glance left and then right as if fearing a reprimand from some invisible source. Looking at Janet again, she timidly extended her gnarled, blue-veined hands. Touched by her defenselessness, Janet put her free arm around Rose's shoulders and carefully boosted her to her feet. The old woman felt more fragile than the bulky swaddling of her clothing had led Janet to expect.

"Are you all right now?" Janet asked. "If anything hurts, we should get help before you try to walk."

"Fine, fine, everything fine," Rose asserted in a singsong, holding on to Janet as she stepped in the direction of the latticed porch.

"Let's go around to the front," Janet said. "The back porch has too many steep steps."

"Sister," Rose said.

"You want to see your sister? Let's see if she's inside. We can ring the doorbell."

"Sister," Rose repeated.

"We'll find her," Janet assured, hoping that Muriel was indeed at home. Rounding the side of the house, Janet was relieved to see the black Oldsmobile sitting in the front drive. She tried to assist Rose up the wide, shallow steps to the porch, but Rose shook her off. The woman's progress was slow, but she was determined. Ready to help if needed, Janet held her breath until Rose was safely on the porch.

Standing beside the woman, Janet rang the bell.

Muriel answered and immediately said, "Oh, no! Miss Fairweather, was my sister out in the street again? Please, come in."

"She wasn't in the street," Janet said. "She fell on the grass."

Muriel nodded. Taking Rose's arm, she beckoned Janet into a spacious entry hall that contained a polished mahogany staircase. The big double doors to the right were closed, but to the left was a formal dining room. From somewhere overhead came the sound of classical music, a dramatic selection, played at a high volume. Muriel waved for Janet to follow as she led Rose into the dining room.

The woman put her sister on a chair and knelt to check for injuries much as Janet had already done. The nape of Muriel's neck showed not a wisp of upswept dark hair out of place. Diamond rings winked with the motion of her slim fingers.

"She seems fine," she said to Janet as she stood, "but the fall has no doubt shaken her."

Janet noticed that Muriel was more at ease in her home than she had been that day on the street. "My husband and I were dressing to go to the pharmacy," the woman said. "It might have been another ten minutes before I discovered that Rose needed help." Shaking her head, she gave Rose a meaningful glance as she added firmly. "Rest assured that my sister will be well protected while we are away."

Rose uttered a choked cry. She said something in her foreign tongue, then in English. She gave Janet a pleading glance and then turned back to her sister. "No turn the key." Her voice cracked with fright. "I will be good. No turn the key."

"Hush!" Without raising her soft voice, Muriel's hissing admonishment was nevertheless sharp. "You know you cannot be trusted." Remembering her visitor, she flushed. "Forgive us, Miss Fairweather. There are times when my sister forgets her promises and must be locked in her room. It is always for the shortest possible time and it is not a punishment. Please understand."

As they talked, the loud music abruptly ceased.

"Yes, of course, I understand," Janet said, seeing that Rose had resumed wringing her hands. It was obvious that she had a horror of being confined.

"Mrs. Renner," Janet said, impulsively, "if it would help, I could stay with your sister while you're away."

Muriel's gold-brown eyes looked hopeful, but then she shook her head. "The imposition is too great."

"No, I'm entirely free," Janet said, wondering if her offer was based more on a desire to avoid returning to her desk than any noble impulse, but staying to help suddenly seemed of vital importance.

Expression indecisive, Muriel frowned in the direction of her sister. As if presenting an answer to the dilemma, Rose pointed at Janet. "She give me flower." She revealed a sly, toothless grin. "A flower, not a rose."

Janet was delighted by what she took as a pun, but the weary smile flitting across Muriel's face indicated that the jest was well-worn. "She does like you, that is true," she murmured to Janet, still undecided. "She has saved the flower you gave her—"

Muriel turned her head as sounds came from beyond the arch leading to a room beyond the dining room. "That is my husband," she whispered. She straightened as if standing at attention.

The gloomy light coming through the dining room windows gave the scene the murky faded tones of an old photograph as an elderly man moved into view, his walk rapid and shuffling, like that of a wind-up toy. When he reached them, he stopped and shakily grasped the back of Rose's chair for support. Janet half expected his feet to keep churning ineffectively even though he no longer moved forward.

He appeared to be in his late seventies. His black suit fit his shoulders well, but his shirt collar gaped about his stringy neck. His white hair was wispy, and his pale skin was stretched tightly over gaunt features. He reminded Janet of pictures she had seen of an ancient Egyptian Pharaoh.

"This is our neighbor, Miss Fairweather," explained Muriel as Janet stepped up to greet him. "Twice now, she had extended kindness toward our Rose."

The doctor inclined his head, peering at Janet through the top of his round, frameless trifocals. "Ah, yes," he said. "I saw you from the car."

He spoke with polite disinterest in a voice that was stronger and steadier than Janet would have supposed. Releasing the chair, he reached to take her hand. She noticed that his fingernails, curved and yellowed, extended beyond his fingertips. He bowed over her hand in the Continental fashion. "I am Dr. Herman Renner."

Janet responded with her own name, thinking that the doctor's dry, leathery palm was like the skin of a lizard. Withdrawing, she said, "I believe you've already met my sister and brother-in-law, Fran and Warren Elwin?"

"So I have." Nodding, he again grasped the back of Rose's chair. Janet recalled Fran's remark concerning the doctor's condescending manner. Even though he had taken her hand, Janet felt it was a formality rather than a true greeting.

"Miss Fairweather has offered to stay with Rose while we go out for your medicine," Muriel said. "It is kind of her." A certain wistful note suggested that although she would like to accept, she was resigned to her husband's veto. Instead, he seemed to give the matter thought. "Indeed?" He lifted his brow.

Muriel explained about Rose's fall. "Although she doesn't appear to have been injured, it seems unwise to take her out. But confining her is so upsetting, and since Miss Fairweather has offered . . ." Allowing her words to trail away, Muriel awaited her husband's decision.

He gave Rose a quick, dismissive glance and then said to Janet, "It would be no inconvenience?"

"No, as I explained to Mrs. Renner, I have the time free. While you're out, you might want to run other errands as well."

He smiled, showing elongated, discolored teeth, but despite the smile, there was a coolness in his eyes that suggested that whatever he did or did not do was none of her business.

"It would set my mind at ease if Rose wasn't here alone," Muriel said. "That is, if it's all right with you."

Without glancing at her, the doctor nodded. "Very well."

"It is all right, then?" Muriel said.

"I agreed, did I not?"

Turning, he shuffled toward what Janet assumed was the entryway coat closet.

"Well, Miss Fairweather," breathed Muriel softly, obviously surprised at her husband's decision. "Let me hang up your rain coat." Returning from placing it in a front hall closet, she boosted Rose to her feet. "Come now, she said to her. "Let us show Miss Fairweather around."

Janet said, "Please, call me Janet."

Muriel acquiesced. "Of course—Janet," she said, but the informality seemed to make her feel ill at ease.

Her arm around Rose, Muriel led the way through the dining room and into a study. A television screen showed a game show in progress, the sound turned off. Janet glimpsed a kitchen in the room beyond.

"Rose is usually most content sitting right here," Muriel said, helping Rose to sit in a rocking chair. She moved to turn on a radio that was part of an entertainment system. A voice emerged, giving call letters to a music station.

Signaling Janet to again follow as she left the room, Muriel said quietly, "She likes the pictures on television—the program doesn't matter. She rocks for hours, watching pictures and listening to her music. We keep the television sound off unless there is a program my husband wishes to watch."

Muriel paused in the dining room. Janet wondered if they ate their meals there. It seemed too far from the kitchen.

Continuing, Muriel said, "Rose also has a little battery radio that she sometimes likes to hold. She will know where to find it. It is tuned to the same station as big radio." Muriel gave Janet a look that pleaded for understanding. "Rose's mind has become slow and simple; she can be reasoned with, but I'm sure she will be satisfied to sit with her music."

"We'll be fine," Janet assured, accompanying the woman to the entry hall where Dr. Renner had pulled winter coats from the closet. Muriel helped him with his black alpaca and then slipped into a peach-colored cashmere that softened the austerity of her dark, classic beauty.

Pausing at the door to pull on white kid gloves, Muriel's face knit as she obviously tried to think of anything else Janet should know. "If Rose wishes to go upstairs, insist on the rear stairs that lead up from the kitchen. A stair lift has been installed there for Dr. Renner's convenience. Rose dislikes the device, but after today's fall, it might be best for her to avoid climbing steps."

Janet followed them to the porch as Muriel led her husband to the car, which was parked with the passenger side facing the house. She assisted her husband into his seat, then stepped around the vehicle, giving Janet one last anxious look before taking her place behind the wheel. As the big car moved, Janet glimpsed Muriel lean forward so she could look around Dr. Renner. Her white-gloved hand lifted in brief farewell, the pale image seeming to flutter like a trapped moth inside the big car.

Chapter 12

JANET TURNED FROM THE FRONT DOOR and stepped into the dining room. She saw Rose moving furtively in the study. She then disappeared behind the door frame between the two rooms. Her black-swathed head reappeared, her neck stretched like a turtle's. When Rose saw that she was observed, she grinned and ducked back. Janet realized that the old woman was playing a game. She could imagine Muriel being embarrassed and scolding her sister for such antics. It seemed best not to encourage her.

Rose peeked around several more times, but when Janet did nothing except stand and watch, she turned away. Janet followed as the woman settled herself in a rocking chair, facing the soundless TV.

Music came from the stereo that Muriel had switched on. Janet had expected a soothing old tune or maybe something classical. Instead, it was Pat Benatar belting out "Hit Me With Your Best Shot." Rose started rocking back and forth. Fascinated, Janet saw that when the song changed to "Woman in Love" by Barbra Streisand, Rose's rocking movements didn't change. Apparently, she rocked in the same rhythm regardless of the tune or the beat. Her gaze was fixed on the TV where the actors in the soap opera, *The Guiding Light*, moved in their soundless world.

Taking a seat on the couch, Janet picked up a copy of the *Wall Street Journal* from the coffee table. She leafed through it, skimming an article on energy conservation that made her think of Ben.

Laying the paper aside, she studied the room. The furnishings, except for a rosewood secretary with glass-fronted bookshelves, were nondescript, but the walls held antique-looking oil paintings with elaborately gilded frames. One was a still life of a dead pheasant hanging over a table that held fruit, flowers, a dead rabbit, an ink well, a quill pen and a half-written letter. Fine for a museum, Janet thought, but not what she'd want in a room where a family would gather. The other two paintings were charming. She remembered from an article she'd once written, such scenes were called *petit genre*, ordinary nameless people involved in their lives.

She glanced at Rose. Rocking steadily, the old woman's attention was on a soundless rerun of *The Golden Girls*. Advertisements came on. A rubber-faced waitress blotted spilled coffee with the best paper towels and then a pretty blonde in high heels served her beaming family canned soup. Rose rocked steadily, her attention on the silent screen unwavering.

Janet stood to examine the townscapes, each with dancers in an open square, but up close on one of them, the illusion of costumed figures was reduced to blobs and swirls. The second painting had a similar subject, but with that one, the closer Janet moved, the more fine details she saw. She wished she had a magnifying glass. The faces of the tiny figures even appeared to have eyelashes.

Moving to look at the books, Janet saw that the volumes had tooled leather bindings. Instead of titles and authors being printed on their spines, there were numbers. A narrow, cloth-bound journal lay on a shelf. Janet figured the journal recorded the book titles, but when she tried to check, she discovered that the glass doors were locked.

Disappointed, she found her attention drifting back to the detailed painting. The expressions on the tiny faces were so perfect it was uncanny. It would be easy to believe the artist was a sorcerer who miniaturized his victims and trapped them forever. At least they looked happy, frozen behind the varnish with smiles on their faces, dancing for all eternity on shoes that would never wear thin.

She turned from the painting and saw Rose scowling. "My music," she complained, gesturing as if cupping an object in her hands. "Upstairs. My music."

"Your battery radio?" Janet remembered what Muriel had told her.

"My music. Upstairs," Rose repeated, her toothless lisp adding emphasis to a newly stubborn tone. She stood. When Janet saw she Rose was turning as if to go toward the main staircase, Janet moved to touch the woman's arm. "If your radio is upstairs, your sister said you must use the stair lift."

"Steps good. Like steps," Rose said.

"Okay, but show me the lift," Janet said, trying to sound enthusiastic. Muriel had warned that Rose might be reluctant. "Is it like an elevator? I'd like to see it, but I don't know where to look."

Rose acted as if she wanted to refuse, but then, jaw set, she led Janet into the kitchen. Begrudgingly, she pointed out a steep staircase. Along one side of the ascent, a chair and footrest contraption was bolted to a metal track.

"Isn't this nice!" Janet raved. "So much easier than climbing steps. So very nice—it must be fun!"

In the face of such exaggerated approval, Rose folded her arms and glared. "Fun. You go."

The unexpectedness of the woman's sarcasm took Janet by surprise. "Do you hate it so much? All right. I'll get your radio, but I'll go up the front stairs, okay?" Janet's real reason was that she wanted to look through the house. She would go up the front, have a quick look around, and then go down the back way.

She realized that while she still admired the house as a fine example of its architecture, she felt none of the passionate longing had possessed her that day when she held Becky clasped in her arms. Why had she ever felt it was where she wanted to live? Her only emotion now was curiosity.

"Where will I find your radio?" she asked Rose.

"Room. Always my room."

"I don't know where it is," Janet said, patiently. "You must tell me."

Rose's wrinkled face showed confusion at the prospect of giving directions. Then, her eyes glinted ingeniously. "See my flower."

Janet guessed Rose might mean the saved chrysanthemum. "Okay. You wait here. I'll find your radio."

The front stairs turned halfway up and ended at a wide second-floor landing that was bright thanks to the central front window. Looking back, Janet saw hallways running down either side of the staircase and then coming together to form a hall leading to the rear of the house. Even more interesting, the front stairs turned again and led up to the belvedere atop the roof. From the outside it looked large, but was it? Janet wanted to see.

The steps were steeper than the other steps. There were polished wooden handrails on both sides with turned wooden spindles. There was a gate at the top of the steps. Janet opened the gate and stepped up into the room where railings around the stairway opening prevented an accidental fall. Before her were books on a small chair beside a chaise lounge with several blankets and pillows. The books were women's fiction in English. Muriel's little hideaway? Janet doubted that Rose was much of a reader and surely not in English. Besides, how could she climb all the stairs? Then again, despite her fall, she had stubbornly climbed the outside steps to the porch.

Because of the spread of the house's roof, the front windows gave only a view of the treetops in properties across the street. The side windows were patterned with orange, yellow and remaining green foliage from the nearby trees. The view to the rear yard, however, caught and held her interest.

She saw the back of the Renner yard where the evergreens met the end of Fran's property. The branches of copper beach tree obscured the houses to the right, including the Stockton house, although she could see a corner of the sandbox.

She leaned forward, wondering if she would see Gina. She remembered how the child darted in and out the bushes when playing with the cat. Was she there now? She shook her head. If Gina was there, she would know it. Immediately, she realized how foolish that sounded.

Shaking her head again, she descended to the second floor landing. The space was generous, as large as the foyer below. Sunshine poured through the window. Janet basked in the warmth for a moment and then turned her attention to the open door of room that was on the left front corner of the house.

She found a bedroom, an attractive space that led to a bathroom and then to a sitting room as large as the bedroom. The suite had an unused air. Reserved for guests? Had the bathroom been part of the original structure or had it been put in later? Warren had guessed the house dated to the middle of the previous century. Was there indoor plumbing then? If people were wealthy enough, she supposed.

Coming out, she saw a closed door further along that section of the hallway. She ventured down to look and found a long room that had the space to create a second suite behind the first. The existing suite and the long empty room probably went over the three rooms downstairs: the dining room, the study and the kitchen. Space for a family that possibly also had servants, making it no problem that the formal dining room wasn't next to the kitchen.

She returned to landing, passed by the large front window and found herself on the threshold of the master bedroom on the right front corner of the house. Janet was delighted by the romantic décor—sheer curtains, hanging plants and a cream-white satin chaise, perhaps a twin to the one in the belvedere. An oil painting of a peacock posed in a mythical Eden hung above the white satin bed. The painting glowed with the richness of a museum piece. The lustrous draperies, full enough to be closed over the sheers if desired, were patterned with fruited vines, echoing the tones of the painting.

Looking across the room's blue carpet, Janet saw a partly opened door that led to its bath. She moved to it, seeing décor that was neither masculine nor feminine. She stepped through the bath to another room, as large as the master, but drab, with a ponderous desk and a heavy-looking work chair. Bookcases and file cabinets lined one wall. Dr. Renner's office, Janet thought. A stereo and record player stood in the corner with an album cover facing her. Finally, some color in the room.

She moved closer. The red and black album cover showed the strong features of a brooding man. The text in red against black spelled the title: *The Flying Dutchman*, by Wager. Was it the dramatic music she had heard earlier?

A door in the office led back to the hallway on the right side of the house. There was another closed door beyond the doctor's office. It opened to a storage room with boxes and odds and ends of furniture. Leaving the room, Janet noticed the metal handrail that ran from the office along down the hallway to the rear of the house. Probably there to assist Dr. Renner's shuffling steps as he made his way to the stair lift.

Rose's room must be down that way.

She moved toward the wide areas where the two front hallways met. A glimpse of motion to one side caused her to turn. Nothing was there. She stared toward the large front window. Had a bird just flown past the glass?

She turned back to the railed hallway. Did it appear darker than before? Had it dimmed, like something seen in a spooky film? She shook herself. What next, eerie music? That black and red album cover with that brooding face . . . The legend of the Flying Dutchman came to her; the story of a cursed ship captain who had defied God's power and was doomed to sail on stormy seas until the end of time. Old legends. Janet laughed at herself. The corridor simply appeared dark because she had just stared toward the sunlit front window.

She continued down the corridor and realized she felt tense. Of course, she did: she was prowling around in somebody's house. Her reasoning didn't help her relax. She moved forward and came to the opening to the rear staircase to her left. She cautiously peeked down, seeing a steep staircase with the lift contraption bolted to one side. Just that. Nothing more.

What had she expected? Rose leaping up with a mad screech, black rags flying?

Shaking her head over her imagination, she turned to the room opposite the rear stairway. The open door revealed a room with brightly colored magazine cutouts of kittens and puppies taped to the walls. A small radio sat on a table next to a single bed. There was also a vase holding a wilting marigold. *Rose's room.*

Janet smiled gently, thinking that Rose, who seemed so alone and lost, must draw comfort from the pictures of the animals. She wondered if she had cut them out herself. With battery radio in hand, Janet stepped back into the hallway. She again caught movement from the corner of her eye. She whipped her head around and saw, definitely *saw* something move.

Transfixed, she stared toward the big front window. There in the landing's left corner. Something was there. It was gone before she could focus on it. Her pulse jumped. There it was again! Only this time, the motion had come from the right of the window. A flutter of motion. Then it was gone.

What could appear and disappear so quickly? She suddenly became aware of a faint rustling sound, like silk brushing against a screen, an unworldly whispering draft.

The hairs on Janet's arms lifted and a sweaty, sensation crawled along her nerves. Breathlessly she waited, ears stretched, eyes smarting from the strain. She heard a car going by outside on the street. An ordinary, mundane purr of an engine, totally unrelated to the eerie sounds heard only a moment before. But what had she heard? Or seen for that matter? It was nothing but her own peekaboo imagination, playing a game that Rose might enjoy.

Rose. Oh, my! Better get down to her at once.

Rushing to the back steps and racing down, Janet burst into the kitchen. Rose sat at the table, a finger in her mouth. Eyes round and startled, the old woman's face was filled with guilt. A sugar bowl sat before her, spilled sugar all around. She snatched her wet finger from her mouth and tried to hide it. Then, cunningly, she took the offensive.

"Too long, too long," she scolded, making it clear that anything she'd done in Janet's absence was Janet's fault.

"My music," Rose said. "I want my music."

Out of breath, Janet sank into a chair, relaxing now that she was downstairs again. The kitchen, with its white-painted cupboards, red Formica countertops, and contentedly humming refrigerator, a modern Kenmore from Sears like the one Fran hid away, offered a soothing, practical atmosphere. Any fanciful moods in this room would be confined to an extra bay leaf in the stew or frosting twirls on a cake.

"My music," Rose repeated petulantly.

Still catching her breath, Janet pushed the radio across the table.

Rose turned the "on" knob. Grains of sugar still clung to the arthritis-swollen joints. She smiled blissfully as the lively hard beat of "Funkytown" filled the air.

Chapter 13

IT WASN'T UNTIL AFTER JANET CLEARED away the mess on the kitchen table and had Rose settled in her rocking chair again that she figured out what had unnerved her upstairs. The downstairs window showed that a brisk wind had sprung up, sharp gusts swirling orange and blood-red leaves as high as the trees from which they had come. She remembered her thoughts about a bird flying across the upstairs window and suddenly, the answer appeared: what had appeared as phantom movements in the corridor were shadows cast by leaves blowing past the sunlit glass. A shadow here, a shadow there, gone before she could focus upon them. The sounds had been caused by leaves as well. Dry, windblown leaves rustling and fluttering against the windows.

With this explained, she reasoned she should go upstairs and prove her theory; except that after she returned to the front of the house and stood with a foot on the first step, she couldn't make herself do it. Turning from the staircase, she told herself she shouldn't leave Rose alone again. When left alone before, the woman had made a sugary mess of the kitchen table, hadn't she? Who knew what she might get into next?

Janet returned to the study where Rose was now using her battery radio. The radio in the stereo cabinet was still playing and even though they were tuned to the same station, the sound had unpleasant echoing quality. Janet shut off the radio in the cabinet. Still standing, she glanced at the TV, seeing an episode from a previous season's *Rockford Files.* Rose rocked in her chair, her expression placid. She seemed to be absolutely, totally, one hundred percent content. Janet frowned. How long would it have taken her to run upstairs again, have a look around and come right back downstairs? No time at all. Rose would have been fine.

Janet reluctantly admitted to herself that her real reason for not going back upstairs was because in retrospect, the atmosphere of the second floor seemed, well . . . eerie. Okay, so the sights and sounds she'd noticed had been caused by blowing leaves, but regardless, hadn't something been out of kilter up there? Hadn't there been an aura that was unwholesome? Mocking herself, she listed what the aura of an old house, any old house, was really composed of: stale air, musty carpets and beams riddled with wood rot silently decaying behind flaking plaster. Unsavory images indeed, but nothing more.

Despite this reasoning, uneasy doubt still itched at the back of Janet's mind when the Renners returned. Dr. Renner came in as Muriel paused behind him to shoo away the Stocktons' Siamese cat, which apparently mistook any opened door in the neighborhood as an invitation.

"Has Rose been a problem?" was Muriel's first anxious question when finally inside.

"She's in the study with her music," Janet answered. "She's been fine."

"I will let her know we are home." Muriel left to see for herself without putting down the bag she carried or slipping out of her coat. She returned a moment later, looking more relaxed.

"She seems quite content," she told her husband, placing the bag on the telephone table. She helped him off with his coat and hung it, then hung her own. To Janet, she said, "We were able to visit several different shops for things we needed and to take a little time. We appreciate your kindness."

Dr. Renner nodded in apparent agreement as he shuffled mechanically to no apparent purpose.

"I'm glad I could help," Janet said. She took her jacket from the hall chair and put it on, saying to Muriel, "Rose refused to use the stair lift, so I went upstairs to get the radio for her." With deliberate ambiguity, still scratching away at the thought that there might be something odd about the upstairs of the house, she said, "She seemed almost afraid." Janet thought that if Muriel had ever noticed anything odd herself, the comment would provide an opening.

"Yes," Muriel said, deaf to Janet's cue. "She does dislike the lift."

So that was that, concluded Janet, amused at her disappointment. She slid into the raincoat that Muriel removed from the closet and handed it to her. Imagine, Janet thought, hungering for tales of ghouls in the attic.

That's when she became aware of Dr. Renner's attention. He had ceased shuffling and now stood with his head tilted so he could see her properly through his trifocals. Earlier, she felt he viewed her like a piece of furniture; something convenient but not worthy of his further interest. Now, he studied her with fixed intensity. It was as he waited for something to happen, something unpleasant; like a dangling spider about to drop upon her head. Uncomfortable, she focused back on Muriel, who had continued to speak.

"For the past week," mused Muriel, "Rose has been restless in a way I have never seen before. Things are so difficult for her."

That evening at supper, Janet told Fran and Warren about being in the Renner house. Buttering one of the biscuits she had served with the stew, she said. "I felt like I was babysitting, like I was teenager again." She shoved away any thought of there being something weird about the upstairs of the house.

"What's the inside of the place like now?" Fran asked. "If I remember correctly, the living room is huge."

"I never saw it," Janet answered, thinking it must have been behind the paneled door to the right of the entry. "We sat in the other side of the house. Except for a bookcase and some paintings that looked like valuable antiques, the decorations are nothing special—except for the ones in the master bedroom. When I went upstairs to get something for Rose, I peeked in. Spectacular!"

Warren, who was ladling himself more stew, interrupted, his black-bearded face questioning. "Anybody want more of this while I'm at it?"

"I do." Fran passed him her bowl. "What was so special about the bedroom?"

Janet described it in glowing terms. "Only two of the bedrooms are in use. It's a big house for three people." She thought of Kirby Orchard's contention that similar types were drawn to certain houses. "Did older folks live there before?"

Fran shook her head. "The Fiorellos, who were there before the Renners, were a young family. They had five kids, but one son was crippled with a muscular disease. He died not too long before they moved away."

Janet winced at the pain of their loss. "Still," she said, "it does seem like a house for a young family, doesn't it?" She was still dwelling on Kirby's theory.

"Wasn't there another couple with grown-up kids in that house when we first came here?" Warren said to Fran, "What were their names? Seems like they suffered some kind of tragedy too."

Fran opened a packet of Sweet'n Low and poured it into her coffee. "Several tragedies—a real run of bad luck. I met the woman—Mitchum, Mary Ann Mitchum. Her divorced sister had been killed in an accident and they took in her daughter. The niece lived with them a year or so, but then she drowned on a camp outing. Very sad."

That night in bed, Janet kept remembering the neighborhood sorrows Fran and Warren had spoken of. Sternly, she told herself that dwelling on the misfortunes of strangers served no good purpose, just as dwelling on the loss of Becky served no good purpose. She adjusted her pillow for what seemed like the hundredth time and stared into the darkness, trying to turn her mind to more peaceful thoughts. She remembered that Ben had said he would call before the weekend. But the weekend was still two days away.

Sighing, she rolled over again and at last felt herself starting to relax, sinking down, knowing she was slipping into a dream even as she felt her consciousness surrendering . . .

In her dream, the taxi stopped and she got out. The driver, who appeared to be Dr. Renner, called her attention to the fine architecture of the school. She felt it would be rude to tell him it looked like plain concrete block, not even as nice as her own plain school had been. Inside, Muriel sat behind the director's desk. She told Janet that she was to work in the nursery.

The nursery, which was lit by a row of jack-o'-lanterns, was filled with the cribs of sleeping children. A door at the far end stood open to reveal the Renners' back garden and the copper beech tree.

The person who had been caring for the class until Janet's arrival was Gina. She wore a nun's habit and kept a vow of silence because it had enabled her to use a special sign language that was most effective with the children.

The children may start crying, Gina told Janet, her hands moving in their special way.

Gina disappeared and Janet was alarmed as the infants and small children in the cribs did begin to cry. The cries became shrill and panic-stricken. Nothing Janet did soothed them. She frantically prayed for their mothers to come. Something terrible would happen if the mothers didn't rescue their children.

The explosion was as unexpected as it was terrible. The force of it threw the jack-o'-lanterns into the air where they bounced like severed heads, flames darting out of their empty eyeholes, red-hot tongues bursting from their jagged mouths.

Fire! The nursery was on fire!

Janet awoke.

Or at least she thought she had.

Maybe she only dreamed she had awakened, because as she turned over and slid back into sleep, she could smell the stench of burning pumpkins and hear the roar of advancing flames as the children shrieked in horror.

Their mothers—where were their mothers?

Gina's hands moved urgently in Janet's mind. *Take the children to the beech tree! came the order. The beech tree. That's where the children will be safe.*

Chapter 14

"I LIKE THAT ONE," BEN SAID, POINTING. "I was big on vampires as a kid." He showed his teeth in a leer and Janet laughed.

It was Saturday afternoon and the two of them strolled along Nassau Street, viewing the Halloween scenes that high school art class students had painted on the windows of shops and business establishments. In preparation for the weekend, the paintings had been completed and judged. The project was an annual community effort that had been started years before to cut down on Mischief Night vandalism and had become a tradition.

Janet studied the judge's card taped to the painting in question. "Somebody else agrees with your artistic taste. This won a third prize. Only it was probably the idea of a certain kind of victim and not the vampire which captured your adolescent imagination." The skillfully handled work showed a fanged, bat-winged monster floating through the bedroom window of a sleeping blonde who resembled Dolly Parton.

"Wrong, wrong, wrong," Ben said "The only thought on my mind was supernatural murder. The more gruesome, the better. Now, have a look at that one."

The next painted window showed insect-like creatures carrying cocoons to their spaceship. Protruding from the mummy wrappings were human hands and feet.

"Yuck." Janet shook her head. "Was science fiction another one of your interests?"

"Was, is, and always shall be. Don't say you haven't been warned." Smiling down at her, he tucked her hand in his as they continued walking. Janet found the gesture companionable rather than pushy and made no move to withdraw. Although the air was cold enough so their breath showed as frost, there was plenty of sunshine and no wind. She felt comfortable wearing her coat open.

They viewed yet another painting of a bloody-fanged creature wearing a cape, this one presiding over a laboratory where modern guns and bombs were being created.

"It's well done, but more like a political cartoon," Janet complained. "Where's all the fun of Halloween?"

"Right this way, my lady." Ben tugged her hand. "I saw one earlier that has a theme I know you'll approve of."

"I bet." With a show of reluctance, she dug in her heels so he had to pull her along. "It's a werewolf, right? A werewolf with a laser gun?"

"No, this is old-fashioned Halloween. It's too bad it's not on the main street where traditionalists like you couldn't miss it."

He dragged her around the corner and toward Palmer Square, where the historic Nassau Inn was located. Taking her past the famed bronze statue of the Princeton tiger, he led the way along Colonial-style storefronts to a brightly painted window.

"How's this?" he asked with a flourish.

The scene showed an old house on a hill, a graveyard and a witch sailing across the face of a full moon. In the foreground, a huge black cat leaned against a pumpkin that had cutout eyes and a smiling mouth.

"Perfect, right?" he demanded. "No monsters, no X-rated gore, no threat of global or intergalactic war. Just old-timey stuff, a little ghost in a white sheet floating above a tombstone. As innocent as candy corn."

"Exactly my idea of Halloween," Janet agreed. "But look, it didn't even win an honorable mention. It's awfully well done. So what if it isn't so original? I would think . . ."

Her voice trailed off. After a moment of silence, Ben prompted, "You would think what?"

"Nothing really. The picture reminds me of something, only I'm not sure what. Perhaps something to do with staying at the Renner house." Earlier, she had told Ben about "baby-sitting" for Rose.

"The cat maybe?" he said. "Doesn't the cat in the picture look like the Siamese I found in the Renner yard?"

"Honestly, Ben! Where were your eyes? That Siamese wasn't black. It's a light tan."

"Oh?" He lowered his voice, teasing suggestively, "In the dark, don't all cats look alike?"

She shot him a glare of mock disgust and then returned her attention to the colorful window. "That pumpkin . . . " She stiffened. For an instant, it seemed that the odor she had smelled at the Stocktons' party had wafted across her nostrils: burning pumpkins, the sickening-sweet stench of their scorching flesh. Then the smell was gone, and she remembered the jack-o'-lanterns in her dream.

"I've got it!" she cried, shrugging off the memory of the phantom scent of burning. "It was the Renners themselves that I dreamed about. About being with them in their garden or somewhere. It was decorated for Halloween. Sort of a nightmare, really."

"Was I in it?" Ben repeated his Dracula face.

"I'm serious. You know how dreams are. Bits and pieces were all muddled together."

"If I don't remember a dream when I first wake up, it's probably gone forever," he said.

"If that painted jack-o'-lantern hadn't jogged my mind, this one would have been gone too," Janet said. "Wish I could remember more. Not that it would make much sense. Seems like it was the kind of dream that didn't make sense even while it was going on."

Seeing that she was shivering, Ben admonished gently, "Better fasten that coat." He turned her around to face him. She stood with her hands at her sides, allowing him to draw the coat shut and loop the belt snuggly about her waist. "Looks like you could do with a cup of coffee," he said. "Or maybe hot chocolate."

"You sound like my sister," Janet said "To her, hot chocolate is a cure-all, like chicken soup."

"She's probably right." He looked into her eyes. "There's a nice restaurant at the inn called the Greenhouse. We could go there, or we could go to my apartment instead." He paused, his expression questioning, saying more than his words. "It's only a few more blocks. You told me the other night that you missed my Arizona slides at the Stocktons' because of a headache. I can fix us something hot to drink and show you the slides this afternoon."

A lock of his crisp-looking hair had fallen over his forehead and she found herself again wondering if it would feel soft to her touch. She felt a rush of physical yearning at the thought of being alone with him and her voice was suddenly unsteady. "Is this an invitation to see your etchings?"

Her coat collar was still open at the throat. He drew it closed and held his hands gently against her face. "I suppose it's just an invitation."

She liked very much the combination of self-confidence and honesty that she read in his gray eyes. Gazing at him, her blood seemed to race with a quickening, breathless thrill, but then her eyes shied away from his. "Suppose we take a rain check for now," she told him softly. *Later*, she thought, *later, when they knew each other better*.

He looked ready to argue, then didn't. "The Greenhouse it is." Swinging an arm about her waist, he led the way to the inn.

Over coffee, he explained with chagrin that he would be leaving again for Pennsylvania the next day. A problem on his job had developed and he wouldn't return until the end of the coming week. "I've been invited back to that adult class to answer questions about solar energy and now I have to cancel." He grinned. "Hope your newsletter won't include a note about my unreliability."

The lift of her brow emphasized the exotic tilt of her eyes as she teased, "Seems you're awfully concerned about what might appear in that newsletter."

"Hey, I really wasn't, but now that you've said that, I am."

She laughed. "Your bio is in there because you must have agreed to help out with that class, but that's all there is about you."

"Not even anything about me being resourceful and brave?"

"I'm afraid not. My task is to edit what students write for extra credit, not write it myself. And I'm supposed to lay it out so it looks professional, and believe me, that's enough for me now."

"Hmmm," he said, "and here I've been paying attention to you because I thought you could write marvelous things that would advance my career."

"Nope," she said. "No such luck."

"Not even if I shell out for a scrumptious high-class dinner tonight?"

"Oh, I can't. Fran's planned one of her special meals." It was true enough, but Janet was glad for a ready excuse. Ben was charming and amusing and she did like him, but extending their time together into the evening wasn't wise; she was sure of it.

"All right." His gaze was measuring. She felt she juggled her defenses like balls in the air and he was trying to slip them away from her one by one.

"I'll scale it down," he said. "How about lunch tomorrow?"

"I thought you were leaving for Pennsylvania."

"Not until later in the day. I'll pick you up at noon. We can have lunch and then drive out for a look at my company's latest house. All energy efficient and on a terrific building site." He winked. "I teach a class in the spring. By then I'll have you persuaded to punch up anything a student writes to sing my praises."

She laughed. "Aren't you the clever one!"

"So, lunch tomorrow is a date?" His grin told her he was sure she was going to agree.

"Okay." She smiled back at him, then said, "I'll walk back to Fran's when we done. I'm sure you have things to do."

He studied her for a moment, the nodded. When they parted in

Palmer Square, he gently brushed her lower lip with a fingertip, a soft, butterfly stroke that left her flesh tingling. His voice was low, as he said, "See you tomorrow at noon."

She headed home, her lips remembering his touch. She wondered, as she knew he had intended, what his kiss would have felt like instead. She suppressed the direction of her thoughts, reminding herself of the wisdom of taking things slowly—advice she wished she had followed during her first few months in college.

Back then, so marvelously free of Fran's constraint, she had eagerly flung herself into whatever experiences life had to offer, and Clay Fairweather, a devastatingly handsome honor student with an air of superiority, had her awestruck.

When he led her back to his room after their first date, she never questioned that giving him her virginity was anything but fated. Neither did she question his jealousy, his short temper, or his explanation that he had few friends because his intellectual gifts and serious interests were misunderstood by those who only wanted to waste time on frivolous pursuits.

Janet's friends didn't like Clay, but they fervently approved of her taking a lover. After all, if a woman found a man attractive, why not? The only puzzle was why she'd waited until she was a junior in college. Enjoy, they had encouraged over Cokes and pizza. Indulge. This was modern times, not the almost forgotten age when a "good girl" believed she had to be in love before she could enjoy sex. But Janet, a modern good girl, unwittingly believed that once she had found good sex, then she must have fallen in love! And sex with Clay had been very good indeed.

Drugged by rapture, they went into marriage after his graduation in 1983 thinking they knew everything about each other, but the only thing they had known was the intensity of their physical relationship; an intensity that faded quickly once Clay entered the world beyond the classroom. There he discovered he was the sun, moon, and stars to no one since the recent death of his widowed mother. Janet soon became the scapegoat for all his frustrations.

Had he not brutally cast her aside after Becky's death, Janet supposed she would have been with him yet, hopelessly trying to satisfy his impossible needs, still believing her failure to do so was all her fault. Time and distance had lent perspective, but her marriage had taught her to distrust quick attraction. How ironic it was that if Ben had appealed to her less, she would have trusted him more. Or perhaps, trusted herself more. She frowned, suddenly doubtful. Seeing him two days in a row might not be wise after all.

Deep in thought, she neared her sister's street, not seeing Gina playing on the Stockton lawn until the child, throwing aside a small bamboo rake, ran to her.

"Gina . . . hello!" Janet was surprised and pleased to be greeted like an old friend. She was even more pleased when Gina shyly reached for her hand. Delighted, she tucked the small, sweaty hand into her own. "Have you been working, Gina? Raking leaves?"

Nodding proudly, the little girl brushed strands of dark hair from her face. Her cheeks were flushed and her eyes, a deep, melting brown, sparkled with life.

Hailing cheerfully, Veronica came from the house. "Janet, so great to see you again!" Her hair, now worn in a long, puffed up pageboy style, partly concealed the width of her jaw. "Your sister tells me you're now the editor of the adult school newsletter. I planned to take the class in French cuisine. Every year I say that, but then I get so busy with other things!"

Although Veronica was gushy, the ensuing conversation was down-to-earth. Janet remembered Fran saying she was always more bearable when her husband wasn't around. But then, noticing the way Gina clung to Janet's hand, Veronica scolded, "Sweetheart, don't hang on people! Think of how dusty and rumpled you are. Go inside and tell Ozzie to get you washed for dinner."

The child flashed Janet a smile and obediently ran off. Pagoda, who had been hiding under the shrubbery, raced her to the house and both cat and little girl disappeared inside together.

"I'm sorry," Veronica apologized. "She just hangs on people."

"I didn't mind." Sparks of annoyance crackled over Janet as if she were a cat and Veronica's words had stroked her the wrong way.

Sensing disapproval, Veronica defended herself. "She needs to touch to communicate, I know that. But not everyone understands." She gave Janet a sharp look. "You are aware of her handicap, aren't you?"

"My sister told me she can't talk," Janet answered shortly. She hoped Veronica would deny Fran's contention, but instead, she nodded.

"It's a result of shock. Tommy and I had thought—had even been told—that she would come out of it when she felt secure again, but we've had her for almost two years."

Janet's conviction that the child could at least whisper remained unshaken, but all she said was, "Well, it's obvious she has no trouble understanding things."

At last Veronica gave evidence of pride. "She's really a bright little girl. Her tutor says she's learning to read and write very well, especially because she's doing it in English." The smile that had softened her features suddenly thinned and grew critical. "Still, there's no denying the handicap. And it will only become a greater problem as she grows older."

What kind of problem? Janet wondered. It sounded to her as if Veronica was mostly concerned about social impressions. She and Tommy had been promised that Gina would someday be perfect, yet here the child was, making a nuisance of herself, "hanging" on people. Janet wished the couple could be made to understand what a treasure Gina could be to their lives.

On impulse, she spoke up, hardly knowing what she was about to say until hearing herself. "How about letting Gina spend tomorrow afternoon with Ben Yates and me?"

Veronica looked startled to think anyone might deliberately seek Gina's company. "You mean take her someplace?"

Janet struggled to hide her irritation. "Just for a few hours, a bit of an outing."

"Well, I suppose . . . if you're willing." Veronica still sounded nonplussed. "This is very nice of you. What time should I tell Ozzie to have her ready?"

"About noon." Janet outlined a sketchy plan. "For lunch and then a Sunday drive. As I said, only a few hours."

The women talked a few more minutes, then parted. Continuing home, Janet realized she should have okayed things with Ben first. Well, it was too late now. She squared her shoulders. Veronica and Tommy had to be shown that Gina was not an embarrassment, and if Ben refused to go along with her impulsiveness, she would stay home and find a way to entertain the child herself.

When she reached Ben by phone later that evening and explained about her invitation to Gina, he was silent a moment, then, "Sure. Why not? Sounds great."

Relieved, Janet blurted, "You're not annoyed, are you?"

He chuckled. "Maybe I'm even flattered."

She was puzzled. "Why?"

"To think you feel you need a chaperone."

"Oh." She supposed he had a point. Although she hadn't consciously reasoned it out, inviting Gina along had relieved her mind on two counts: being able to do something for Gina, and keeping Ben at a bit of a distance. And seeing it, Ben had understood. When she replaced the receiver, she was smiling. Without a doubt, Ben Yates was a very nice man.

Chapter 15

JANET TOOK HER PLACE IN THE PASSENGER seat of Ben's Cavalier. Gina, dressed in a red hooded sweatshirt and candy-striped slacks, her dark hair held back with the usual red ribbon, settled in the rear as if she belonged there, not casting a look back toward her house as the car left her street.

"She's a cute kid," Ben observed quietly to Janet. "A friend, Edgar Lightfoot, works for the church agency that helped place her with the Stocktons. He told me she was a charmer." He shot Janet a grin. "I'll have to introduce you to Edgar sometime. I owe him my thanks. It's because of him that you and I met."

"How so?"

"He once invited me and the Stocktons to the same party and we started discussing ecology. It led to Tommy and Veronica asking me to give that presentation at their house." His smile became meaningful as he continued. "I now think of it as my lucky night."

"Oh." The personal note caught her off guard. Looking into the back seat at Gina, she found herself trying to shift the emphasis by including the little girl. "I guess I have to thank Edgar too. Gina and I are really looking forward to this afternoon."

Smiling, Ben gave a glance back at Gina and then said to Janet, "Do you and Gina have any idea where you'd like to have lunch?"

"I haven't been here long enough to know the local restaurants," Janet said and then, surprisingly, the thought of the perfect spot popped into her mind. "Wait—if we keep on this road a few miles, we'll come to a place Gina really likes."

"Sounds good," Ben agreed cheerfully.

Janet found herself frowning. How had she known about the restaurant? She decided that Veronica must have mentioned it the previous day. Turning in her seat, she met Gina's sparkling eyes.

"Oh, you heard us?" she teased. "Heard where we're going to stop? Bet you already know what you want. Either a hot dog or a hamburger, right?"

Wearing a tucked-in, mischievous smile, Gina gave her head a negative shake.

"Oh, am I to guess? Let's see . . ." Thinking of what a child might enjoy, she suddenly visualized Gina sitting before a plate of chicken fingers. She could imagine her lifting a succulent morsel of the crisply fried chicken as clearly as if it were happening before her eyes. She was positive she was right, but to come out with the answer so quickly would ruin the game.

"I know," she said, deliberately making a different choice. "A tuna sandwich. With pickles. Right?"

Vigorously, Gina shook her head *no*.

"Ummm. Spaghetti? Spaghetti with meatballs?"

Gina's brown eyes danced as she again shook her head.

"This must be the place," Ben announced, pulling into the parking lot of a log cabin-style restaurant.

"Looks nice." Janet was thinking that any place Veronica and Tommy frequented was bound to come up to a certain standard. She got out and had Gina's door open by the time Ben had circled the car.

Bending, he called inside, "Gina, if it's lobster you want, tell me now. I can't take shocks to my wallet without warning."

The little girl shook her head in gleeful denial.

Pleased over Ben's easy manner with the child, Janet figured the game had gone on long enough. "I've got it! You want chicken fingers, don't you? Chicken fingers are your very favorite. Am I right?"

Gina's delighted expression proved that Janet had hit the correct answer. She scrambled out of the car and into Janet's arms, giving her an exuberant hug.

An hour later, having finished lunch, the three arrived at the hillside where the construction site was located. The house was still at the framework stage. Seeing Gina's disinterested expression, Janet gave the child permission to go exploring. "But don't go any farther than that wall," she cautioned, indicating a tumbledown fieldstone wall bordered with thickets of milkweed and scarlet sumac along the property line.

Ben ushered Janet into the unfinished structure to give a grand, guided tour, his booted feet thumping across the boards with a confident familiarity that testified to his deep involvement.

It became immediately obvious that he was showing off his dream house. If he didn't plan to make it his someday, he at least looked forward to having something exactly like it in the future. Was it a home she might someday like? She cut off the thought.

Standing in what would be the master bedroom, he waved a hand in the direction of rolling countryside. "See what I mean about this view? Imagine starting the day off like this! Who wouldn't wake up feeling wonderful?" Moving on, he pointed through an open wall to a private patio and announced the future location of a hot tub. "Energy saving, of course," he amended.

"Come on," she joked. "A hot tub? After the way you criticized conspicuous consumption? You're just trying to justify hedonistic impulses."

"Not really. In winter, circulating water will be heated by the wood stove, which would be burning anyway. In summer, the sun's rays will do the job. Marvelously efficient."

"If you say so," she said, although she had no doubt that he knew what he was talking about.

After they finished touring the house, Janet made sure that Gina was still harmlessly playing and then rejoined Ben, who sat on the sun-warmed deck, his long legs stretched out comfortably. A tilted sheet of plywood provided protection from occasional gusts of wind.

He smiled up at her as she stood before him. She saw how the slant of the sun cast intriguing shadows on the strong, irregular lines of his face, the muscular width of his throat made more evident by the open collar of his shirt.

Looking at him, Janet suddenly reviewed the implied intimacy of going to see a house under construction, that traditional sign of the nesting impulse. A stunning sense of longing flooded through her and she averted her eyes, fearing her thoughts would be revealed.

What was she doing? Was she looking at him as if he could supply what was missing in her life? The idea frightened her. Her failed marriage certainly taught the error of such thinking.

He beckoned. "Come and sit down."

She did his bidding, but kept a distance between them, sitting with her arms wrapped about her up-drawn knees. The afternoon was shaping up to be a mistake. He was putting out all the signals of a man ready to get involved, but despite their mutual attraction, the timing was wrong. She was too burdened by emotional baggage to do anything except move slowly, and it wasn't fair to expect him to understand.

The silence suddenly seemed unbearable. Casting for something neutral to say, she said, "So then, is . . . is this the type of housing project you're working on in Pennsylvania?"

He groaned. "Don't I wish."

When he volunteered nothing more, she said, "Well, what is it that you're doing then?"

"Installing solar panels in an already inhabited condominium." He made it sound like hard labor with only bread and water.

She didn't know why he was being so cryptic. "What's so awful about that?"

"You wouldn't want to know."

"Why not? What are you talking about?" She was annoyed.

He grinned. "That's better, yell at me. I'm not so fierce. For a moment there, I thought you were afraid I would bite."

"I thought no such thing," she defended, coloring as she realized he had deliberately led her on. "You're being ridiculous."

"See? Call me ridiculous, but do I get mad?"

She found herself laughing. "I'm going to call you worse if you don't explain." She realized she felt more at ease and knew that's what he had been aiming for. Charm, plus a knowledge of psychology. A dangerous man indeed. But in a nice way. "Come on, what's so dreadful about the condo job?"

"It isn't so awful," he admitted, smiling. "It's just that a certain amount of labor has to be done from inside the homes. Trying to work around the homeowners' schedules has caused more holdups than I care to think about."

"And tomorrow will be more of the same?"

"Afraid so." Shifting, he rested on an elbow as he gazed at her, his expression open and warm. Janet felt she had never known anyone else with eyes exactly his shade of gray. "But, he said, "I'll be home next weekend, I was wondering if—"

Whatever he had intended to say was interrupted as Gina rushed up, bringing a fistful of pebbles.

"Oh, how pretty!" Janet exclaimed as the child spread the stones on the wooden surface of the deck. It was obvious that Ben wanted to make plans for the coming weekend, and she didn't know how she wanted to respond. She reached for one of the stones.

"Look, Gina," she said, "this is a piece of quartz. See how clear it is? When you hold it to the sun, you can see rainbows in the light." As the little girl squinted through the cluster of crystals, Janet felt Ben watching her. It made her feel as transparent as the quartz. She quickly picked up another stone. "Look, honey, see these sparkling glints? This is mica. Isn't it pretty?"

When the child scampered off to find more stones, Ben observed, "You're good with kids. Come from a big family?"

"No, just me and my sister." Because of their past conversations, she knew things about his family: about his mother and father, who had lived in New Jersey until their retirement to Naples, Florida; his sister, presently in Germany with her husband, a career Army man. But obviously, she hadn't told him as much about herself.

"There were aunts and uncles on my father's side," she said. "All much older than Dad. We never kept in touch." Lightly, she discussed her growing up years, the deaths of her parents, emphasizing the good parts, skimming over the bad, taking pleasure in Ben's appreciative responses when she related funny things that had happened.

There was a silence, then he ventured, "Tell me, what happened when your—"

She winced and turned her head, feeling all her contentment of the last few minutes drain. She remembered what Fran admitted she'd told him. She didn't need a crystal ball to know he had intended his sentence to end: *when your baby died.*

"Janet . . ." He reached for her hand. She tried to pull away, but gently, firmly, he refused to let her go. "Janet," he ordered softly. "Janet, look at me."

Reluctantly, she did as he asked.

His smile was gentle. "It's okay," he said. "It's all right, really, it is."

He relaxed his hold so that she could have moved her hand away had she wanted to, but it suddenly no longer seemed necessary. She gazed at him, his words echoing in her mind: It's *okay. It's all right.* Simple phrases that could be virtually meaningless, yet when combined with the way he had spoken them told her all she needed to know about his patience and understanding. A sweet confusion of emotions rushed through her. She felt joy, yet at the same time, she felt close to tears. There had been no need to feel apprehensive about their afternoon together, she realized that now.

Smile tremulous, she said, "About next weekend when you return—"

He grinned. "Lady, are you trying to maneuver a date?"

She laughed. "Something like that."

"Sounds good to me. I like aggressive women." His voice was teasing. "Any ideas of what to do?"

She shook her head.

"Okay, tell you what," he said, giving her hand a squeeze. "Starting Monday, I'll call you every night next week. By Thursday, we should have figured out something. How's that sound?"

She laughed again. "It sounds fine."

"Okay, then, it's a promise." Standing, he pulled her to her feet. "As much as I hate to say it, it's almost time to go. But there's one more thing I want you to see." His arm slipped easily about her waist. "There's a perfect spot for a gazebo, a view that can't be seen from inside the house. An extra dividend to the site."

Feeling easier with him than she would have thought was possible, they had started walking when she abruptly stopped. "Wait a second. I'll be with you in a moment, but Gina wants me."

Leaving Ben, she headed toward the property line, picking her way around fallen stones that would be gathered and reassembled when the landscaping began. Nearing the wall, she frowned, unable to see the little girl. The red-garbed figure jumped into view from the other side of a bush.

"What did you find?" Janet called.

Gina held up a pebble pinched between her fingers.

"Let's have a look." Going closer, seeing the clarity of the stone, Janet feared she would have to tell Gina her discovery was only a weathered chip of glass. But upon close inspection, it indeed proved to be quartz, the color faintly tinted with rose.

"Maybe you should save that, honey," Janet advised. "Someday in science class, you'll study various kinds of rocks. Your teacher will talk about this kind and you'll have your own sample, all ready to show."

"What's up?" Ben asked, reaching them.

Gina happily displayed her treasure.

"Very nice," he approved. His voice was warm, yet to Janet's ears, it also held an odd note she couldn't define. "Hate to call things short," he reminded her, "but as soon as we take a look at the gazebo view, we have to be on our way."

"Okay." She turned to Gina. "If you want to keep any of the other stones, you had better get them now."

Puzzled, Ben looked after the little girl as she hurried off. His gaze shifted to Janet. "How did you know she wanted to show you something?"

Janet thought back. "She must have motioned. I guess I saw her out of the corner of my eye."

"But we were together, and I swear there was no sign of her." He frowned. "I don't know how you could have seen her at all."

Chapter 16

JANET HEARD THE SCREAM OF A SIREN as she finished her lunch. It sounded close, but by the time she reached the door and looked around, all was silent. Whatever the emergency vehicle had been, it must have gone on up the street.

The weather was a disappointment after the sunshine of the previous day. The afternoon laid chill and corpselike under a sky the color of lead. At least it was the right atmosphere for Mischief Night.

Returning to the kitchen table, Janet surveyed her folder of newsletter material with a jaundiced eye. She'd been to the school enough so she felt reasonably proficient although there were times when she still needed Crystal's help. Her problem at the moment, however, was how far to go in editing student's material. Some just weren't as good as the others, but she didn't want to come across as discouraging. It was a complication she didn't have with material written by the former editor. There, she could spark up dull, mechanical copy with no worries. She finally decided that the best thing was to do was take the originals along with her editing suggestions and discuss them with their teachers.

Her thoughts flew back to that day with Ben and Gina.

On the way home, the child had fallen asleep in the car and Janet and Ben talked, telling each other about their lives. She realized she probably knew more about Ben than she'd ever known about Clay when they'd been dating—their physical attraction had left no space for what she realized now was far more important—learning about a person's hopes and dreams and what life meant to them. One person could never know another person completely, but how blind she'd been about Clay when compared with what she was getting to know about Ben.

She shook her head and told herself to put her mind back on the job. She would spend the rest of the afternoon getting her work in order. The next day she would go to the school and tell Ida her plans to discuss the students' work with their respective English teachers.

As if the vow in itself was an accomplishment, she felt self-satisfaction as she carried a fresh mug of tea into Warren's office and sat before the typewriter. Fran was coming home late that day, so Janet was preparing dinner. Three uninterrupted hours stretched before she would start work in the kitchen.

The phone rang.

The high-pitched, strained voice on the line was Muriel's, her jumbled words filled with apologies for her "imposition" and the fear that she was "taking advantage." Janet finally understood she was being asked to come over.

"Yes, of course I can come, Mrs. Renner," Janet said. Putting the siren sound she had heard together with Muriel's agitation, she asked, "Has something happened to your sister?"

"No. I need someone to stay with her. Dr. Renner has suffered a possible heart attack. I must go to the hospital with him. I need someone to be with Rose."

"I'll be there in a flash." Janet hung up the phone, snatched her work folder from the desk and ran for her jacket.

By the time she reached the front entrance of the Renner house, the stretcher carrying the doctor was being placed in the ambulance. The Oldsmobile sat ready in the drive, engine running. Muriel, wearing her peach-colored coat, met Janet on the porch.

"Forgive me, but I did not know who else to call upon." She pressed Janet's hands. Her complexion was pale, with a chalky undertone. "Dr. Renner's condition may not be terribly serious, but with his medical history, we could not afford risks. Please, there is no way to know how long I will be at the hospital."

"The hospital here in Princeton?" Janet asked.

"Yes, it is close, and his heart doctor knows people here." Eyes fearful, she glanced at the ambulance. The men were closing the rear doors. She gave Janet an imploring look. "I am imposing, I know."

"Don't worry, I'm glad to help. Now, go on to the hospital and don't worry about your sister."

"Yes, you are so good with her." Distracted, Muriel saw that the ambulance was ready to leave. She seemed torn between the responsibility of her sister's welfare and attending to the care of her husband. "You will find Rose in the study. Fortunately, this is a day when she is interested in her picture collection. She—"

"If you want to go with the ambulance, you had better be on your way," Janet said gently. "Don't worry about Rose. Don't worry about anything here. Everything will be fine."

Janet watched from the porch as the ambulance pulled smoothly from the drive. As the Oldsmobile followed, Muriel cast a look back. Janet waved and smiled reassuringly.

When she re-entered the house she noticed that the doors to the right of the entry were open to the living room. She looked in and saw canvas spread on the floor and two tall ladders. The air smelled of paint. Janet conjectured that the Renners probably intended to redecorate the entire house, room by room. When they were done, it would probably all be as magnificent as the master bedroom.

She cast a cautious glance up the staircase and then went through the dining room to the study. Rose had magazines spread upon a card table. Her black headscarf was tied like a shawl across her shoulders and sagging bust. Working with blunt-tipped scissors, she was industriously cutting a kitten picture from an advertisement for cat food. When Muriel had said Rose was busy with a picture collection,

Janet had mistakenly assumed she meant photographs, perhaps snapshots from their home in Argentina.

The stereo played and the television was silently tuned to a soap opera, the screen showing a middle-aged blonde actress with enormous blue eyes in bed with a curly-haired man who appeared much younger.

Rose looked up. Not questioning Janet's presence, she showed her gums broadly, her smile puffing up smooth apples in the wrinkles of her cheeks. "More for my room," she announced, indicating the picture. "More, always more."

"Yes, that's a nice one," Janet said, wondering if Muriel had taken time to explain that she and her husband were going to the hospital. Perhaps Rose didn't even realize that the man was ill. She decided to make no reference to it unless Rose brought up the subject herself.

The final clip of the scissors severed one of the kitten's paws. Unconcerned, Rose placed the cutout on top of similar ones and lifted a fresh magazine from the pile.

Janet watched as the woman leafed through the pages, her gnarled, swollen hands surprisingly dexterous.

"More!" she crowed triumphantly, having come upon another ad for cat food. She reached for her scissors. It didn't seem to matter that the picture was identical to the one she had just clipped.

Curious, Janet asked, "Do you just like the pictures, or do you also like real cats?"

Rose cackled and spread her arms. "Open door and in comes cat—surprise! Hide in cupboard, hide under bed—surprise!"

Janet smiled. Pagoda was definitely a sneaky cat. "So you chased it out again? I once saw you shoo a cat from your yard."

It didn't appear that Rose was would continue the conversation, but then, in a tone that somehow managed to be sullen and sly at the same time, she said, "Doctor Herman be angry." With her accent, the word "Doctor" sounded like a first name, not a title. "Doctor Herman, when he goes, cat can come. Cat and little girl come all days."

"Little girl? You mean Gina?"

"Little girl won't talk."

Privately, Janet wondered, won't talk or can't talk? The distinction intrigued her, but what she said aloud to Rose was, "Why would Dr. Renner be angry? Doesn't he like cats?"

Rose cackled as if Janet had purposely made a joke. "Cats, he no like. Children, he hates."

The turn of Rose's phrase seemed out of character. For a moment, it was as if a different person had spoken from her withered lips—perhaps the person she had been years before.

To that person, Janet said, "I don't understand. How could he feel that way? I thought he was a child psychologist."

"Sister say Doctor Herman be re tired." Rose made the word "retired" into two words, then smirked. "Take tire and roll away."

Startled, Janet realized the woman had made a joke using a play on English words. She wouldn't have thought her capable of it.

Then Rose said, "I say little girl, go home. Doctor Herman be angry. Now whistle wagon rides him away. Little girl can come all days if Doctor Herman be dead."

Janet realized that "whistle wagon" was Rose's name for ambulance. The woman's blunt, matter-of-factness when discussing her brother-in-law's possible death was a shock.

"You shouldn't talk that way, Rose," she chided, realizing even as she spoke that Rose had detached herself from the conversation. Calmly, the old woman finished cutting the picture and added it to the others. In that one the kitten's paws were intact, but the tip of an ear was cropped. Returning to the magazine, she resumed flipping through the pages. "Dog food," she muttered, as if she could command the magazine to produce the ad she desired.

Realizing that she still wore her jacket, Janet slipped it off and took a seat on the couch. On television, a chubby brunette puffed a cigarette and flirted across a restaurant table at a man with his hair in a mullet, the top a four-inch puff of curls that had to be permed because the back hung straight to below his collar. When he looked into the camera, he turned out to be the youth who had been in bed earlier on the show with a blonde woman.

Janet opened her folder to the articles she had to edit. After several minutes of trying to devise a title for one student's article, she started thinking about the dinner she had intended to prepare. There was no telling when Muriel would return. Perhaps she should phone Fran and suggest she bring home something already cooked from the Spoon.

There was a phone in the room, but it was next to a stereo speaker. The radio volume could be turned down, but there was no point in doing anything that might disturb Rose, who was contentedly clipping away.

"I'm going to use the phone in the hallway for a minute," she told the woman. Busy with the scissors, Rose gave no sign that she had heard.

In the hall, call completed, Janet started to return to the study and then paused to look up the staircase. The polished mahogany leading to the top of the steps gleamed with a cold, austere formality in the sunless afternoon. The words, "a beckoning chill" leaped from the dark casket of Janet's imagination: ominous remnants from childhood spooky tales lying in wait for weak moments.

Annoyed, she remembered her apprehension the last time she was in the house and decided it was time to put speculations to rest. It would only take a second to climb up and prove there was nothing odd about the upper hallway. She would do it now. Quickly, while Rose was safely occupied.

Chapter 17

HALFWAY UP THE STEPS, JANET HEARD the sounds.

Soft, breathy rustlings.

The leaves, she reminded herself. Leaves caught against the window screens, shifting gently in the wind.

She mounted a few more steps. Peering through the spindles, she could see the smooth, polished wood of the second-floor hallways where they joined. She reached the turn in the steps. Her gaze went to the large window on the front wall of the house. On that overcast day, the light had a hard-edged glare, as cold as the glow from an alien moon.

The sounds came again. She couldn't tell from where they came, but the sounds held a distinctive cadence. Her flesh tingled as hairs on her arms and the nape of her neck lifted.

What she was hearing didn't have the irregular randomness of wind shuffling through trapped leaves. It was something different. Something with an eerie sort of rhythm.

Breath held, she strained to find a pattern to the soft sounds: Da-da-ta-ta-da-da. No, not quite right. The accent fell strongly on the fifth count: Da-da-ta-ta-DA-da? Yes, that was it.

Uneasy, yet curious, she tapped a finger on the railing in time with what she was hearing: Da-da-ta-ta-DA-da. She felt as if she accompanied a ritual chant. A chill slithered its way down her spine. There had to be a reasonable explanation for the sounds. The heating system must be creating vibrations. Yet, could steam and water coursing through pipes produce so measured a tempo?

Cocking her head, she tried to be analytical. Imagination could transform even the mundane ticking of a bedroom clock into a message: tick-tock—wake up; tick-tock—get up. She tried to suppress the creative part of her mind. All she wanted was the bare skeleton of the sounds.

It suddenly occurred to her that she might be hearing something related to music from the stereo downstairs. Just as a distant marching band can sound all drums and no tune; whatever currently played for Rose might have bass notes that were being carried through the house.

Listening intently, she became more and more certain she was right. She nodded to herself. Yes, some echo or trick of architecture made the sounds seem to issue from the second floor. When she returned to the study, she would find that the song being played on the radio had bass notes matching the beats she'd heard.

But by the time she returned to the study, a love ballad with soft violins had begun. Nothing like the rhythm she'd heard upstairs. Disappointed, Janet leaned against the doorjamb, watching Rose thumb through yet another magazine. The woman gave no sign she was aware of anything outside her own narrow world. A program of children's cartoons had supplanted the soap opera. *He-Man and the Masters of the Universe* showed the blond-headed giant in a gladiator's costume battling a dragon. Watching the colorful action on the screen without really seeing it, Janet impatiently waited for the next radio selection.

After another misty love song, a boisterous rendition of "Hello, Dolly" began. Janet's eyes sparkled. Vigorously tapping her foot, she counted out the energetic beat: ONE, two, three, four; DA-ta-ta-ta. Distinctive and easily identifiable.

Quickly, she left the room. Now, while the song had another minute or two to go, she would become a detective.

She reached the dining room arch and could still clearly follow the "Hello, Dolly" melody, but the moment she rounded the corner to the foyer, the music cut off so abruptly that she stepped back to make sure the radio still played. It did.

Reassured, she began to ascend the steps.

Unconsciously, she sang the words, "Hello, Dolly! How are you, Dolly!" under her breath. Then, hearing herself, she stopped, feeling spooked. She had seen too many films in which a merry background tune gradually assumed ominous, minor notes, fraught with warning. She shook her head, annoyed with the sinister twist of her thoughts. Her endeavor was nothing alarming. It was a harmless investigation. She would go halfway up the steps and find that some auditory trick of the old house did indeed transmit the underlying beat of "Hello, Dolly." She would hear it and be satisfied. What could be simpler?

She reached the second-floor landing, went past the steps that led up to the belvedere and then on past the master bedroom until she came to the joined hallway that led on to the rear of the house.

She listened intently. There was nothing but silence.

Frowning, she bit her lower lip between her teeth. The sounds must have been from the heating system after all, and now, the furnace must have switched off. Her theory about the radio had been wrong.

Then she heard it.

Her heartbeat caught in her throat.

That soft, breathy pulse. It wasn't louder than before, yet it was somehow stronger. Determined. Da-da-ta-ta-DA-da! Da-da-ta-ta-DA-da! Nothing like the boisterous, lighthearted sound of "Dolly." Nothing like that at all.

The sounds seemed to come from behind her. She turned to face the big window. Hands gripped tightly against her breast, Janet shrank against the wall.

Earlier, she had likened the sounds to chanting but had dismissed the thought, but a chant was what the syllabic cadence most resembled.

One composed of a multitude of small, soft voices in unison. Voices as soft as a whisper.

Whispering. Yes! Her blood froze. That's what she was hearing: whispers! A whispering chant, like the doxology of a phantom choir.

Fear crackled along her flesh like an electric current. Now that her mind grasped what she was hearing, the beginning words began to separate themselves, taking on meaning. "We are—" The rest dissolved into the incomprehensible . . . ta-ta-DA-da. "We are ta-ta-DA-da."

Suddenly, off to the far side of the window, she caught sight of a small, glimmering blur. She didn't know if the whisperings ceased in that instant, or if her senses were so transfixed by the glowing whirl of motion that everything else faded away.

The blur blossomed into a shapeless mist, and then slowly coalesced, taking the form of a faintly illuminated pillar about two feet high. The pillar wavered and then began to drift away from the harsh daylight of the window. As it entered the shadows, details, like etchings upon glass, began to emerge from the misty vortex. Part of a face, a cascade of dark ringlets, the curve of an arm, a rounded stomach . . .

Janet stifled a cry. A small girl . . . a mere toddler, now stood in the corner of the hall. Her body, not fully materialized, seemed to be garbed in a shift-like garment. And then, beside the girl, another glowing shape! Taller, congealing more rapidly.

With a fascination that was beyond fear, Janet watched spellbound as the second child came into view. Thin, and nearly naked, the belly swollen. A little boy.

The same little boy she had seen that night in the garden with Ben.

\

Chapter 18

THE VISION BEFORE HER WAS SO beyond comprehension that Janet simply stared. The glowing shapes shimmered before her eyes. Then they were gone, as completely as if they had never been. In breathless disbelief, she continued to stare, waiting for something to happen. Something . . . anything . . .

There was nothing.

Legs trembling and threatening to give way, Janet moved to the bottom of the belvedere staircase and sank to sit on a stair step.

Ghosts, she thought, her mind still whirling. This house is haunted. I've just seen two ghosts. She realized she felt no fear. How could she be afraid of children? Ghosts, yes, but children all the same. The Renner house was haunted by ghost children.

She was still in a daze when she descended the stairs. What was the meaning of what she had seen? What event in the house had caused it to be possessed?

Downstairs, she found Rose still at the table, lovingly stroking a cat picture as if her fingers could feel the soft texture of animal fur. Biting her lip, Janet studied the old woman. Had she ever seen the ghosts?

Even if she had, she probably made little distinction between reality and unreality. In any case, she wouldn't know any history of the house to help explain it. Muriel probably wouldn't know either.

Janet suddenly thought of the one person who might have some answers: Kirby Orchard. He had asked her to go to the adult school with him that night to sit in on film class and she had agreed. On the way home, she would ask him what he knew about the Renner house.

But that night, after adult school and riding home with him, Janet found that her earlier enthusiasm had cooled. If she hadn't seen the ghosts with her own eyes, she wouldn't believe in them, so why should Kirby? Besides, the strange memory of what she had seen felt special; she didn't want to hear it mocked. It wasn't a subject to rush into headlong. On the other hand, assuming such a house would have collected a reputation over the years, she felt safe in asking, "What sort of research have you done on Dr. Renner's place?"

"Well, I know its recent history because it's on the block across from where I grew up, but I've done no special study." Kirby gave her a curious glance. "Why do you ask?"

Janet found herself prevaricating. "I . . . I was there earlier today and saw how the Renners are putting a lot of money into fixing the place up. It made me wonder about it, that's all."

She couldn't believe that no resident had ever seen the ghost children in the past. Kirby's ignorance on the subject must mean the witnesses had kept their mouths shut. And it was probably smart for her to do the same. People gave suspicious looks at individuals who claimed to hear and see the things that go bump in the night. Besides, as illogical as it might be, she felt that seeing those ghostly figures represented a mystical privilege, one she wanted to protect. It was just as well, she decided, that any investigation with Kirby had come to a quick impasse.

Redirecting the conversation, she asked him if he had lived in Princeton all his life.

"I grew up here and never lost touch as long as my parents were alive." He seemed to enjoy the opportunity to talk about his past. "I had left to study in Los Angeles when I had a career as a film director in mind. I saw myself traveling importantly between Hollywood and Cannes, as dashing as Errol Flynn, as sardonic as George Sanders, as urbane as David Niven. And thin." He shot her a playful glance. "Take note that the three aforementioned gentlemen all had board-flat stomachs."

He talked of being drafted into the Army, being wounded and then coming home to finish his degree. "I was here when my father died and soon after, my mother. I stayed, knowing that this is where I belong."

"And you live in the same house where you grew up?"

"The very same. It's small and perfect for a bachelor like me. It belonged to my parents, and my mother's parents before that, bookish, sedentary people: scholars, educators, and ministers. And all plump. It's in our genes. As with them, my proper milieu is the classroom and the library. I've made some dear friends in the cinema, but it's what's written on paper about films that holds me rather than the flickering images themselves."

Kirby's use of the words "flickering images" vividly recreated in Janet's mind the scene in the upper hall of the Renner house.

I've seen a ghost, she repeated to herself, still awestruck with the wonder of it. And not one ghost, but two! She recalled her attempt to figure out what had illuminated the boy that night in the garden, and now understood that his small form glowed with an energy of its own. In the dark garden, he had appeared flesh and blood, but by daylight in the hallway, both he and the little girl stood revealed as apparitional.

Closing her eyes, she smiled at the remembered images. Then, with jarring suddenness, came the intrusive memory of the chant. Mind's ear working like a tape recorder, it seemed she was hearing those eerie whispers all over again: We are ta-ta-DA-da!

Her eyes flew open. She had forgotten until now that there had been something profoundly disquieting about those measured sounds.

So determined, almost threatening! She shivered. What were the rest of the words?

It wasn't until Kirby slowed for his drive that she realized they had reached his home, just a short distance from Fran's. His cottage was brick, with white shutters. A post lamp made a bright circle of welcome by the entrance. She previously had told him she would walk home, but in her present mood, the darkness hovering just outside the street lamp light took on the aspect of a lurking, pulsing thing. It was almost as if she could feel its chilling breath.

Turning off the engine, Kirby said, "Your mention of the Renners reminds me that this afternoon, I saw an ambulance turn the corner that goes to their house."

Janet grabbed at the chance to delay her walk home. "I should have thought to tell you, you being a neighbor. Dr. Renner was taken to the hospital. I sat with Rose most of the afternoon, but Muriel came home with good news. Dr. Renner's EKG shows no new damage, although he's going to stay a day or two for observation. As I said, the Renners have been fixing the place up. The doctor suspects that his attack was actually a reaction to paint fumes."

Kirby said, "And being in the house today made you inquire about it?"

The return to the subject of the house caught her off guard and she blurted, "Well, sure, after the things that—" Having revealed more than she had intended, she found her defenses crumbling. In a reversal of her feelings, she knew she wanted to share what had happened at the Renner house or at least share a part of it. She felt she could trust Kirby to lend a sympathetic ear, if she didn't stretch credulity too far.

"Actually," she said, "I asked because I wondered if the place had a reputation. I mean, as a place where strange things have happened."

Kirby murmured in interest. With his double chin a soft roll above his collar and the lamp light glinting off his glasses, he looked like a spectacled Buddha. "You mean you've experienced something strange there?"

"There was something," she admitted. "Today was the second time

I stayed with Rose. The first time, when I had to go upstairs, I felt there might be something . . . disturbed about the second floor." Her laugh was nervous. "Or maybe I get goose bumps too easily."

"What unnerved you? Something you saw, something you felt?"

"Maybe both. I saw flickers of motion out of the corner of my eye, but when I looked, nothing was there. And I thought I heard soft little sounds." She had been twisting the strap of her purse as she talked and now discovered she had cut off the flow of blood to her hand. Untangling the strap, she worked the circulation back into her fingers as she concluded her story. "I decided it couldn't be anything except the shadows and sounds of dry leaves blowing across the windows."

"But is that what you really believe?"

Her throat felt suddenly tight. "I don't know."

"And what about today?"

"More of the same, I guess."

"Maybe I've missed something about the house." Kirby said. "If you can spare a minute, come inside while I consult one of my area history books. We might find some interesting mention of the Renner property after all."

Janet agreed, making a mental note not to say anything that might lead Kirby to believe she was carrying her imagination too far.

Inside, in the small, neat kitchen, an overweight little Boston terrier yipped in welcome and wheezed in from an adjoining room as Kirby hung their coats.

"Oh, what a cute little dog!" Janet knelt. "Does she mind if I pet her?" Answering in doggy body language, the animal shoved against Janet's extended hand and grunted blissfully as her head was scratched.

"Let me introduce Trixie," said Kirby fondly. "She's nine years old, aren't you, old girl?" He reached to pat the dog's rump. "Go on back to your bed now, Trix."

As the dog obediently puffed off, Kirby led Janet to his office. The room was outfitted with a rolltop desk and an overstuffed couch and sofa from a long-lost era. A handmade rag rug covered the floor. One wall was all bookcases, and a table on the opposite wall was piled both above and beneath with papers and more books. The framed film posters over the sofa looked like originals: Fay Wray in *King Kong*, Shirley Temple in *Little Miss Marker*, Bogart in *The Maltese Falcon*. On the other large wall were faded family photographs in dark oak frames and a large map of Princeton Borough, individual houses marked along the streets.

"Sit anywhere," Kirby directed with a vague wave. As Janet pushed aside newspapers and made a place for herself on the sofa, he knelt to paw through the books under the table, his bald head reflecting light from the desk lamp. Even though he was dressed in a suit and tie, all Janet could think of was a monk rooting through scrolls in a moldering monastery library.

She said, "Fran told me that the people who sold to the Renners were named Fiorello. And the people before them, the ones who had a young relative who drowned. They were named Mitchum. But they didn't know of anyone before that."

"The folks before them were named Crammer." With a grunt, Kirby dragged out a box. "That was when I was back and forth. I never really got to know them."

Janet noticed a folder on the desk with the name "Stockton" typed on it. "Did Veronica and Tommy ask you to research their house?"

Kirby glanced to see what she was looking at. "No, that's another family, over in West Windsor. No relation. Tommy enjoys talking about the Stockton name being prominent in Princeton history, but he has no interest in researching his house. It's like that when people expect to relocate."

"Relocate?" Thinking of Gina, Janet felt distressed. "Where do they plan to go?"

"Overseas. Tommy is with a company that installs data processing systems worldwide. His outfit has been working out a government deal, something to do with embassies. Tommy will become the company's chief foreign representative and he and Veronica will move abroad. From the start, they've been prepared to leave as soon as Tommy's new position is assigned. It's kept them restless, unable to put down roots.

Oh, drat!" He peered up at Janet. "I just remembered where that book is. I lent it to someone."

"Oh, no! Can you get it back?"

"Of course," he said with a grin. His knees cracked as he got up and sat in his desk chair. "A friend has kept it for months." His expression was impish. "I'll give him a call for lunch, and guilt over keeping the book will have him picking up the tab. Speaking of food, would you like something hot to drink? And a slice of pie, maybe? Dutch apple, I think. Anyway, the kind with raisins." He stood, placing a hand on a stomach that strained his vest buttons. "Or, at least, keep me company and make sure I don't sneak an extra slice. I'll repay your vigilance by telling you all I know about the people who have lived in the Renner house."

Over pie and cups of lemon herb tea in the kitchen, Kirby kept his promise. "Now, when I was a kid, the first people I remember there were named Patrick. I started school with the Patrick kids. They moved when I was in the third grade and the house sat empty until the Roberts arrived. They didn't leave until I was away. Maybe there were more people after them, but I probably wasn't home enough to pay all that much attention."

Hoping that Kirby would remember something significant as they talked, she asked, "Were they all young families?"

"You mean were the same kinds of people always attracted to the house? No, it doesn't seem so. The Crammers and Roberts were middle-aged. The Roberts moved in young but stayed until after their kids were grown. Same for the Mitchums. More pie?"

When she shook her head, he said, "Good girl." He grinned, patting his plump stomach. "If you'd had more, I would have had to join you to be polite. But at least have more tea."

He filled both their cups from what remained in the pot. "No," he said, "I can't see a common pattern among the residents of the house. Take the Renners now, three older adults—an unusual family in any case. I've seen the sister from a distance." He tapped his head. "It appears her brain has gone a bit soft."

Janet was disappointed that the talk had come to nothing. "Then in all the years you've lived here, there has never been a hint of disturbance?"

"None that I know of, but of course, that book may turn up something." He nudged his glasses back into place. "Have others in the household noticed anything amiss?"

"Hardly. When I fished around the subject with Muriel, she didn't know what I was talking about."

"Well, not everyone is sensitive to psychic phenomena. The fact that Muriel senses nothing actually means very little."

Janet's look was doubtful. "That's hard to believe."

"Not if you think about it in somewhat different terms. I'll give you a common example." He fluttered a pudgy hand over the tabletop. "We could both agree that nothing but empty air occupies this space. But if we turn on a TV, we would discover that this 'emptiness' is filled with an energy that will cause a television to show images and messages. Just as a TV is sensitive to certain energy waves, some people are sensitive to other types of energy." He peered at Janet. "Have you had many psychic experiences in the past?"

"Me?" Having the focus shift from the house to herself confounded her. "What do I have to do with it?"

"Because in this case, you're like the TV. If paranormal energy exists in the Renner house, it's apparently passed unnoticed. But now, something may have revealed itself to you, making you as much a part of the puzzle as the house itself." Pushing aside his empty pie plate, he folded his arms on the table, studying her with lively interest. "Any former psychic episodes may lend us valuable information."

"But I'm not psychic," she argued. "You mean weird experiences since childhood, or just knowing things? No, there's never been anything like that." As she said it, she thought she could have avoided a lot of mistakes in life if she could have read a crystal ball.

Her voice became reflective. "You know, the very first time I saw the place, it drew me like a magnet. That's when it was for sale two years ago. If the plans to move to another state hadn't been already set, I would have fought tooth and nail to make it mine."

"Is that how you feel now? If it goes on the market again, you want it?"

Janet didn't hesitate. "No, I wouldn't."

"Didn't you once tell me you would like to settle in this area, near your sister?"

"Yes, but I wasn't considering that house." She twirled the spoon in her empty teacup. "I mean, it never crossed my mind to watch for the time when it might become available again." Not understanding herself, she knit her brow. "You'd figure I would have still wanted it, wouldn't you, with property adjoining Fran's and all? It's too big for me, of course. But when I first saw it, it could have been four times as large and I can't tell you how I longed to have it."

"Maybe your attitude has changed because you now suspect it's haunted."

She shook her head. "No, my feelings about the house had cooled before I ever set foot in it. I was merely curious about it when I came here to live with Fran. It interested me because of what I had once felt, yet any desire to live there had evaporated."

"Are you leery of going back inside again?"

Smiling, Janet ran a hand through her dark curls. "If I am, I'm in big trouble. I promised Muriel I'd stay with Rose tomorrow afternoon while she visits her husband in the hospital. Of course, it won't be just Rose and me. Men will be working in the living room. Muriel wants the painting finished and the place thoroughly aired before Dr. Renner returns."

"Okay, so you're not fearful as long as others are around. But, do you still feel drawn to the house?"

"Only in the sense of being curious. It's a puzzle, and I want to understand—" Breaking off, she frowned at Kirby. "Say, you're still studying *me*, aren't you?"

His smile made twin moons of his fleshy cheeks. "Yes, but I promise to get that book back. If anything in its history explains a possible disturbance, we should have the answer within the next few days."

Chapter 19

BEFORE JANET WENT TO BED THAT night, Ben called from his motel room in Pennsylvania.

"Happy Halloween Eve," he greeted warmly.

"I never heard it called that," she said, thinking how wonderful it was to hear his voice. "This is Mischief Night."

"Well, I didn't want you thinking of mischief unless I was around. Miss me?"

"Terribly." She spoke lightly, as if kidding, but, it was true. She found it hard to believe she had known him for such a short time. "I went to see the adult school director tonight. Kirby Orchard gave me a ride there and back."

Standing in Fran's kitchen, leaning against the ridiculously ancient refrigerator, Janet decided to say nothing about the Renner house. It had been enough of a venture to confide a part of the story to Kirby. There was no telling what attitude Ben might take. The risk seemed too great. But she did tell him about Herman Renner's attack and how she had stayed with Rose.

"When Muriel came home, she brought me a gift basket of fruit from the hospital gift shop. I had already told her I wouldn't accept payment, but I can't be getting a gift basket every time, so I said she could pay me. The idea of accepting charity gets under her skin. I bet they had servants galore in Argentina."

Ben asked, "Who do they have to help out now?"

"Nobody. That's why she had to call on me. Fran says she's seen a cleaning service van parked at their house. But that kind of help is awfully impersonal compared with having a housekeeper live in. Muriel must do the cooking herself, and I know she does the food shopping. When people come from a foreign country, it probably takes a long time to find the kind of help they feel comfortable with."

It wasn't until after they hung up that she realized she had forgotten to tell Ben what Kirby had said about Tommy Stockton's career plans. The thought of Gina moving away gave her an empty feeling. Maybe it was best not to mention the move. Ben was aware that she hardly knew the child. He might think her foolish to have become attached so quickly.

She went to bed still thinking of the phone call and the sound of Ben's voice. Thoughts of the Renner house waited just outside the rim of her consciousness and she held it there. Her talk with Kirby allowed her to postpone the matter until he contacted her. Thinking only of Ben, she drifted into sleep.

In the middle of the night, she roused to what sounded like a baby crying. A lingering dream, she told herself, even as the small voice seemed caught in that strange echo that seemed to multiply the sound. The illusion faded quickly, but she couldn't get back to sleep for a long time.

She recognized that a part of her wakefulness was due to her growing interest in Ben Yates. Her attraction to him had allowed her to start closing the door to the past. It was something she wanted to do, *had* to do, if she were to have a future, yet the adjustment brought pain. Whether with Ben or with someone else, a new life would place her among those who could only know Becky as a photo in an album, as anonymous as the birth announcement she had once proudly clipped from the newspaper. No matter how strongly she might desire it, no one would ever be able to share with her the love she felt for her lost daughter. Her feelings for Becky would remain an important part of her forever, but that small personality could exist only within her heart. Assailed by loneliness too deep for tears, she laid wakeful for hours.

Suffering in the morning from lack of sleep, she headed for the school, glumly thinking ahead to meeting with two of the English teachers whose students' articles needed work, plus meeting the student who was the newsletter photographer.

As Janet walked to the Renner house that afternoon, she was in a much brighter mood than she had been in that morning. The teachers were pleased with the efforts she'd put into sharpening up their students' work and the photographer, Annabelle Chu, turned out to be a delight.

Of Chinese descent, Annabelle was a high school junior, a lively, pretty girl with extraordinary camera skills and an effervescent manner. When the newsletter talk was finished, Janet had admired the showy earrings the girl wore in her double-pierced ears, and Annabelle had responded with a dramatic sigh. "What I want is three earrings per ear, but my mother refuses. Little needle holes and she calls it butchering. Ever hear anything so ridiculous? My great-great-grandmother had bound feet! My lobes could look like IBM cards and who should care? Butchering. Can you imagine?"

As Janet rang the Renners' front doorbell, she wondered if she weren't so taken by Annabelle's theatrics because it distracted her from thoughts of the afternoon ahead. Despite her brave words to Kirby, perhaps she did feel apprehensive about being in the Renner house. A haunted house; a house inhabited by ghosts. She was thinking how unreal that sounded when Muriel opened the door.

"How's Dr. Renner doing?" Janet asked, hesitating only a second before stepping inside.

"He is fine, thank you, but not quite ready to return home." Nervously, Muriel fingered the white braid on her navy Chanel jacket.

"I am sorry if I kept you waiting. I was busy writing instructions for the workmen when they return from lunch. All morning, they have had nothing but questions! It is a wonder they have made any progress, but as you see, they have."

She directed Janet's attention to the room to right of the stairway; a room she had only glimpsed when Dr. Renner had been taken to the hospital. Funny, she thought. With all her explorations on the house's upper levels, she'd never bothered with this downstairs room behind closed doors.

Moving closer she saw what Fran had meant about the size of the room. It was big enough to be a ballroom. She figured it must run under all the second-floor rooms on the right side of the house. There were two fireplaces, one against the outside wall of the house and one at the far end. The ceiling near that fireplace had wires hanging down.

Seeing where Janet was looking, Muriel said, "I had this space all planned, the color scheme, the carpet, the furniture and the artwork. The ceiling and wall were being painted and then, as I think I told you, the paint fumes were harmful to my husband."

"Janet nodded. "Yes, that was a shame, but there was no way you could have known."

"Of course not," Muriel agreed, "but with him not at home I thought I could get the painting completed. The two chandeliers that belong here were taken away for cleaning and it was discovered that the wiring for one of them was faulty. Now the ceiling can't be finished until the wiring is repaired." She pointed toward the dangling wire that Janet had noticed. "The electric wire runs under the flooring in an upstairs store room. Fortunately not in any of the rooms that Dr. Renner and I use."

Muriel sighed. "It will be so lovely . . . off-white ceiling, cream-colored walls and darker cream woodwork. I have chosen a figured rug in pastel colors. The couches and chairs will be a cream shade, accented with colors picked from the rug, and I am having suitable artwork shipped from storage in New York City. Now that's all been postponed."

"It sounds lovely," Janet said, wondering when the Renners

would use the room. She hadn't gotten the impression they ever entertained.

Muriel stroked a beringed hand across her forehead as if she had a headache. "I am not at my best. During the night, I was kept awake by Halloween mischief-makers."

"Oh, my," Janet murmured in sympathy, thinking that she and Muriel had apparently been companions in sleeplessness, although for entirely different reasons.

"When I was out earlier this morning, "Janet said, "I saw toilet paper draped on trees and pumpkins smashed along the street. Mostly a nuisance. Was any of your property damaged?"

"Apparently not." Muriel folded her hands, as if in thankful prayer. "I understand it is a custom for young people to roam on that one evening a year. They must have been in my rear yard, shining flashlights at the house. I heard sounds and opened my bedroom door a crack. Just enough to see their lights."

"Oh?" Attention sharpening, Janet was suddenly thinking of the light emitted by the ghost children. Could that have been what Muriel had really seen? But the thought slid away as Muriel raved on, showing far more expression than usual. "Halloween! What an unwelcome custom! Had Dr. Renner been at home, he would have been terribly distressed."

Janet ventured, "Your sister said he didn't care to have children in his yard."

Muriel shot Janet a surprised, almost furtive look. "The tree is an attraction," she explained defensively. "He worries that a child might try to climb it and become injured. He would not want that to happen. And then, in this country, there are also the lawsuits."

The phone in the hallway rang, and while Muriel answered, Janet peered up the staircase. She found it incredible that no chills went along her spine. All she felt was a sense of loss. Although she was positive of what she had seen, she wondered if in future years, she might look back upon the incident and say, "Yes, there was a time once when I saw two ghosts—or at least, I think I did." Shaking her head, she thought that wouldn't happen. She didn't want to repeat the experience, yet neither did she want to lose the feeling that she had been granted a privileged moment.

When Muriel hung up the receiver, Janet said, "Is Rose busy with her pictures again today?"

"No. She seems content with her music, but perhaps you can take her outside for a while. The air will be good for her. That was Dr. Renner's physician on the phone." The call seemed to have cheered her. "Tomorrow, he will make the journey from Manhattan to the hospital here to perform his own examination. He is an outstanding man in his field, one in whom Dr. Renner places great faith."

"It's great that he's willing to make the trip," said Janet, wondering about the cost of having a top specialist travel to a patient rather than the other way around. Without stopping to think, she asked, "Since you came to this country to be near your husband's doctor, why did you two settle so far from the city?" Then, embarrassed, she stammered, "I'm sorry. It's none of my business."

She expected Muriel to loftily ignore her prying, but instead, the woman smiled faintly. "We had our furnished hotel suite waiting for us on Park Avenue. Dr. Renner visited Princeton only to meet with an old friend who was speaking at the university. After their reunion, they drove through the town, enjoying the sights. I was not with them, so how they came to this street, I do not know, but as soon as Dr. Renner saw this house, he wanted it."

Still wearing that faint smile, she gazed at Janet, the rare beauty of her gold-brown eyes seeming to hint at unfathomable secrets. "From that one brief look, this house became an obsession. He claimed it called to him. Nothing else would satisfy. Since it was available, there was no impediment. We had shipped items from our home in Argentina for our apartment, but this house was already furnished by the previous owners. The items we brought here were mostly books and paintings and other treasured valuables. Since we have been here, I have been slowly working to make this house look more like our home should be."

Muriel paused and seemed to be waiting for a response.

Janet, not sure what to say, thought of the lovely master bedroom. Muriel must have started her redecorating there, but of course, she couldn't admit she'd been snooping and had seen the room.

Feeling awkward, Janet said, "This is a beautiful house and the work you're having done will surely show it at its best. Your husband will be very happy here."

"Perhaps," Muriel said, her smile mysterious.

After Muriel left, Janet pondered the odd way the woman had replied to Janet's comment about Dr. Renner's future happiness in the house. The entire exchange was as perplexing as Muriel's Mona Lisa smile.

Chapter 20

IT WASN'T UNTIL LATER, AS JANET sat in the study with Rose, that she realized Dr. Renner's feelings for the house sounded similar to what hers had been that long-ago spring. *Obsession*. The word had been Muriel's, but it was accurate enough.

She wondered if the strength of Dr. Renner's attraction would fade as hers had done. It probably would. Just when Muriel finished the last room exactly to her taste, old Herman would announce it was ridiculous not to live closer to his heart specialist. Not that moving to an already furnished Park Avenue apartment was a trip to lower Siberia.

Park Avenue. Janet let her eyes roam the study. There would be no room like this at a fancy Manhattan address. The gleaming bookcase with its glass doors and the paintings surely belonged to the Renners, but the sagging brown couch, Colonial print draperies, and rag rug must have been left by the Fiorello family. Rose's rocker, although good solid maple, needed refinishing. It looked as if somebody's dog had teethed on the rungs.

Of course, viewed in a different way, the study wasn't so bad. Actually, she thought, it was the gilt-edged artworks that made a basically cozy, if ordinary, room look shabby by contrast. Exchange the oils painting for plainly framed country prints, put plants on the wide sills and toss around a few corduroy cushions and the room would have a pleasant, lived-in appeal. In fact, that was probably how the Fiorello family had it. Fran had said they had five children. This had probably been their family room.

How warm and friendly it must have looked with a crowd of youngsters flopped on the rug before the TV. Except, perhaps, for the poor boy who Fran said was crippled. Maybe he had been in a wheelchair. Janet sighed at this reminder that she wasn't the only person to have lost a child. Maybe that's why the Fiorellos moved away. After their son died, it had hurt too much to stay.

She glanced at the TV, which advertised a home computer. Rose, who wouldn't know a computer from a crockpot, kept her eyes glued to the screen as she rocked. Occasionally, the workmen could be heard over the sounds of the stereo. Although Muriel hadn't asked Janet to check on their progress, she supposed she should take a look now and then. Still, she didn't feel like getting up at the moment. She yawned. Muriel kept the house too warm, yet the high temperature was perhaps best for Rose and the doctor. She yawned again. Her busy morning had tired her. So far, she had been able to keep a step ahead in her new job, but it was a strain.

Mind drifting, she thought how she looked forward to Ben's telephone call that evening. She would tell him about Gina . . . about how Gina . . .

Startled, she straightened, losing the trail of thought. Blinking, she looked around, realizing she must have been on the verge of dozing. And she must have been thinking about Gina, because the child was in her mind: fuzzy impressions, with no degree of clarity. Frowning, she remembered Muriel suggesting that Rose should go outside. It certainly seemed an ideal time for it. The fresh air would benefit her as well as Rose.

Rose evidenced no objection to getting into her coat. Tying her babushka herself, she shuffled along with Janet through the kitchen and toward the latticed back porch. Janet unlatched the door and stepped out, then smothered a startled gasp. Gina waited at the foot of the steps, smiling as if she had known they were about to appear.

I must have heard her playing, Janet told herself, recalling how thoughts of the child had so suddenly popped into her mind. "Hello, honey," she called. "Miss Rose and I are coming down the steps. Please keep out of the way while I help her."

Making certain that Rose had a good grip on the railing; Janet guided the arthritic woman safely down even though it seemed that Rose might have managed without her help. When they finally stood on the brick path which led to the lawn, Janet gave Gina a tentative look. "I'm glad to see you, sweetheart, but I really don't think this is where you should be."

"Okay—is okay," Rose stated. "Doctor Herman not here." Reaching out a tender hand, she touched the child's shoulder. The gesture surprised Janet until she remembered Rose had spoken before of the little girl being welcome if the doctor wasn't around.

"That may be so," Janet told the old woman, "but neither he nor your sister want the responsibility of children in the yard. They're afraid someone might get hurt."

"Nobody get hurt," Rose answered. "This America."

Seeing no purpose in responding, Janet said, "Gina, you can stay for now, as long as I'm with you, but when I go inside, you must leave." The little girl nodded to show her understanding, and Janet smiled. "You come here often, don't you?"

Gina nodded even more vigorously.

"Well, it is pretty here," Janet said as she walked Rose over to sit on a bench where the pines sheltered her from the wind. With that done, Janet looked around appreciatively. Even with most of the trees denuded, the yard retained a fairy-tale quality. There was a narrow opening in a privet row off to one side that suggested an enticing maze just beyond, and the property border of evergreens could in a fantasy world mark the start of an enchanted forest. And, as Muriel had pointed out, the copper beech, with its smooth gray bark and low-growing branches, begged to have someone climb it. Janet saw a place about seven feet off the ground where the arrangement of limbs offered the perfect setting for a tree house. Enticing indeed.

Now that she was outside, it was difficult to think of anything unnatural happening anywhere on the property, either inside or out. Memories of the scene on the second floor faded under sunlight. When Kirby regained his book, would there be even the slightest clue to help her understand what she had witnessed?

Gina's cat, Pagoda, crept from under the evergreen hedge, his shifting eyes large and inquisitive. A gust of wind stirred a leaf under the beech tree. Instantly, the animal crouched, tail switching. When Gina went to stand watch with her pet, Rose said: "Girl. Like my Lili. Next time, keep close."

Janet frowned. "You had a little girl, Rose?"

"Lili. Long time, long time . . ." Voice fading, the old woman lapsed into an inward silence, her eyes becoming as opaque and unseeing as tarnished tinfoil.

Janet reasoned that if Rose had a daughter, she would now be middle-aged. Or did Rose mean she had died years ago? A burden of stale memories seemed to hover around the bent shoulders of the old woman. Janet decided not to probe further. She looked across the yard to where Gina and the cat stood under the beech tree. Eyes still fixed on the leaf, muscles rippling under its coat, Pagoda made ready to pounce.

Janet narrowed her eyes. *The beech tree, hide under the beech tree . . . it will be safe under the beech tree . . .* She didn't know why the words came to mind, but the promise of safety was disquieting rather than comforting. She was relieved when Gina lost interest in the cat and came to the bench. She wore the same red flannel jacket as on Sunday, and her cheeks and the tip of her nose were red.

"Are you warm enough?" Janet asked. "Let's see—oh, you have a nice, thick sweater on underneath. But here, let me fix that hood. It's letting cold air in around your ears." As Janet fussed over her, Gina inclined herself forward, allowing Janet to smooth her rippling, dark hair and retie the ribbon around her ponytail. Janet then drew up the coat zipper and made sure its hood fit snugly.

"There, now," Janet said. "Isn't that better?"

Sounds came from the street. Looking through decorative shrubs to one of the houses on a side street, Janet saw a small clown and an even smaller Smurf skip along the sidewalk, trick-or-treat bags on their arms. "Oh, look at the cute costumes on those children!" Janet exclaimed.

"Children," Rose intoned. "They were with us, then gone. All gone."

"Yes, that's right," Janet agreed absently, leaning forward to follow the last glimpse of the children. "They've gone on up the street."

With a grunt of effort, Rose got to her feet and moved toward the lawn. With the grass dry and most of the leaves blown away, Janet figured it would be safe to allow the woman to walk by herself. Keeping one eye on the aged figure, she smiled down at Gina. "What's your Halloween costume, honey?"

Janet expected her question to lead into another guessing game, but she saw blankness on the small, triangular face that she hadn't anticipated.

An unwelcome suspicion edged into her mind. "Gina . . . you do have a costume, don't you?"

The child shook her head.

"Oh, my." Janet felt terrible. She had never considered that Gina might not be prepared for Halloween. Although the event received a certain amount of attention in public school, a private tutor might not think to do anything about it. Which left everything up to Veronica, who apparently hadn't thought to do anything either.

Gina's chocolate brown eyes showed troubled uncertainty. Janet realized that the child couldn't be totally ignorant of Halloween, not if she watched television. But perhaps she hadn't understood it was something she could be expected to take part in. Until I opened my big mouth, Janet thought.

Suddenly, she brightened. She could call Veronica later for permission to take Gina around to a few houses on her own. Smiling in anticipation, she knew she could rig up a costume of some kind. Oh, she did hope Veronica would go along with it! She realized her happy smile must have conveyed something good, for Gina reached for her hand and smiled back.

They sat contentedly for a few minutes before Janet began to feel concerned about Rose. The woman had started out as if she were enjoying her stroll, but then she had begun that strange, hypnotic circling of the yard, the expression on her lined face anguished. There was no telling what went on in her troubled mind, but Janet couldn't believe it was beneficial. Far better for her to be peacefully rocking in her chair, lost in her music.

"I'm going to take Miss Rose inside now," Janet told Gina, getting up. "It's time for you to go home. I want you to promise that you won't come back in the yard after I've gone inside, okay?"

Gina nodded solemnly.

Turning, Janet went to Rose.

"All gone," Rose muttered, her words thick and guttural as Janet urged her along. "They were with us, then all gone. Hot. Everything burning hot. They were with us, then all gone." The woman suddenly became aware of Gina, who still lingered by the bench. Jerking her arm free, Rose clapped her hands sharply. "Go home!" she ordered, her voice frightened. "Doctor will catch you! Go home!"

Although startled by this outburst, Janet managed to maintain a comforting tone as she said, "Gina is leaving now, see?" To Gina, she said, "I'll see you later, honey, but for now, go."

Gina scurried off, and Janet had no further difficulty getting Rose around to the front of the house where the steps weren't so steep, nor in getting her inside, even though she kept up a constant, unintelligible mumble. When helping her remove her coat, Janet finally realized the woman was repeating the word "dangerous," the first syllables issuing from deep in her throat in a foreign way, the final "s" sounds hissing because of her missing teeth.

"What's dangerous, Rose? What are you worried about?"

Becoming excited, the woman uttered a low, almost animal-like wail. "Dangerous! Doctor will see. Dangerous if little girl comes, I keep her safe!"

"It's all right," Janet soothed, beginning to fear that Rose was getting out of control. "The little girl has gone home now, remember? And the doctor doesn't know she was here. He's gone to the hospital, remember?"

"Dangerous," Rose repeated, but then, to Janet's relief she fell silent as the reminder of Herman's absence apparently percolated into her brain. By the time Janet got her settled in her rocking chair, the woman's mood was restored to tranquility.

After assuring herself that Rose would be all right, Janet left her long enough to see how the workmen were doing. The electrician had just arrived. He was to replace the living room ceiling fixture and needed to trace the original wiring, which had been installed through the floor of a second-floor storeroom. Carrying his toolbox, he mounted the main steps. As he neared the top, Janet found herself holding her breath, waiting for a hesitation or some other sign that he had sensed something amiss lying ahead. But his boots tramped firmly upward, and he was lost from her sight.

Annoyed by a vague disappointment, Janet released her breath. Going back to the dining room, she paused in the archway to the study. She saw Rose still rocking peacefully. She decided to take the opportunity to telephone Veronica.

It was the housekeeper, Ozzie, who answered. After Janet explained, the woman said, "Gina would love it—that's something I hadn't thought about. Veronica's in New York with the mister. Where are you calling from? If I can reach Veronica, I'll call you back."

Janet explained, and within a half house the Renner's phone rang, but instead of it being Ozzie, it was Veronica.

"Your plan sounds wonderful," Veronica gushed, "Gina will have the time of her life!" She gave no sign of realizing that as the child's foster mother, she might have planned something for Gina herself.

"Are you sure you'll have something for her to wear?" Veronica said. "I could call Ozzie to go out and buy a costume."

"No thanks," Janet answered, trying not to let her feelings shade her voice. "Homemade costumes are fun."

After it was decided what time she would pick up Gina, Janet hung up the phone, feeling an inward ache. Veronica's lack of true interest in the child was unmistakable. A tragedy. If only there was some action she could take. But if the Stocktons eagerly awaited relocation, it would only make things harder for Gina if she became too involved. She sighed heavily, thinking that being the child's friend was the best she could do.

Hearing the electrician pounding away upstairs, Janet gave a glance toward the study to reassure herself that Rose was still settled, and then she was drawn up the steps. Moving from the landing to where she'd seen a storage room, she saw boxes and loose odds and ends piled outside the door.

When there was a pause in the pounding, she called, in through the doorway, "Is everything all right? Were you able to reach the proper wires?"

"What's that?" called a startled voice. The electrician, a thin, bearded man, appeared in the doorway, his eyes a bit wide. "Oh, it's you. You surprised me." He glanced around. "I'm making a racket slamming nails out of a floor panel. Didn't hear you come up."

"Sorry. Please remember not to leave anything lying in the hallway. An elderly man lives here, and I wouldn't want him to trip."

"No need to worry, ma'am." After another glance around, the man disappeared back inside the room and the pounding commenced.

Janet remained as she was, testing the atmosphere. Had the electrician seemed uneasy? Had he been aware of something he couldn't explain? She stared into the dark corners, finding nothing out of the ordinary. Once again, she experienced that strange sense of loss. Shaking her head, she waited a moment more before going downstairs.

Chapter 21

WHEN BEN CALLED JANET THAT EVENING, she bubbled over with news of her adventures with Gina.

"Fran and I fixed her up like a little witch. She wore my black skirt over her shoulders for a cape and Warren gave us an old black fedora that we stretched into a pointed hat. With her face powdered white, and frowning eyebrows and a scowling mouth painted on, she looked terrific. Gina herself got the idea for the finishing touch—horrid big freckles drawn on her cheeks with my eyebrow pencil."

"Hey," Ben chided. "Why not a princess or a snow fairy? I thought you didn't like Halloween monsters."

"This was different. She looked adorable."

Ben's sound of mock despair traveled over the wire. "A spotted kid with a scowl and a weird hat? Remind me not to ask you if I ever need help with my appearance. How did Gina like trick-or-treating?"

"She loved it," Janet said with a delighted laugh. "I forgot there were so many kinds of candy. We went to houses on this block and to the facing houses around it, which included Kirby's house. Let me tell you, she made out like a bandit. Veronica was away when we got back, but Ozzie was waiting for us. When I left them, Ozzie was sitting with Gina at the kitchen table as they sorted everything out. I'm so glad we went."

"It would have been a shame for her to miss it," Ben said.

"It would have! And it brought back so many nice memories of Fran walking me around on Halloween night when I was a kid. She's been a great sister, Ben. I appreciate her more now than ever." Then she added a bit ruefully, "Of course, that doesn't mean she's perfect."

"Oh? This sounds like complaint time."

"Not really. It's just that she can be such a know-it-all. It rankles, you know?"

"What's she done?"

Janet hesitated and then decided there was no reason why she shouldn't tell him. "Remember that night she hauled you off to tell you I had imagined hearing a baby cry?"

"Sure. And I realized it was that Siamese cat."

"Yes, only it wasn't. A cat's cry might resemble that of a baby, but not enough to fool anyone comparing it with the real thing."

"But, I thought—"

"Look, the first time I heard it, it seemed possible I dreamed the cry, but then I kept hearing it. Fran insists there's no baby around, but she's obviously mistaken." Janet twisted the phone cord as she talked. "Maybe someone cares for a child overnight, only periodically. Anyway, this evening, when I was out with Gina—"

"Oh-ho!" Ben's chuckle traveled over the miles. "I'm way ahead. When you and Gina went from door to door, you took an impromptu survey to find out which house had the baby. And now you're all primed to show your sister that she doesn't know everything after all, right?"

"Yes, only—" Janet's voice reflected chagrin. "I didn't get my bright idea until after we were halfway done. I obviously missed the right one." She felt warmed by Ben's understanding groan. "And I had dreamed up such clever ways to ask!" She could see the funny side of her failed scheme. "You would have been proud of me."

"At least you've eliminated the wrong houses," he said.

"There is that," she agreed.

Before they hung up, Ben said he would be returning to Princeton late on Thursday. "I'll check in at work on Friday morning, but I can take off early in the afternoon," he said. "We can drive around, and I'll show you more of Princeton, then we can have dinner if you're free. "

Janet's teasing smile was in her voice as she said, "Well, I think I can arrange it."

The first of November came, and the next few days passed uneventfully. On Friday afternoon, Ben picked Janet up outside the Renner house, pulling his car up behind a parked van.

"Perfect timing," she said, climbing into the Cavalier. Too eager to wait for him to come to the door, she had rushed out as soon as she had seen his car.

Despite how she had looked forward to being with him again, she was unprepared for the impact it would have upon her. She had forgotten how appealing he was, forgotten the strength of his face, the warmth of his smile. The force of his presence caught her unawares. For a trembling moment, she was on the verge of throwing herself into his arms, and then caution seized her. Back-pedaling her emotions, she floundered for something to fill the awkward moment.

"I'm so glad I called you to meet me here," she told him, speaking too rapidly. "Muriel just returned from the hospital a little while ago."

His knowing grin was gentle. "I missed you, too."

Her breath caught in her chest. She wondered how he could do it, how he could see through her that way. "Oh, Ben . . ." Her voice was unsteady. Another thing she had forgotten was how clearly he made her see the barriers she had built about herself. He opened his arms, and this time, she didn't allow herself to hesitate before she was cuddled against his chest.

"Oh Ben, I did miss you," she confessed, her eyes closed, her words muffled against his shirt. "I missed you very, very much."

"That's better," he said softly. She could feel his breath in her hair. After a long moment, he released her, saying, "So what's this about the Renners? More trouble with his heart?"

"Partly," Janet answered with a shaky laugh, thinking that after the snug security of Ben's embrace, she was the one with heart trouble. How wonderful it was to be held in his arms. She reluctantly shifted her thoughts to the Renners. "He didn't actually have another heart attack, but he's a lot weaker than before. Muriel says his color is awful. His specialist tried to argue him out of coming home tomorrow, but his mind is made up."

When Ben was starting to pull his car out into the street, he glanced at the electrician's van. "I guess the work you said Mrs. Renner wanted isn't completed yet."

"No, it's not. The first electrician did enough so the painting is done, thank goodness. Now the house can be aired out before the doctor returns. And the two chandeliers have been rehung, but one won't work until the electrical connections have been finished in the room above it and that's what's going on now. The first electrician came only once and didn't show up again."

A frown marred Janet's forehead as she wondered if the man had indeed sensed something odd on the second floor. "Muriel asked me to phone him, and after mumbling some excuse, he hung up on me. She had to find somebody else to finish the job."

Over the phone, Ben had said something about showing her more of Princeton and the famed university buildings, and now, wanting to change the subject, she said, "This sunny afternoon is perfect for that tour you promised me. I've often wondered about that huge stone building on Nassau Street—a library, I think. It looks so modern."

"You must mean the Firestone Library, at the corner of Nassau and Washington. It was built in the fifties, so for around here, thirty-something years makes it practically brand new. They always have a book or photography exhibit on display. We'll go see."

After seeing the Ansell Adams exhibit at the library, they went on down the road. "For contrast," Ben said, "we'll look at the University Chapel. It was dedicated in the twenties, so it's hardly ancient, but the Tudor-Gothic style makes you feel you've stepped back in time."

"It's magnificent!" breathed Janet in a hushed voice a few minutes later, craning her neck to view the chapel's high, vaulted ceiling and awe-inspiring display of stained glass. "I don't think I've ever seen church windows as impressive as these. But this place is huge! It must seat almost two thousand." She looked at Ben. "When you said 'chapel,' I imagined something tiny and quaint."

"For that," he said, "I've got to show you Faith Chapel. I had an aunt who used to belong when it had an active congregation, but now it's been taken over by the historical society. I don't know if it's open to the public on weekdays, but I hope so. I'd like to see it again myself."

After a drive that took them out of Princeton Borough and into the larger, more sparsely populated township, Ben stopped at a steepled Colonial-style frame church that was surrounded by a graveyard. Set along a country road, the old building reminded Janet of a church in a miniature village set, the kind placed under a Christmas tree with cotton batting snow and a mirror for a little pond.

They exited the car and Ben led Janet up the steps. The doors were unlocked. Inside a custodian said he was there to sweep and turn on the heat in preparation for a wedding.

"It's a pretty little church for a small ceremony," he told them. It sounded as if he thought that's why they were scouting out the place. Janet and Ben exchanged amused glances. While the man continued his work, they walked down a carpeted aisle that was flanked by oak pews that could accommodate no more than forty people.

"Now, this is my idea of a chapel," Janet said, throwing a smile at Ben, who leaned against a pew, watching her explore.

Janet neared the gray marble baptismal font. Looking over the prayer rail, she touched the font reverently and read the inscription and the date, 1874 to 1877. She said, "This is dedicated to the memory of Gregory and William Hickok. Two little boys who must have been twins. Born in the same year and then died in the same year,"

Probably some disease that was going around back then," Ben said.

'Yes," Jane said touching the font. At first, the satiny marble was cool against her fingertips, but then it seemed she felt a warm vibration as if the years of sacred service had invested the font with blessed power of its own. She remembered Becky's baptism, the child's eyes wide with wonder, the sprinkles of water on her downy head like droplets of holy dew.

Ben walked up beside her, bending to read the date. "Only three years old," he mused. "They're probably buried in the churchyard outside. Want to go see?"

Janet shook her head. "No, I don't think so."

Thanking the custodian, they left. Ben drove back toward Princeton and on down Washington Road again, driving in and around a lake. He pulled off where there was a good view and stopped the car.

"All the maps and brochures call this Lake Carnegie," he said, "but I've lived in this area most of my life, and never heard anyone call it anything except Carnegie Lake."

Janet smiled. "That just goes to show that the natives never know anything." Seated on the lake side of the car, she opened her door to the warm sunlight. Neither of them made a move to get out.

Ben said. "My grandparents were from around Grover's Mill, just a few miles from here. I loved to hear them tell about the Orson Wells radio broadcast, 'War of the Worlds', which used the Mill as the supposed Martian landing. Millions across the country believed that Martians, armed with death-ray machines, had landed there. Of course, most natives recognized it as just a good story."

"And you love science fiction," Janet said.

He grinned. "Indeed, I do." He angled about in the driver's seat. "Let me share some of that sunlight, lady." He put his hands to her waist as she shifted about and there she was, resting comfortably against him as he thrust one of his long legs out to receive the sunlight streaming through the opened door.

They sat as they were for a few moments and then he said, "That bothered you in the church, didn't it—when I suggested we go out into the graveyard."

With her body resting against his, she knew he must be aware of her sudden tension. "Yes, it bothered me."

"What was your baby's name?"

Her voice was no more than a whisper. "Becky."

"Tell me about her," he urged gently. "Tell me about Becky."

She was quiet for a long moment. "You couldn't really understand without knowing some things about Clay and me."

"Tell me. I want to know."

She was quiet again, and then said, "As soon as we knew I was pregnant, Clay bragged to everyone it would be a son. Medical knowledge aside, I knew it would be a black mark against me if I failed to produce the desired male heir. But when Becky was born, Clay's reaction was poorly disguised relief. It dawned on me that he had only talked of a son because it was the macho thing, but for him, a daughter was best. Becky was named after his mother, who had just passed away. There was something fiercely intense about Clay's love for the baby. I think he believed Becky would grow up expressing that same uncritical admiration for him that his mother had always shown, almost a sort of worship. I could see trouble ahead, but while Becky was so little, it was a beautiful time for us. Except for when we were first married, Clay and I were never happier."

She shifted, feeling Ben's chest against her back. A band of sunlight kissed one ankle, bared beneath the hem of her slacks. She was aware of the cradling security of Ben's arms, the lulling rhythm of his breathing. Resting her head back against his shoulder, she closed her eyes, continuing to speak.

"When Becky was four months old, I went in early one morning and found her lying still and bluish in her crib. Her skin was unnaturally cold. I snatched her up and tried to force her to breathe, to force her heart to start beating again. I guess I screamed for Clay.

"The next thing I remember, the ambulance was there, and the police. I didn't want to let Becky go, but they took her away, and the police started asking questions.

"They were very kind, very polite, but it was just a little backwoods Alabama town, with outsiders like Clay and me coming in because of new industry in the area. If any of the townsfolk had ever heard of Sudden Infant Death Syndrome, they most likely figured it was a fancy excuse for an ignorant mother who either puts her baby to sleep face up and it chokes on spit-up milk, or she puts it to sleep face down and it smothers." She uttered a small, mirthless laugh. "Let me ask you, how could a person win either way? One of the policemen even said: 'We know how hard it can be on a mother's nerves when a baby keeps fretting, depriving a mother of sleep. A mother doesn't really want to hurt her baby, all she wants is to get a little rest.' Nobody made any direct accusations, but still, I was an outsider. People don't want to believe an apparently perfect baby could suddenly die. It made them feel better to view me with suspicion."

With a shudder, she fell silent again.

Ben caressed her arm, his touch comforting.

Finally, in an unsteady voice, she continued, "Whenever things went wrong, all Clay knew to do was cast blame. In this case, it was pitifully easy to blame me. In shock, I had withdrawn and was seen by the town as cold and uncaring. Typical Northern woman, I guess. Clay, however, was openly tearful and a thankful receiver of every religious platitude handed out. He was seen as their kind of people. I don't mean to make light of his suffering, but when he became the center of attention, he wallowed in it. Suddenly, he was accepted, while I was not. It was his nature to try and ingratiate himself further by making sure they all understood that he saw me as an outsider too. Finally, divorce was the only answer for either of us."

After another pause, she told him the rest of it. "We signed the divorce papers. We still had the house but didn't want to be there together. Besides, he now had status in the town, and I didn't. I had saved enough for furniture before we bought the house. He gave me what that amount had been and I moved to another town. I rented a room and worked in a restaurant and grieved. I finally got enough sense to stop being stubborn and to come back here to Fran. I never told her any of the details that I just told you. She hadn't wanted me to marry Clay and I thought she would say she told me so. But she didn't; she just took me in."

When Janet fell silent, she and Ben remained sitting quietly for a while. Then, without discussion, they got out and walked along the lake. Neither of them spoke until they returned to the car, when Ben said he figured it was time to think about dinner.

He took her to a place he knew near New Brunswick which was quiet and pleasant and had excellent food. He did most of the talking during the drive up, and by the time their salad was served, Janet, more at ease with him than ever before, knew how good it was that he had encouraged her to be open about the past.

It was dark and starting to get cold by the time he took her home and walked her to the door. They stood talking in the shadows, his arms lightly encircling her waist.

"You'd better go in," he finally said. "You're starting to shiver."

"I don't feel at all cold," she said, realizing the moment she had spoken that her words could have a double meaning.

He chuckled. "You know, you're a lady I could become addicted to very easily."

"Addictions are a terrible thing," came her answer as she looked up at him.

"There are certain exceptions." He inclined his face toward hers.

His kiss was gentle and undemanding. She reached up, touching his hair. The texture was soft, just as she had known it would be. She felt a tremor of emotion and fervently wished she were the kind of woman who could be more open with her feelings: one who could say, "Benjamin Yates, I think there's a very good chance I'm falling in love with you." But she wasn't ready to say it. Even so, their next kisses were passionate.

"Lord," he groaned, "I wish I could be with you again tomorrow instead of having to attend that energy conference I told you about. I don't know if I can last till Sunday."

Snuggling against him, she thought of his invitation for Sunday dinner and then a party at the home of some of his friends. Breath warm against her ear, he murmured, "I'm looking forward to showing you off, you know? Wear that light orange dress, okay?"

She smiled. "Apricot."

He kissed the tip of her nose. "Right, that's the one. Okay?"

"Okay," she promised and went on inside.

As she closed the door, Warren came out through the kitchen and switched on the light. He smiled paternally as she blinked against the glare, instinctively smoothing hasty fingers through her tousled curls. She felt like a teenager coming in from a date and she wondered if she had any lipstick left.

"The phone just rang for you," Warren told her, "and I said to hold on because I thought I heard you coming in. It's Kirby Orchard. It must be important. He's called twice."

Chapter 22

JANET LIFTED THE PHONE IN THE kitchen, her thoughts having shifted to the Renner house. The fact that Kirby had called twice convinced her he must have turned up something important.

"Kirby, you got your book back, right?" Her words came tumbling out. She hadn't realized she would feel so eager. "What have you learned about the house?"

"Hold on," he admonished with a chuckle. "My friend did return my book, but so far, I've found nothing exciting, nothing like a family curse or an Indian massacre on the land before the house was built. Of course, we can always hope. Anything new with you?"

"No," Janet said. "I've been there every day this week with Rose."

"Well, don't feel downcast," he soothed cheerfully. "After a bit more investigation, I may turn up something on the wild side yet. My book is a local record written by a Princeton resident just before the turn of the century. The writer mentions the names of former residents of the present Renner house, which have directed me to other sources, genealogies, collections of letters and diaries. When you study houses, you're also studying people."

"The people and the families are my interest," she said.

"Yes, but it's not all tied up in a neat package," Kirby said. "Could you come over tomorrow morning?"

Janet was quick to say she could. "But it will have to be early," she added. "Muriel wants me by eleven-thirty. That's when she leaves to bring Dr. Renner home from the hospital."

"Then why don't we meet at nine? That should give us the time we need."

She hung up with a smile. With Ben away all day at the energy conference, Saturday had offered nothing of interest except Dr. Renner's homecoming. Now, thanks to Kirby, the prospects had brightened.

She had no sooner gone into the living room to exchange a few words with Fran when the phone rang again. Warren lumbered from his office, grinning and rubbing his beard in exaggerated perplexity.

"I don't know about this sister of yours," he said to Fran. "She's bewitching all the males in Princeton." Still grinning, he turned to Janet. "The phone is for you again. I'm done working. Go ahead and take it in my office."

The caller was Ben, wanting to say good night. He and Janet talked for a while, their voices low, their words punctuated with soft laughter. She went to bed starry-eyed, thinking only of Ben. But in the morning, as soon as she opened her eyes, she found herself thinking of her meeting with Kirby.

At nine on the dot, she was ringing his doorbell.

"Hello!" Kirby greeted her with enthusiasm as he let her in. He wore rumpled flannel trousers and a flannel shirt that was a bright, leprechaun green. "I see you've brought a notebook. Excellent."

"I'm all set," she said, eager to get down to business. With Trixie in tow, she followed as Kirby ushered the way into his office and directed her to a seat alongside his desk. After she seated herself, he pushed over a small table between her and his desk chair. He then excused himself and returned carrying a tray bearing a teapot, napkins, cups, cream, sugar and lemon. Setting down the tray, he said, "Oh, forgot something," and started for the kitchen again.

"Let me help," Janet said, hoping to hurry him along.

"No, no, only takes a second." He returned with a fussy little ceramic dish that contained assorted wheat crackers and cookies. He held out a piece of broken cookie to Trixie. Wheezing and snuffling, the dog investigated the tidbit thoroughly before daintily accepting it and waddling off.

Eyes following the creature, Kirby shook his head. "Would you believe that had I given that persnickety animal a whole cookie, she would have snapped it up without a bit of that suspicious sniffing."

"Animals can be funny," Janet agreed impatiently, feeling she would jump out of her skin if she couldn't prod him into getting started. "So, did you find out how old the house is?"

"Not exactly," he admitted, pouring the tea.

Finally, as they ate, he turned his attention to the books and papers on his desk and said, "About the age of what is now the Renner house, there is enough information for us to make an intelligent guess." He tapped the open page on his desk. "Elizabeth Parke—that's spelled with a final E—was an orphan who built the house with an inheritance from her adoptive father. He died at Gettysburg in 1863. From another record, I learned that in 1871, the house was standing and occupied. So, we know Elizabeth must have built it sometime between '63 and '71."

"That's about what Warren thought. He said at the time it might have been the only house on the block"

"He's probably right. And for a conservative estimate—" he inclined his head toward her notebook— "let's say the house was finished around 1870."

Janet dutifully recorded the date and then, pen poised, looked up expectantly. "So, the street in front became Parke Street and Elizabeth Parke was the first resident?"

"I think not," Kirby said. "I have here a collection of letters, some of which are from a Parke family relative who resented the division of the inheritance. The writer complained that blood kin had been shorted in favor of Elizabeth, an adopted child. It was also said that Elizabeth

Parke had erected the house to make it a home for orphans, or, as one letter writer snidely puts it: 'Elizabeth was set on frittering away good money on bastards as undeserving as herself.'"

"My goodness!" Janet was shocked. "If the others in the family were always so mean about Elizabeth, maybe that's why she was given a greater share of the inheritance: to teach them a lesson—which they obviously didn't get."

Kirby chuckled. "Yes, but remember we are talking of a Victorian society, where a traceable and unblemished lineage was judged as considerably more important than it is today. In any case, Miss Parke seems to have died before her dream came to fruition, for at a later date, a letter states: 'Her life's blood spent on her folly, she expired of influenza, leaving her shelter for the lost to be bought by strangers.'"

The corners of Janet's mouth turned down. "Then Elizabeth never established her orphanage after all?"

"Apparently not. By 1871, the house was inhabited by a family prominent in the area. They were the ones mentioned in the book my friend returned. It was a reference to the fact that they purchased the 'Parke House' that first gave me the clue to search out Elizabeth." His modest words were somewhat belied by his proud tone. "I knew I had come across the Parke name somewhere, so I searched my collection of old published letters and found what I just told you about Elizabeth."

"And her nasty relatives."

Kirby chuckled, took a sip of tea, then said, "So the Hickoks, the first residents, lived in the house for about ten years, and then—"

Janet interrupted. "Hickok? I just saw that name yesterday. It was inscribed on a baptismal font in a tiny chapel that Ben Yates and I toured. Could it be the same family?"

"Faith Chapel?" Kirby beamed. "Yes, it certainly is the same family. The Hickoks were responsible for a number of community efforts, including the establishment of that church. It fell into disrepair but was saved by the historical society."

"The Hickoks lost twin sons," Janet said. "Their names were on the font. It was dedicated to them."

"Yes, and if I recall correctly, their family monument is in the graveyard outside."

"Ben thought it probably was." She was remembering her feelings when she stood at the font: her thoughts about Becky and the later discussion with Ben by the lake.

Busily consulting his papers, Kirby nodded absently. "Okay, we have Elizabeth Parke, the builder, and then the Hickoks. Next, somewhere around 1888, the Alexander Whitehursts were in residence. We know because it's mentioned in an old record that an Alex Whitehurst, Jr., of that address, was one of those who lost his life in the blizzard of '88. After that, I found no reference until 1910, when an old map shows that a family named Goodsmith lived there. Oh, by the way, I forgot to mention that Elizabeth had named the place The Beeches."

Janet brightened. "There's a huge old copper beech in the yard."

"When I was a kid, there were two of them," Kirby said. "Perhaps at one time, there was a whole grove, a grove of beechen green." Leaning back, he quoted: "That thou, light-winged Dryad of the trees, in some melodious plot of beechen green, and shadows numberless, singest of summer in full-throated ease."

Voice trailing off, and looking looked faintly embarrassed, he said, "Keats, 'Ode to a Nightingale'." He straightened in his chair. "Anyway, from then on, my job was a cinch. A phone call established that the people I knew as a kid, the Patricks, bought the house from folks named Granger. The Grangers were supposed to have been there for years. I think it's safe to assume they purchased the place from the Goodsmiths, so—" He inflated his green-clad chest with pleased satisfaction. "We've come full circle in the investigation."

Janet, who had been recording the family names, lifted her pen. "But we really don't know anything about the people or the things that happened there. I mean, we don't know anything that indicates why the house should be disturbed."

Kirby gave her a sharp stare that seemed out of keeping with his cherubic appearance. "Haunted, that's what you really mean. You're convinced it's haunted."

Flushing, Janet was defensive. "Isn't that why I brought up the subject in the first place?"

Nodding, he adjusted his glasses. "And you told me you thought you saw lights, and you thought you heard sounds. You painted a rather vague and uncertain picture." He tilted his head inquisitively. "You know, there are people who overplay their experiences, but I have a hunch you do the opposite. Could it be that you've been holding something back?" His tone remained mild, yet there was intensity behind it as he said, "Suppose you tell me all over again exactly what you witnessed at the Renner house."

Chapter 23

AFTER A HESITATION, JANET RELATED EVERYTHING. She told him about the whispered chanting and the ghostly figures, including the fact that she had earlier seen the image of the little boy in the Renner back yard.

Kirby listened with absorbed interest, his eyes never straying from her face. When she finished, he was silent a moment, then said, "Janet, I don't want you to misunderstand what I'm going to say. I do believe you, but the fact of the matter is, the children and the phantom voices may not actually have been real."

"I never claimed they were," she defended, bristling. "I mean, they were there, but they were ghosts. Apparitions!"

He cleared his throat. "Allow me to explain. There are several theories concerning the appearance of what we call ghosts. One of them holds that the medium's very presence is what causes psychic energies to assume a specific form. This mysterious energy is real, but not necessarily the form in which it is perceived. Let me give you an example." He picked up his half-finished cup of tea and said, "Can you touch, feel and see this tea water?"

She stared at him and then gave a confused laugh. "Sure I can."

He set the cup on the table and pushed it over to her. "Look into the cup and look the tea."

She obediently did so and then looked up again. He said, "Is the tea water shaped like this cup?"

"Yes, but only because it's in that cup."

"Correct," Kirby said. "Tea water, or any liquid, takes on the shape of its container."

Following his drift, but not seeing the point, she angled the cup. "And if I tipped this over, it would pour out in a shapeless mess."

"Exactly! By itself, liquid has no distinctive shape." He beamed and then arranged his portly form in a scholarly pose. "Now, let's take the example of neon gas, which is also shapeless, plus being odorless and invisible. However, when it's pumped into a glass tube and electrified, it glows red. And then the shape of the neon gas is?" He paused, clearly awaiting her answer.

She smiled, thinking this would be sort of childish fun if it only wasn't so serious. Teasingly, she raised her hand. "I have the answer, teacher. The neon gas takes the shape of the glass tube that it's been pumped into—" She broke off and stared at Kirby. "You're saying that there's invisible energy that most people don't notice but some people do. People like me. And I'm like a vessel, taking this energy in and shaping it to what I want to see and calling the shape real." She narrowed her eyes. "Like I'm a crazy person."

"No, no, not at all, not crazy." He patted the air as if calming her words. "What I'm saying is that we each have our own perspective gained from our life experiences." He learned forward. "When I say 'little children, or little child,' would it have a special meaning?"

Janet hesitated, unable to keep her tears, those damned betraying tears, from springing to her eyes. "My little daughter died. She . . . she was only a few months old."

"Ah." Kirby's tone was sympathetic. "I am sorry to hear that. Had she been sickly since birth?"

After Janet briefly explained, he studied her. "The terrible shock of her sudden death could be responsible for opening your mind to psychic awareness."

Janet hated the way his explanation drained the magic from what she had witnessed. "Didn't you say there were other theories?"

"Yes, although I hardly think they apply here. Hauntings may be a psychic record of an actual past event. Say, a woman who hanged herself in a certain room might keep appearing in the room and be seen as a ghost. Without prior knowledge of the actual event, witnesses will give identical descriptions of the woman. It's as if the distraught suicide victim has caused the event to indelibly shape the psychic ether. What's created is a sort of psychic imprint."

Perplexed, Janet asked, "Does that sort of ghost communicate with people?"

"No, it's like an imprint on the atmosphere." He frowned ruefully. "It's like the food stain I got on my favorite tie. I thought the stain had been laundered out, but there it was again. It wasn't the experience of how it happened, which was me being careless. It wasn't the experience happening all over again. It was simply the mark left by the experience."

She thought a moment. "Okay, I guess I can understand that, like certain conditions bring it out again, like the stain on your tie. What those people are seeing is not a true ghostly being."

"Exactly," Kirby said. "Then, in traditional literature, a ghost is a human spirit trapped in this world after death instead of moving on to the spiritual realm. Such a ghost exhibits an independent personality and often is said to communicate with mediums in a séance."

Kirby rocked back in his chair, folding his hands across the mound of his stomach. "There is enormous evidence that intangible energy exists, yet few keys to help us understand its true nature. But at least in your case, we can be pretty certain we're dealing with the first explanation: the ghost children are most assuredly a projection of your own mental state."

It was clear to Janet that Kirby's mind was set, and for a brief instant, she wondered if he could be right. Then she shook her head.

What she had seen had been absolutely real. But she couldn't blame Kirby for not believing what she had seen. Ben probably wouldn't believe, either. Thank goodness she had kept her mouth shut with him, not even mentioning that Kirby was researching the house.

Accepting the futility of further argument, she attempted a laugh. "Maybe it's the electrician I should talk to."

When Kirby tilted his head in question, she waved a hand, dismissing her words even as she spoke them, figuring there was no way Kirby would listen with an open mind. "It's just that the electrician Muriel hired only worked upstairs a few hours on one afternoon and then he refused to come back."

"What were his reasons for not returning?" Kirby said.

"He didn't have a reason, at least nothing that made sense. When Muriel had me phone him, he said he had to work someplace else. He made it sound like a religious avocation."

"Oh? What were his precise words?"

Janet shrugged. "You'll think it's crazy, and I guess it is, but it sounded as if he said he was 'born to call'. That's what made me think of religion, you know, a religious calling. But he mumbled and I must have heard him wrong."

"Think back," Kirby encouraged, excitement creeping into his tone. "Instead of saying, born to, could he have said born with?"

"Yes, I suppose so." Kirby's unexpected interest surprised her. "But he must have been drinking. 'Born with a call' makes no sense."

"Not spelled C-A-L-L." Kirby looked like a man who had won an unexpected prize. "The word is C-A-U-L. 'Born with a caul' is also termed 'born with a veil.' It refers to a baby born with the afterbirth membrane covering the face. In folklore, such a child grows up possessing second sight, or what we term a psychic gift. It sounds as if the electrician was trying to tell you he believed himself sensitive to the unknown and had no wish to return to the Renner house."

Janet felt sudden hope. "If he saw the children too, then you would have to believe me!"

"But I do believe you. It's just that neither of us is sure how to interpret what you saw and heard. In any case, since your experiences have not recurred, there's no reason for you to feel wary."

"Who said I did? I don't feel wary of the children. It's the chanting that sounded so threatening."

He pondered this. "The ghost children themselves . . . you weren't the least afraid of them?"

"Little children? Of course not!"

He was puzzled. "But isn't it the children who utter the chant? You made out words. 'We are, we are . . .' Who else is the 'we' except the children?"

Unsettled, Janet drew back. "It—it's logical, but . . . I never thought of it that way."

"Perhaps you hesitated to think of the children as the source of something frightening."

"I guess that's true." She looked at her watch. Although there was a half-hour before she was due at the Renner house, she no longer wished to continue the discussion. The idea of the children being the source of the chant had shaken her, but why try hashing it out if Kirby believed it was only a figment of her imagination anyway?

Standing, she said, "I'd better leave. Muriel might need me early."

Kirby also stood. "What's the name of the electrician? Perhaps he'll be willing to talk with me."

His request encouraged her. As she found the electrician's name in the phone book, she decided she might have judged Kirby too hastily. Maybe his mind wasn't such a closed door after all.

"You know," she said slowly, sitting down again, "there's one other thing I've begun to wonder about." She told him about the crying baby. "I figure someone in the neighborhood cares for the child on an infrequent basis, which is why Fran doesn't know about it. But to be honest, there's something weird about the cries. Although I've never heard them when I've been in the Renner house, could they have something to do with the ghost children?"

Then, before Kirby could reply, she shook her head and spoke again, "But no, I forgot, Gina heard the baby too."

"Gina? Oh, you mean the Stocktons' foster child." Kirby frowned. "I understood that she's unable to talk. An emotional trauma from being in an earthquake. And now she's recovered?"

"Not to a full extent." Janet spoke with sudden heat. "The Stocktons were assured her speech would return when she felt secure again, but they've done precious little to give her that needed security."

Kirby was thoughtful. "She's the little girl you brought to my door on Halloween night, isn't she? A lovely child."

Janet was pleased. "Yes, she is. And when the mood strikes her, she can speak, even if only a few words."

"Then, she's spoken to you on several occasions?"

"Yes, she . . ." Janet corrected herself. "No, to be strictly honest, I have to say it was only once. It seems more because we get along so well, but I guess there really was only one time. However," she wagged a finger, "I really heard her, so don't start calling it some neon gas fabrication."

With a rumbling chuckle, Kirby spread his hands. "I wouldn't presume to argue."

At the door, he said, "I'll let you know if the electrician has anything interesting to add to this mystery." His tone grew heavy. "And a word to the wise. Regardless of the cause of an apparent haunting, one aspect seems to be common to all. The force of the disturbance tends to increase in direct proportion to the time a sensitive person spends in the area, dwelling upon it. Don't be afraid of the Renner home, but on the other hand, don't linger in the upper stairway listening and watching. Although your vigilance may be rewarded, you also may get more than you bargained for."

Chapter 24

JANET CROSSED THE STREET IN FRONT of Kirby's house and started along the sidewalk that would take her to the Renner's end of the block. She reached a point where the view led across a series of back yards. She saw Gina and Pagoda playing hide-and-seek in the Renner's row of evergreens.

Oh, my! Janet thought, envisioning the doctor coming home to see the child and suffering a relapse.

Cutting across the intervening yards, she called Gina's name.

The little girl turned, a smile illuminating her face.

Janet's heart melted like taffy, but she struggled to maintain a stern expression. "Gina, the man who lives in that house is coming home from the hospital. I think you know he doesn't like children in his yard."

Ignoring Janet's words, the child ran forward to give her an enthusiastic hug, jumping up as she did so, almost as if she wanted to climb up her body.

"You little monkey!" Janet laughed. Her session with Kirby had been draining, but Gina's cheery openness refreshed her spirits. She untangled the child's arms and set her on the ground again. "You think

155

you can charm me, do you? Go on home, now. I have to go inside and take care of Miss Rose while her sister's away. I'll see you later."

Gina peered up at her quizzically.

Janet laughed at the child's expression. "Yes, honey, I promise. I'll stop by your house later. I know how long and dull a Saturday afternoon can be when there's nothing special to do."

As she said this, she was thinking that spending time with Gina would be a lot healthier than mulling over Kirby's ghost theories. How dumb to have looked forward to the session when it turned out to be upsetting. It made her angry to recall Kirby's belief that the ghost children were created by her mental state. Unfortunately, the supposition that they uttered the chant was harder to argue with. Those eerie whispered sounds . . . she couldn't suppress a shudder. Maybe the chant wouldn't sound so ominous if she could make out all the words.

She shifted her attention back to Gina. "When I come over, we'll take a walk, or you can show me your schoolwork." Placing her hands on the child's shoulders, she turned her about to face the back yard of the Stockton house and gave her a little push. "See you later, young lady, but for now, skedaddle."

With a quick grin over her shoulder, Gina raced off, hair ribbon flying, Pagoda at her heels.

Muriel met Janet at the front door. She was dressed to go out; a high-born South American lady. She wore a short mink jacket over a claret-colored suit and a fur hat pinned to her sleek black hair. Black gloves, a black leather purse and matching shoes completed the stylish ensemble.

"I have persuaded Dr. Renner to make the trip by ambulance," Muriel said, explaining he had adamantly refused to allow a bed to be set up for him on the first floor of the house. "He insists he will be comfortable nowhere except in his office with his books, so I thought it would be best to have him carried directly upstairs. He does not realize how weak his hospital stay has left him."

"What he should realize is how much harder it will be for you to care for him if he is upstairs," Janet said impulsively.

Muriel gave her a look of cool reprimand. "I will manage." She changed the subject. "Rose is in the kitchen with her lunch. Perhaps you would also care for lunch. I regret to warn you that her mood today is restless."

"Does she know your husband is coming home?"

"I have told her. But I think she is edgy because her sleep was disturbed last night, as was mine. Those mischief-makers returned again." The woman's eyes reflected her anxiety. "I don't know how Dr. Renner will react if they persist. It will upset him terribly."

Janet decided Muriel must mean genuine youngsters that were still playing Halloween pranks. Doubly glad she had sent Gina out of the yard, she said, "If it happens again, Mrs. Renner, you should call the police. It's their job to take care of such problems."

Muriel shook her head. "When one is a foreigner, one does not call in the authorities."

"There's nothing to fear," assured Janet. "Besides, if kids get away with causing trouble, they become even bolder. If you're bothered again, ring up the police. You'll be doing the entire neighborhood a favor."

Muriel's wry smile was polite but disbelieving. "Thank you. I will remember your advice." Glancing at her watch, she reached for the door. "Look for our return within the hour."

Leaving her jacket on the entry hall chair, Janet went to the kitchen where she found Rose noisily eating a bowl of soup. A white napkin tucked under her chin protected the inevitable black dress from dribbles.

Looking up, the woman blotted her mouth. "Good soup." She gestured toward the stove. "Want soup?"

Janet saw that there was plenty left in the pan on the stove. Without having given much thought to it, she had decided to wait for lunch until after returning to Fran's, but if she was to spend time with Gina later that afternoon, it would be better to eat now.

"Sounds good," she said, turning on the heat under the pan.

After the two of them finished eating, Janet had started to clear the table when Rose stood. "Music," she intoned. "Want my music."

"I heard your music playing when I came in," Janet said. "You can go on into the study by yourself, can't you? I want to wash these dishes. Your sister will have enough work without clearing up after us once her husband is home."

"Doctor Herman," Rose mumbled, with such scorn that Janet turned to gape at her. "Doctor Herman," the woman repeated, then mimicked spitting on the floor.

"Rose," Janet scolded. "I hope you don't act like that when your sister is around. It only makes things harder for her."

"Doctor Herman," Rose repeated in that same derisive tone. Abruptly, she reached for Janet's arm, her manner becoming urgent. "Come, you see! Must see!"

Janet allowed the woman to lead her into the study, figuring she would settle her with her music, and then go back to finish the kitchen chores. Only instead of going to her chair, Rose hobbled to the rosewood secretary.

"Look!" she ordered, pointing to the upper bookcase.

"Yes, all right, I'm looking, Rose," Janet said patiently. "What do you want me to see?"

With a cackle, the woman reached around and triumphantly produced a key from behind the secretary.

"Look!" she ordered again, fumbling the key into the lock.

"Now, Rose . . ." Janet chided, not liking the situation. "If that bookcase were any of my business, it wouldn't be locked."

Ignoring her protests, Rose opened the glass doors and tore out a volume.

"No," Janet said as Rose thrust the book at her. "I don't want that. Put it back."

But with desperate intensity, the woman shoved the book forward. Janet had to take it to prevent it from falling. It was heavy, with glossy, pages filled with headings and sub-headings in a foreign language.

"This must be one of Dr. Renner's textbooks," Janet reasoned aloud, curious despite herself. "The language of Austria is German, isn't it? Are these his old psychology books?"

"Yesss, yesss," verified Rose, the s sounds hissing like steam from a boiling teakettle. "Doctor book." She showed Janet another book that was much the same, then opened and presented a cloth-bound journal. As Janet had assumed earlier, the journal correlated the numbers on the books with titles, also written in German. The fading ink showed mechanically precise penmanship, the sevens slashed in the European way. The words mütter and kinder were frequently repeated. A likely translation sprang to Janet's lips and she said, "Mothers and children?"

Rose moaned in delight, as if Janet had successfully deciphered a Rosetta stone. "Yes, yes!" Her voice cracked with excitement. "Mother, child . . . the love, all the time!"

Janet stared. It was to be expected that books on child psychology would address themselves to the love found in a mother-child relationship. Such feverish elation made no sense. And how did Rose know anything about the German language? Someone must have told her something about the books. But who? Dr. Renner? That made no sense. The man ignored her.

"All right, Rose, calm down. I've seen what you wanted to show me, thank you." She returned the journal and books to their places and closed the glass doors. Finding a hook on the back of the case, she rehung the key. With a brisk smile, she turned to the old woman. "Why don't you go sit and relax a little after your lunch."

The tension that had been on Rose's face eased. "Lunch. Soup good."

"Yes, it was delicious," Janet agreed, grateful that the woman had been sidetracked so easily. With no further difficulty, she was able to settle her in the rocker. The TV showed an Alvin and the Chipmunks cartoon doing something underwater, and by appropriate coincidence, the radio played "Octopus Garden" by the Beatles. Janet stayed until she was certain that Rose was absorbed in the music and then returned to the kitchen.

Not five minutes later, as she was hanging the dish towel to dry, she heard Rose's shuffling approach. The old woman entered the kitchen, the expression on her lined face as intense as before.

"You must see," she said, her tone emphatic. "Must see."

Supposing that Rose intended to trot out books again, Janet's reply was equally emphatic. "Rose, I refuse to poke into what's not my business."

The old woman squinted her rheumy eyes and worked her mouth. Janet could almost see rusty gears turning in the cobwebbed attic of her mind. With a sly smile, Rose mumbled under her breath.

"What's that?" Janet leaned forward. "I didn't hear."

"I take stair lift," the woman declared, voice growing in confidence. "Sister says no big steps. I take stair lift."

"Rose, that's wonderful!" Relieved they were off the subject of the books, Janet applauded as if for a child.

"You see!" Rose moved to the rear staircase, beckoning Janet to follow. "You go stairs, I go lift. So easy!"

Indulgently, Janet went after her, watching as Rose settled herself on the stair lift seat and pressed a button. With a grinding whir, the chair started to move up along its metal track.

"Come!" Rose leaned forward anxiously, gesturing.

"Don't lean over! You'll fall!" Janet hurried to catch up. "I'm coming, see?" When they reached the top, Janet expected Rose to reverse the action of the lift to go down again, but instead, with a grunt, she staggered to her feet.

"What now?" Janet asked, thinking that Muriel hadn't exaggerated when warning that Rose was restless.

"Must see." Rose repeated, her steps halting, but faster than Janet would have thought possible.

Janet tried to take her arm because she feared Rose would lose her balance, but Rose shrugged her off. Not knowing what was going on, Janet was surprised when Rose moved past her room which Janet had expected to be the woman's destination. She continued following as Rose led her past the storeroom where the electrician had worked and kept moving.

For just a second, Janet looked ahead to the large window at the front of the house; the window where the ghost children had taken form. Kirby's warning echoed in her mind: regardless of the source of the disturbance, her sensitivity to it might cause its force to increase, but that wasn't her present concern. Her concern was Rose.

The woman had opened the door to Dr. Renner's office and was beckoning her. Scolding herself for even a second of delay, Janet hurried ahead, ready to scold Rose for trying to lead her into a room where neither of them belonged.

She stepped to the doorway and saw the hospital bed. Suddenly, she understood why Rose had led her upstairs.

"Oh, Rose, you wanted me to see the room that's been fixed for Dr. Herman, didn't you? It's very nice. Thank you for showing it to me. Now, let's go back downstairs."

But Rose proceeded inside. Frowning, Janet went to bring her back, only to find her unlocking yet another bookcase.

"Oh, come on!" Janet stepped purposely toward her.

"No, must look!" the old woman insisted. Her headscarf had slipped, and lank gray strands hung about her sunken cheeks as she pointed like an oracle toward a shelf of manila folders.

"I'll not look at a thing," Janet declared, annoyed that Rose had tricked her. "What can this stuff mean to me? Your brother-in-law surely doesn't want us here. Come along, now."

"No!" Rose snatched a folder from a shelf. A label bearing the initial P was pasted to the front cover. Her voice rose, cracking in excitement. "See! The love, always the love! Always, he look for the love. So important."

Not understanding but deciding it best in the long run to pretend cooperation, Janet opened the folder. A musty odor wafted up from typed sheets of brittle, yellowed paper. Each sheet bore a different word, probably a name, beginning with a P.

"What are these?" Janet asked irritably. "The doctor's old records?"

Nodding, Rose rifled the pages with her eager, knobby fingers. "See? All gone. All gone!"

Half choking over the moldering smell, Janet closed the folder with a slap. Staring directly into Rose's time-blurred eyes, she said, "Listen! I don't know how to read German. I can't read a word. Do you understand? Nothing on these pages makes a speck of sense. I don't want to see another thing. Understand?"

Rose looked ready to argue but then her shoulders sagged.

Seeing this change, Janet decided she had finally struck the right degree of firmness. "Rose, we have no business being here and we're going to leave. Understand? We're going to put things in their proper places and then go downstairs where we belong." She returned the folder to the shelf.

"All gone," Rose said mournfully, wringing her hands.

"Yes," Janet said. "They're all gone back on the bookshelf and locked away." She ushered the old woman from the room.

Meekly, Rose went down the lift and along to the study, but all the while, she continued a mournful singsong: "Gone. All gone. They were with us, then all gone."

Janet realized she had heard Rose utter those identical words before. Perhaps she was like a computerized doll with all-purpose responses to suit any occasion. Getting separated from her sister in the store, seeing children pass by the house, having the folders locked away, all described as "all gone."

Or could it be that she actually referred to something else? Perhaps something from the past that stuck in her aging mind like a burr.

Chapter 25

ALTHOUGH MURIEL HAD TOLD JANET SHE expected to be away for only an hour, it was closer to two hours before she and the ambulance arrived. Even then, things failed to go smoothly.

Janet, who had thrown on her jacket and gone to help by holding the front door, saw Muriel leave the parked Oldsmobile and climb into the rear of the ambulance. She assumed that Muriel would have her husband brought out momentarily, but instead, nothing happened. One of the ambulance attendants, a tall, dark-haired man, saw her on the porch and came to explain the reason for the delay.

"The wife gave us instructions," he said. "We were to carry the husband in through the front door and directly upstairs to his room. Simple, one, two, three. Now he's telling her he's going to walk."

Janet frowned. "That may be risky, considering his weak heart. I guess he has a stubborn streak."

The driver, who had come up in time to overhear Janet's words, commented, "Invalids don't realize that walking in their own homes is a lot tougher than a nice level hospital corridor with a railing on one side and a nurse on the other. Still, letting him get steamed up over it may be worse than giving him his way."

Muriel must have decided the same, for she emerged from the ambulance with a defeated expression. A second attendant was with her. For the first time, Janet saw Muriel's hair in disarray, strands loosening from her chignon to fly around a face drawn with fatigue. Her diction, however, was as controlled as ever.

Head held high, she addressed the three men: "My husband, Dr. Herman Renner, wishes to use the stair lift, but instead of him walking there, I have convinced him to be carried through the house to the lift location. Once he is upstairs, he can be assisted to walk to his office. In that room, there is a hospital bed already prepared."

"Is there furniture to move out of our path?" asked the driver.

"Probably." Muriel gave Janet a weary look. "Will you please show the gentlemen the way? I will stay here with Dr. Renner."

Janet led them in and then through the dining room and the study and to the kitchen where she pointed out the back stairs and the lift. Rose had followed along and stood with her head tilted to one side, giving the strangers an intent and curious stare.

"We'll have to have enough space in the kitchen so we can help the patient from the stretcher to his feet and to the lift," the driver said.

"Right," agreed the dark-haired man, grabbing a chair. He said something to Rose, probably a caution to keep out of the way, for Janet heard her respond, "I move, I move."

Janet went back through the study and into the dining room. The men shortly followed, the dark-haired man looking back, his expression puzzled.

Janet had already carried the dining chairs to the far side of the room. To the men, she said, "I think you can now shift the dining table over this way to clear the path you'll need."

As the worked, she returned to the study and found Rose, standing with her hands clamped over her mouth. Her eyes were wide and frightened.

"Rose . . ." Janet went to her. "What's the matter?"

With a moan, Rose began swaying from side to side.

Janet asked if anything hurt. Remembering that one of the men had spoken to her, Janet figured he'd said something that had upset her. Rose's only repose was continued moaning. Not knowing what else to do, Janet led her to her rocking chair. Once seated, the woman's moans subsided but she kept her hands tight across her mouth.

Finished in the dining room, the men went to the ambulance for Dr. Renner. Keeping one eye on her charge, Janet stepped to the doorway when the stretcher was carried in, the wasted carcass upon it blanketed to the chin. The bony outlines of the doctor's skull were revealed by his scanty, white hair. The jutting prow of his nose dominated a face that appeared masklike. Only his fiercely darting eyes appeared to be alive.

Withdrawing from the man's strange gaze, Janet stood in the study next to Rose as the stretcher was carried past them and into the kitchen. From the sounds, getting the doctor to his feet caused no problem. She then heard the stair lift.

Ten minutes later, she heard the men coming down the front stairs. Janet got up to catch them before they left. The dark-haired one had already turned toward the dining room when she reached him.

He said, "We're ready to leave, and I was coming to find out how the old gal was doing."

Janet said, "I wanted to talk with you, too. She's calmer now, but what happened? What did you say to her?"

"Nothing much." The man was obviously perplexed. "All I said was—" He spoke a few words in a foreign tongue, then translated: "'Good afternoon, Grandmother.' That's all I said. As soon as I recognized her accent."

Janet was nonplussed. "What part of South America are you from?"

The man laughed. "South America? No part. I'm Hungarian."

Janet was more confused than ever. "Then she couldn't have understood you. I wonder what she thought you said. Whatever, it apparently frightened her. Rose is from Argentina."

The attendant frowned. "Originally? Even with the teeth gone and the way she mumbles, she's got the sound of my old relatives from Hungary. And she knows the language because her answer was perfect. She wished me a fine afternoon. Then all of a sudden, off she runs, her face like death. There's something a bit strange about the old gal, that's for sure."

By the time Muriel came downstairs after settling Dr. Renner in his sickroom, Rose was rocking blandly before the TV with no sign of her earlier distress. Janet made no mention of the upsetting incident, and soon left the Renner house.

On her way to see Gina, Janet thought about Rose. Having been told that Rose was a native of Argentina, she had never questioned her accent. If it hadn't really sounded Spanish, she had unthinkingly attributed it to the woman's garbled manner of speaking and her own uneducated ear, but there was no chance the attendant was mistaken. The way Rose had clapped her hands over her mouth told the story. Her knowledge of Hungarian was a secret. The poor woman had been trying to seal her lips after it was too late.

Janet cut through the yard to the side street so she could approach the Stockton house from the front. As she continued walking, she decided that maybe the sisters were actually from a poor Hungarian family, only that wasn't good enough for Dr. Renner. He not only wanted people to believe his wife had a more elevated pedigree; he wanted it to be exotic. And to him, South America was exotic. With Muriel's dark beauty, the deception was easy enough, and so it was done. The doctor's wishes were clearly law in that household. Janet could imagine him ordering Muriel to scour away any hint of her accent, while poor Rose, who he believed could not be trusted, was bound to secrecy.

That might also explain Rose's knowledge of German words. European countries traded with one another; probably many words became common over time. But that didn't explain the urgency with which Rose had thrust the doctor's books and patient records upon her. There had been such wildness in her eyes. Perhaps she believed his private papers held references to herself and Muriel.

Janet supposed Dr. Renner was aware of how disturbed the poor woman was. Not that he hadn't looked plenty disturbed himself when being moved through the house. Janet reasoned it must be a helpless sensation to be carried strapped to a stretcher. He had probably been terrified that the attendants would drop him. That would explain why he had been so against being carried up the stairs.

Unless—she couldn't help smiling—unless he had been afraid of the front way because of the ghosts.

Her smile faded as she realized she might have struck upon something. Suppose the doctor had sensed an odd atmosphere upstairs. Maybe it had been fear rather than reasons of health that had inspired him to install the back stair lift.

By the time Janet was at the Stockton's front door, she had decided her theory about the doctor was nonsense. Except for herself, and perhaps the electrician, everyone else seemed to consider the upper hall neutral territory. When she wasn't playing games, Rose even preferred the front way. And she had seen Muriel dash up and down there without a thought.

Ozzie answered the bell. Janet explained about wanting to spend time that afternoon with Gina, only to learn that the child had gone out with Tommy and Veronica.

"Of all days for this to happen," the motherly woman lamented. "The child does so enjoy your company."

Glad that Gina was having an outing, but disappointed for herself, Janet was about to leave when the housekeeper suddenly said, "Say, your first name is Janet, isn't it?"

"Why, yes."

"Then I have something for you!" The woman's laugh was jolly. She handed over a piece of paper from her apron pocket. "Gina wrote this and tucked it into my hand as she left. Only I didn't figure it out until now."

Janet saw that the message started with the printed word, "Ganit."

"See how she sounded it out?" prompted the housekeeper. "Because Gina and Janet start with the same sound, she thought they both began with the same letter, only it threw me off. She's a smart little cookie, isn't she? And the message is awfully cute too."

"Yes." Janet saw that Gina had carefully printed:

Ganit I sorry have must go away.

I love you. Love Gina.

Ozzie chuckled. "Isn't that just the sweetest thing?"

"Yes, yes it is." Touched, Janet swallowed the lump that had formed in her throat. "Do you know when she'll be back?"

"Late, that's what Mrs. Stockton told me. She's throwing a party tomorrow. A spur of the moment thing for all the husband's company friends. You'd think she'd be getting ready for guests, wouldn't you? Instead, she and the mister rush off with the little girl, when usually, they never seem to remember she's around." The woman shook her head over the futility of trying to figure out her employers.

Janet entered Fran's empty house. Usually, she didn't mind solitude, but on that afternoon she longed to hear a friendly voice. If only Ben were home! She thought of calling Kirby but didn't want to start thinking about the Renner house again. It was all crazy stuff.

In possession of many notes and comments from the teachers, she worked the rest of the day on the final newsletter.

When checking a word in the dictionary, she saw it had a section of English translations for words in different languages. After a hesitation, she looked up mütter and kinder, telling herself the words had to do with Rose and Muriel and not the haunting. As she had suspected, they meant "mothers" and "children. The word, kinder was German for "children," as found in the word kindergarten. Which had nothing to do with the puzzle of the sisters' origin nor of the house. Good. Because she had already decided not to think about that anymore.

Much later, after polishing off the final copy of her first newsletter, she found leftovers in the hidden-away new refrigerator—Fran only kept cold drinks in the antique one in the kitchen. With nothing else to do while waiting for Fran and Warren to come in, she curled in a cozy chair and watched an old movie, *Myra Brekinridge* on TV. It amused her to see that Fran sometimes still wore her blonde hair like Farrah Fawcett's in the film.

Somewhere in the back of her mind she knew she was drifting off into sleep and starting to dream. She stood in Herman Renner's second-floor sickroom, only it had been cleverly decorated with a bold painting of the beech tree, the broad gray trunk on one wall, the limbs and colored leaves twisting upward to brightly cover the ceiling over the bed. The decorations made her think of a kindergarten classroom. She was somehow still outside the dream and able to remember thinking about a kindergarten earlier.

Abruptly, she became an active participant and the dream became real. She saw that the room wasn't a kindergarten; it was a place for much younger children. A nursery. Where Dr. Renner's hospital bed had been were rows of children's cribs.

A folder appeared in her hand. As she opened it, the typed pages burst into flames. She cast the folder away with a cry just as another was thrust upon her. She wanted to refuse it, but then it was in her hands, opening by itself. Fire burst upwards. Another burning folder appeared and then another. Starting to sob in panic, she struggled in vain to protect herself as the folders flew upon her like birds with incendiary plumage, scorching her hands, her arms, smoke starting to fill her lungs.

It was then she saw fire spring up from inside the cribs and realized in horror that the burning folders had ignited the nursery beds. Feeling her hair and eyelashes start to crisp in the searing heat, she frantically beat at the flames with her blistering hands, but it was too late. The temperature rose to the flashpoint and the curtains, walls and ceiling exploded with a roar. The cribs became a sea of fiery tongues that cried out in agony; crying like lost children, abandoned, trapped and burning.

Chapter 26

ON SUNDAY, JANET WENT WITH BEN for a light supper at a Rocky Hill tavern he knew, and then on to the party as planned. Although she had especially looked forward to meeting his friends, she found it impossible to keep her thoughts on the party. The manner in which the terror of her nightmare had tied in with Dr. Renner's sickroom and the folders Rose had been so desperate for her to see brought back her strange experiences at the Renner house and kept them in the forefront of her mind.

Noticing her distraction, Ben asked if she was all right. She assured him that she was, but then, when driving home, when he asked her again, she felt remorse.

"I'm sorry," she said. "I hope I didn't spoil the evening for you. I should have canceled."

"No. It's just that I can tell something is wrong."

It had been on the tip of her tongue to excuse away her mood by simply saying she hadn't slept well and leaving it at that, but the concern in his voice broke through her reserve. All at once, she was telling him about her dream as well as confessing her belief that the Renner house was haunted.

While she talked, Ben interrupted only to clarify a few points, and when she finished, he was silent, staring straight ahead as he drove through the night.

Unable to help feeling rebuffed, she said stiffly, "Well, you're a good listener, I'll say that." Bitterly, she regretted having been open with him. Hadn't she known all along it would be a mistake? "I guess it's time to move on to a less wacky topic, right?"

"No, it's not that." His tone was unreadable. "I was trying to sort things out. You gave me a lot to absorb all at once. The Renner crew sounds difficult enough without the occult angle." After a thoughtful pause, he said, "I guess what really bothers me is that you never mentioned any of this before. You tell Kirby you think you might have seen ghosts and that you've been frightened by strange chanting sounds, yet you've never said a word to me."

His reaction caught her off guard. She hadn't considered that her silence might seem a betrayal of trust, which still didn't mean he thought her story had merit. Defending herself, she said, "I only told Kirby because it's a subject that interests him."

Looking over at her, Ben said softly, "A subject that interests me is you. If you've had upsetting experiences, I want to know about them." He reached across the seat, his fingers strong and warm as he clasped her hand. "Being able to share things . . . isn't that what caring for each other is all about?"

"Oh, Ben." His words and the touch of his hand deeply moved her. Voice unsteady, she said, "Maybe the fault was that I cared too much. The whole idea of claiming to have had a supernatural experience . . . I was afraid of what you might think."

"Don't ever be afraid of being honest with me." His hand on hers felt warm and comforting. "Maybe I don't understand what you've experienced, but I'm not mocking it."

She sighed, feeling as if a weight had been lifted from her. "I don't know what reaction I expected," she admitted. "If you had shown wide-eyed enthusiasm, I guess I would have thought you too gullible."

"No pleasing some people, huh?" He smiled at her across the

dimness of the car. "Actually, I may have a more open mind on this subject than many because of an experience when I was young."

"Oh?" She was immediately captured. "What happened?"

"When I was a kid, my mother made me take piano lessons. She and her two sisters, Blanche and Norma, had each studied the piano as girls, but Mom had a tin ear and gave it up after only a few months. Norma, had also given it up, but Blanche, who died when she was only a young woman, had been quite talented. Mom hoped I'd take after my Aunt Blanche."

"And did you?" Janet asked, wondering where the story was headed.

"No. I wasn't much good, but when my teacher gave a formal evening recital, I had to perform anyway. It was held in the school, and one of the kids got nervous and threw up. It caused a panic. The stage was empty, with nobody ready to go on, so the teacher asked Mom, who was backstage helping, if she would explain to the audience that there would be a slight delay.

"Mom was always scared to death of being in public, but she managed to stammer something to the crowd. Then, as she was about to escape to the wings, she noticed a music book lying on the piano. She says it was as if she were suddenly in a trance. Feeling as if she were watching herself from a distance, she opened the book to a selection, sat on the bench, and placed her fingers on the keys. Now, this is a lady who hadn't played well and never learned to read notes. My father, who was in the audience, said it was the most amazing thing he'd ever witnessed, because there, in front of a filled auditorium, she played an entire classical selection perfectly.

"Afterwards, backstage again, Mom was a total wreck, laughing and crying. The piece she played, something by Debussy, had been a favorite with Aunt Blanche. Mom swore she had felt Blanche's presence, and that it was actually Blanche who had done the playing through her. She had always been convinced that her sister's spirit had lived on after death and believed that on the night of the recital, she had finally been granted the long-awaited proof."

Finishing his story, Ben shrugged. "I don't know if there's a rational explanation for Mom's experience, but whatever, it was totally outside of the normal range of happenings." Taking his eyes from the road, his smile was gentle. "I don't know whether that's good enough for you or not, but that's what I mean when I say I have an open mind."

Janet's throat was tight with emotion. "It's a beautiful story. I hope it means what your mother thinks." After a silence, she added, "But that still doesn't necessarily mean you accept everything I've told you, does it?"

"What do you want me to say? Accept it on what terms? You've told me Kirby claims there are several possible reasons for what you've experienced. Maybe the Renner house is haunted. I know nothing about things like that, but doesn't it make sense that you might see little children for personal reasons?"

"I lost one child, Ben, an infant daughter. Why should I see a little boy who looks several years older, or a little girl, a toddler with dark hair? Becky's hair was blonde. I don't think it would ever have turned dark. I have a feeling there were more children there too, only they never took on form. And the chanting was definitely made by more than two voices."

"What about the baby you keep hearing?" Approaching a crossroad, he slowed the car. "It sure seems that nobody except you thinks it exists. Maybe the cries are related to the haunting."

"Then you believe there could be a haunting?"

He was silent as they stopped at the crossroad where a yellow caution light blinked. Still paused, he said, "I guess that story I told you about my aunt means I believe in things that can't be explained."

As Ben moved the car on, Janet spoke, her voice strained. "I was about to remind you that Gina heard the baby too. But when I start to think that maybe the crying is related to the haunting, it scares me. If it isn't a living baby that Gina heard, does that mean she's also aware of the ghosts?"

"If there really are ghosts. I bet Kirby would say that if one mind could shape an image, another mind could see it."

"Ben, that's awful! You think Gina might be hearing and seeing illusions from my mind? That's horrible."

"Okay, okay. Maybe the phantom children fit into one of Kirby's other categories of hauntings. They sure don't sound like a happy bunch. All that crying. That's what you said about the little boy that night wasn't it? That he was crying?"

Janet angled herself about to see Ben's profile against the side window. The lines were firm and strong: the face of a practical man. Yet, when speaking of his mother's experience, he had made room in his mind for a cautious belief in the unknown. Perhaps it wasn't fair to demand more.

"You never saw the little boy, did you?" she asked. "It seems impossible that he was so clear to me, yet you didn't see him. Didn't you even sense something?"

"I'm afraid I only sensed that if we didn't get away from where we didn't belong, we'd land in trouble."

Sighing, Janet settled back. "Trouble for me would be another one of those nightmares. Even after I was awake, it seemed I could still hear the children screaming and smell the smoke from the fire. I'm fairly sure there was also something about a fire in that other dream I had. That vague dream I told you about when we looked at Halloween window paintings? I only wish I could remember."

"Maybe it's better not to. Maybe our brains work out hurts and confusions in ways we can't understand. When we poke around, insisting on making interpretations, maybe we interfere. It might be like constantly disturbing a bandage instead of letting healing take place on its own."

Hearing his words and his comforting tone, Janet wished she had shared with him all along instead of holding back. Mentally reviewing their conversation, she realized that being believed didn't count as much as she had thought. What mattered was being able to talk things over openly with someone who cared.

She looked out the window. The car traveled through a rural area a few miles above Princeton, occasional mailboxes along the way offering the only clues to nearby habitation. It must be lonely living so far away from town, so desperately lonely.

Stunned, she realized the drift of her thoughts. She'd always felt that living far out in the country would be peaceful. What had made thoughts of loneliness suddenly cross her mind? It made no sense, especially not when she considered how very close she'd been feeling to Ben only a moment before.

Yet she did feel lonely. Depressingly alone. It was as if a dark fog had seeped into the car, settling over her like a cloak, making it almost impossible for her to breathe.

Suddenly, from the depth of the suffocating darkness, the image of Gina's face appeared, the child's eyes swollen with tears. Janet moaned.

Ben looked her way. "Honey, what is it?"

"I—I saw . . ." It was hard for her to speak. Blinking, she realized that the image was gone. She could breathe again, but the depression, a sense of hopeless abandonment, remained.

"Gina, she—" Struggling to free herself from the lost, lonely mood was like fighting her way through quicksand. She reached toward Ben. The contact steadied her. "Ben." Her voice was hoarse. "There's something wrong with Gina. We must go to her."

"What do you mean? What are you talking about?"

She clutched his sleeve. "Gina needs me, that's all I know." Her alarm was growing. "I must go to her, now. She needs me!"

Ben started to ask further questions and then seemed to think better of it. "All right, we're only a few miles away." He stepped on the accelerator. "Hang on. We'll be there in a matter of minutes." Saying nothing more, he simply drove.

When arriving, Janet saw cars lined up before the brightly lit Stockton house and remembered Ozzie speaking of a party. With a party going on, the Stocktons would have no time for the child. She might have hurt herself and no one would know! Janet was out of the car and running toward the house as soon as Ben stopped. A man stepped out on the porch to smoke his cigar, the sounds of music and laughter following him. Heedless, she pushed past him and burst inside. Seeing her, Tommy Stockton detached himself from the crowd in the living room.

"Janet, hi! I'll tell Veronica you've heard our good news—"

Janet cut him off. "Where's Gina?"

The highly polished plastic of Tommy's handsome features under his full volume hairstyle wrinkled in momentary confusion. "Why, upstairs with Ozzie, I suppose."

Wheeling about, Janet bolted up the stairs. She reached the landing just as Gina shot from a dimly lit corridor like a bullet and threw herself into her arms.

"Baby, baby, I'm here!" Janet cried. Running her hands along the sweating, trembling little body, she started to sob in relief. Whatever was wrong, it was nothing physical. Gina, although clearly upset, was all in one piece, alive and well.

Ozzie appeared. "Goodness! I might have guessed you'd be the one she'd be wanting." She switched on a light. "What a blessing you're here. I haven't been able to do a thing with the poor lamb."

There was confusion downstairs as Ben and Tommy stared at the tableau at the top of the landing. Tommy disappeared and returned with Veronica. They came upstairs, Ben following.

"I didn't know what the trouble was," Janet was saying in a choked voice to the housekeeper. "I had such a powerful feeling that she needed me." By that time, she was seated on the window bench, Gina on her lap, the child's face buried against her breasts, crushing her dress.

"Gina!" Veronica, wearing a broad-shouldered, white tuxedo suit with wide, rhinestone-studded lapels, admonished sharply, "What do you think you're doing?" Embarrassed, she tried to pry the child free, but Janet shook her head. "No, no, it's all right."

"Not really," Ozzie snapped, flashing Veronica a look. "She's been crying for hours."

"Oh, dear," wailed Veronica.

"That's a damn shame, poor kid," Tommy commiserated uncomfortably. "It's going to take her time to adjust. I guess things were sort of abrupt."

Janet, who had been stroking Gina's back, suddenly remembered what Kirby had said about the Stocktons. Staring at Tommy, she accused, "Your new assignment came through! That's what the party is all about, isn't it?"

The entire picture became clear to her in an instant. With their thoughts focused on the excitement of the move and the celebration with their business friends, Veronica and Tommy had never taken the time to give Gina the assurances she so desperately needed.

Hugging Gina even closer, Janet vibrated with outrage. "Did you think you could just spring such changes on the child? Just announce you were whisking her abroad, uprooting her from everything she's familiar with, and not leave her feeling confused and frightened? She's only a little girl, you know."

Tommy's tone was defensive. "We're not going to uproot her. We've found the perfect boarding school. It has a splendid atmosphere and living with other children will be the best thing for her."

Janet couldn't believe her ears. "You're not taking her with you?"

It was Veronica who answered. "We can't, Janet. We're going to keep moving from embassy to embassy, country to country. That would be a lot harder on Gina, you must see that. It's much better to have her settled in one place."

"A very expensive place, I might add," boasted Tommy, stroking the area of his gray plaid suit where his heart should have been. "The best. We toured it thoroughly today and Gina will be extremely happy there." Someone called him from below. "I must return to our guests," he told Veronica. Giving Janet a frosty nod, he retreated down the stairs.

Veronica suddenly looked very forlorn despite her sophisticated hairstyle, curled and fluffed to show off sparkling gold earrings. Then, remembering that she should be in charge, she thrust out her jaw, demanding of Janet, "Just how are you involved in this?"

"Janet is Gina's friend," spoke up Ozzie. "The child was upset and wanted her." Perhaps unaware that Janet had not been invited to the party, the housekeeper had accepted her presence without question. Her statement led Veronica to jump to conclusions of her own.

"Oh, and so you called her over. Well . . ." She rubbed her hands helplessly, clearly in a situation where she was at a loss.

Janet could feel Gina's tension as her small body continued to burrow silently against her like a young animal seeking comfort. Not wanting to risk being asked to leave, Janet kept her tone moderate and her feelings to herself as she offered, "Suppose I take Gina to her room and see if I can get her settled for the night."

Veronica hesitated. "I supposed it does seem like a good idea. I must return to my guests" She nodded as if approving her decision, then gave Janet a vacant smile and left.

Janet watched Veronica hurry down the steps, then realized Ben was still standing there.

"Oh, Ben," she whispered apologetically, still stroking Gina's hair. "I'll probably be a while." She felt torn by two different needs. "This isn't fair to you. I can walk home. You might as well go."

He studied her and the child, a warm but curious expression in his eyes. "It's all right," he said. "Take your time. We'll stay as long as Gina needs you. I'll wait."

Chapter 27

"YOU WANT HER, DON'T YOU," BEN said to Janet. They had left the Stockton house and were in his car on their way to his apartment.

"Yes, desperately." Janet's voice was choked. "You saw how she was, how they treated her."

Ben nodded.

Janet knew he not only saw, he understood. After Gina had been settled and had drifted off, she and Ben had talked softly. Together, they decided they would stay until they were sure Gina was truly sound asleep before they found Ozzie and let her know they were leaving.

Janet had then gone into the bathroom. She passed the bench where Gina's haunting words, I heard your baby; I heard your baby crying, echoing in her mind.

When she stepped back into Gina's bedroom, she saw that instead of the child being in her bed, she lay cuddled on Ben's lap. Hearing Janet come in, she looked up with a sleepy smile and reached out her arms.

"Guess we know who's the favorite," Ben said, with a smile as he handed Gina over.

After they were sure the child was deeply asleep, they had found Ozzie as planned and said good night.

"You were holding Gina," Janet had said once they were outside the Stockton house. "Did she just go to you?"

"Yes. Since she'd seen you with me, I guess I was a good guy too."

Now in his apartment, Janet couldn't forget Gina's hopeless sobs. "The Stockton's have no idea what it means to be parents," she said. "They never should have taken her in the first place."

"Don't be so rough on them, honey. Taking her was a lot better than letting her stay in an orphanage. Edgar said that little Italian town where the earthquake happened was already on the edge of poverty. Her family was gone and with her handicap, Gina's future there wouldn't have stood a chance."

Janet's eyes widened. "I forgot you knew someone from the agency that placed her. Have the Stocktons adopted her or is she still a foster child?"

"As far as I know, she's still a foster child. I could ask Edgar and find out for sure."

"Oh, would you?" Janet looked up into Ben's face. Tone suddenly uncertain, she said, "Do you think I'm acting crazy for wanting her?"

He shook his head. "I have no trouble understanding it."

"But how do you feel about it?" Her voice quavered. "My thoughts have been occupied with Gina, but not . . . not about us. She's important to me, Ben." She realized she had been trying to keep her feelings for Ben and her feelings for Gina on separate tracks, but circumstances had now placed the two interests on what might be a collision course.

She searched his face. Although she wasn't ready to make a commitment, she didn't want to risk losing him.

"There's something I want to say to you," Ben said.

Her senses went on alert. This was going to be it, she thought. He was attracted to her, he cared for her, but he'd been alone long enough and wanted to share his life with someone. He was ready and she wasn't. And if that wasn't bad enough, she had what he thought of as a weird fixation on the Renner house and notions about ghosts. And now, he knew she was thinking of bringing an eight-year-old into the mix. It was too much, and she saw why he wanted to say goodbye.

"I've been thinking," he said. "We've spent a lot of time getting to know one another and we've learned a lot in a short time. Maybe you even know more about me than the man you married, and I can say without hesitation that I know more about you than the girl I married even though we had dated all through high school."

Janet wasn't sure where he was going, but she figured it was rambling somewhere downhill. Letting her down easy, that's what it was. It made her want to say, "Just get it over with and dump me," but all she could do was listen while he struggled with his words.

"I was too young then, not knowing what I wanted." He talked on and then he smiled faintly. "It's different now. I've grown up and know where I want to go in life."

"Your career is important," she said, finding that the more he talked, the more she belatedly realized the mistake she'd made in not admitting to herself that Ben had become the man she could imagine spending the rest of her life with. She had been a fool to hold back. And now it was too late. Forcing herself to speak she continued. "What you do is valuable. It's work that makes a difference to people."

His smile widened. "And you have your interest in journalism. You told me once you could see yourself someday working for a newspaper or a magazine. You didn't say it, but I will, maybe even on TV."

She had to smile. He was really doing a good job of it, saying they were each on different tracks; moving away from each other. Sure, she got the point. She just wished he'd get it over with.

"I understand you're not ready," he said, his voice slightly husky, "but I want you to know that if Gina's important to you she's important to me too." He shook his head as if amazed at himself. "I thought from the start was a cute kid she was, but when she roused, saw me and just came to me. Let me tell you, she won me over, just like that." He snapped his fingers. "Her family might have been poor, but she was loved. She trusted the people around her to take care of her and love her. That's not what she's getting from the Stockton's, but it's what she could get with us."

Janet blinked, not sure what she was hearing as he continued.

"You want Gina, and approval should come easier if we could offer her a home with two parents." Ben's hands were on her arms, his touch firm, but gentle. "I'd like to use the situation to allow me to put a ring on your finger, but I can't take advantage of you like that."

"A ring on my finger?" she echoed in disbelief. Did she have this all wrong? He wasn't backing away from a commitment because he wanted to be free—he was holding back because he didn't want to pressure her?

"Ben . . ." Tears that mingled joy and relief made her eyes shine like stars. "You mean you think you might want to marry me?"

"Not *might* want to, *do* want to, but I know how hard things have been for you, and knowing how you feel—"

She started to laugh. "I don't know how I feel, except happy. I love you, Ben." Fingers closing on the lapels of his jacket, she pulled him closer. "I love you and I no longer want to put a hold on my life. If you want me, yes, I'll marry you."

"Are you sure?"

"Yes, I'm sure. And it's not because of Gina. It's because of who you are and what you are. I mean it when I say I love you." But then, she stopped for a sobering moment and said, "Ever since I met you, I've been thinking I should take it slow. Is this all going too fast?"

"Maybe it seems so, but that doesn't make it wrong, does it?"

"No, it doesn't," she whispered. "I was the one who was wrong. If it's right, then it's not too fast."

Ben smiled. "I want you here with me, to move in with me. But maybe we shouldn't announce our engagement until there's that ring on your finger. It might help convince your sister of my best intentions."

She laughed, realizing she was happier than she'd ever thought she could be. "Fran's a good sister, the best," she said, "but when it comes to me, she's still big-sister bossy. I've known from the start that I couldn't stay with Fran and Warren forever. And now, well . . . " She gave Ben a tremulous smile. "Now I can be with you and that's perfect. And if we could have Gina it would be super perfect."

It was then that he moved back slightly and said, "I suppose this means that if Gina becomes ours, you'll want to take the cat, too."

Taken aback, her words stumbled out. 'But the cat is Gina's! If you saw how she and Pagoda play together—" Then, seeing the twinkle in his eyes, she put her fists on his shoulders. "Are you teasing me?"

He laughed. "I just figured if we're getting married, we should at least have had our first fight and gotten it over with."

"Wait until you hear this," she said. "When you started talking, I thought you were working up to say it was time for us to go our separate ways."

He was stunned. "So all the time I was talking—"

"I was thinking you were saying goodbye."

He chuckled. "Then we already had our first fight before I brought up the cat, only that fight was all inside your head." His manner turned serious. "We both want Gina, but it's not a sure thing. She's hardly being neglected in a legal sense."

"But she is!"

"She's deprived emotionally. What that means as far as the law is concerned, I don't know. And we don't have much time to find out. Didn't Veronica say they're scheduled to leave in two weeks?"

"Oh, God, yes," Janet said. "Could you reach Edgar tomorrow?"

"I'll be working out at a site for the next couple of days, but I'll try to reach him tomorrow at lunchtime." He touched her hair with a gentle hand. "There's no telling what Edgar will say."

"But you'll try to make him understand?"

"Definitely. Because of her handicap, Gina's case is unique, and the special rapport you have with her should count heavily in your favor. The agency will probably back our efforts, but we have to be careful in the handling of the Stockton's. Tommy might put up a fight."

"But he doesn't care about her!"

"He's a competitive guy," Ben said. "He might view Gina as a game point and battle hard not to lose. "

"Oh, boy. Then I'll be dealing with both him and my sister."

Ben touched her face gently. "You know, you have a tendency to act as if you're all alone in the world, having to make all the hard decisions on your own." He looked at her with eyes that were serious and filled with caring. "I'm saying that you're not alone. Whatever we're in, we're in it together."

Together. Peace flowed through her as if a soothing hand had quietly turned off her racing anxiety. She touched his cheek, her love for him quickening her blood, her desire reflecting in her eyes.

"Oh, yes, Ben," she whispered. "Together. We're together."

She ended up staying the night, but as planned, they woke up early, when it was still dark outside. Resting warmly next to him, she wondered if Fran had discovered that she hadn't come home. Probably not, she thought. When Ben stirred, she turned to him. He opened his arms and enfolded her. After that, she was only thinking about him and them and being together.

Later, while it was still dark, she and Ben got into his car. They had decided that she would move her clothes and other items to his apartment, but the fact that he'd be away for several days meant she would stay with Fran until he returned. As to how and when she would tell Fran, she hadn't yet decided.

They reached the corner of Quince Street so Janet could walk home without the sound of the car disturbing Fran and Warren.

"Thanks for bringing me home so early," Janet said, as she reluctantly withdrew from his arms and the last of many goodbye kisses. "There's only a small chance she'd realize I wasn't home, but I don't want to risk worrying her." She thought of something he's said earlier. "What did you mean about Gina and me having a special rapport?"

"I'd call rushing through the night because of a powerful premonition that she needed you rather special, wouldn't you?"

"It was strange, wasn't it?"

"You're darned right, and it's not the only example." He reached to touch her hand, as if comforting her because he knew his words would be disquieting. "That day at the house site, I swear she sent a mental message for your attention."

"No, I explained that. She beckoned or made some other move to catch my eye. Anything else is impossible, Ben."

"You still say that after hurrying to her last night?"

Her answering tone was hushed, almost fearful. "There have been times when things about her have surprised me. Things I ignored. At the time, I didn't attribute them to anything unnatural."

"Because she's deprived of speech, perhaps she's found other ways to communicate."

"Can things like that really happen?" As she spoke, a vague, dreamlike scene floated across her mind. Gina, dressed in black and white, hands sending secret messages . . . the beech tree, its branches spread protectively . . . The images fled as swiftly as they had come.

Her throat felt tight. "This conversation makes me feel awful. Like you're saying Gina's a freak, and that I am too."

"I'm saying she has a gift," Ben said. "Deprived of one sense, she's been granted another. And thankfully, you seem to be able to answer to it. I also think she's the answer to something else for you. She could never take your daughter's place, but she could answer your need to love and protect a child. The need that now is probably expressed in other ways."

She was uncertain. "You mean the ghost children?"

He nodded.

"And what if you're wrong?" she demanded with a sudden surge of emotion. "What if the apparitions are totally independent from me? Something truly real?"

"I don't know." His lips moved gently along her cheek. "I don't know what that would mean, but I don't think it's anything we have to worry about."

"Because you think you're right."

"Yes, honey, because I think I'm right."

***

Inside Fran's house, Janet moved through the silence to a window with a view out the back yard. Her breath made a white mist on the pane as she looked out and located the beech tree, its highest bare limbs swaying gently above the yellow house rooftop. Was the house truly haunted, or were Kirby and Ben right about the disturbance being a product of her mind?

Ben's certainty about the ghost children rankled. Although she still basked in the blissful memory of his embrace and knew that he was right man for her, that didn't mean he was perfect. Maybe his theory about the haunting was correct, or maybe it wasn't, so how could he sound so dratted sure?

On impulse, she opened the back door and stepped out into the misty half-light. Pressing the catch so the door wouldn't lock behind her, she went across the back lawn, the thin November light brightening as sunrise moved closer. Crisp, frozen blades of grass crunched under her feet, and she could feel clammy morning air deep in her lungs.

She reached the row of evergreens and breathlessly stared through a gap and into the Renner yard. For an instant, it seemed that she glimpsed sparks of bright light amidst the branches of the beech tree. The words of the poem Kirby had quoted came to her: thou, light-winged Dryad of the trees . . .

The cold began to settle around her and she retraced her steps to Fran's back door. She had just slipped inside when a soft touch against her ankle turned her to stone, a scream strangling in her throat. Then she heard the soft, plaintive cry.

Pagoda. Shaking with relief, she reached down to lift the cat into her arms. "Oh, my," she murmured against the animal's soft fur. "What you did to my nervous system!" Pagoda started to purr.

"You sneaked in when I held the door to snap the lock, didn't you? Well, now, you're going right outside again." She deposited the animal on the stoop, locked the door and wondered what she had expected to see in the Renner yard. The spirits of the ghost children under the safe shelter of the copper beech? The Beeches. Kirby said that had once been the name for the Renner house. She wondered where the thought that the beech tree provided safety had come from. From her forgotten dream, perhaps?

She recalled her strange feelings that day she had watched Gina playing under the tree. Gina, who went too frequently to the Renner yard. "Dangerous," Rose had warned. Starting to shiver, Janet thought she would do anything to protect Gina. If there was danger, whatever it was, she would protect her.

Chapter 28

JANET TURNED IN HER COMPLETED NEWSLETTER, her fingers crossed, while Ben was away. He called her that night, saying he'd set up an appointment with his foster child agency friend, Edgar Lightfoot. Later that week, he was able to break away long enough for the two of them to meet with Edgar in his office in the afternoon.

The meeting went better than either of them could have hoped for—the only disappointment was that Ben would go back to his job site soon after they had an early supper. He dropped Janet off at Fran's. After their lingering kisses, he reluctantly left.

Fran and Warren had just finished their dinner and were still in the dining room after clearing the table when Janet came in. She said she had something to tell them, her tone serious.

"You better sit down again," Janet said, talking her usual place at the table. When they did, she said, "I need to tell you some things and I don't want you to interrupt until I'm finished." Janet's gaze was mostly on Fran.

She told them everything about the Stocktons' plans for Gina, and that she wanted to take the child.

Putting up a hand because she saw that Fran was about to speak, Janet continued. "I've found out that the school in Princeton has a class for children with disabilities, and Ben and I are moving in together. My divorce has been granted. I didn't pay much attention to it when the paper came because it didn't seem to matter, but now it does. Ben and I plan to marry and so far, things seem to be falling into place." Again, she held up her hand. "I know I'm doing the right thing."

Fran, whose expression had grown more and more guarded, looked at her with eyes clouded with concern, and said. "Are you finished now?" She didn't wait for an answer. "I can see that the boarding school Veronica and Tommy want would be bad for the child, but what about you? You're taking up with a man you've only just met and now talking about marrying him! He's a good person, I'm sure, but it's too fast, and you're adding to it by planning to take on the responsibility of a stranger's child—one with problems.

"This is all wrong for you at this stage of your life," Fran continued. "Besides, there's no reason to believe the agency will consider you as a foster parent. You're getting your hopes up for nothing."

"I told you that Ben and I have already spoken to Mr. Lightfoot, the agency representative." Janet's tone was patient but firm.

"But, Jan," Fran objected. "I don't see how I can let—"

Clearing his throat, Warren interrupted. "I don't know as Janet is asking our permission, sweetheart." Hunching his burly shoulders, he added quietly, "She's certainly given the matter careful thought, and if it's what she wants to do, I think we should support her."

Braced for further argument, Janet was surprised and relieved when Fran, after a thoughtful silence, nodded. "You're right, of course. Jan, I'm not going to say I'm wholehearted about this thing, that would be lying. But you're an adult and if it's what you want, okay." She squared her shoulders. Her eyes, which had been soft a moment earlier, turned flinty as she narrowed them. "What I have to do now, is plan. I'll talk to the Stocktons. Veronica can be sensible, but Tommy's going to be tough. And I won't have much time to soften him up. The best thing is for me to have a private talk with Veronica first."

Hearing those words, Janet's relief at Fran's acceptance of her plan turned to dismay. She recognized both her sister's look and her tone. Fran had just transformed herself from the chief antagonist to the chief in charge the campaign. Janet flashed a desperate look in Warren's direction. She could imagine Fran racing over to Veronica's with all the best intentions, innocently creating the very stumbling blocks they must avoid.

Warren, his thoughts apparently running along the same lines, spoke up. "Since Veronica's unlikely to be the problem, let's leave her out for the moment. Tommy's the one to work on."

"Sure, Warren," Fran complained testily, "but I never get a chance to see him."

"Maybe not, but I do. When he's in town, as he is now, I pretty much know when he'll be at the brokerage office in town, keeping his eye on the market. I can wander in and ease into a discussion of his career success. I'll point out the advantage of having an interested local party, Janet, of course, to care for Gina while they're abroad. Knowing Tommy, he'll quickly calculate how much cheaper it will be to have her in a private home rather than in a boarding school."

"Yes, yes I see!" approved Fran, her tone registering the surprise she always showed when someone presented a solution she judged as good as anything she might think of herself. "

Excited, Fran turned to Janet. "Isn't it a wonderful plan? And once Tommy starts thinking that way, it would be only a short jump for the Stocktons to work with the agency to move you from being an approved guardian to appointing you as an official foster parent."

"Definitely," Janet said. "I think you're right. We should leave everything up to Warren." She uttered a silent thankful prayer. Wait until she told Ben of the narrow escape!

With her concerns placed in Warren's capable hands, Janet was free to turn to other matters when Muriel Renner phoned later that evening.

"I must take Rose out shopping tomorrow afternoon," Muriel explained. "Dr. Renner's recovery has been smooth, but I am not feeling peaceful about leaving him alone in the house. Could you come over for several hours?"

Viewing Muriel's request as a gift wrapped in gold ribbon, Janet agreed at once. Even before she had replaced the phone, a plan had leaped almost full-blown into her mind.

So Mr. Benjamin Yates thought he knew all about hauntings, did he? Well, she soon might have a surprise for him. A surprise that would badly dent his theory concerning her part in the disturbance of the Renner house.

Chapter 29

JANET ASKED FRAN TO DRIVE HER to the high school the next morning. There, she learned that Annabelle Chu was in a study hall in the auditorium. To pass the time, she went to the main office. Ida beckoned her in.

"Got to tell you," Ida said, bending to tap her cigarette on the rim of a wastebasket, "everyone loves what you did with the newsletter."

"Thanks," Janet said. "I'm glad you took a chance on me. I learned a lot and it was fun working with Crystal."

"Yes, she's something, isn't she?" Fluffing her hair, Ida took another puff of her cigarette. "I was going to call you. There's a full-time clerical position coming up. I'll recommend you for the job if you want it." Wearing green stirrup pants under an oversized red sweater with a wide green belt cinching her waist, Ida waved an arm. "Also, the job will include the spring newsletter. Everybody liked how you worked with the teachers and the kids to get the best out of them. I'll send the details in a couple of days."

"That's terrific," Janet said. "I'll be looking forward to hearing more." Such as the hours and salary, Janet thought as she parted from Ida and headed toward the auditorium. Soon, if all went well, she would be caring for a child and have a full-time job right there in town. She and Ben had discussed hiring the tutor who'd been working with Gina so there wouldn't be the change of a new school right away. For the same reason, they wondered if Ozzie would have any time for them after the Stocktons left. The woman had been important to Gina—keeping that link would be helpful to the child.

She reached the auditorium as the doors opened. Annabelle came out with the crowd, her shiny black hair up in a high side ponytail, revealing there were still only two earrings per lobe. Seeing Janet, she stepped to one slide and left the flow pass behind her.

They greeted one another and as the hall quieted, Janet asked the girl if she had a camera to rent.

Annabelle waved a hand expansively. "Rent? No, but you can borrow one. What kind of pictures are you planning to take? Snapshots?"

"Not exactly," Janet hedged, wondering how Annabelle would react if she confessed she wanted to photograph a haunted house. She didn't even know if her plan was feasible, although she had once seen a TV documentary in which a camera had supposedly captured faint, ghost-like figures that had been invisible to the naked eye. Because of his film background, she would have liked to discuss the phenomena with Kirby, but when remembering his warning against dwelling upon the disturbance, she was sure he would throw cold water on her idea.

Giving Annabelle the story she had fabricated, she said, "I want to take interior shots of how some rooms are decorated, only there's not much light. And I can't use a flash. There are a number of mirrors, and reflections would be a big problem."

"I could lend you stands and lights."

"Thanks, but I don't want to go to that much trouble. I just need a camera and light-sensitive film. Something fast."

The corners of Annabelle's mouth pulled down as she shook her head. "You don't need fast film for still pictures of rooms."

Janet improvised. "I'm nervous with a camera and my hands tremble or something. My pictures are always coming out blurred.

Anyway, that's what I want to try, something fast, and something that will allow me to catch plenty of light."

Shrugging, Annabelle led her to the media center, but the camera she wanted had already been borrowed. She selected a substitute.

"This will make automatic adjustments for light, but watch the way the motor drive advances the film. Maybe I should disconnect it. It's a bad feature if you're shaky. You could end up ripping off a bunch of shots of the same thing before you know it."

To Janet, that sounded perfect. "No, leave it. And now, what kind of film should I buy?"

She walked from the school to a camera shop in town and two hours later, with the freshly loaded camera making a lumpy outline in her shoulder bag, she walked to the Renner house.

The morning sun had given away to threatening clouds. Rose wore a black London Fog that lost all its style the moment the woman pulled on her headscarf and awkwardly knotted it under her chin. Muriel was also prepared for foul weather, a veritable fashion plate in a mulberry-colored raincoat with gray boots and matching accessories. Her complexion was pale, with shadows of fatigue under her eyes, yet there was an anticipatory excitement in her manner as she stood in the entry smoothing on her gloves. Janet suspected that after several days of being cooped up with a husband issuing demands from his sickbed, she was more than eager to escape for a few hours.

More chatty than usual, Muriel pointed to her sister's feet. "See how thin the leather has worn? Today, we buy new shoes. More chatty than usual, Muriel pointed to her sister's feet. "See how thin the leather has worn? Today, we buy new shoes. With her arthritis, it is not easy to get them perfectly fitted." She spoke as if discussing a child with an intriguing problem. Obviously relishing being the center of the conversation, Rose smiled broadly.

Nodding to show her attention, Janet placed her shoulder bag on a chair and laid her jacket across it. As she listened to Muriel's speech, she tried in vain to detect an accent. A certain stiltedness and too perfect pronunciation marked her as not being native-born, but that was all.

"How is your husband's heath?" Janet asked. "I only glimpsed him when he was carried in."

"His recovery has been remarkable and at this time of day, he usually works at his desk. In case he needs anything, I must provide the opportunity for him to say so. He has a bell, but I suspect he would be too proud to ring it."

Should I check on him anyway?" Janet asked.

Muriel's expression revealed sudden discomfort. She lowered her voice. "In about a half hour, could you please pour a bottle of mineral water from the refrigerator and take it upstairs?"

Wondering why this was hush-hush, Janet nevertheless lowered her own tones. "No problem. Does he need it to take his medicine?"

Shaking her head, Muriel whispered, "Dr. Renner is a very self-reliant man. He would be angered if he knew I asked you to look in upon him. But if you tell him I instructed you to bring him a drink that should be all right."

Janet nodded wryly, feeling that Dr. Renner had a selfish way of being self-reliant. He no doubt enjoyed being waited on hand and foot. Muriel's fatigue testified to that. What he didn't like was the suggestion that any weakness on his part made it necessary.

"You should know that if you use the back steps to take up the mineral water, Dr. Renner's sickroom will be several rooms down on your left. You will see a handrail that stops just before his doorway. Don't open it. Knock. He will call you in." Muriel pointed to a notepad on the phone table. "Here are the phone numbers of Dr. Renner's physician and that of the ambulance, although you should not need them."

Muriel's manner suggested she felt she imposed upon Janet's good nature, but Janet was delighted. She had planned to carry the camera up the front staircase, creeping along, hoping against hope that the doctor wouldn't hear her prowling. Now, she had a justifiable reason for being on the second floor, which she was a lot more familiar with than Muriel realized.

After the two women departed, Janet took the camera into the study. She reviewed its workings and her plans to use it: going up the back stairs from the kitchen, she would carry the water to the doctor. After leaving him, she would head toward the front, taking photos around the big window. He might hear her footsteps, but coming up one stairway and going down another was certainly nothing to question. Even if he kept his door open, the lack of a flash would do nothing to draw his attention, and the electronic advance would enable her to simply point the camera and sweep its eye smoothly, taking pictures in rapid succession. She would then go downstairs, her mission successfully completed.

Ben had called her while she was still at Fran's that morning to say he would be home that evening. She had smiled to herself while they talked; thinking that when she had photos that showed the ghost images, how surprised he was going to be.

Still, as confident she felt, there were nervous butterflies in her stomach. She hadn't realized the house would be so quiet without Rose's radio. The silence increased her edginess. Dr. Renner was home. Why wasn't he playing his loud music? After returning the camera to her purse, she noticed that the front of the rosewood secretary had been dropped down to form a writing surface. An untitled book lay there. Curious, she examined it.

A glance into the bookcase showed several empty spaces. There was no sign of the ledger. She reasoned that the doctor had called for his records so he could request certain books. The one on the desk either waited to be taken upstairs or had been brought back because he had finished with it.

Feeling no restraint against examining a volume left in plain sight, Janet leafed through, finding a slip of paper listing the book she held as well as other titles, the doctor's code numbers carefully written next to each. Impulsively, she copied the foreign titles. Although Rose had said that the books were the doctor's text books, the titles might prove interesting if translated.

Twenty minutes later, when she was in the kitchen opening the mineral water, Janet glanced out the window and saw Gina and Pagoda playing. Unmindful of the worsening weather, Gina, wearing jeans and a red slicker, was bareheaded, her dark hair pulled back in a ponytail and tied with the usual red ribbon. Because of the doctor, instead of greeting Gina warmly and spending time with her, she must immediately send her away. Would the little girl understand, or would she feel that once again, someone she trusted had rebuffed her?

Raindrops spattered against the window. Almost at once, the glass was sheeted. Peering through the wavy wetness, Janet could barely make out the cat darting off with Gina in tow. The last glimpse of the red slicker disappeared into the rain as the small figure tore off in the direction of the Stockton property.

With Gina safely away, Janet slipped the strap of her bag, the camera safely inside, over her shoulder and put the tumbler of mineral water and a napkin on a tray and went up the back steps to the upper floor. The silence of the house struck her as ominous as she neared Dr. Renner's room. Standing outside his closed door, she let her bag slide soundlessly to the floor. Drawing a deep breath, she stood like a servant and knocked.

"Yes?" The doctor sounded testy, clearly annoyed at being disturbed. His voice was stronger than she had expected.

"It's Janet Fairweather, Dr. Renner," she said, suddenly timorous. When he said nothing more, she cautiously pushed the door open.

The doctor was seated at his desk, pen in hand. As he peered up through his trifocals, his expression was inscrutable. He wore a rust-colored woolen robe, the long sleeves enveloping bony wrists that seemed as if they could be snapped like matchsticks. Although a lamp illuminated his workspace, his gaunt, cadaver-like face was in shadow. The outline of his head, backlighted by the window, made his skull appear semitransparent and as fragile as an egg. Before him on the desk lay outspread folders. Janet saw he must indeed be reviewing his old patient files. Off to one side was the ledger.

Stepping in, she nervously explained, "Mrs. Renner asked me to bring you this mineral water." Looking for a place to set the tray, she saw a side table with an open book upon it.

Following her gaze, the doctor's face hardened. Quickly, he reached to close the book. It had shown a diagram that Janet had glimpsed, and it was clear that he hadn't wanted her to see it.

Whisking the book away, he directed, "Put the tray here," and gave her a smile that was conspicuously false, his long, yellowed teeth catching the light. From a forgotten fairy tale, silent words popped into Janet's mind: Why, Grandmother what big teeth you have!

She set down the tray, the water and a napkin, aware of the intensity of his stare. It seemed as if the force of his personality was a tangible thing. The atmosphere of the room felt as if it was thickening, making it hard for her to breathe.

"Is there anything else you need?" she asked, looking up, trying not to flinch. When he made no reply, she stammered awkwardly, "If not, then . . . then I guess I'll go."

He nodded coldly and returned his attention to work on his desk.

After closing the door behind her, Janet still found it difficult to catch her breath. She would not have believed she could be so intimidated by the command of a man who was physically frail and infirm. No wonder Muriel showed him such submissive respect.

She lifted her shoulder bag from the floor and was momentarily tempted to postpone the rest of her plan, but then she stiffened her resolve. She was upstairs now. What time would be more fortuitous?

Taking a few steps toward the big window, she paused and looked left and right at the space as big as the entry downstairs and saw nothing that looks odd. But that's why she had the camera, she told herself, to capture more than her eye could see.

With the camera in position, she started to move ahead and was ready to press the shutter when she heard something off to one side and behind her. She tensed and looked back. There was nothing to see. But that sound . . . Was it that breathy rustling she had heard before? That prelude to the whispering voices?"

"And what do you think you are doing, Miss Fairweather?"

With a gasp, Janet whirled toward the voice, the camera clutched to her chest. The doctor stood in the doorway to the master bedroom. The sounds she had heard must have been him moving quietly from his office and through the connecting bathroom to the master room.

"I did not hear you leaving immediately and so I wondered," he explained mildly. To her immense relief, he did not seem angered, only curious. His eyes fastened on the camera.

"Were you perhaps planning to take my photograph?"

"No, no! I just wanted—" Frantically, Janet tried to think of some excuse. She could hardly tell him what she had told Annabelle. Nothing in the upstairs had decorations worth photographing, except the master bedroom, of course, and saying she planned to take photos of such private quarters would hardly get her off the hook.

"The . . . from the window," she stammered, pointing toward it, her shoulder in the general direction of the front window. "There's a good view from here. The trees of the houses across the street, the sky, I thought it might make a pretty picture."

He nodded. "Ah, yes, and a rainy day is so ideal for an amateur to take a few harmless snapshots, isn't it?" Even in biting sarcasm, his tone remained mild. "May I see your camera?"

Wordlessly, she handed it over.

His hands, with their thick, horny nails, turned the instrument as he examined it from all angles as if it were a rare thing. "Pictures of the houses of the people who live across from me?" he questioned.

"Well, not because of they live across from you, it's because . . ." Her words ran out.

He looked at her and waited.

She found herself babbling. "A friend of mine on the newsletter is a photographer and I thought I could take a few shots and she could tell me what was really good. I mean . . ." Her laugh trembled like a thin wire. "Rainy day and all. You're right. Not a good time at all."

He nodded. "Perhaps not the best time, but as good a time as you thought you might get, hmmm?" His smile was almost benign, his tone cajoling. "Who is your newspaper friend? Someone local whom I've met unknowingly, perhaps? And of course, he knows others of his ilk. Journalists, so hungry, sniffing like hounds for greasy tidbits."

"Not newspaper," she corrected, repelled by his description of the press. "Newsletter. The adult school newsletter. News about the night school."

Shrugging as if she hadn't spoken, he returned his attention to the camera. "Made in Japan. I remember a time when all fine optical equipment was from Germany." Shaking his head, he peered at her sadly. "I live in the past," he lamented. "Too much in the past."

As he spoke, he looked so pathetically ill and wasted that Janet wondered how she could have ever found him intimidating. A strange clicking and whirring sound suddenly startled her. Momentarily, she felt only confusion and then she realized the noise came from the camera.

"Oh, no!" she cried, belatedly realizing she was hearing the motor drive. Never having experimented, she had no idea it would be so loud. "The pictures! You're pressing the shutter, the film—" She grabbed for the camera, but he twisted about, holding it from her.

"The film!" she repeated, snatching again for the camera. As the last sound faded, he released the instrument into her hands. She looked at the counter and then gaped at the doctor in disbelief. "You used the film. It's all run-out. Film for twenty-four photo! You used them all!"

"Did I?" He mimicked surprise. "My, my, twenty-four photos of the floor." His lips exposed his teeth in a feral sneer. "I wonder what your newspaper friend will say."

"Not newspaper," she insisted, upset and confused, but sensing that it was important to explain. "The newsletter is only for the high school, for their evening teaching program for adults. It's—"

Her words broke off as she saw that instead of listening, the doctor stared at something behind her.

Thinking that Muriel had returned and had come unnoticed up the carpeted steps, Janet turned from the doctor, but instead of Muriel, she saw pinpoints of light.

An icy fist clutched her stomach as ever so faintly, she heard the whispered chant: "We are ta-ta-DA-da. We are ta-ta-DA-da!"

The sounds breathed seemingly from everywhere, soft sounds and more shimmering lights. She whirled, looking past the doctor and down the corridor to the back of the house . . . shimmering lights were everywhere, behind her, ahead of her . . . With a flickering, misty swirl, one of the lights in the gloomy corner off to the side of the window began to congeal.

All at once, Janet saw the toddler, the small, dark-haired girl, garbed in a shift-like garment. As before, the figure did not seem to take complete form, but then, aghast, Janet saw the reason: the child *was* fully materialized; it was her body that was not complete. One shoulder and arm were perfect, but the other arm stopped at mid-elbow in a bone-jagged line of torn, bloodless flesh. As if aware of Janet's horrified observation, the child turned in her direction.

Janet uttered a choked scream as she saw that one eye, the left one, was wide and bruised. But there was no right eye. There was no right side of her face!

Then, beside the toddler, appeared the little boy. His nearly naked body was not as thin as Janet had remembered, but his bloated belly still gave evidence of malnourishment. Although he stood on both legs, one of them was bent in an unnatural angle, as if it had been broken. No longer crying, his eyes were clear, and his lips moved as if he were about to speak.

More ghost children leaped into view. Youngsters huddled together, some of them holding infants. And all of them were damaged, arms broken, bodies contorted, faces disfigured. Maimed. All of the children were maimed.

And then she heard the chant again, the sounds suddenly becoming clearer: "We are ta-ta-DA-da! We are grow-ing-DA-da!"

Yes, that was it—*growing*. That was one of the missing words! *Growing*. With a sense of benumbed shock, Janet listened, finally hearing the last word, finally hearing the chant in its entirety: "We are growing stronger."

The rhythm steady and unstoppable; the chorus of the phantom children:

We are growing stronger!

We are growing stronger!

WE ARE GROWING STRONGER!

Chapter 30

JANET DIDN'T KNOW HOW LONG she stood transfixed by the specter of the mutilated children, their eerie, otherworldly chanting dinning against her ears. She lost all sense of time. Then, other sounds intruded: a strangled, wheezing from behind her and a thump.

With effort, she tore her gaze from the sight and turned to see the doctor had fallen back against the wall, a feeble hand extended in an inarticulate plea to keep him standing upright. His complexion was bluish, and as she watched, his eyes rolled upward and his legs began to fold.

With no time for thought, she lunged to support him as his body sagged, a dead weight in her arms. His head rolled lifelessly, and she felt a drooling wetness on her shoulder.

He's dead, went through her mind, he's dead from shock. He saw the ghost children and his heart stopped.

With that thought, she managed to look back along the corridor and then to the front again. There was nothing there. Nothing. And, except for her labored breathing, nothing to hear.

The doctor groaned and Janet felt him weakly scramble for renewed footing. With a thick, guttural muttering, he lifted his head and attempted to stand on his own. He looked at Janet without recognition and mumbled again.

"Go easy!" she cautioned, holding him propped against the wall, still certain he had suffered a heart attack. "Don't try to walk."

With surprising strength, he levered his body upright and turned from her. Tottering, he turned and stepped into the master bedroom. She could only hurry along at his side, making sure he didn't fall as he proceeded on through the bathroom, holding onto the door jams as he came to them and finally reaching his office that had become his sick room.

By the time she had assisted him to his hospital bed, the awful blueness had left his face, although he still sucked air in wheezing gasps. As she lifted his feet and pulled a blanket over him, she began to realize his collapse might have only been a faint.

"Muriel . . . my wife, where is she?" he demanded with effort, still viewing Janet without apparent recognition.

It took Janet a moment to get her thoughts straight, to think of people doing ordinary things in ordinary ways. "She's gone to the store," she told him. "She went to buy shoes for Rose."

He stared. "Miss Fairweather? What are you doing here?" His speech was easier now. He lay back against the pillow. For an instant, Janet felt she saw a glint of calculation in his eyes, then it was gone. "I was working at my desk," he said. "At my desk, that's where I was." He closed his eyes, murmuring, "Working at my desk."

Janet realized he was saying he had no recall of finding her with the camera, or of seeing the ghost children. Could that be true? She remembered that momentary glint in his eyes and found herself doubting, but either way, he'd had a shock.

Leaving him, she hurried to the door and stared toward the window. There was nothing to see except rain streaming down the glass. She then turned toward the railed hallway. Nothing. Nothing to be seen in either direction. But there *had* been. Those disfigured forms . . . they *had* been there. And Dr. Renner had seen them too. Whether he was admitting it or not, she became positive that his collapse had been caused by what he's seen.

She heard the front door open. Muriel's voice floated up. Stopping only to gather her bag and tucking in the camera, Janet flew down the front staircase.

"Dr. Renner might be having a little problem," she said to Muriel.

Muriel dropped the package she'd been holding and rushed upstairs.

Hands shaking, Janet helped Rose take off her wet raincoat and guided her into the study.

When Muriel reappeared a few minutes later, she said that her husband seemed to be a bit tired, but otherwise just fine. "He did admit to lightheadedness," she told Janet. "He thinks he may have gotten up too quickly after working at his desk, causing the blood to rush from his head. He thinks he lost consciousness for a minute or two."

Feeling light-headed herself, Janet decided that if that was what the doctor wanted his wife to think, she would go along with it. Saying she was relieved his spell hadn't been serious, she smiled and nodded mechanically as she was shown Rose's new shoes and heard about the shopping excursion. As soon as tactfully possible, she left the house, unmindful that the rain still fell heavily. It was as she crossed the Renner back yard that she began to experience the aftermath of shock.

The emergency of the doctor's collapse had for a time blanked out her reaction to the horrifying appearance of the children, but now, when standing in a world that was so very real, raindrops upon her face, wind singing through the evergreens, that the full impact of the dreadful vision settled upon her.

Swaying sickly, she leaned against a tree, her head spinning.

Children, ghost children. Not two or three, but at least ten or more. Children of various ages. Damaged. Bodies twisted, starving, swollen. Grotesque. Parts missing, eyes gone, limbs broken, torn away. Like the leavings of some hideous accident.

And, what had the chant meant? *Growing stronger.* Growing stronger in number? More children to join their dreadful little band?

Children from where?

From what source had the ghost children been assembled, and why in the Renner house?

Lost in confusion, she leaned her aching head against the tree, heedless of her rain-soaked hair and the rivulets of water running down her collar. She knew Ben was away and busy, but oh, how she yearned for his comfort, to be in his arms. Even if he couldn't help her make sense of what she had seen, she desperately wanted to be with him, to talk with him.

Close to tears, her thoughts spun disjointedly. Good old beech tree . . . She felt the smooth hardness of the wet trunk against her forehead. Safe. So safe under your branches.

Beech tree. *The Beeches.*

She stepped back and craned her head up to see the great branches twisting above her. Slowly, she turned to view the yellow house. Seen through the grayness of rain, everything about it has lost its charm; it had been transformed into a brooding hulk, a witch's house, its gingerbread and sugar masquerade melted away.

The history of The Beeches came to the forefront of her mind, and suddenly, with horror, she knew—

She knew who the children were, and especially, she knew why they made the Renner house their home.

Chapter 31

JANET'S FRANTIC POUNDING BROUGHT KIRBY Orchard to his door.

"Janet!" His round face showed alarm as he stepped back to let her into the tile-floored entry. "You're soaked!"

"The children . . ." She stood dripping, violently shivering. "I saw the ghost children, heard them . . ." Her words ran together unintelligibly.

"It's all right, it's all right," Kirby soothed, patting her arm. Trixie, not liking the commotion, whined for attention and did an agitated toe tap on the tiles.

When Janet, teeth chattering, tried to explain again, Kirby decided, "It can wait. First, get yourself warm and dry."

He hustled her down the hall to the bathroom where he switched on an electric heater and opened a linen closet. "There are plenty of towels. And here, look, a nice thick terry robe. Put it on and leave your wet clothes on that rack and pull it in front of the heater so they can dry." Moving to the door, he went out, taking Trixie, who had tagged along. Over his shoulder, he said, "I'll have a hot drink waiting for you in my office."

When Janet, came into the office, robed with her dark hair still damp and curling tightly about her face, she was calmer, although the undercurrents of panic still ran close to the surface. She told herself that while Kirby couldn't give her the comfort she so desperately needed, he would understand what she had to say far better than Ben. Sitting on the couch, she accepted a hot, rum-laced mug of tea with a trembling hand.

Kirby watched with concern as she tucked up her feet and took an unsteady sip of the tea. "I've just gotten home from a meeting," he said. "Got into as much bad weather as you, but at least I was wearing rain gear."

She managed a weak smile. Seeing she was recovering, he leaned back in his desk chair. "From what you said at my door, am I to assume you've persisted in investigating the Renner house?" His tone was chiding, but gentle.

"Oh, I remembered your warnings all right." She drew a shaky breath. "I also remembered how convinced you are that the apparitions only take the shape of children in my own mind. That's why I went over with a camera, to gain evidence to show to you and Ben."

"You took photos?" Kirby couldn't hide his interest. "They might not show what you hope to see, but still, there are cases where films have recorded unusual signs—"

"No, no," Janet interrupted. "What happened with the camera is another story, but, oh, God! If I'd only had the camera ready when those children appeared."

"You saw them again today?"

"Saw them and a whole lot more. Ten at least, and a number of them were babies." She started to lose control again. "Babies, Kirby, innocent babies! And I heard them . . . that awful chanting . . . Kirby if only you could have been there!"

"Now, now," he soothed, moving his chair closer.

"It wasn't just that there were so many of them, Kirby, it was their condition. This is going to sound incredible, but the ghost children are damaged, mutilated."

Taking a deep breath, she described the horror she'd seen.

"My Lord!" Kirby had gone pale. "I've never heard of anything like that. Never."

She pushed a hand through her hair. "That wasn't what sent me running over here like a madwoman. What happened was, I suddenly realized who the children are." Her voice lowered. "Kirby, they're victims of the house. The ghosts are the captured spirits of children who have lived and died in that house."

He drew back. "Victims of the Renner house? I don't understand. Where did you get such an idea?"

"From the very history we've discussed. I've finally figured out the common denominator among the residents. We didn't think there was one, but there is. Time after time, people have moved in there, and then lost a child. Don't you see? The house lures families, kills their children, and holds fast to their spirits. And I can prove it. Remember the boy I saw in the garden, the crippled boy I later realized must be a ghost?" Her eyes held a challenge. "Think about the last child who lived at that address, the Fiorello boy. What do we know about him?"

Looking pained, Kirby admitted reluctantly, "Timmy Fiorello was crippled."

"And what eventually happened to him?"

Kirby waved in protest. "He died. But the house wasn't responsible. He was afflicted from birth with a muscular disease that progressively worsened. When the family came here, he already suffered from it."

Janet set that objection aside. "The important thing is, the house is where he died. And now it has him forever."

"That's an unhealthy idea, Janet, and totally without foundation. You shouldn't even explore such a notion."

"Why? Because it's so frightening? Ignoring the truth doesn't change things. Think of the family before them, the Mitchums. A child came into the house with them, and shortly thereafter drowned."

"But not on the property, Janet. It was on a school outing, if I recall."

"The child had lived there. It was her home, and when she died, the house had a claim on her spirit." Janet's tone was certain. "And she's still there, along with the other victims. I know it."

Disgruntled, Kirby sat back in his chair. "All right, so two children at that address have died. Children do die on occasion, sad as that fact might be. That hardly means their homes keep their spirits in bondage."

"Oh, but The Beeches is special, remember?" Janet spoke with bitter irony. "Dedicated to the care of children, right? Examine your notes. Back in the 1800s, Elizabeth Parke built it as a home for orphans, a shelter for the lost. Remember how self-righteous and cruel that relative was when writing about her? Elizabeth was an orphan herself, a bastard, despised and scorned in her stringent Victorian world. How she must have suffered! It would be enough to drive her insane, and I think it did. When she died before her house could fulfill the purpose for which it was built, I think she continued her mission from beyond the grave. The house now carries on as she intended, only in a sick, twisted way, because the children it now shelters are ghosts. And for the house to gain them, living children become its prey."

The expression on Kirby's round face was dour. "Even if you're right about Elizabeth being mad, I can't believe it would have the effect on the house that you claim."

Janet put her empty tea mug on the table and pushed it aside. "Can't you? Look at what's happened to the families there. The Hickoks, the very first residents, lost three-year-old twin sons."

"You're claiming they were the first victims?"

"Exactly. And after them, the next family lost a son to a blizzard."

Goaded, Kirby found his notes. "All right, yes. The victim was an Alexander Whitehurst, Jr. But that doesn't mean he was a child. 'Junior' doesn't tell us his age. He could have been an adult."

Janet remained adamant. "And he could have been a five-year-old, gone out to feed his pet pony in the barn. Unable to find his way home in a fierce blizzard, he froze to death before he could be found."

Kirby scrubbed a helpless hand through his scanty fringe of hair. "But you just made that up. We have to deal with facts."

"Facts? Come on, Kirby. The first residents lost two children, the second residents lost one, age uncertain, and the last two families lost one child each. That's four dead children for sure. How's that for facts? Let's look at the other families." Leaping up to see the list, she pointed to a name. "After the Whitehursts came the Goodsmiths. What about them?"

"We don't know if any of their children died or not." Kirby's manner was stubborn. "But there's one thing I can tell you, the people living here when I was a child suffered no such tragedies. Their children were my playmates."

Janet narrowed her eyes. "The Patricks and the Roberts, right?"

"Indeed. As for the family the Patricks bought the house from, the Grangers, we know nothing about them. You may have found a few coincidences, but nothing to build a sound theory upon."

"No? Suppose we take a closer look at the Grangers." She jabbed a finger at their name. "You've written that they lived in the house from about 1910 to 1924. That's not the Dark Ages. Having lived here most of your life, you must know some senior citizen who remembers them."

He thought a moment, then said, "The lady who lived next door to them is now in a nursing home. Nettie Laine. I paid her a visit only a month ago."

"Fine. Give her a call."

The corners of his mouth turned up impishly. "Pretty sure of yourself, aren't you?" He reached for the phone. "Don't be surprised when you're wrong."

Resuming her seat on the couch, Janet folded her arms as Kirby greeted his old friend. After a moment of folksy chatter, he inquired about the Grangers. "Do you recall them, Nettie? I'm researching a genealogy and a question has come up. Would you know if the Grangers had any children who passed away?"

As he listened, Janet saw his face slacken. When he hung up, the eyes he turned to her showed baffled shock. "Mrs. Granger lost a child to diphtheria."

"I knew it!" Janet said in mournful triumph.

"There's more. When the child died, Mrs. Granger was pregnant.

Grief apparently sent her into early labor and the infant died soon after birth."

"Then that baby was one of those that I saw!"

"The thing is, now I remember something else." Shoulders sagging, Kirby drew a heavy breath. "I insisted there were no deaths of children in the families I knew. But, when I was little, the Patrick kids were supposed to get a new brother or sister. I remember Mrs. Patrick looking very fat. Then I was told there would be no baby after all. It didn't mean anything to me then, but now, I realize the baby must have died."

The full implication gripped Janet like a clammy hand. Her voice dropped to a whisper. "Now we've traced two of the infants trapped with the other children in that house."

Kirby mused, "Could they be the ones you've heard crying—" He snapped his lips like a trap, pinching off the words. "Drat!" he cried. "Now you've got me tangled in your yarn!"

Janet leaned forward. "Open your mind, Kirby! What if you're wrong about the children being figments of my imagination? If they exist, they had to originate from somewhere."

"I suppose you have a point," he admitted, then scowled. "I still don't know. As far as I can recall, the Roberts lost no little children. A few years ago, I did hear that the oldest daughter, Meg, had died. But that was the result of an accident in the place where she worked, and it happened long after they left here. She was nearly my age."

Janet speculated, "Maybe she isn't a ghost then, or maybe age doesn't matter. Suppose that what counts is that the house was her home when she was little? Could the house somehow retain a part of her after death? The childish part of her spirit?"

Kirby grunted. "Unlikely, I'd say." He pursed his lips. "You told me that at one time, you were desperately eager to live there yourself. Had you done so, the death of your baby might be another point for your argument. But you didn't move in and your baby died anyway." He hesitated. "Do you believe the house had something to do with your child's death?"

"Becky?" she said, stunned. After a silence, she said, "No! Maybe I was wrong about the house actually killing the children. Maybe it senses those who are doomed. Maybe that's why the house called to me. It sensed that Becky would die." Her eyes grew haunted. "It's hard now to recall my enchantment with that house. At the time, had you told me that the beech tree meant anything bad, I would have been outraged. Clay and I wandered into the rear garden that day. Everything I saw made me feel that the three of us, Clay and me and Becky, had found a place that was rare, magical, and unbelievably beautiful, like in that poem you quoted: some melodious plot of beechen green. I wished the moment would never end."

She clasped her hands, which suddenly felt icy. "But now I know that had I moved in, Becky would have become part of the house's terrible history." Swallowing, she added fiercely, "But I didn't move in, so, thank God, she was at least saved from that."

Kirby searched her face. "You don't feel she's there?"

"As one of the ghost children? No, Kirby—definitely not! Believe me, I would know." After a long, agitated moment, she got herself under control. Her eyes enlarged as a new thought came to her. "Kirby, I think the loss of my desire to live there is significant. Once I no longer possessed a child it wanted, the house no longer tried to attract me."

"You speak as if it has a personality."

"Perhaps through the spirit of Elizabeth Parke, it does."

"What about the Renners? There's your exception to the rule. They have no children."

His comment gave her pause. "Yes, and that's puzzling because he was apparently drawn to the house much as I was." She explained how Muriel had described the doctor's strong attraction. "An obsession, she called it." Thoughts of the camera returned to her mind. "He's a strange man. The reason I wasn't able to use the camera today was because Dr. Renner appeared and stopped me."

"Oh my, how did he react?"

"He had the idea I wanted to photograph him. I've learned he has secrets to hide." Her tone downplayed the awesome force of the man's personality. In some odd way, she felt that to acknowledge his power might pop the cork from a crusted bottle and release the foul, oily smoke of an evil genie into the cozy room. "I found out that Rose and Muriel probably aren't from South America, but from Hungary. For reasons of his own, the doctor has them living a charade. It's a wonder they stand for it. Rose makes no secret of despising him. She spent most of an afternoon trying to discredit him in my eyes, only I never understood what she was trying to get across."

Remembering the book list, she pulled it from her purse. "She insisted on showing me his old textbooks. I thought she confirmed my guess that they were on child psychology, but maybe I didn't understand. I copied down titles. If some are in a different field, Rose might have been trying to indicate he's flying under false colors."

Shoving his glasses into place, Kirby studied Janet's list. He consulted a dictionary for several words, then peered up at her, his expression puzzled. "I suppose these books are indeed in the doctor's line of interest, only they study a peculiar type of abnormal psychology."

"Found in children?"

"Not likely. They're cases in which the victim believes he or she suffers from supernatural afflictions: possession, clairvoyance, thought transference, that kind of thing. Of course, Freud and Jung showed an interest in the occult, so there's a certain amount of tradition for this."

Janet's brows knit. "The doctor had a book in his room that he didn't want me to see. It showed an odd diagram."

"How did it look?"

"Sort of a star, with writing on the various points."

An inspired light suddenly gleamed in Kirby's eyes. He jumped up and pulled a book from a shelf. "Like this?"

She didn't understand his excitement. "Something similar. I didn't see it well."

He showed her the title: *Encyclopedia of Witchcraft.*

Janet's mouth dropped. "Dr. Renner is weird, but not *that* weird."

Kirby spoke excitedly. "Suppose it was the doctor's study of the supernatural that drew him to the house in the first place? He's presumably had his books a long time, so it's not a new interest. Suppose his occult studies enabled him to sense its paranormal atmosphere from the start?"

"You mean his so-called obsession could have actually been intense curiosity?"

Kirby beamed. "Why not? Starting before the Second World War, there was a resurgence of the occult in Europe. It's well documented that Hitler consulted astrologers. There were even rumors that he hoped to tap unseen mystical powers to help him gain world rule. With this sort of thinking in the air, Dr. Renner could have gotten caught up in it in his youth." He waved the book. "I bet he's been going through his books anew in the attempt to understand the aura within the house."

A mental picture of the ghosts came into Janet's mind. Except for the boy who had been crippled, there was nothing in the history of the residents to explain why the children had appeared as mutilated. She winced from the sickening memory, thinking it was almost better to believe that Kirby was right about her perceptions being distorted than to believe what she had seen. Remembering the chant, she realized she hadn't told Kirby that she had finally heard all the words.

"'We are growing stronger,'" he echoed reflectively after Janet had explained. "But whatever does it mean?" His next question echoed the thoughts that had lurked in Janet's mind like loathsome intruders ever since her experience that afternoon. "Growing stronger in what way? And for what purpose?"

Chapter 32

JANET ARRIVED HOME AT FRAN'S AND FOUND her impatiently waiting.

"Lord, girl!" the older woman exclaimed, brushing back her sprayed-high mass of blonde hair in frustration. "I rushed back here early with good news and then had no idea how to find you. When I called Mrs. Renner, she said you had left an hour ago. At that time, it was raining cats and dogs. Where did you disappear to in the middle of a storm?" Not waiting for a reply, she rushed eagerly on. "Just wait till you hear!" She helped Janet slip out of her wet jacket and headscarf, hung them across a chair back, sat Janet down at the kitchen table and excitedly revealed she'd had lunch with Veronica at the Spoon.

Oh, no, Janet thought in dismay, her stomach tightening. Fearfully, she listened as Fran said, "She came in just by chance. I knew Warren had been working on Tommy, so I figured it was time to bring up the subject with her."

Everything discussed with Kirby went out of Janet's mind in the immediacy of the moment. Had Fran unknowingly undone whatever progress Warren had made?

"You told her I want to have Gina?"

"Yes, and I think she was relieved to discuss it. She knows she and Tommy haven't done right by the child. When she told me that they had been reviewing possibilities other than boarding school, I knew that Warren's talking had done some good. She and I talked, and now, just a little while ago, she phoned. She says she and Tommy have definitely decided to make arrangements to leave Gina in your care. I know that Tommy has a lot of contacts and knows how to pull strings."

Janet felt limp with relief. "Oh, Sis, you did a good job." She couldn't wait until Ben heard the good news.

Fran rubbed her hands. "Big sister sure doesn't let the grass grow. They want to settle thing tonight. You shouldn't go alone—Warren and I will go with you."

"Oh, but Ben should be back this evening," Janet said. She hesitated, and then added, "I appreciate the offer from you and Warren, but Ben and I should go alone."

Fran frowned, then smiled and nodded. "You're right," she said, only then, what had been a pleased expression faded. "Jan, am I doing the right thing? I know it's what you think you want, but will it work? A new marriage is one thing, but for you and Ben to take on a handicapped orphan . . . it's not going to be easy."

Lovingly, Janet reached across the table to touch Fran's arm. "It is the right thing, Fran. Not only for Gina, but for Ben and me too."

But despite her gladness, this reminder that Gina was an orphan had her remembering the orphaned Elizabeth Parke and the yellow house. Kirby's contrary opinion hadn't shaken her conviction that its dedication as a shelter for lost children had become horribly perverted. All she had to do was remember the appearance of the ghost children to be sure of that.

What direction might the thwarted desires of the house take with the childless Renners as residents? A horrid question forced its way into her mind: had Gina's frequent visits to the property put her in jeopardy? She recalled that Rose had kept repeating the word, "dangerous." Said it like a warning. Did Rose mean danger from the house itself? A danger for Gina?

She had no more time to mull it over because, to her delight, Ben arrived shortly before dinner. They ended up eating with Fran and Warren and after that, she and Ben went to the Stocktons' home.

"Let me tell you," Tommy said to Janet and Ben as he passed around drinks, "this thing with Gina has worked out beautifully." He spoke as if the idea had been his all along.

Veronica had brought out snacks that nobody needed. The four of them sat on the white couches in the white living room with its arresting sparks of color, while in the background, Whitney Houston softy sang, "Saving All My Love For You."

"After all," Tommy pointed out, "it's hardly as if we adopted her and changed our minds. But even if she's only been a foster child, we still want her to have what's best. I've talked with people. I've given each of you fine recommendations and the agency has given you two its approval."

Tommy reached for Veronica's hand. "We agree that you're the best one to step in and take over for us."

Veronica nodded. "Yes, there's absolutely no doubt in our minds." She then said, "Oh, and congratulations Ben, and best wishes to you, Janet, on your impending marriage. Fran told me all about it." She patted Tommy's arm. "Marriage, it's wonderful. I'm so happy for you."

The following conversation was mundane, and Janet allowed her mind to drift, thinking that Gina had undoubtedly been put to bed already by Ozzie. She imagined the time when the precious job of tucking the child in for the night would be hers.

She thought she heard herself being called. She glanced around, half expecting to see Ozzie, but no one was there.

With everything settled, everyone was finally on his or her feet and Tommy and Veronica were leading them toward the door.

They were in the hallway when Janet felt it happen again. *Felt*, not heard. In some strange way, totally apart from normal conversation, she realized that she had been beckoned.

There came a pattering of footsteps and Gina appeared at the top of the stairs, eyes sparkling. Dressed in a white nightgown, she so resembled one of the ghost children that for a moment Janet felt her heart almost stop. The child danced down the steps and leaped straight into her arms.

"What's gotten into that girl?" Ozzie demanded rhetorically, coming into view upstairs. "I'm sorry, but I thought she was asleep. All at once, she was out of her room and going down the steps."

"Seems as if some little person has been listening to grown-up conversation," said Tommy in a hearty tone. "It's good to know she's happy with this arrangement. Can't blame her for a little eavesdropping."

But Janet, holding Gina close, was aware that there had been no eavesdropping, at least, not of a physical kind. Stunned, she realized that everyone else had been right all along. Gina was indeed mute. That first night, those words: *I heard your baby crying,* had been spoken directly into her mind.

Chapter 33

JANET AND BEN TALKED ALL THE way back to his apartment, and once there, they were so glad to be together again that they went into one another's arms and then there was nothing but the two of them. Afterward, however, Janet lay awake.

Over breakfast, she told Ben what she'd been thinking about in the night. "You've been right all along about the connection between Gina and me." She spoke with wonder, still adjusting to the fact. "Kirby has said that severe shock can enhance psychic abilities, and being caught in an earthquake should certainly qualify. It explains any number of things that have happened to her. I felt something strange the first time I saw her, and then again at the Stockton's party, as if we shared a bond."

Coffee cup in hand, Ben nodded. "I wouldn't be surprised if we all don't have flashes of psychic insight now and then. It probably is a lot stronger in Gina because of being unable to talk, and also there's her need. With the Stocktons as parent figures, she badly needed a loving friend." He picked up toast. "And I guess this also solves the puzzling question of the crying baby. Gina never actually heard it. She simply tapped into your strong emotions at the time."

Janet stiffened. "What do you mean, she never actually heard it?"

"Well, it was just something she picked up from you, right? When you met her upstairs in the Stockton hallway that night, she tapped into your feelings and mistakenly assumed you had really just heard your own baby crying. Your emotions were projected so powerfully that it must have seemed to Gina that the crying was real and that she must have heard it too."

Janet stared across the table at him. "Okay, so Gina thought the crying baby was mine because Becky was so much in my thoughts. But we each heard the crying independently."

"Honey, I really don't think so." His tone was patient. "Remember what you told me, how you felt ill at the Stockton party and started thinking about Becky? You felt depressed and thought you heard a baby crying. When you went upstairs and met Gina, you were in a heightened emotional state. She simply picked up on it."

Janet shook her head. "You've got it backward. The sound of crying came first. I went outside the Stockton house, heard the sound of the baby, and then started thinking about Becky. Besides, I had already heard it that first night at Fran's."

Ben shrugged, obviously wanting to drop the subject. "Either way, it doesn't matter, does it?" he said. "What counts is that Gina will soon be an official part of our lives."

Janet said nothing and he went on with his breakfast until her silence made him look up. That was when she told him what had kept her awake in the night.

"I'm scared for her, Ben." Knowing he didn't understand and resenting him for it even though it wasn't his fault, she tried to keep her voice steady. "If the crying sounds are related to the haunting, the fact that Gina heard the crying means she's in unconscious contact with whatever possesses the Renner house."

Ben looked pained. "Honey, isn't it obvious to you what's really been happening? It's just as Kirby said: the loss of your daughter has gotten mixed up in your mind with the history of the Renner house." His tone became grim. "And a big part of the blame goes to Kirby. I know he's all wrapped up in this stuff, and maybe there's merit in his theory about free-flowing psychic energy. But he should have been able to see that his theories were only encouraging you in the wrong direction."

"Oh, God, Ben, you're so wrong!" Janet cried. "Let me tell you what happened there yesterday."

The retelling of the horrid, second sighting of the ghosts and her dreadful conclusions about them left her exhausted. When she was finished, Ben's reaction was to get up for more coffee.

Feeling resentment, she looked at his broad, muscular back. This was the man who was here for her when she needed him? Feeling abandoned, she stared woodenly as he filled their cups and sat down.

Correctly reading her manner, he reached across the table, his caressing touch offering comfort as well as strength. "I'm trying to understand," he said. "But somehow I got stuck when you started explaining that the house was evil. Even if this Elizabeth Parke person was insane, which nobody can prove, that hardly establishes the house as wicked."

Her hand tightened on his. "Oh, Lord, Ben! People move in there, their children die, and the spirits of the children stay in the house. Children, tiny babies . . . I've seen them, and it's horrible! What more do you need to start looking for evil?"

"I don't know," he said.

The lamp hanging over the table cast solemn shadows under his high cheekbones. She released his hand.

"You sound like Kirby," she said.

"He feels the same way?"

"Just about. Only neither of you can judge because you weren't there. If you had been, you would've realized something unspeakably wicked has afflicted those children. It was as if they were victims of some diabolical creature."

Ben cocked an eyebrow. "Why not a fire?"

"Fire?" She spoke as if it were a foreign word. "Why fire?"

"Because several times you've mentioned catching whiffs of phantom smoke. And you dreamed about a fire."

The dream can back to her, in full. "Yes, there were folders that burst into flames."

"And along with some cribs," Ben said. "It seems to me that nursery beds should symbolize children."

She blinked. "I don't understand my dreams, but Kirby's house research would have shown if there had been a serious fire at the house. Besides, a fire would have only harmed the children of whichever family were resident at the time, but all the children are damaged, Ben, not just one or two."

"I have a tough time believing in disembodied evil. Evil is something that people do. It doesn't exist on its own, as a force."

"Ben, how can you say that? Of course, people may not want to believe in it, but—"

He interrupted. "Actually, I think the vast majority love believing in evil forces. It's a handy scapegoat. But that argument is neither here nor there. Right now, what I'd like to learn more about is Dr. Renner. His dread of photographs and his assumption that you were a reporter makes it sound as if he's hiding something newsworthy."

Janet saw he was angling the subject away from the haunting. Tone stubborn, she said, "One of the things he's hiding is knowledge of the ghosts."

Ben stuck to his own line of conversation. "I never met the man. What's he like?"

Admitting defeat for the moment, Janet answered his question. "Despite being infirm, he radiates power. Even when he's trying to be charming there's a creepy sense of it, and yesterday afternoon, he was downright frightening. It's no wonder Muriel walks the line."

"If she's actually a native of Hungary she has secrets of her own. A lot of things happened during the war," Ben said.

"Fran says the doctor claims he left before the war started."

Ben's expression was skeptical. "He might have fled to Argentina under a cloud, fleeing trouble. For that matter, maybe he didn't leave Argentina so recently because of his health. Maybe somebody found out about him."

"No, he's really ill, Ben."

"You thought he faked that faint."

"No, the faint was genuine. I said I thought he was faking when he acted as if he didn't remember finding me with the camera or seeing the ghosts. Those were issues he didn't want to deal with, so he pretended his memory had blanked out."

"So, we've gone full circle," observed Ben with a bleak smile. "We're back to the ghosts, with you now insisting that Renner saw them too."

"Definitely." Janet stuck to her point. "I also feel Kirby was right about why Dr. Renner bought that particular house. He sensed the haunting and he *had* to move in."

Ben's mouth tightened. "And naturally, he did this because he was compelled by mysterious forces."

Janet glared. "I don't like Dr. Renner. There's something strange and scary about him. But as little as I care for the man, I think I'd get further talking to him than either you or Kirby." She jumped to her feet. "Don't you understand, Ben? Haven't you listened to a thing I've said? The house feeds on little children. Ever since Elizabeth Parke's death, the house has been a mortal danger to youngsters, but never more so than it is today. It's hungry, Ben, hungry and thwarted, because for the first time in generations, the family living in it has no children."

"Honey, listen," Ben said, getting up himself. "Don't you see that you've disproved your own theory? A house that hungry for victims wouldn't settle for anything less than a family with kids. A power to attract should ensure an equal power to repel. If that pile of wood is as conniving as you say, it never would have allowed the Renners to move in. How can you explain that kind of goof?"

Janet bit back a sob. "Ben, can't you see that's what terrifies me? The house made a mistake, but it won't have cheated itself if it can take Gina. If it can somehow draw her in, the house will have its prey after all!"

Chapter 34

HAD IT NOT BEEN FOR JANET'S fears about the Renner house and its threat to Gina, the next few days would have been among the best in her life.

Her new position at the high school had come through and Ben was welcomed by Fran and Warren as a future family member. As for Gina, official regulations went smoothly. Child services people from Edgar's company met with Gina, Ben and Janet at Ben's apartment and approved where the child would live. Then the parties concerned met at Edgar Lightfoot's office. Papers were signed, and Gina became Janet's and Ben's foster child, effective on the date Tommy and Victoria were to leave for Europe. After that, when Janet and Ben were married, the next step would be adoption.

There was a single holdup. Although Janet felt it safest to immediately remove Gina from the vicinity of the Renner house, Tommy, in a trumpery of paternal devotion, had insisted that Gina stay under his roof, until, as stated in the legal agreement: "that sad day, when my wife Veronica and I release her into the care of Janet Fairweather and Benjamin Yates."

He would not be budged from this and what could Janet say? "But

Mr. Stockton, as long as she stays on this block, she may be in danger from the ghost children." She had no doubt that such a statement would have Edgar Lightfoot viewing her with entirely new eyes. "Wicked little ghost tykes, Mrs. Fairweather?" he would say. "Perhaps we should discuss this a bit further before continuing with the proceedings."

And so, although Janet still feared that the haunting might have an adverse influence on Gina, she bit her lip and said nothing.

On the following Monday morning, when Ben was at work, Kirby phoned in a jovial mood. "I knew to call you at Ben's apartment number," he said with a chuckle. "In case you weren't already aware, Princeton can be quite the small town. The grapevine informs me that you and Ben Yates plan to marry and start off with a ready-made daughter. Congratulations."

"Thanks, Kirby. Everything seems to be working out so very well, except—" She hesitated, and Kirby guessed the reason at once.

"Your mind is still on that house?"

With an uneasy laugh, she admitted, "When I heard your voice, I hoped you were calling with fresh information."

"Actually, I've been juggling around the facts we've already uncovered. You know, examining things from a different angle."

Her eyes brightened. "You've found something new after all?"

"If you can call a different approach new, yes."

"Oh." Janet knew what that meant, a new way to persuade her that she should simply erase the matter from her mind.

When Kirby suggested that she and Ben come over that evening for a chat, she begged off, explaining that she and Ben were having dinner together that evening. She was glad for the excuse. The idea of the two men ganging up to "talk sense" into her was more than she could bear.

The call completed, Janet nearly dropped the phone as she went to hang up. Her hand had broken out in a nervous sweat and she realized how much Kirby's words, had upset her. She was suddenly angry. For how long was she supposed to go around with the question of the ghosts unresolved? It was time to find some answers, and if Kirby couldn't help, she knew who could.

Lifting the phone again before she could change her mind, she dialed the Renner number. The one person who would take her concerns seriously was Dr. Renner. He might have his secrets and his frightening manner, yet he had not only witnessed the ghost children, but that book he'd tried to hide from her showed he was making a study of the phenomena.

Determination increasing, she listened to the phone ring. Due to the misunderstanding about the camera, she figured there might be difficulty in getting an interview, but once he understood her mission, he would probably be as eager to speak with her as she was to speak with him. First, she would explain the situation to Muriel. Half the battle could be won, she felt, by enlisting Muriel's aid. As intimidating as the doctor could be, his field of child psychology surely testified to a deep and caring concern for children. Janet couldn't believe he would turn his back once she explained her concern that the house might be a danger for a living child in the neighborhood.

As she had anticipated, it was Muriel who answered the phone. To her delight, the woman was surprisingly receptive to a meeting.

"But let us not meet for lunch," the woman said in response to Janet's invitation. "It would be too difficult with Rose. Suppose we go out in the automobile? Rose always enjoys that." Her refined tone was low and guarded, as if she feared being overheard. "Would it be possible for me to pick you up in about an hour?"

Janet gave Muriel Ben's address, and an hour later, she was climbing into the Renner Oldsmobile. She responded to Muriel's quick, nervous greeting, then looked to the rear to say hello to Rose.

The elderly woman sat with her radio clutched against her black-coated midriff, her eyes as blank and faded as the painted eyes of an ancient doll. She stared out the window, seemingly unaware of Janet or anyone else. A thin wire ran from the Walkman to lightweight, orange sponge earphones, a comical anomaly when compared to that wizened, babushka-framed face.

Muriel eased the car from the curb. "We will park on the main street. Rose can watch the traffic and pedestrians while we talk."

Once again Janet had the feeling that Muriel was as eager for the meeting as she. Puzzling this, she said nothing more as the black car rolled toward the center of town past neatly kept yards and houses, the ride so smooth and effortless that the wheels might have been magically pulled along a predestined route.

Fortunate to find a space on Nassau Street, Muriel parked where Rose could observe patrons bustling in and out of a row of shops. She switched off the engine. Then, with a spasmodic gesture, she switched it on again.

"It is too cold not to have the heater running. It is such a terrible thing to be cold." She fluttered a slender hand apologetically and fell into an awkward silence, staring at Janet with wide eyes that held the expression of a long-caged animal that still had moments of remembered freedom.

"Mrs. Renner," Janet began, but Muriel held up a hand, stemming Janet's words as she spoke herself, reeling out what was obviously a well-rehearsed speech.

"Miss Fairweather, you have been a great help and comfort to me and my sister. We have appreciated your kindness, but Dr. Renner will no longer allow outsiders inside our house."

At the abrupt announcement, Janet stared dumbfounded, able to think of nothing except her thwarted plans. Then, remembering the doctor's reaction to finding her with the camera, she asked boldly, "Does his rule really include everyone, or just me?"

A flush stained Muriel's olive complexion. "He is not well. For no apparent reason, he forbade me to call upon your aid again. I thought it was a whim, but it apparently is not. I felt I owed you an explanation." Before Janet could explain what had happened regarding the camera, Muriel added, "There is another matter we must discuss." The caged look in her eyes had intensified. "Do you remember my complaints about the mischief-makers?"

At this turn of conversation, premonition rippled along Janet's spine. She asked, "The flickering lights, the sounds . . . have they troubled you again?"

"Yes." Muriel's voice dropped to a whisper. "I do not think they are neighborhood pranksters as I once believed." The smooth oval of her perfect face looked carved from marble, beautiful, but bloodless. Her lips barely moved. "I think they are not of this world."

At Janet's gasp, Muriel's eyes sharpened. "Ah, Miss Fairweather, you know of what I speak!" Eagerly, she leaned forward. "This is the other reason I needed to see you. Something incorporeal has possessed my house. You have been there, you know it is true, is that right?"

"Yes, yes," agreed Janet, trembling with relief to know that Muriel was also aware of the ghosts. Here was proof that the haunting existed outside her perceptions. Now, more than ever, it was crucial to meet with Dr. Renner. Perhaps Muriel didn't suspect that her husband was equally aware of the haunting, but once she realized that his occult knowledge might save the children who were under the influence of the house, she would surely arrange a meeting as quickly as possible.

Trying to suppress her excitement, Janet knew it was still important to pick her way carefully. "On the second floor and perhaps also in the back yard," she said. She paused to gauge Muriel's reaction. Then she added, "But especially before that big window in the front."

"And what did you see?" Muriel's gaze, watchful, intense cat's eyes, tiger's eyes, waiting, as if their owner were ready to pounce.

"Children," Janet whispered.

"Yes," breathed Muriel. "Yes, wraiths of long-dead children."

Janet swallowed, knowing there was no reason to hold back any longer. "I saw a small boy, and a smaller girl, along with others." It was morbidly comforting to share the experience. Words burst from her. "Mutilated. The spirit children's bodies were mutilated!"

She expected Muriel to confirm this horror, but instead, she drew back with surprise. "I saw nothing like that."

Janet was confused. "But you must have! The boy was crippled! And the little girl, her one eye was gone, one entire side of her face."

"A bruise perhaps," said Muriel. "A slight bruise on the side of her cheek. But two eyes, definitely, for both shone brightly."

"But the damage was there," insisted Janet, her voice rising. "I saw it clearly. And the other children were harmed as well, even the babies, bodies crushed, limbs torn . . ."

Muriel gave her a cautioning glance. After checking to see that Rose had not been disturbed, she conceded quietly, "There were many children, you are right. In my state of alarm, I did not study them closely. I was too stunned, you understand?" She was clearly reluctant to argue. "The harm you saw, it is possible, only I did not notice. But we can agree we have seen the ghosts of children, can we not?"

"Yes," Janet said. "We can agree."

The air in the overheated car was claustrophobic. Janet wondered how two otherwise sane women could be discussing a haunted house.

A glance from the car window showed a woman with a red muffler and a brown coat emerging from a travel agency. Despite knifelike gusts of wind, her smile was blissful, as if she envisioned herself already off on some tropic holiday. She carried a canvas purse and Janet wondered if there were ticket reservations tucked inside. Oh, if only she could scoop up Gina and run with Ben to some safe and faraway place!

She turned to Muriel. "Did you hear the words the children chanted?"

"I heard rhythmic sounds, but not words."

Janet repeated what she'd heard of the chant. Muriel shook her head. "I heard nothing clearly enough to understand. For what purpose would they increase in strength? Does it mean an increase in number?"

Janet twisted the strap of her purse. " Yes, that's exactly what it sounds like to me." She related the history of The Beeches, telling about the resident children who had died there over the years. She then revealed her dreadful certainty that the misguided wishes of Elizabeth Parke had endowed the house with an evil that distorted the spirits of the young victims it held.

She concluded, "Denied the child of a resident, the ghost children might now seek—" She was unable to voice Gina's name in this context. "They might seek some other child to join them."

Falling silent, she realized that for some incredible reason, Muriel seemed to have been calmed by hearing the history of the house. The tension had eased from her face and her eyes were almost tranquil. Arching a perfectly shaped brow in thought, she asked, "Then this haunting apparently results from a long-existing pattern? One dating back almost to your Civil War?"

"Yes." Janet couldn't understand Muriel's reaction. To her mind, one of the most dreadful aspects of the haunting was that the deaths had continued undetected for so many years.

"Ah, for so very long, over a century." Muriel's sigh sounded strangely satisfied. "No concern of ours then."

Janet couldn't believe what she was hearing. "Oh, but it's very much our concern! There may be some way we can stop the tragedy from ever happening again." Sensing it was the time to put Kirby's theory to the test, she asked urgently, "Mrs. Renner, has your husband ever studied the occult?"

The question jolted Muriel. "Why ask such a question?"

"Because I think it explains why he bought the house. From the first time he saw it, he must have sensed it was haunted. The desire to explore it must have proved irresistible."

Muriel wet her lips as if about to argue, then after a hesitation, said thoughtfully, "You may be right. It is true that he has studied the psychic realm. An interest from his younger days." Her smile was mirthless. "The location of the house was impractical, so far from his physician. Why would he make such a move? But your theory explains the mystery. As you say, it would have proved irresistible."

Encouraged, Janet eagerly pressed on to the moment she had been waiting for. "If your husband has studied the haunting, he may have gained knowledge, even influence, over its powers. That's why I wanted to see you today, to ask you to arrange a time for me to speak with him. He may be able to help me."

"Help you?" Muriel's amused laugh was like an old gate swinging in a lonely wind. "He can help no one, Miss Fairweather. He is beyond help of all kinds."

"You don't understand. It's desperately important that I talk with him. Once I explain—"

Muriel cut her off. "He would not see you. Have I not already made that clear? You, of all people, he would not see." Her tone was adamant. "He is a man with a great need for privacy."

Thrown into confusion, Janet couldn't fathom Muriel's reactions. The woman knew her house was haunted, and certainly could see it held potential danger. Could she be so self-centered that she saw danger only when it threatened her personally? Suddenly furious, Janet wasn't going to accept a runaround. If she had to act tough, that's what she would do. "He needs privacy all right, Mrs. Renner, privacy to keep his secrets! Only some of his secrets are out." Her eyes bored into Muriel's. "For example, you, Mrs. Renner, are not as he claims. He tells everyone you're a high-born South American lady, but that's not so. Your homeland is actually Hungary."

Muriel stared at Janet as if some evil moon had risen and transformed her. "Oh, God," she whispered, clutching her heart. "How did you know? Rose . . . you learned this from Rose!" She gestured in despair. "Her speech is so unclear, and for so many years she has never allowed anyone close to her. Never . . . until you." She reached out, the gesture imploring. "Are others also aware?"

Shaken, Janet decided that the ambulance attendant hardly mattered and that the information was safe enough with Kirby and Ben. "No, I'm the only one." In the face of Muriel's distress, she was ashamed of her ruthlessness, yet determined not to lose her advantage, not when Gina's safety was concerned.

She spoke with a calculation born of need. "Everyone else believes you're from South America, born in Argentina, just as they've been told. There's been no question." Her tone softened persuasively. "But since I've guessed, well, I know there is more to the story."

Janet was thinking that Muriel had no idea how much she knew of their past. She could be imagining anything, good, bad or even worse. Perhaps what was hidden had been a burden to Muriel and unveiling it would be a relief. If Muriel explained the truth about her past, would that erase the reason the doctor had against meeting with her?

She watched as Muriel closed her eyes briefly and then reopened them. "Yes," she said, "I will tell you. It has not been healthy to bury the past, to pretend it never existed. That has been wrong, so very wrong."

Breathlessly, Janet waited to hear more.

Chapter 35

MURIEL AND JANET EACH GLANCED TO make certain that Rose was still absorbed in her music. The old woman's earphones were in position, her faded eyes fixed on the traffic and passersby as if her window were a flickering screen rather than reality.

Assured, Janet and Muriel turned to face one another. Muriel began to speak. A soft radiance suffused her lovely face, her voice holding a faraway tone. "We lived in Hungary, near a city where my father was a professor at the university, but we also knew the country, for our holidays were spent at the villa of my grandparents on Lake Balaton." Her smile was reminiscent. "There, fields of lavender lay full on the hillside. Oh, to smell them again! We were seven, two girls and five boys, Rose the firstborn, I, the last. Pretty bookends, Papa called us. Life has taken its cruel toll, but when young, Rose was pretty indeed, although not in a popular way. Shy and nervous, she felt ill at ease mingling with those her own age. Since there are sixteen years between us, it suited her to occupy herself with me like a mother." She shook her head sadly. "It was to my benefit that she gave me her youth."

The picture Muriel painted of a richly coddled childhood was one that Janet had originally imagined, only in Argentina. Her later notion that they had been from a poor family and the doctor wanted to elevate them by pretending they were from a wealthy family in Argentina was wrong as well. How many other things had she been wrong about? What Muriel was saying now, had to be the truth. Every gesture of Muriel's was to the manor born. An educated father, wealthy grandparents, a child loved, even pampered by an adoring older sister. Yes, it all rang true. How could she have thought otherwise, even for a minute?

"At that time," Muriel continued, "Our nation was caught between the powers of Russia and Germany. Many leaned toward fascism, and in an outbreak of ugliness, one of my brothers and his best friend, who later became Rose's husband, were seriously injured. My father sent them to a trusted colleague to Vienna to recuperate. Rose went along as a nurse, taking me with her. It was there, in the spring, that we met Dr. Renner.

"An acquaintance of my father's colleague, he and his wife were house guests. Even though I was barely on the threshold of womanhood, I was aware of Dr. Renner's particular attention, his gaze constantly fastening upon me. He was extremely handsome, very masculine. Young as I was, I was flattered, and found it pleasing to think that his fair-haired wife, so pink and white and rounded, resented the notice I received." Anxiety darted over Muriel's face as she hastily amended, "You must understand that I imply nothing improper. He rarely spoke to me directly. The most personal moment was when I once overheard him telling my father's friend that I would someday be a lovely woman. That was all.

"Matters quieted at home and by the winter, we had returned. Two years passed, then things changed abruptly. Restrictions clamped like iron. We could go nowhere, do nothing, without special permission. Because of the annexation of Austria, Germany was our neighbor. Their rules became ours. Some found ways to leave, others tried to fight. My brothers and their friend, by then, Rose's husband, were accused of working with the communists. They were taken for questioning and never returned. On her own, Rose, so courageous and resourceful despite her shyness, wrote to Dr. Renner, asking if he might use his influence to help us." Color stained Muriel's face as she added, "She enclosed my photograph.

"If Dr. Renner responded, we did not have time to learn of it, for my father, terrified by the disappearance of his sons and son-in-law, arranged train passage for Rose and me to friends who promised protection. Our parents, my brothers' wives, and their children were to follow the next day. We never saw any of them again.

"Our train was stopped by the Gestapo. Rose and I, along with others, were taken to a small village which had been emptied and given over as a holding place for refugees. There, we were kept for some months."

"Kept?" asked Janet, incredulous. "You mean, like prisoners?"

Muriel seemed amused by Janet's tone. "I do not think you can understand. We were guarded. We had been stripped of everything except the clothes on our backs. The only thing Rose and I had left of value was each other."

Her eyes darkened. "Since the disappearance of her husband, Rose's mind had grown increasingly unsound. In the village, she met a man whom she fantasized was her husband returned to her. She became pregnant but had not yet begun to show when troops arrived. The elderly and the infirm, mothers and young children, were gathered in the square. All those able to work were forced into trucks. The last of us to leave saw the remaining soldiers firing their guns at those huddled in the square."

Ignoring Janet's horrified gasp, Muriel continued, "It was winter. We were crowded into the trucks without food or water or warmth and many died on the way to our destination, including the man Rose believed was her husband. When we had been back in the village, we had heard frightening tales of where people like us might be taken. When the trucks finally stopped, we thought the worst had come true, that we had been brought to Auschwitz."

"Auschwitz?" It was a word Janet had heard, but until that moment it had never seemed real.

This time, Muriel gave attention to Janet's horror. She arched a brow, her smile cool, and blade thin. "Yes. Have I neglected to mention the crime of our little band? Our sin was being Jewish."

Once heard, Janet found this truth also self-evident. There could be no other explanation for the inhumanity Muriel described. In some confusion, she asked, "Then, Dr. Renner . . . is he Jewish as well?"

Muriel's eyes glittered. "He is not. A far different story if he were. Rose and I are both his glory and his shame." Without enlarging on her cryptic comment, she went on.

"We found we had actually been transported to a work camp for a munitions plant. To describe the conditions, I only need say that new workers were brought in daily to supplant those who died during the night. As to Rose and me, our situation became reversed. Although I was fifteen to her thirty-one, I became the senior sister. I managed to help her hide her pregnancy, although it was to no purpose. I had already seen it happen to another woman—there was no time for rest, only for work—she and the child would be destroyed."

Paying no attention to Janet's anguished gasp, Muriel continued. "Then, what seemed a miracle intervened. I was called by name to the commander's office. When he was satisfied as to my identity, he said I was to be moved to a new location. I remember crying that I could not be separated from my sister." She gave her head a helpless shake. "Whatever was I thinking? To imagine anyone would heed my tears! My mind as well as Rose's must have become unhinged.

"The commander laughed and had Rose brought to him. Anyone who really looked at her could see that she was pregnant. I realized my foolish plea had signed her death order." Remembered wonderment crept into her voice. "Yet, within the hour, we were taken to a car. Coats were given to us." Unconsciously, she stroked the coat she now wore. "They were coarse and soiled, but to us they felt like the richest fabric. The vehicle was heated. I had forgotten such luxury could exist."

Breaking off, she smiled strangely at Janet. "You have guessed so many things expertly. Can you guess the name of our savior?"

Janet moistened her dry lips. "Dr. Renner?"

"Ah, yes. But that wasn't really so difficult, was it? I gave you so many clues. Yes, Dr. Renner. He had received Rose's letter, but his inquiries to locate us failed. His interest was piqued and he redoubled his effort. He is a man who dislikes being thwarted. Thoughts of us began to occupy his imagination. Learning our fate had become a quest."

It was clear to Janet that it was Muriel herself who occupied the man's imagination. As Rose had cleverly planned, the photograph had done its work. A lovely child had become a breathtakingly beautiful woman, exactly as the doctor had predicted. He became determined to find her again.

It was a romantic tale, especially when viewed against the backdrop of the brutal Nazi regime, romantic despite his lies about Muriel's background and those of having left Europe before the war.

"The doctor had friends, important connections," Muriel continued her tone now dreamy. "His search was aided by the fact that detailed records were often kept. Eventually, his search was rewarded. Through special influence, he had us moved to the place where he was."

"And he helped you escape the country?"

"Yes, but not immediately. Such things take time. He had to be careful not to arouse suspicion. Getting the proper papers, shipping his books and written records, tying up loose ends, gathering sufficient funds." Muriel's smile twisted as she repeated with irony, "Ah, yes, the tying of loose ends and the gathering of funds."

"And Dr. Renner's first wife?" Janet remembered reading of the bombing of German-held cities. "She died in the war?"

Muriel's shrug was oddly unconcerned. "Much was lost in the war."

Janet frowned inwardly, thinking of Ben's speculations that the doctor left Europe under a cloud. From what Muriel was saying, the doctor fled Germany while war still raged. Smuggling out his belongings, gathering "funds," which Muriel seemed to hint might not be his to take—and probably leaving a wife behind. The doctor's deeds could have won him bitter enemies, enemies who would not, even after all these years, forget.

Still, there was the romance! The influential German doctor smitten by the lovely Jewish girl and she, so adoring of her knight in shining armor. He had not only pried her from the jaws of certain death but was also willing to rescue her demented sister. Muriel must have worshiped him. Yet it was clear her feelings had changed over the years. She gave him care and obedience, yet Janet had never seen evidence of warmth. What had gone wrong?

In some corner of his mind, had the doctor despised himself for loving Muriel? Raised in an anti-Semitic society, his attraction could have been mingled with shame. Also, Renner and Muriel had known virtually nothing of each other before fate and circumstances bound them together. He saw only her physical beauty, while she saw only his power to act as her deliverer. When their illusions faded, there might have been little left to build on. Yet, they had stayed together. Muriel's clothes and jewels showed his continued pride in her loveliness; and if for no other consideration than Rose, Muriel owed him a great debt.

Abruptly, Janet asked, "What happened to Rose's baby?"

Lost in her thoughts, Muriel was startled. Turning her head, she stared blankly out the window. "After its birth, it died. That was the finish for Rose. Her mind became then as it is now."

Janet felt an anguished pang, understanding how destructive the forces of grief could be. Then she reminded herself to fasten her concerns on the living. Enough of old history. It was time to return to her reason for wanting to learn more about the doctor.

Straightening her shoulders, she offered a proposition to Muriel, "I'll hold everything you've told me in the strictest confidence, but I urgently need to talk with your husband. Not about the past. That's private between the two of you and can stay that way. But I need to talk with him about the house and the fact that it's haunted. You said that in his younger days he studied the occult—"

Muriel cut her off. "Yes, long ago. It need not be discussed."

"But it must be!" cried Janet. "We've already agreed it explains his interest in moving into that particular house. Listen, please, I must make you understand. There is a child in the neighborhood, one who has been repeatedly drawn to the property. She—"

Again, Muriel interrupted. "The little girl who has that cat? Such an annoying animal!"

Janet blinked. "Well, yes. The girl's name is Gina, and—"

Her shoulder was gripped from behind. She whirled to see Rose sitting on the edge of her seat. Unnoticed, the elderly woman had stirred, and the earphones now hung loosely about her wattled neck. She leaned forward, her face only inches away.

"Dangerous!" she hissed. "Dangerous." Flecks of spittle landed on Janet's cheek. That knobby, arthritic hand gripped her shoulder with a force that must have been as painful for its owner as it was for the one who was held. "The little girl! If she comes, this time I keep her safe."

Coming to Janet's aid, Muriel tried to loosen her sister's grip. "It is all right, Rose. It is all right."

Succeeding in lifting Rose's hand. Muriel clasped it between the both of hers, gently, tenderly, as if comforting a child rather than a grown woman. "Hush, now, do not worry."

Rose stared at her in blind confusion, peering down the dingy chambers of a long-lost past. "All gone, all gone! They were with us, then they were all gone!"

"Yes," Muriel soothed, stroking her sister's hand. "But now it is all right. We need not worry about them anymore."

"No!" Rose struggled to free her hand. "No, no!"

Seeing that the old woman was on the verge of becoming out of control, Janet quickly spoke up. "Mrs. Renner, perhaps you should get in the back seat with your sister. I'll drive the car to your house. I can walk back from there."

"Yes, thank you," the woman said gratefully, and did as Janet had suggested.

Janet soon pulled the vehicle to a stop before the front door of the yellow house, Rose had quieted. Muriel, who had been crooning to her in a foreign tongue, allowed Janet to assist them from the car. Then, at the front doorway, she said in a dismissal that was distracted rather than rude: "Thank you, but we are all right now," and proceeded to take Rose into the house.

Helplessly, Janet watched the door close behind the two figures. Feeling upset and frustrated, she returned to Ben's apartment. But no more than twenty minutes later, Muriel phoned.

Without preliminary, she said, "Miss Fairweather, I have been giving thought to your concerns. It may be possible that my husband might be persuaded to speak with you after all."

"Oh, Mrs. Renner, thank you!"

"I promise nothing," Muriel said quickly. "It will be no easy task. As I have explained, his mind is most set against you. If you desire this meeting, you must be patient. Can you be that?"

"Yes, of course. But—"

"Good. I cannot talk further at this time. I will do my best. Please, I beg of you, be patient."

The phone clicked softly in Janet's ear as Muriel broke the connection.

Chapter 36

THAT EVENING, JANET EXPRESSED DISBELIEF when Ben led her into The Black Swan, the most elegant of the restaurants housed in Scanticon, Princeton's renowned Danish hotel and convention center. "We're having dinner here? Did you come into an inheritance? What's the special occasion?"

He grinned. "Wait and see."

"Give me a hint at least." Was she dressed up enough for this? She wore a green plaid jumper over a white sweater. Ben wore a tan suit with a black and brown striped tie and a white shirt—the same thing he might wear to work, but a man in a suit and tie always looked dressed up.

"Well," he said, "this isn't the main reason, but from the way you sounded earlier over the phone, I felt we needed something extra special to fortify us when you tell me the details of your meeting with Muriel."

The formally garbed waiter ushered them into the red and black dining room where the centerpiece on each table was a tall crystal vase of cut tulips, the velvet-black stamens dramatic against the scarlet petals.

"Oh my goodness," Janet exclaimed. "Tulips in November!"

Ben smiled. "A special night for a special lady. Now, here's the main reason we're here. When I was away overnight, I was close to where my mother's sister lives. I stopped to see her, and she already knew about our engagement, thanks to my parents."

Janet nodded. She had already spoken to Ben's parents in Florida over the phone. They were planning to visit New Jersey and meet her before the wedding.

"In talking with my aunt, she learned you don't have a ring yet," Ben said. "So, my Aunt Norma told me that when my grandmother died, she and Mom divided her jewelry, and my aunt had their great grandmother's engagement ring, passed down in the family. She said that since you didn't have a ring yet, I could give this to you, and it's yours--even if you want a different engagement ring."

"A family heirloom?" Tears came into her eyes. "Oh, Ben!"

He reached across the table to touch her hand and then he took a small jewelry box from his pocket, opened it and handed her the ring.

She could only gasp in delight. She's seen many engagement rings with big flashy diamond solitaires, but this was far lovelier to her eye, a modest diamond with three smaller diamonds and three smaller emeralds arranged evenly around it.

"Your eyes are hazel," Ben said, "but sometimes in the right light, they look green. The emeralds seemed right for you."

"Oh, and it looks as if it fits. Here—" She handed it to him and extended her left hand. "Try it and see."

He slipped it on her finger. "Perfect," he said. "Officially engaged." He smiled with pleasure. "I'll order champagne to go with our double celebration: being engaged and having Gina join our family."

A few of Janet's tears did fall then. She patted them away, and then they simply clasped hands across the table and gazed into one another's eyes until the waiter appeared.

After ordering, Ben said, "So now, let's hear about your afternoon with Muriel." He smiled. "Afternoon with Muriel. It sounds like a soap opera. Did you talk about ghosts?"

"Yes," Janet said with a little laugh, "Actually we did, but that isn't what I wanted to tell you about."

She supposed he should know that Muriel had confirmed the presence of the ghosts, but she wasn't going to press the point. Muriel's promise to arrange a talk with Dr. Renner had lifted a weight from her. Dr. Renner not only knew about the ghosts, he also might have some way to exorcise their threat. At the moment, whether or not Ben truly believed in the haunting no longer seemed so important.

"Well?" Ben said with a smile.

"Okay, yes, Muriel said she's aware of the ghosts. They're there, whether you and Kirby believe me or not."

Ben frowned. "Okay, so something in that house is strange. I guess I can't argue with that. I mean, I believe such things might be possible. But did you and Muriel actually see the same things?"

"She did say 'children' without any prompting from me, but there's no way we can settle it either way, so let me tell you about the things Muriel and Rose experienced during the war. It was horrible, and I'm sure there was more that she left out."

"How did the war touch them in Argentina?"

"That's part of the story," Janet said. Their food arrived. Once the waiter had departed, Janet related Muriel's story, ending with, "It's a wonder any of the survivors found the courage to live again. And you were right about Dr. Renner having reasons for hiding. Maybe 'Renner' isn't even his real name."

Ben said, "If he's Herman Renner, Viennese child psychologist, his professional credentials are in order."

Janet's eyes widened. "You checked on him? What did you find?"

Ben looked pleased with himself. "Nothing except that he's who he claims to be. Which still means he could have loaded a Swiss bank account with stolen funds and knocked off his first wife before leaving Europe."

"Ben!"

"Ben!" he mimicked good-naturedly. "Think of what Muriel told you: the last thing the doctor did before leaving Germany was to tie up loose ends."

"Murdering a wife could hardly be described as *tying up loose ends*. Muriel couldn't have meant anything like that."

"Are you so sure? I get the impression she drops veiled hints instead of saying things straight out. The way the doctor reacted when he found you with that camera proves he's guilty of something."

"Oh, yes, about the camera. I had intended to tell Muriel about that, but it was forgotten when Rose became so upset." She knew she was returning to the subject of the haunting, but she couldn't help herself. "Tomorrow, I'm calling and explaining my real reason for having the camera. Once Muriel tells Dr. Renner I was after pictures of the ghosts, it should make it a lot easier for her to persuade him to see me."

Ben looked up from his steak au poivre. "I wish you'd stop thinking that Gina is in danger."

"I don't want to, but today is the second time that Rose gave me a warning."

"Honey, the woman's mind isn't sound. She probably has Gina mixed up with someone from her past." His tone was persuasive. "It doesn't matter what's happening in that house, whether it's haunted or not. By next Tuesday, Gina will be ours. She will be in our apartment, sleeping in the room we're fixing up for her, blocks from the Renner place. Only a week more to wait."

"Eight days," Janet corrected, but privately, she admitted that he was probably right about Rose. The woman was hardly what she would call reliable. Thoughts veering off, she thought of how Edgar Lightfoot had reviewed agency medical reports, giving the opinion that Gina should someday speak normally.

Looking at Ben, Janet said, "You know, when I was talking with Edgar, I realized that even though I kept insisting that Gina had spoken, I never once tried to coax her into talking to me again."

"I figured you felt it best not to pressure her."

"I guess that's what I told myself, but I think I feared proving she really couldn't do it. But now, I've brought up the subject with her. I've told her that someday, the words will just start popping out. She hates being different—she wants to be able to join in with the other kids.

But I also made it clear that no matter what happens, she's okay in my book."

"Did you make any mention of communicating without words?"

"I doubt she realizes it happens. Or perhaps she assumes it's an ability everyone possesses. I don't understand enough about it myself to attempt a discussion." Strain came into her voice. "I don't understand any of this, Ben. Don't you see that's why I want to talk with Dr. Renner?"

Ben's ruggedly handsome face reflected sympathy, yet his answer was emphatic. "No, I don't see. This very moment we're sitting in a restaurant located on grounds belonging to Princeton University, a world-famous institution of learning. The Forrestal Research Campus is here, packed with engineers and scientists. Then there's all the other University schools, plus the Institute for Advanced Study—that's where Einstein was, for God's sake. If you want to investigate, Kirby Orchard could probably find you scores of people who know more about the supernatural than Renner ever dreamed of."

"But they wouldn't know about the haunting, Ben. They wouldn't know about that particular house."

"And you think that paranoid bigamist does? The house may be disturbed, but I doubt that the doctor or anyone else has power over it. Nor do I believe that ghosts have powers over the living. I admit there may be something odd about the number of resident kids who have died there, but Gina's occasional romps in the yard don't put her in that category. You're worrying for nothing."

Expression suddenly contrite, he reached over to place his hand gently upon Janet's, his gray eyes showing love and concern. "Honest, I'm not making light of your concerns, but I don't believe there's any reason for them. Now, how about finishing your shrimp Copenhagen and then let's have a look at the dessert menu."

****

The next day when Ben was at work and having heard nothing more from Ida about the job, Janet phoned Muriel to explain why she had taken a camera into the house.

Muriel was silent a moment, then: "Ah, yes. Now I understand. I will explain this matter to him. But he must be in the proper mood before I make the attempt. Do you understand?"

"Yes, but you will explain?"

Muriel's response was testy. "Have I not told you so? Again, I ask you to be patient."

Not satisfied, yet feeling there was nothing else she could do except trust the woman, Janet tried to turn her mind to other matters. Even though there was no word from Muriel during the rest of the week, everything else was going so smoothly that almost despite herself, she began to relax.

Saturday morning, she and Ben drove to the Quaker Bridge Mall and shopped for kitchen items she would need for cooking in his kitchen, plus extra linens for the bathroom and master bedroom and two rugs. They also purchased furniture for Gina's room. Janet looked ahead to future shopping with Gina, deciding together on a color scheme and then choosing the paint, the wallpaper, curtains and other items.

The store windows in the mall were decorated for Thanksgiving, with displays of squashes, apples, and nuts spilling in abundance from giant cornucopias. Eagerly, Janet found herself looking forward to the first holiday meal that she, Ben and Gina would share as a family.

Ozzie, who was to continue living at the Stockton house until it was sold, was delighted with Ben's and Janet's plans to continue having her remain a part of Gina's life, like a part time nanny. She would be there for Gina after school before Ben and Janet came home from work.

On Saturday afternoon, Janet and Ben brought Gina to see the room in the apartment that would be hers. Ozzie had brought over some of her clothing to hang in the closet and put in the drawers, so it would show her it was her new home. A book shelf held newly purchased books, toys and games that Ben had selected. Gina looked around the room, sat on the bed, and then went to the bookcase. She touched and played with everything, but settled for the longest time playing with a farm set with a barn and smaller buildings and plastic animals: cows, pigs, a horse, a dog, and chickens.

Two hours later it was time to take Gina back to the Stockton house so Ozzie could get her ready for dinner with Veronica and Tommy.

The toys you selected were perfect," Janet told Ben later. "Especially the barn set. I wonder if there were farm animals where she lived in Italy."

"I wondered the same thing when I picked it out, but she seemed to like everything." He grinned. "Maybe I'm an expert in eight-year-olds. The presents I mailed to my nephew on his eighth birthday made a big hit too. When Gina gets me for a father, she's getting someone with a proven track record as a gift selector. And you selected the doll. She played with the toy animals, yes, but she kept the doll in her lap."

"She did, didn't she?" Janet said, pleased. "Mothering a little doll."

"And soon she'll have her own mother, you," Ben said.

"Mamma Mia," Janet said, laughing as she thought of the ABBA song of the same name, She wrapped her arms around Ben's waist. "Oh, Ben, I love you. To think I ever worried I'd have to choose between you or Gina."

He held her close. "The two of you are a package deal. I couldn't ask for anything more." He hesitated, then added, "Except, maybe someday, a baby brother or sister for Gina?"

"That sounds good, Ben," she said softly, knowing that she no longer feared the slipping away of the past as she began her new life. "That sounds perfect."

Although Gina couldn't be with them on Sunday, it was yet another blissful day: going over to have dinner with Fran and Warren and the families of two of Warren's married children. All in all, perfect days, a perfect weekend, thought Janet.

That evening, she fell asleep with nothing except good thoughts on her mind. As she started to dream, it first seemed an extension of her contented mood. She and Gina and Ben were walking through the mall, looking at the rich heaps of produce in the Thanksgiving displays. In her dream, she turned to speak with Ben, but he was gone. Gina and all the other shoppers were gone as well. Janet found herself alone before a window that showed a cinder-block wall. In front of it were crates of turnips and cabbages, and a wheeled cart heaped high with knobby, orange-red squash.

Strangely fascinated, she moved forward. Abruptly, she was on the other side of the wall and inside a crude room. As a hint of sulfurous smoke curled from a secret corner, Janet saw that the room was filled with children in their cribs. They slept restlessly, the night broken here and there by a plaintive cry.

Like my dreams, Janet thought, knowing even as the thought formed that this was also a dream. The nursery, the children's restless cries, the smoke . . . all from her dreams. She sensed that something bad was about to happen, something her other dreams had warned her about, something terrible . . .

The force of the explosion slammed into her like a fist, numbing her, turning her into stone. With a thunderous roar, a corner of the room collapsed. Trapped in their cribs, the children screamed. Aghast, Janet watched helplessly as the ceiling fell, timbers and rubble tumbling down upon the victims of the nursery, tearing flesh, smashing bone, caving small skulls.

Where are their mothers? a voice inside Janet shrieked. Why don't they come to save them?

Flames leaped with a deafening roar. Through the exploded wall spilled the orange-red globes of squash, rolling and smashing into the thick of the fire, filling the air with the pumpkin-like stench of the burning squashes.

Where are the mothers?

A searing light erupted. All went dark.

There was only the dark, the acrid smoke, and the fading screams of dying children . . .

Then all was silence. Silence as deep as a grave.

Janet slept on.

In the morning she awoke with a vague sense of unease. I must have dreamed, she thought. Not a dream, a nightmare. Lying in bed, she tried to recall what it had been. Then she remembered Ben saying that it was probably best to allow troubling dreams to lie undisturbed.

Ben's right, she said to herself as she arose. There was only one more day to go before Gina officially became her child, and she didn't need the worries of mysterious night phantoms. As she dressed, she decided that Ben was right about a lot of things. Whatever went on at Renner property had nothing to do with her, or with Gina. If she wanted to concern herself with the welfare of its future residents, she would have plenty of time for that after she heard from Muriel.

Later that day, Kirby phoned to suggest that she and Ben drop over later that evening for coffee and or a drink. Janet recalled that his previous invitation had been to discuss the Renner house. She figured this was the same—the rotund little man parading forth additional reasons as to why the Renner house couldn't possibly be haunted, which would be what Ben wanted to hear.

In an indulgent mood, she gave in. "All right," she said. "Ben and I will drop by."

She was thinking that even though Kirby was all wrong about the house, he had been a good friend. Since he really seemed to want this meeting, it would do no harm to go along.

Chapter 37

ON THEIR WAY TO KIRBY'S THAT evening after supper, Janet was on cloud nine, able to think of little except the fact that by the next morning, Gina would officially become theirs. Even the unexpected call from Ben's boss, which meant he would have to leave soon for an evening meeting, didn't take the shine from her evening.

Mischievously pressing against him as he rang Kirby's doorbell, she said, "I've got your number, Ben Yates. Last week it was dining at Scanticon and this week it's a quick bite from a neighborhood deli. Now you claim you have work to do and leave me at the house of another man. Clearly, you've grown bored and you're trying to let me down easy."

Laughing, Ben gave her a hug. "Gosh, and I thought I was being subtle."

When Kirby answered the door, Ben explained why he wouldn't be back until later. "I hope I won't be long, but you know what meetings are like. I'll be here as soon as I'm able."

"Don't hurry on our account," Janet purred sweetly. "Kirby and I get along just fine."

Looking at the other man, Ben shrugged helplessly. "She's been a handful all evening. For dessert, she wanted pickles and ice cream."

Kirby beamed. "Oh, yes, Janet—tomorrow you become Gina's mother. Are you all going with the Stocktons to see them off at the airport?"

"No, we will meet them at their house early tomorrow before the limousine picks them up. We'll say our goodbyes and Gina will become part of our family." Joy sang through her voice.

After Ben left, Kirby said, "Did you already have dessert?"

"No, there wasn't enough time." Janet giggled. "And even if there had been, I wouldn't have had pickles and ice cream."

"I have some cake I think you'll like," Kirby said. "Go into my office and take your coat off and I'll bring it in."

Kirby appeared with slices of chocolate cake topped with vanilla ice cream. Not until they had finished eating and he'd returned the dishes to the kitchen did he sit down and bring up the subject of the Renner house.

The expression on his round face earnest, he said, "I told you over the phone that I had a new slant, a different way to interpret the deaths of those children. I think we looked at things from the wrong angle."

Settled comfortably on the couch, Janet was so confident she could anticipate what he was about to say that she decided to beat him to it. "During the past few days, I've decided just about the same thing," she said brightly. "Regardless of what's happened over the years at that house, or what's there now, it has nothing to do with me, or Gina. You tried to convince me of that and so did Ben. Finally, I've accepted that you're both right."

"Oh, my." Kirby pursed his lips. "I feel like I'm in an O'Henry story—the one where she sells her hair to buy him a much needed watch chain, while he sells his watch to buy her combs for her lovely long hair."

Janet frowned "What do you mean by that?"

"I mean is we may have been working at cross purposes." He shifted his bulk in his chair. "First, I owe you an apology. I finally reached the electrician, and you were right. There's more to the haunting than just your own perception of it."

She was suddenly wary. "You're saying he saw the ghosts too?"

"What he had was a strong feeling of being watched. He said he kept going to the hallway outside the room in which he was working, and on each occasion, he felt he had just missed a glimpse of some movement out of the corner of his eye. He also complained of hearing sounds. He described them as being very faint. Similar to singing without actually being a song."

"You mean the chanting." Her voice was flat. This wasn't what she had expected to hear, and it certainly wasn't what she *wanted* to hear. Not now, not when she wanted to devote her attention to joyful matters.

"Yes," Kirby said. "I asked him if it could have been a chant, and he agreed that it might have been."

Reluctantly, Janet asked, "What did he see?"

"Apparently nothing meaningful." Kirby adjusted his glasses. "Or maybe he didn't want to admit what he really saw. He did say that if he were his Irish grandfather, he would think the house bewitched by wee folk. That means fairies, of course, but I suppose he could also have meant ghost children."

Janet's lighthearted mood had fled. "That's what he meant, all right," she said. "I haven't told you—I didn't think there was any point, but Muriel has seen the ghost children too."

"And you kept quiet because you didn't think I would believe you," Kirby said.

"And you wouldn't have," Janet said. "And when I told Ben, he seemed to think Muriel and I were trading hallucinations." Distraught, she put a hand to her head. "I don't need this. In the past few days, my fears have seemed to evaporate. I felt critical of Muriel because she wasn't concerned enough about the haunting, but now I understand. She has enough concerns in real life, and so do I. All I want to think of is having Gina, getting married to Ben, and being happy and now...." On the verge of tears, she became furious.

"Why did you stir this all up again, Kirby? Okay, so the ghosts exist apart from my own imagination. Terrific. I knew that all along. But it doesn't matter. Whatever is or isn't in that house, its influence doesn't extend beyond the property. That's what counts with me."

Kirby leaned his portly body forward. "But the last time we talked, you were concerned over a possible threat to Gina. My new understanding of the haunting should relieve your fears."

"I no longer have those fears. And even if I did, my worries will be over by tomorrow morning when Gina joins Ben and me. Regardless of the powers of the ghost children, she will be safe. There's nothing more to discuss."

"I think there is," Kirby said. "Are you going to feel comfortable taking Gina to visit your sister when it's so close to the Renner house? Will you have a secret dread that the hours Gina has spent in that yard have harmed her? I want to dispel those anxieties." He paused, then dramatically intoned, "Janet, I hope to prove to you that the influence of the house is not evil, but good." He handed her a sheet of paper. "Take a look. Listed in order, those are the names of the resident children who have died."

Janet wished she could refuse the list, but she couldn't; the subject had been important to her for too long. A new entry seemed to leap from the paper at her. "What's this?" She pointed to the dates after a name. "You now have the age of Alexander Whitehurst, Jr.—dead at twenty-three. How did you discover that?"

Kirby couldn't restrain his cherubic grin. "Played a hunch. I looked in the graveyard of Faith Chapel. The Whitehurst plot wasn't too far from the burial place of the Hickok twins. Young Alexander was born in 1865 and died in 1888. If you look further down, you'll find something additional about the Crammer family."

Janet gasped. "They lost a daughter? But weren't they people you knew? You told me they had never suffered a loss."

"I never knew about it. The girl was born with problems and never mingled with other children. The family moved there when she was young and left after she died somewhere late in her teens.

It all happened when I was away. I don't recall ever knowing she existed."

Janet stared at the list another moment, then looked up, her hazel eyes wide and shocked. "The Goodsmiths lost a child too?"

"A fully grown daughter, a widow who died during childbirth. Her infant, also a girl, thrived under the care of her grandparents at The Beeches and eventually married a senator from Virginia."

Janet was aghast. "Regardless of age, the Goodsmiths lost a daughter. That means that every family who ever lived at The Beeches lost one or more children. Every single family!" She was horrified. "And to think you said you'd discovered no new information."

"Had I revealed this to you without having time to explain the interpretation, you would have become upset."

She jumped to her feet. "And I'm not upset now? God, Kirby! Child after child, lured to that wicked house!" She brandished the paper. "Everything I worried about, everything you tried to convince me didn't exist is true. And there's no longer any guessing—here's the proof!"

Kirby remained as unruffled. "Proof of certain deaths, but not necessarily of youngsters. What family doesn't have members who have died? And in any case, where is the proof that the house is wicked?"

"Isn't that self-evident?"

"No, it is not, and if you'll sit down again, I'll explain."

Sitting, she looked at the list again, her face pale. "You thought this would relieve my mind? Incredible!"

He leaned back in his chair, folding his hands across his stomach. "You were the one who gave me a clue as to what the truth might actually be. That, along with a reading of the letters written by Elizabeth Parke."

"I thought the letters you had were about Elizabeth. Written by a disgruntled relative."

"Yes, by one made angry because she spent her father's inheritance building the house she called The Beeches. If you think back, you may remember feeling sympathetic toward Elizabeth. The idea that she built a home to shelter children who needed help appealed to you."

"That was before I realized she was dangerously demented. Before

I realized the house had become a torture chamber for the spirits of the children who died there."

"And did you believe the house actually killed them? Think back, now. Remember how you reacted when I asked if you felt the house was responsible for your own child's death?"

"I know what you're talking about, but I don't see the point of quibbling. I decided the house didn't murder the children outright—it sensed children who were doomed and drew them in by making their parents want to live in the house."

"Exactly. You said you felt that's why you initially found the house so appealing. You said the house sensed that your baby would die and it 'called' to you."

"So? What really counts is that once the house had those children, it wouldn't let them go. And what does any of this have to do with letters written by Elizabeth?"

Grunting as he reached over, Kirby passed an opened book across the desk to her. "Elizabeth had a friend named Thelma Flock. This is a collection of records from the Flock family, which includes letters written by Elizabeth. In them, she comes across as a kindly, compassionate woman with deeply felt spiritual values. She wanted her life to count for something good."

"When she was young, sure, but that doesn't mean she didn't become crazy and vicious when old."

"She never had the chance to grow old. She died of influenza at the age of forty-two, the same year in which one of her letters is dated. Elizabeth wasn't demented. The woman in those letters was incapable of creating the twisted legacy you ascribe to her."

"Then why all those dead children?"

"In part, you've already stumbled upon the answer. The house that Elizabeth built has the power to recognize children in deeply troubling situations. It may lure their families, yes. Beckon them, seduce them, if you will, but for a good purpose: to ensure happiness for the children, to bless their lives."

After a hesitation, he said, "Janet, I know nothing of your past other than the loss of your infant daughter and that your marriage ended in divorce. When you first saw the Renner house and wanted to live there, was your marriage secure, or did it need healing? Would it have provided for Becky the nurturing necessary for her happiness? Remember how you described your feelings as you stood on the Renners' property? You felt surrounded by something rare and magical, that it was a moment of unbelievable beauty."

Remembering, Janet felt a lump in her throat. Reliving the experience, she whispered, "Yes, I said that the moment was perfect. Perfect. I said that I wished it would never end."

"If your husband was with you, did he sense it too?"

"I think . . . Yes, Clay responded, I'm sure of it. For just that moment, yes."

Kirby spoke softly. "As I thought. And I believe that transcendent moment existed because of Elizabeth Parke's determination that the house be dedicated to the welfare of children. It reached out to you because of an unhappiness it wished to heal." He pointed to the list Janet still held. "The Beeches sheltered those children, my dear. Whether their time on earth was measured in months, days, or years, their childhoods were made beautiful. And I think I can prove it."

Janet's emotions were at war. On one hand, she vividly remembered the feelings of warmth which seemed to emanate from the house, yet the hideous conclusions she came to later were equally as vivid. She stared blankly at Kirby's posters, seeing Shirley Temple curtsy prettily, and King Kong staring in bafflement at a miniature Fay Wray. Stiffening her spine defiantly, she said, "Okay, let's hear this oh-so-convincing proof."

Kirby was undisturbed by her skepticism. Calmly, he said, "The last child who died here was Timmy Fiorello. I knew the family, and I can tell you that when they moved in, Timmy was the most unresponsive eight-year-old you could hope to find. He never smiled, he never showed interest in anything. Then, he began to change. Ask your sister, if you doubt me. His physical condition didn't improve, but his attitude did. On more than one occasion, I heard his mother speak of it as a miracle, for while living in that house, ill as he was, crippled as he was, Timmy became a happy child."

"And you're giving the house the credit?" Janet demanded.

"Yes, because Timmy is not the only case. The little girl who later drowned, the relative the Mitchums took in, is another. She came from a neglectful background, a child virtually raised on the streets. Eleven years old when orphaned, she already had a history of being in and out of foster homes and shelters for playing truant and shoplifting."

"At age eleven?"

"Yes, so the Mitchums were prepared for trouble. Only it didn't happen. The child responded beautifully to her new environment, did well in school, and made many friends. There were never any difficulties."

"Obviously, it was the Mitchums themselves who made the difference."

"Exactly the point: when the Mitchums first moved in, they had short tempers and exacting expectations for their children. Had they still been like that when taking the little girl, there would have been trouble, I'm certain. As it was, they seemed to have learned patience and understanding. The conflicts ceased. Their own kids turned out fine. They're all grown now and leading good, productive lives. By the time the little girl entered their household, the Mitchums knew how to provide the environment she needed. I'm giving the house the credit, yes. And then there's the case of Dorinda Crammer."

Janet held onto her resistance. "The Crammer girl? I thought you didn't even remember her."

Kirby wagged a sausage of a finger. "Ah, indeed, I didn't remember. It was my old friend, Nettie Laine, who told me the story. After our recent conversation, I paid her a visit at the nursing home and quizzed her about everything she could recall of folks who had lived at The Beeches. I learned that there were many troubled children there whose futures turned out surprisingly well. For example, one of the Granger young cousins, might have ended up in jail had not his aunt and uncle not taken him to live with them at The Beeches. He straightened out, and now he's retired after a long and successful career as a lawyer. She also told me about Dorinda Crammer."

"And Nettie claimed the house cured the girl, right?" scoffed Janet, folding her arms.

Kirby smiled. "Not exactly. She said that when the Crammers moved in, Dorinda was afflicted with violent spasms. She had suffered brain damage at birth that resulted in episodes in which she behaved like a wild animal, throwing herself against the floor, kicking, biting, and screaming.

"Because she was young, her parents could physically control her during these emotional storms, but they knew that when she reached her teen years, only drugs could prevent her from harming herself or others. But, from the time they moved into the house, Nettie says Dorinda improved. Against all the expectations of her doctors, the number of spasms and their violence lessened. After a few months, they ceased altogether.

"Dorinda was never a normal child. Her mind wasn't right, and she had severe respiratory difficulties. She was never able to withstand the excitement of playing with other children or going into public situations, but in the familiar surroundings of her home, she was at peace. She was, until the time of her death from pneumonia, a serene and contented individual."

Kirby tapped his balding head. "Nettie called the beneficial changes in the girl 'miraculous.' I started thinking. What happened to Timmy Fiorello had also been called a miracle, and perhaps the changes in the Mitchum family were miraculous as well. I began to see the house in a new light. Yes, some children who lived there died, but many others went on to enjoy full, productive lives. There is great evidence of happiness and emotional healing. Whatever the explanation, the way life changed for so many children and their families seemed a fitting tribute to Elizabeth Parke's intentions when building the house."

Gazing at Janet, he said gently, "That's what I hoped to make you see—not only does the house hold no dangers for you and Gina, but that its history speaks of beauty rather than ugliness."

Janet looked away. She knew Kirby was trying to be helpful, yet everything he said increased her turmoil. She wondered what Ben would think about Kirby's theory. Sneaking a look at her watch, she wished he would hurry and rejoin them.

Shifting restlessly, she said, "Kirby, the trouble with your idea is that it ignores a very important point about the ghost children. Remember how I described them? Their bodies were torn, broken, mutilated." It made her feel sick to remember it. "How does that fit in?"

He pushed out his lower lip. "I guess it doesn't."

"Darned right it doesn't." In the past few moments, a strange uneasiness that had nothing to do with the discussion had begun edging up upon her with the relentlessness of a dark tide creeping up a beach. Something was wrong, she thought. Had Ben run into some sort of trouble? Surely it was time for him to show up. There was nothing she could do except wait.

She picked up her end of the discussion.

"I realized that the house was evil because of those damaged spirit forms," she said. "It may appear to nurture troubled children, to introduce bliss into their final days, but it's an illusion." Her voice gained intensity. "Only an illusion, Kirby, because whenever these children die, something terrible happens to their spirits, something cruel and hideous starts feeding on them."

Kirby frowned. "You said Muriel also saw the ghosts. Did she also see them as damaged?"

"Yes." Janet's reply was emphatic. Then, remembering the actual conversation, she recalled that Muriel had only admitted to seeing bruises. From the poster, the darling Shirley-moppet showed a smile as dazzling as sunshine. Janet thought of the little girl whose face was partially battered away, her one eye completely gone. That couldn't have been the same little girl Muriel had seen as only bruised. And for some reason, Muriel had also missed seeing the crippled boy.

Angrily, she dismissed these discrepancies as irrelevant. Why waste time talking? She wasn't going to convince Kirby any more than he could convince her.

"Muriel didn't see the children enough to examine their appearance. She was too frightened." Janet openly consulted her watch. "It seems like Ben should be here by now."

"He's been gone less than an hour," Kirby said.

Janet's nod was brusque. The feeling of something being amiss grew stronger, as if she stood in deep water with scuttling creatures she couldn't see gathered about her feet, nagging, nibbling.

"I'm going to Fran's," she said. Grabbing her jacket off the chair back, she headed toward the entry. By the time Kirby jumped to his feet and caught up, she had reached the door.

Janet? What's the matter?"

"After our discussion tonight, how can you ask? It's late. I'm going to my sister's house."

Trixie had followed, watching with her round, protruding eyes.

"Why the rush?" Kirby reached for his coat. "I'll walk you."

"It's not necessary." She turned the doorknob. "When Ben arrives, tell him where I am."

Without waiting for Kirby's reply, she hurried outside, breaking into a jog as she reached the sidewalk. The air was frigid, and she realized she hadn't buttoned her coat. Distraught, she found that the clear night air did nothing to calm her. She felt as if she were on a treadmill, the adrenaline racing without purpose through her veins.

How could Kirby defend the Renner house? His arguments made no sense. How could he imagine that a house with such a gruesome history could have a beneficial influence?

She considered all the families from The Beeches who had lost children. How well she knew the pain of such a loss. Those babies, all those helpless children. She suddenly wondered if the older victims had somehow managed to escape the curse after death. The ghost children were so pitifully young! The crippled boy, who looked about four, seemed the oldest. She remembered Kirby saying that Timmy Fiorello was eight when the family moved in. How old had he been when he died? In any case, it seemed that the crippled ghost boy couldn't be the spirit of Timmy. She didn't recall seeing any twins, either. Of course, if the Hickok twins weren't identical, there would be no way of recognizing them.

With Fran's back door in view, she ran the last few steps. It suddenly seemed vital that she get inside as quickly as possible, but once she was there, she stared about the kitchen in confusion. This was not where she wanted to be, *needed* to be.

Fran stood at the kitchen counter setting the coffee timer for the morning, Turning, she said, "Oh, Jan, you're never going to believe this. Ozzie called to say that the Stocktons had phoned from yet another party to say they're staying overnight with friends and leaving for the airport from there." She rolled her eyes. "Imagine! Their big farewell scene with Gina tomorrow has all been forgotten."

Janet had no time to absorb this before the phone rang. Fran answered, and from her expression, Janet was positive the call brought bad news. She felt something vital give away inside her. She had been right, there was something wrong. Desperately so. *Ben*, she thought. Something awful had happened to Ben. She felt hollow, a cold wind blowing through her.

Perplexed, Fran turned from the phone. "It's Ozzie again. She said Gina's bed is empty and the back door is unlocked, so she's wondering if she came over here to find you. If she did, I've seen no sign of her."

"Let me talk to her." Janet snatched the phone.

"Gina's not with me, I haven't seen her," she told Ozzie. "She can't have gone out at this hour. She must be hiding somewhere inside. I'll come and help you hunt."

"No, she's gone out," Ozzie said. "Her jacket and boots are missing. If she's not with you, I bet I know where she went. Her cat hadn't come in by bedtime and I think she woke up, found it still missing, and went out to hunt for it. Naughty of her, but the last few days have been hectic, and she finds the creature a comfort."

Fear slashed through Janet like a blade. All she could think of was the Renner yard. "You say you know where she's gone?"

"Yes. There's a house on the next street with cats and we've found Pagoda there before. I'm sure that's where the child has gone. Why don't you come along? We'll probably meet her bringing the cat home."

"No, no Ozzie." Janet could hardly speak past the fear that clogged her throat. "There's another place where she and Pagoda play. I'll check there instead." She now understood the reason for her powerful feelings of unrest: *Gina*. Gina was in trouble and calling out to her.

Cursing the peaceful days that had lulled her instincts of menace lying in wait, Janet was out of the house before Fran could ask questions. Heart hammering, she raced across the rear yard, heading toward the barrier line of pines.

Chapter 38

BREATH RASPING IN HER THROAT, JANET wove her way through the evergreens that stood between Fran's and the Renners' properties. The crisscrossing, starlit shadows cast by the beech limbs transformed the Renner yard into a maze. A huge harvest moon rose above the house, but did little to help her make sense of the shadows. Nowhere in the tangle was there any sign of Gina or the cat, yet an increasing sense of urgency convinced her that the child was nearby.

As if responding to a silent call, she started toward the house then stopped, her heart squeezing as the night air that was suddenly clouded with foul-smelling smoke. Smoldering pumpkins? No, squash. Orange-red globes of burning squash . . . Her forgotten nightmare flooded her consciousness, the memory so vivid that it almost seemed to be happening again: the nursery beds, the cries of helpless children, the explosion and the devastating fire . . .

The air cleared. The odor was gone, but the memory of the nightmare remained. Sickened, Janet tried to clear from her mind but the images continued burning in her brain. There was no record of fire at The Beeches. Had her dreams been a portent of the final evil the house would inflict: flames and destruction sweeping through a haunted nursery, devouring even the phantom remnants of the spirit children?

Her eyes focused on a lighted kitchen window where Muriel stood at the sink. Like a quick cut in a film, Janet's mind moved from her waking nightmare to the here and now: the Renner house and Gina. A conviction grew within her that the child must be inside the house.

Moving once again, she rushed across the lawn and up the steps of the latticed porch. At her wild rapping, the outside light came on. Recognizing her caller, Muriel opened the door.

"Miss Fairweather, Janet . . ."

"Gina's missing!" announced Janet, entering without awaiting permission. "The little girl who has the cat, is she here?"

Flustered, Muriel shook her perfectly groomed head. "Why, no." Dressed in a lace-collared, full-length lavender dressing gown, she looked like a portrait of Renaissance royalty come to life. "I have been downstairs all evening. Had anyone knocked, I would have heard."

"Gina wouldn't have knocked. Her cat is missing, but she couldn't have said what she wanted." Janet thought of the allure open doors held for the animal. "Mrs. Renner, have you been outside? If you left the door ajar, the cat could have sneaked in. Gina could have come in, looking."

"I have been inside all evening. Except, I did go out and around the house to the refuse containers. I might have stood there for several moments; the moon tonight is almost overwhelmingly beautiful."

Muriel frowned. "I am remembering that my sister enjoys both the little girl and the cat. I have cautioned her against encouraging them to come into the yard. My husband becomes very angry. But if Rose saw the little girl out the back, she might have called her in. She could have taken her upstairs before I came back inside."

"That's what must have happened," Janet said, pressing forward. "Gina is upstairs."

"But, no!" Muriel's eyes widened in alarm. "Miss Fairweather, my husband is in his office, relaxing before bed. He cannot be disturbed. Wait here. I will go to Rose and see."

Lifting the hem of her dressing gown, Muriel turned and hurried up the back steps.

Janet could hear orchestral music, dramatic, yet muffled, as if from behind a distant door, yet the sound of violins seemed to cry up and down, the perfect accompaniment to her vision of leaping flames, pulsing and rising to the final end for the haunted children. Did the house need Gina's presence before it could enact this last, dreadful curse? Her heart thudded painfully. She told herself that if Gina was in Rose's room, she was all right. The danger for her would be in the area near the front window. As long as Gina stayed away from that area, she was safe. Janet had to believe that.

Muriel was taking too long. Janet was about to start up the steps when Muriel came down, her expression distressed.

"Gina wasn't there?" cried Janet.

"No, and Rose isn't there either. She has taken some pictures from her wall," she said, her tone puzzled. "The little cats and little dogs." Muriel's eyes widened. "There is a small room that sits on top of the roof. Rose knows I called it my secret place. I scold her when she goes up because of the many steps, but she has gone up there when I'm busy in the house elsewhere." As if speaking to herself, she said, "Could Rose be there with the child? Maybe that is why she took pictures, to entertain the little girl."

Convinced that was exactly what had happened, Janet reminded herself that had not sensed anything harmful when she'd climbed up the third flight of stairs. The threats he had feared were on the second floor. If Gina was in the belvedere with Rose, she was safe from danger.

Unless there was danger from Rose herself.

Chapter 39

WITH MURIEL LEADING, THEY WENT THROUGH the house to the front stairway. "We must be quiet," Muriel cautioned. "My husband must not know that you are here. This way we will not have to pass by his room."

The front hall light had been on. Muriel switched it off as she started up the steps, Janet following. They made the turn and faced the front window, which now presented an expanse of impenetrable blackness. Janet twisted to see the doctor's corridor, now inky black. She reasoned with relief that his door must indeed be shut.

Muriel put a finger to her lips as if her husband could hear them above the muffled rage of music as they started up the narrow flight to the belvedere.

Janet was on Muriel heels as she opened the gate. With the taste of fear sharp in her throat, Janet followed. What she saw ahead was an answered prayer. Pale lamplight showed Gina, sleepy-eyed but smiling, curled upon the chaise. Rose reclined beside her, holding Pagoda on her lap. The child looked up in delight as Janet rushed to her.

"Oh, Gina! Baby, you're all right!" Tears wet on her cheeks, she sat on the edge of the chaise and held the child close. Gina reached up

266

to touch her face and Janet felt thoughts move and shift in her mind, thoughts like pictures, placed as if by phantom fingers: the ending of the little girl's anxious search for her pet, the invitation into the nice old lady's house. The pictures increased in pleasure. In her mind, Janet heard the purring warmth of Pagoda, Rose's soft crooning, tasted the sweetness of chocolate . . .

Janet smelled chocolate. The mental connection broken, she held Gina away from her, seeing chocolate at the corners of the child's mouth. Sticky smears also marked her fingers and the lacy bib of the white nightgown she wore under her unzipped jacket.

"My, you've had a feast!" marveled Janet, her laugh shaky. Still reeling from the stunning oneness with Gina's thoughts she saw the empty candy papers on the bed and the floor.

"Lili. Chocolates for my Lili," crooned Rose, stroking the cat, but showing a fond, toothless smile at the child. "Chocolates, good. Never when she was my little baby, but now, always. For Lili, always."

Muriel, who had remained near the gate after quietly closing it, shook her head. "Not Lili," she corrected gently. "The little girl is not Lili. She is a neighbor child."

"My Lili," Rose emphatically repeated. "A big girl now."

"That was her baby's name, Lili," Muriel explained to Janet, her soft voice filled with regret.

Pagoda tensed its body skittishly, giving Muriel a suspicious glare as she came nearer. Placing a loving hand on Rose's shoulder, Muriel said to Janet, "She only wanted the child's company, do you understand? She did not intend to cause you distress."

Janet gazed upon Rose's wrinkled face shadowed harshly by the folds of her black headscarf. For a moment, she seemed transformed into the witch with the gingerbread house. "Come in, come in," the old crone had beckoned, and lured by sweets, the unsuspecting child had answered her wicked call. The fanciful image faded, leaving only a bewildered old woman who desperately grasped for a lost dream.

Gina was now drifting sweetly toward sleep, one small hand, palm up, resting trustfully upon Rose's lap.

Janet's gaze lifted to Muriel.

"Rose meant no harm," Muriel said.

Nodding, Janet's attention returned to Rose

Speaking in a singsong, the old woman stroked Pagoda's sleek coat. "Sister say, no cat inside. So soft and nice. Sister say, no cat. Sister say no little girl." Her emotions burst forth and her chin jutted. "Children be safe. Doctor Herman do nothing, know nothing."

She moved her hand from the cat to Gina, who opened her eyes briefly to give her a sleepy smile. "Mother, child," crooned Rose, her voice cracked and tinny. "Love, always love. My Lili come back safe with me. Safe. I keep her safe."

At these words, Janet darted Muriel a swift and anxious look and Muriel repeated, "She means no harm."

Gina was now clearly asleep, the blue tracings of veins delicate on her closed eyelids, the lashes, long and thick. She shifted, burrowing her body, drawing up her legs, her red rain boots showing under the hem of her nightgown.

Janet whispered to Muriel, "Does Rose believe Gina is her child returned, as she once believed a stranger was her husband?"

"Apparently." Muriel gave her sister a tender look. "We may speak before her. There are blessings to her condition. She is content with the child and cat. For the moment they are her entire world."

Moving from Rose, Muriel closed the gate that protected the stairway and stood firming in front of it, blocking the way to the steps.

"Miss Fairweather," she said, "you once asked about Dr. Renner's study of dark mysteries. You were insistent in believing he could help you. To hold you off, I said I would consult with him about this. But I had no intention of doing that."

You had your reasons," Janet said." She didn't care about the woman's excuses. She only wanted to take Gina and leave.

"Yes, I had my reasons," Muriel said, narrowing her eyes, "but it is time for you to learn more."

Janet got to her feet. She was done with the Renners, done with the yellow house, and she also wanted to be done with Muriel. A strange, almost vengeful note had crept into the woman's voice. Janet didn't know what it meant, but she saw that there was no way for her to pick up Gina and safely get past the woman and the closed gate.

"All right," Janet said. "I'll listen, then Gina and I will leave."

"Sit down," Muriel ordered. She gestured to the chair by the chaise. "Sit and I will tell you what you wanted to know. Once you hear it then you can judge for yourself the help that Dr. Renner could give you."

Janet started to speak again, but Muriel's look quelled her. Not knowing what else to do, Janet sat, but not on the chair but on the chaise, so she could stay in contact with Gina.

"There is more I did not tell you about the place where Dr. Renner had Rose and me moved to during the war," Muriel said, her eyes glittering with a light that struck a coldness through Janet, even while holding her spellbound. "The car took us to a compound where he had his quarters. Now I tell you that in his work with children, he had come to believe in a psychic bond between a mother and child. He developed a theory that a mother and young child communicate through psychic channels. He wished to prove it." Her voice sounded as if chips of glass were in her throat, grinding, cutting her words. "You may have heard of other doctors during the war who wished to prove similar theories about twins."

Instinctively, Janet drew the sleeping child closer. "I've heard of hideous experiments."

"Ah, believe them, for they are true," Muriel softly answered.

"You don't mean that your husband—"

"Not medical experiments but in its own way, no less cruel."

Janet's thoughts whirled. "Then how could you marry him!"

Muriel moved to sit on the other end of the chaise. "I knew nothing about this until I came upon his records after we were in Argentina." Her sigh was like the sound of sand sifting through an hourglass, and her fierce tone had changed to one of poignant regret. "By then, we had been together for over twenty years."

"You mean his work in his folders?"

"You know of them?" Her smile was thin. "No wonder he wished to keep you away. By the time I learned the truth, it was all part of the past, the same past in which he had saved Rose and me. How could I compare those dry written records with my vivid memories? Or with my gratitude. Perhaps I have not told you that the compound was outside a death camp. There was a wall between the camp and us, yet no walls could keep out the distant outcries or the constant stench of death. Is there any way I can make you understand my fear? I was only fifteen, and from all that horror, he had delivered me. And he had also delivered Rose. Life with him was all I knew. He had become my life."

Janet looked at the woman before her; face still unlined, every strand of her blue-black hair perfect. Could an individual pass through what Muriel spoke of and remain sane? Her vocal cords strained with tension, Janet asked, "He was a Nazi?"

"He did not consider himself political. He thought of himself as a scientist who benefited from the military machine. Through high-ranking friends who believed his theories might have military use, he had been allowed to set up a laboratory. He called it his nursery. Rose was placed in what he assured me was a safe hospital for the birth of her baby, while I lived with him in a private apartment."

"Did his wife know about you?"

"His wife?" Muriel's tone suggested that the question was irrelevant. "She had already left him to marry another man."

"But I thought—" she began, thinking that settled Ben's theory about the doctor leaving behind a wife, perhaps dead by his hand, when he fled Europe.

"But it is interesting," mused Muriel, "that you ask about her, for the blow of her betrayal had changed him from the man I had met as a child. Only when we were together privately could he reveal his softer emotions. Years before, he had developed a passion for me, the strength of which had never waned."

Her tone became ironic. "Perhaps because I was Jewish, and not quite human in his mind, he saw me as if I were a pet; one before which he could reveal any flaw or weakness, and like a pet, I would remain uncritical, adoring. Odd that he should have turned so cold in all other respects, for his research depended so strongly on emotion."

"The love between a mother and child?"

Muriel, nodded, her golden-brown eyes holding Janet steady as she continued. "From his records, I learned he had snatched mothers with young children from the gas chambers and thus considered their lives his possession. He put them in separate, soundproofed rooms and then stationed himself to secretly view them both. He ordered his assistants to subject either the child or the mother to distress while he studied the other party for a possible reaction. The aim, of course, was to see if messages could be transported by psychic means."

Janet's voice quavered. "Messages of distress?"

"Yes, on the theory that the primitive reactions to pain and fear were the strongest of all emotions, and therefore, the most efficiently communicated."

"What—what sorts of pain and fear?"

"He employed simple measures, like leaving hungry infants to cry in isolation for hours, or pricking tender flesh, or placing a suffocating hand over a baby's face until it was in a panic, starving for air."

Muriel's emotionless tone only increased the sickening impact of her words as she continued. "With the older little ones, he employed more sophisticated techniques, such as having masked and horror-garbed attendants awaken them in the middle of the night. Skillfully, he created for them an existence of living nightmares. The methods used on the mothers were similar. In torment and fear, we all become as little children."

The intensity of Muriel's gaze mesmerized Janet as the woman continued. "His studies proved that a powerful psychic bond flowing between both mother and child was possible, but extremely rare. Unknown distress in one party caused no consistent response in the other, except in some cases of extremely young infants. He became convinced that as these infants reacted to stress, it altered their mother's heart rate and the amount of oxygen in her blood. The sound of the mother's heartbeat and the richness of her blood are meaningful to the unborn child. He thus deduced that a response to these factors persists for some weeks after birth."

Smile twisted, she said softly, "It was all scientifically done. No one could fault the carefulness and the details of his research."

Janet's eyes were wide. "And he was able to hide this from you?"

"I believed him when he said he was using psychiatry to help the children he had saved. I had visited the nursery and saw how the children adored him. The babies in their cribs turned eagerly toward the sound of his voice and toddlers rushed to cling to his legs when he entered the room. They had no idea he was the father of their pain. They loved him. Perhaps, in an odd way, he loved them too. I know that the memory of their suffering has haunted him, never allowing him to rest." Again, that twisted smile. "Perhaps, because with the children, as with me, he felt safe in revealing tender emotion."

"Tender emotion! When he tortured them?"

Muriel seemed to savor Janet's revulsion. "I do not explain it. I can only tell you that the memories have never allowed him to rest."

"What of Rose and her baby? Were they also part of this—this experiment?"

"Yes, but with her mind as it was, she was incapable of telling me. Perhaps she only cared that there were times when she and the infant were allowed to be together."

"But the baby eventually died?"

Muriel's face was drawn, still perfect and unlined, yet ages old, her eyes empty of all but pain. "There came a time when men like Dr. Renner realized the war had turned against Germany. His research had been completed to his satisfaction and he wanted only to escape. He, along with others in his position, had used funds robbed from war victims to establish fortunes in foreign banks. His dilemma was to leave before the Allies arrived and yet not appear to be a traitor to the Nazi regime.

"His original plan was to send me on ahead, but I refused to leave without Rose. He finally allowed this, but he held back the child, saying he'd bring her, and a nurse, to join me and Rose later. When he arrived, he was alone. He said that the Russians had attacked, firing upon his laboratory, and destroying the nursery.

"Only later did I learn that he himself had destroyed the nursery with explosives, buying time for his escape by making it appear that he was dead as well. The children, including Rose's baby, were blown to bits. If the mothers in the other part of the building survived the explosion and conflagration, they were probably put to death by the main camp authorities before the arrival of the Allies."

Muriel's shocking words returned Janet's mind to her nightmares of fire, explosion, and violence. Stunned, she realized that in her dreams, she had seen what Muriel had described. Through her dreams, she had witnessed a psychic replay of those final, horrid moments in Dr. Renner's nursery.

Her mind grappled to find answers for the multitude of questions that poured in upon her. Had Dr. Renner's guilty memories so permeated the atmosphere that the past took on tangible form? Yet why had she been privy to it? Was it because it concerned children? Still raw from the tragic loss of her own child, perhaps she had been open to messages from children lost and hurting. The sound of the crying baby, no babies, which had haunted her for so long. Those cries, along with the smell of smoke, had they been fragments recreated from a hideous time in Europe that had happened before her birth?

It seemed to fit together. But still, there remained unanswered questions. The gruesome history of The Beeches must play some part in what she had experienced. That too involved children. The ghost children, there must be some connection.

Her thoughts were interrupted as Muriel moved from her position and opened the gate. "So, now, Miss Fairweather, you have been told of my husband's great knowledge of the dark aspects in this world. I think you no longer have things to ask him, am I correct?" She did not await an answer. "It is time for you to take the little girl and go home."

She moved to touch her sister's shoulder and bent to speak her. "Rose, you are tired. Time for bed."

Rose looked up and then looked back at the sleeping child.

"Time for bed, come along." Muriel held out her hand.

Like an aged turtle tucking into its shell, Rose drew back. "I stay here. This my bed with my Lili. This, thisss," she hissed.

Still dazed from the revelation of Muriel's story, Janet shook her head, trying to clear her thoughts. The image of flames still scorched behind her eyes. Blinking, she looked at her watch. How long had it been since she left Kirby's house? It seemed a million years. Ben must have returned from his meeting. By now, he must have to gone to Kirby's, then to Fran's looking for her and then learned that Gina was missing. Would he know to look for her at the Renners' house? After all her concerns about the place, she was sure that he would. He might show up at any moment. She would take Gina outside to meet him.

"My Lili," she heard Rose repeat to Muriel, her tone stubborn.

"Such a lovely name," murmured Muriel. "You may call the little girl Lili, but I will call her Gina." She gave the child a gentle shake. "Come little Gina, wake now." The child's eyes fluttered open. "Come, Gina."

Together, Muriel and Janet helped the groggy child to her feet. "You had a nice time with Rose," Muriel told her. "I know you will want to visit again."

"Visit," Rose echoed, seeming to like the sound of the word and accepting it. "We visit, we look at pictures." She pulled kitten and puppy cutouts from under a blanket. "See pictures?"

"How nice!" exclaimed Muriel, signaling Janet to leave. "May I look at them?"

From the floor below, the music ceased.

"Quiet now," Muriel warned, her tone fearful. "With the music stopped, he might hear you."

With the old woman distracted, Janet moved toward the steps and through the gate. That was when the child remembered Pagoda and turned back. Seeing what Gina wanted, Muriel reached for the animal.

As Muriel's hands touched the cat Rose grabbed at it also, pleading, "Soft, don't take!"

Startled awake, Pagoda, its eyes stretched wide in fright, uncoiled and sprang to the floor. Muriel reached for the cat, tried to grasp it. With a yowl, the creature broke free and darted down the steps. Gina, her booted feet clumping, followed before Janet could grab her.

Janet descended in time to see the cat shooting across the second-floor landing stair landing, turning as it ran to race down the hallway and past Dr. Renner's sickroom and continuing on, lost in the darkness that led to the back stairway.

Gina, who had been in fast pursuit of the animal, came to a stop as Dr. Renner's office door flew open and crashed again the wall.

There was a long, frozen moment. Then, Muriel, who had followed, breathed, "My husband . . . Dr. Renner . . ."

A dim rectangle of light fell across the corridor. Dr. Renner's figure stood elongated in the pallid glow, his robe hanging loose over his long nightshirt. His proud head looked too large for the frail support of his neck as he leaned forward, squinting without his glasses to better search the gloom, the dry, mummified flesh of his skeletal face making him a Ramses disturbed from an ancient sleep. He moved forward in rusty steps and then stopped. He focused on Gina, who stared as his threatening form stepped closer.

Janet, on stairway descending from the belvedere, saw the doctor silhouetted in the light from his doorway. She looked to Gina, the outline of her corduroy jacket hanging comically over her white nightgown, but there was nothing comical in the grating accusation that emerged from the doctor's throat.

"*You!*"

Gina seemed to become smaller, shrinking in upon herself, stepping back toward the big front window.

The hoarse, menacing voice carried clearly. "*You!* You are one of *them*?" The doctor advanced another menacing step. "Why are you here? What do you want of me?"

Chapter 40

FRANTIC STEPS BROUGHT JANET ALMOST TO Gina's side, then she faltered as a confusion of flickering lights suddenly appeared. They floated above and about in the darkness, coming from everywhere, from the hallways, down from the belvedere, floating like phosphorescent creatures adrift in a midnight sea.

Janet blinked as the lights assumed familiar forms. Rapidly, with breathtaking speed, the ghost children appeared: the little boy, his limbs now straight and sound, his thin chest filled out, plump and healthy; the toddler, her flesh restored to wholeness, smiling, her eyes glowing like dark and lovely stars. Marveling, Janet saw that all the children, the babies, the older ones, all of them, were sound and whole and beautiful. Their lips moved, and she felt the whispered chant weave through her. *Felt*, not heard, subtly changed now, full and victorious, the rhythm transformed into a hymn of praise.

Stronger, Stronger, We Have Grown Stronger. Stronger, Stronger, We Have Been Healed.

The psychic message echoed in Janet's brain: *Healed*. Glowing insight burst upon her. The strength yearned for in the chant had been the strength of healing. Day by day, the healing had progressed until now it was fully accomplished.

Staring at the luminous figures, she finally realized the full impact of the story Muriel had told her. These ghost children . . . she now knew who they were. Kirby had been right. The house did not hold the souls of resident children. The forms before her were the phantoms of Dr. Renner's experiments, the victims of his nursery. They had loved him, Muriel had said. Because he had shown kindness when in their presence, these innocents had given him their trust. In the stricken violence of the explosion, their spirits had rushed to him; he who had become central to their tortured lives, and throughout the years, they had continued to cling. The final, mutilated images of themselves in life had been impressed upon their psychic bodies by the shock of their dreadful deaths. Yet now that the doctor had been drawn to the house Elizabeth Parke had dedicated to the care of the lost, they had been made whole again.

Janet knew she had been right in believing that the house had deliberately enticed certain families. But Kirby had been right as well. The Beeches bestowed not harm, but spiritual hope and healing upon its children. Under its shelter, they had been miraculously touched. And in drawing the doctor and his invisible following, the house had extended its powers even beyond this mortal life.

Dr. Renner's hoarse cry returned Janet's mind to the scene before her. Gina had turned to stare at the ghost children with wide-eyed wonder. The doctor's attention was also fixed upon them, but his expression was one of horror. "You're dead!" he screamed at the misty figures, shaking a trembling fist. "You've all been dead for a lifetime! What do you want?"

His cracking voice was drowned as the joyous chant began again: *Stronger, stronger, we have grown stronger. Stronger, stronger, we have been healed.*

Breathlessly, Janet watched the apparitions advance upon the old man. She could only think they sought vengeance for their suffering, but instead, they wove gaily about him, extending their arms, twirling as if to display their newly perfect forms. Watching with stunned disbelief, Janet realized these innocents still saw the doctor as the loving center of their lives. They wanted him to share in their delight!

But he, without understanding, attempted to fend them off, frantically striking at the nearest figure, a three-year-old girl who held a baby that looked too big for her to carry. She moved before him as if proudly presenting the infant for his inspection. Flailing, the doctor reached futilely through her vaporous form. The little girl turned, laughing, as if believing the doctor played a game. More children drifted toward him.

As if frozen, Janet watched as he snatched first for one, then another. It happened in a whirl, his wild-eyed panic increasing as the wraiths eluded him like smoke. Cursing, robe flying, he staggered drunkenly among them until one of his thrashing arms contacted Gina. Feeling her solidness, he spun with a grating caw of victory to seize her throat.

"Janet!" came the child's frightened message. "Mamma!"

Janet bolted forward. Peripherally, she felt there was yet another figure off in the direction of the stairs, yet as she rushed forward, there was no time to look. She fell upon the doctor, her fingernails stabbing into his flesh. He struggled, then a regathering of the spirits overwhelmed his attention. With a gasping screech, he allowed Gina to slip free as he confronted the spectral figures anew. Clutching Gina's limp body to her breast, Janet sank to the floor as the phantoms swirled through and past them.

Sobbing, Janet crouched over the stricken child, seeing the welts which marred the whiteness of her slender throat. "Gina!" she cried in wild despair, and blessedly, the dark lashes fluttered. Gina's eyes opened to gaze up into her face.

A cry from the doctor caused Janet to look up as the ghost children surrounded him like a flock of eager starlings, hungrily seeking to embrace him, to hug his frantically kicking legs.

"But I was kind to you! I never really hurt you!" he babbled hysterically, twisting and jerking like a demented scarecrow. "I was your friend!" Their ethereal hands pawed his chest, grabbed at his arms, floated to cover his lined and horror-distorted face with smothering caresses.

Raw, spasmodic shrieks, in German now, whistled with a terror that pierced Janet's ears. The doctor's strained, rattling breathing seemed to fill the room as the figures billowed thickly around him. Writhing, he clutched his chest, his face contorting into a mask of agony. He issued a final, tortured squall, and then, as if his bones and flesh had become as insubstantial as dried paper, his body slowly crumpled to the floor to sprawl in grotesque disarray, lifeless and still.

There was silence, then small murmurings of alarm from the ghostly children. In confusion, they drifted away from the corpse. Their whispers, as thin as the rustling of wind through treetops, were bewildered and frightened. Hugging Gina protectively, Janet saw that Dr. Renner's death had broken his ties with the children, yet, with him gone, what fate was left to them now?

As if in reply, a soft illumination began to radiate gently upon the small, spectral forms. The frightened tones of their whisperings changed, becoming questioning, expectant. The light increased and Janet saw additional phantoms appear. More children? But no, for as the outlines became more distinct, she saw the figures of women. One of them who had a broad, sweetly smiling face reached toward the toddler. A hesitation, then the child eagerly accepted her hand. More women appeared, welcoming children into their arms. *Their mothers,* thought Janet with a thrilling surge of emotion. Their mothers, come at last to gather their lost little ones.

"Lili," came a hoarse whisper. Rose, who had stumbled down the last of the belvedere steps, moved past Janet, reaching toward the three-year-old who held the baby.

Lili," Rose repeated, reaching with yearning toward the infant. As her trembling fingers traced the hazy outlines of the small face before her, the corners of the infant's rosebud mouth lifted as if in delighted recognition.

Pathetically, Rose fell to her knees, attempting to grasp the small form, but her shaking hands only moved through vapors.

A woman materialized to sit and take both the three-year-old and the baby onto her lap. She touched the infant's hand, then gestured first toward Rose, then to her own breast. Her expression was questioning. When Rose reached toward the baby again, the woman repeated her gestures.

Slowly, Rose sank back on her heels. She nodded. "Lili," she said hoarsely. "Yes. When I come."

The misty host of figures wavered before Janet's eyes. Like a morning fog before the coming of the dawn, the phantasms evaporated, mothers and children reunited, gone as swiftly as they had appeared, disappearing shades of the doctor's tortured memories, resolved at last, fleeing with his soul. Spectral light faded and became one with the shadows.

"Janet!" Just as she recognized Ben's voice, he bounded up the stairs and was by her side. Stunned, she stared at him, realizing that the figure she had seen so briefly on the stairway had been his. Had it been only seconds ago that she had unknowingly glimpsed him as she rushed toward the doctor? It must be, yet it seemed as if eons had passed.

"Gina! Is she okay?" As he touched the child's cheek, he was rewarded with her smile. "Thank God!" he exclaimed fervently, helping the little girl sit up although she remained in the circle of Janet's arms. His voice shook. "Thank God, she's all right."

Getting himself in command, he directed his gaze to the doctor's limp form. "That's Dr. Renner? He's dead, isn't he? It must have been a heart attack." Voice still rough with emotion, he shook his head. "Your sister said you were probably here. The back door was unlocked. I stepped in, the cat zipped past me and I heard voices. I followed the sounds until I reached the second floor.

"I could hardly figure out what I was seeing. I guess the doctor grabbed Gina to keep from falling, then went into convulsions. What an awful experience for the poor kid. The shock must have overwhelmed her."

Janet couldn't understand. Did Ben think Gina had simply fainted?

If he had been on the stairs when the doctor collapsed, he must have witnessed the ghosts. Why did he seem so ignorant of all that had happened?

"Didn't you see?" she demanded. "Didn't you see?"

"See Renner's death throes? Sure. Thank God you were there to snatch Gina out of his way." Excitement grew in his voice. "Then, on the stairs, that's when I heard Gina."

Janet stared. "Heard her? But no, unless—" Did he mean that the frightening experience of the doctor's attack had made Gina's psychic call reach out to him?

"Yes." He laughed. "Heard her. Don't tell me you missed it! She called, 'Janet,' and then, 'Mamma.'" He smiled down at the little girl, tenderly stroking her dark hair. "Yes, she's your mamma, all right."

Gina's small hand tugged Janet's wrist. When Janet looked down, the child, her eyes shining, hesitantly whispered, "Janet." The sound was halting as she tasted the word upon her lips. She spoke again: "Mamma." Her voice was husky. Then, with a tremulous smile, she spoke more clearly: "Janet, my Mamma."

Hearing her, actually hearing her speak, Janet burst into tears. "Gina, you can talk! Oh, honey, you really can!"

Ben's tone was filled with wonder. "When the doctor lunged, she must have felt desperate for help. She had to call out. We knew she could do it, and this was the breakthrough."

Or the house, Janet thought, joy winging through her. *The healing shelter of The Beeches.*

From the corner where Muriel hovered over the doctor's body, Rose intoned, "My Lili was with him. Now, my Lili be free."

Dark head bowed, Muriel held the older woman close. "Now we are all free. Perhaps, even him."

As if from a distance, Janet heard Ben say, "We should call an ambulance for the doctor's body."

Muriel turned. The smooth oval of her face was now as peaceful and pure as alabaster, the tiger fires of conflict no longer blazing from her eyes. "I will make the necessary calls. Do not be concerned." Her soft voice was rich and firm with dignity. "There is no need for worry. Everything is all right now for my sister and for me."

Ben hesitated and then nodded, helping Janet to her feet. "We had better let Ozzie know that a certain little girl is safe and sound."

Shifting his gaze to Gina, he extended his hands. The child reached up, holding on as he swung her easily up into his arms. "We call that 'upsy-daisy'," he told her, giving her a squeeze. Can you say that?"

"Upsy-daisy," she repeated parrot-like, her voice still husky. She gazed at him a moment, then rested her head on his broad shoulder. Her eyes were heavy-lidded with the need for sleep. She reached for Janet's hand, and holding it, contentedly smiled.

Hugging the child close, Ben reached out his other arm to include Janet. His voice deepened. "I'm thinking of Gina's bedroom ready and waiting. Let's say we have a few words with Ozzie and your sister and then take our Gina home."

Leaning against him, Janet looked into the space around the large window, so hushed, so silent. She knew what she had seen. *She knew.* But in this life, none of it had the reality of Gina's hand so sweetly clasped in hers, and the warm, earthly comfort of Ben's embrace.

"Yes," she told him softly. "Yes, let's take our Gina home."

Dear Readers,

"The Chanting is a love story with supernatural elements that increase as the story progresses," said one of my readers, a comment that hit the mark with me.

I hope it does for you. In case it didn't or you have other things to say about *The Chanting,* you can reach me at HaafBeverly@gmail.com

The first version of *The Chanting* was published under my married name, Beverly Haaf. To distinguish this new release and its changes from the previous one, the new one is published under my maiden name, Beverly Terhune. This will please my Princeton friends and acquaintances, plus my relatives who live in that area.

Beverly Terhune Haaf

Also, under the name, Ivy C. Leigh, I write the *JumpRope Chronicles* series, which is about mysteries, romance and murder, in a small New Jersey town that exists only on its pages. My husband, John, jokingly calls its residents and visitors, my *imaginary friends.*

My home is in Beverly City, NJ, a town with my first name—is it any wonder I sometimes use a pseudonym? While living here I started a monthly newspaper, the *Beverly Bee,* and yes, named for the town and not for me.

I work and live in an old Victorian house—not haunted as far as I know. A friend who visits frequently, whispered to me, "The ghosts may have a different opinion."

That's it for now,
Thanks.

Beverly Terhune/Beverly T. Haaf/Ivy C. Leigh
HaafBeverly@gmail.com)

Books from JPI
Jersey Pines Ink
https://www.jerseypinesink.com/

TREES, a collection of all bark and bite dark stories
edited by Dina Leacock

The Chanting, a Supernatural/Romance Novel
by Beverly Terhune. (Beverly T. Haaf.)

Honeycomb Fire, Romantic Adventure
by Beverly T. Haaf

Just a Drop In The Cup, A Collection of 42 Speculative Short
Horror and Fantasy Stories
by Diane Arrelle

Seasons on the Dark Side, a Horror Short Story Collection
by Diane Arrelle

Crypt Gnats, an Anthology of Horror Stories
You've Been Itching to Read,
edited by Dina Leacock

WhoDunit, A Collection of Intriguing
Mystery Short Stories,
edited by Dina Leacock

JumpRope Chronicles Novels by Ivy C. Leigh

Death Behind the Lilacs
Death Counts the Golden Coins
Death Spins an Indigo Web-
Death Wears Red Roses

E-Book: *Jump Into:* three short JumpRope stories

www.ingramcontent.com/pod-product-compliance
Lightning Source LLC
Chambersburg PA
CBHW031112030726
47496CB00002BA/513